Chioma Okereke was born in Benin City, Nigeria and moved to London at the age of seven. She started her writing career as a poet before turning her hand to fiction. Her work has been shortlisted in the Undiscovered Authors Competition 2006, run by Bookforce UK, and in the *Daily Telegraph* 'Write a Novel in a Year' Competition 2007. *Bitter Leaf* is her first novel.

Bitter
Leaf

Chioma Okereke

virago

VIRAGO

First published in Great Britain in 2010 by Virago Press

Copyright © Chioma Okereke 2010

The moral right of the author has been asserted.

A CIP catalogue record for this book
is available from the British Library.

ISBN 978-1-84408-627-6

Typeset in Sabon by M Rules
Printed and bound in Great Britain by
Clays Ltd, St Ives plc

Papers used by Virago are natural, renewable and
recyclable products sourced from well-managed forests and certified
in accordance with the rules of the Forest Stewardship Council.

Mixed Sources
Product group from well-managed
forests and other controlled sources
www.fsc.org   Cert no. SGS-COC-004081
FSC   © 1996 Forest Stewardship Council

Virago Press
An imprint of
Little, Brown Book Group
100 Victoria Embankment
London EC4Y 0DY

An Hachette UK Company
www.hachette.co.uk

www.virago.co.uk

For my father
(and his imaginary friend Bill)

O gifted men, vainglorious for first place,
how short a time the laurel crown stays green.

Dante

One

Many things distinguish a place, its rolling hills or turquoise waters. There are civilisations that wear plates in their ears and others that wear hoops of gold. There are even cultures that kill their old before they become burdens on those that remain. Rituals are carried out all over the world at any given moment; some that everyone can relate to and some as foreign as a fire-walk in lands surrounded by snow. But many things unite people universally: births and deaths, gains and losses, departures and arrivals.

If there was one thing Mannobans knew about, it was leaving, and they hadn't arrived at this way of thinking simply. Once upon a time, hundreds of years earlier, there had been much wailing and gnashing of teeth at the exodus of a loved one. Plenty eye-water had spilled into their red clay, contributing to its fertility and binding the people closer to the earth. Gradually, they learned that leaving wasn't always such a bad thing. Leaving engendered possibility, and allowed the growth of another emotion: hope. Hope and faith would always bring about return.

When people left the village these days there was, of course, a spirit of sadness in the family of the departing one, and naturally that melancholy permeated neighbours and friends, but the tearing of clothes and extraction of hair was merely a custom that had been passed down from elders long gone. This extraordinary behaviour actually helped: the pain of shed follicles distracted people from the immediate loss, from the figure retreating in front of their eyes, blending into a blurry horizon and out of sight. But tears dried quickly once a person was gone, the realities of life far more demanding than wilfully issuing salt water from ducts so rarely used.

Returns were celebrated with pounding feet. A villager carried news of the approaching arrival to their neighbour, and the information spread like an outbreak of typhoid. This was quickly followed up with heightened voices, calling up to gods or anybody that could hear, and then Mannobans displayed their palms to the sky in happiness. Arrivals were always welcomed, but returns were *heartfelt*.

If arrivals triggered people's hospitality, returns offered no such politeness. Once the traveller was knocked to the ground by the force of a parent's embrace, their dirt was removed with the tears and saliva of all well-wishers. Immediate sustenance would have to wait, as fresh animals were killed, cleaned and cooked in a feast that would draw even those unconnected to the returnee to the compound with watering mouths. The party would carry on well into the days to come, with more and more food being cooked and consumed. People dropped in to witness a reunited family's joy and the returnee would regale all those present with stories from their journey, embellishing achievements or making light of troubles that had befallen them. Mannobans needed little excuse for a celebration and when one of their own came back home after a spell away,

2

the villagers rejoiced as if they had uncovered the secret to life.

But this kind of spectacle didn't suit everyone, even if they had been born and raised on Mannobe soil. For some, to return under such scrutiny was akin to coming back to the village naked. They preferred the cover of nightfall, returning as shadows. They would creep up on unsuspecting family members, hoping to ambush them into a tight embrace before any sound could spring from their lips. Even though news of their arrival would inevitably trickle through the night to be announced in the morning, at least they would be spared the mass hysteria.

It wasn't only those who had shameful secrets they didn't want to see dispersed as casually as farmers' grain: some people simply preferred a quieter life, free of the local hullabaloo if they could help it. They were the most surprised when their return caused a stirring among the people, especially those whose presence had been largely overlooked when they were residents. In their focus on trying to enter the village in darkness, unnoticed, they always failed to see the one thing, or the one person, standing in front of their eyes: Mama Abandela.

Jericho swore as her grip on the bag handle slipped again and let the bag fall to the floor with a heavy *thunk*. Sitting on top of it, she sighed gratefully at the brief respite, although if she rested too long she'd lose the strength required to make it the full way home.

She peered into the darkness, waiting for shadows to identify themselves. She was tired, anxious but also happy at being back – not that she'd seen much of the village with her night-time arrival. The smell had been the first thing to hit her, akin to the shock of a toe-dip in the river during Springtemps. There weren't enough preparations in the world for that dare.

3

The fragrances as she'd journeyed homeward had been the first greetings of family, minus the frenetic outbursts. It was the first thing she'd forgotten in the city – the potent odour of earth that struck, before making way for subtler essences to penetrate; trees and plants, the richness of the Belago, animal life along with the varying smells of community.

People came to mind as her thoughts rested on the village, familiar faces taking shape like the nature around her, and she was grateful for her decision to return at a late hour. As soon as her mother knew, it would begin – the rejoicing, the endless questions and, of course, the expectations. She would officially be home, back from La Ciudad d'Angel.

She got off her bag and opened it carefully. She removed her medical certificate from the wrapper she'd bound it in to protect it. She couldn't read it in the dark and didn't want to light her lantern yet, but its very existence was a tangible weight in her hand. Smoothing away imaginary wrinkles, she wrapped it up again, anticipating her mother's pride.

She returned the wrapper to the bag but before closing it she extracted a handkerchief, brought it to her nose and inhaled deeply. It smelt of her, but she pretended it was still rich with the long-lost, citrusy scent of its owner as her fingers traced the raised black thread where his initials stood in the corner.

Jericho tucked it inside her clothing, quiet laughter burning her chest alongside her secret. She allowed it to join the sounds of nature, laughing harder when an animal she couldn't see mimicked her sound somewhere in the nearby trees.

She'd brought a piece of the city with her. That would have to suffice until it came for her.

Mama Abandela had been walking at nightfall for as long as she could remember. She preferred the softness of the air at that time, and her stiffening limbs preferred it too; it allowed her body to relax after the day's toil before she waited for sleep to pass over her house. She'd begun to take to the road after cleaning her last cooking pot and helping her eldest son to bed when he returned from the workshop. Mannobe was different in the darkness; the earth underfoot fragile, as failing eyesight rendered the dips in its surface alien.

Sometimes, she had to stand still to catch her breath and would be surprised, wondering where the holes were on her body that it had trickled out from when she wasn't looking. Her mother had always said old age was something you had to shake off, like a gecko that tried to land on your head. It didn't belong there, so you couldn't settle for it. The moment you did you were done for, because it would swiftly call the rest of its family to join it.

Mama knew that at some point she must have lost her concentration and it was at that precise moment that a family of geckos had sneaked into her hips. It was their presence that were causing her joints to misalign. She'd tried fervently to shake them ever since, but they were there for good.

She kneaded the flesh on her side and managed to dislodge a reptile temporarily, allowing her to continue her walk. Ah, the things she'd seen on her nocturnal trails! Enough to make the blood boil. Still, she managed to keep most of them to herself, poring over them in bed when sleep failed to visit her. Only the things that were too juicy slipped from her mouth on to others, for that's exactly what they were: *slippery*. Not that Mama ever blamed herself. The geckos burrowing into her midriff were trouble enough without worrying about her lips as well.

It was not the first time he'd had to hold on to a tree to right himself. His grip tightened as bubbles of booze rode

5

up his bloodstream and popped, causing flickers of light behind his eyelids. Babylon laughed conspiratorially with the tree trunk, waiting until the wave of nausea passed over him. He breathed deeply and when he felt able to balance without the aid of a weighty prop, he began to zigzag home.

The scratchings of night along with the graze of trees added an element of danger to his trip that he enjoyed. Excitement pierced his belly. It was a game he liked to thrill himself with as he tried to imagine the sensations of the dark. When his foot ran over a jagged rock he said out loud, 'That was softer than the arch of Tete's foot.' When his body brushed past a burr bush, he thought, 'That is what the touch of Magdalena Codón's hair must be like.' Every nocturnal scent percolated through his nostrils and triggered a memory of a woman; each memory of a woman ignited a spark inside him that illuminated his way home in the darkness.

Babylon was so enveloped in his thoughts that he didn't see the aged Mama making her way around a corner until he collided with her soft, wide frame. His apology was overtaken by a vinegary burp and once Mama Abandela had finished slapping him off her waist, her mouth ran off a million words as if she'd stored up her life's worth of insults for this very occasion. Sensing he was unable to placate the old woman in his current state, he began to back away slowly until he noticed her attention had left him and had moved on to something else. Following her gaze, he picked up noises in the distance.

It took Babylon a few seconds to realise that the light he saw wasn't a figment of his intoxicated mind. He watched the prism of amber floating through the dark, bringing trees into view before they disappeared again, and made the connection that someone was walking in the night with a lamp. Ordinarily, that wouldn't have interested him, but he was intrigued by the intensity of the older woman's curiosity. He didn't know about the geckos in her side that made her moving off after their collision difficult; he was simply content to take in the occurrences of the darkness with someone else.

Babylon hummed gently, a tune that had been working its way through him all day, and realised that his humming helped regulate his coordination. It was strange how music could unhinge and right a person at the same time. He was pondering this when the light cutting through the darkness flashed. Sounds came from the opposite direction and he noticed another lamp.

Even before the two lights were united he heard it. A good friend had said that musicians are conduits of love, and as a musician, he knew first hand the power of a note. He'd seen grown men rendered catatonic at a piano's trill, and even the most hardened players fainting at the moan of a lyre.

An exclamation cut through him like an erroneous chord and Babylon watched as the lamps formed a large halo on the dark road. He saw the profile of a stranger's face, the soft features, that wide mouth, and his stomach dipped dangerously. The two women hugged each other tightly, and when they pulled apart he followed their separating voices to find the one that had stirred him. She turned in his direction, almost as if she'd sensed his unspoken need to see her face, and Babylon felt his throat go dry.

'*Who*?'

'Pardon?'

He turned to the old woman at his side, as if seeing her for the first time and startled by her proximity. Her voice had erupted from her chest as acrid as cricket-song.

'Who's that?' He pointed.

Mama Abandela squinted in the way all old people seem to do, even though she was quite accustomed to seeing clearly in the half-light.

'Penny Aze—'

'The other one,' he interrupted rudely.

'Mcchhheeww,' Mama kissed her teeth at him. 'Edith Lwembe's girl. Who went to the city. Jericho.'

'Jericho?' he repeated slowly.

'Yes. Are you drunk *and* deaf?' she spat out.

Watching the lights dance through the dark, he caught Mama Abandela's heavy step as she moved off. He'd wanted to offer to escort her home, it was the least he could do after frightening her, but he knew he wouldn't remember his lack of chivalry in the morning. Babylon let her shuffle off at her turtle's pace and then stared into the pitch black. The woman had disappeared, but he could still see her face.

He took a careful step in the dark and resumed his game, muttering her name all the while as if it was the only word he knew.

Two

Jericho sidestepped as the woman in front of her spat on the ground before repositioning the chewing stick at the side of her mouth. The market was a heaving mass that only an expert could navigate effectively, as people shoved each other away to secure the best bargains and the freshest produce. It took years of practice to be able to interpret the hideous choir of shouting vendors who coaxed prospective customers with endearments like 'Auntie' and 'Sister', trying to outdo their competitors as well as the musicians who performed then opened their palms wide for payment.

She coughed as she walked past the dilapidated stall of an old woman smoking fish. The trader looked like she'd blackened herself alongside her wares from many years in front of the dangerous outside oven, and Jericho observed the skilful way she fanned herself along with the fish she hoped to sell. It was called Manuel's Meat Market, but it offered everything from beans to clothing. Its layout made absolutely no sense, except to the vendors who saved space for other traders near to them; they thought nothing of selling clothing next to roast chicken or mountains of spices next to fuel. Just as it made perfect sense that directly after buying pawpaws and three cupfuls of rice, someone would turn their body ninety degrees and argue over the price of a pair of slippers made from old tyres. But to a foreigner it was a labyrinth of stalls; intricately assembled goods to dazzle the eye and detract from the putrid ammonia smell emanating from the muddy streets and pockets of refuse. A circus where sacks of wheat and semolina were piled so vertiginously high that they resembled cutting-edge architectural installations. Young women balanced wooden planks laden with stock on their heads and ran through the stalls, and sleights of hand confused customers into taking the substandard goods vendors wanted to offload.

The city's market had been equally populated but there had been a sense of order. To Jericho, everything in the village seemed more exhausting. Her work away had felt different, more rewarding. Since she'd come back, the simplest chore felt like an inconvenience. When her mother placed the broom in her hands the very next day, it had been weightier than a tree trunk. When she sent her to the market for their food, the journey appeared longer than the one her best friend's brother used to have to do every day to collect water for their family. But all her protestations had fallen on unsympathetic ears.

'What, you think you're a Dorique?'

Her mother had laughed richly at the statement the villagers used to chide each other with whenever they felt someone had developed ideas above their station, and Jericho had quickly bit back the words on her tongue.

She'd taken her time getting to the market owing to some locals who had stopped to talk to her following her return and the young men whose eyes shone like torches upon seeing her, so that she'd whiled away time at Cook's Monument before heading back. The sundial in the square was as breathtaking as she remembered. The moment it came into view she recalled the story they'd passed around as children, the story told to them by their elders, and she imagined Mr Dorique's face, overcome with emotion, as he rooted the dial into Mannobe earth.

Although the sun obscured much of her vision, Jericho played her game in silence, chewing on her bottom lip nervously. She willed a piece of shade to come and slice the dial in two: if the shade appeared, then the man in her heart would be the one she carried for ever. Her excitement grew as she felt the gentle breeze pick up around her. It was only a matter of seconds before a dark cloud would appear, she was convinced, but then a group of people blocked her view of the sundial. Jericho shrugged at her game's premature ending. There would always be another chance to play.

She stopped for a packet of boiled nuts and popped a handful into her mouth greedily. They tasted as familiar on her tongue as her mother's soup. She knew it was more than the nuts themselves; it was the paper they were wrapped in, the cone-like shapes they manipulated the paper into so they could be eaten on the go, the warmed ink leaking into the kernels and the smoke from everything that was being cooked on site adding to their flavour. She smiled to herself as she crunched through them until her fingers came up empty. Just when you thought you'd had enough of the village it had a way of creeping up on you and piquing your appetite, leaving you hungry for more.

There were more people by the dial on her return journey than she expected, but then she heard music. It actually sounded good; lots of local musicians had perfected one song and played it endlessly before opening their hands, wanting something. She was convinced people only paid them so that their hands were occupied with money – which they would blow on millet brew – and the villagers would be momentarily spared their playing.

Something about the music was familiar yet strange at the same time, and she found herself straining to hear over the audience's approving shouts. Jericho wished she hadn't been so quick to finish her snack. She could have listened to him while eating; each activity would have been improved by the other.

When the song came to a stop, the crowd split as people moved off while others joined to view the performance and she caught a brief glimpse of the attraction. He'd placed his guitar on the ground and stood up to shake the locks from his eyes before scooping them up into a pony-tail. She took in the definition of his legs from the tight trousers he wore. His face was striking, and she wasn't one to give compliments easily. She supposed he would be considered attractive if she liked that sort of thing, which she didn't, she confirmed, sneaking another generous glance. His features looked as though they'd been carved out of Cooroo Mountain.

Jericho believed that science held many truths the human mind was incapable of fathoming, for example the curious pink moon that caused the women of Mannobe's feet to prickle with pins and needles. So when she walked past as the music resumed, she thought nothing of the fact that her breath quickened at the quiet trill of the Spanish guitar. When her breasts swelled suddenly so that they fought with the constraints of her top, she simply waited for the moment to pass.

As the musician moved his body out of profile, she felt her heart spasm in her chest. She thought she'd accidentally locked eyes with him and her body flooded with unexpected warmth. It was difficult to tell – from the distance he could have been looking at anyone. Then the moment was gone and as the richness of his voice floated around the square she knew she'd imagined it. The fists in her chest relaxed when the music man's grainy voice was out of earshot.

Jericho touched the handkerchief resting underneath her clothing before picking up her sack of groceries and heading home.

Mannobe had been a laid-back, fruit-off-the-vine place for as long as people could remember. Even when the trappings of burgeoning civilisation successfully seduced the neighbouring villages, Mannobans held on resolutely to their traditions like barnacles to a ship: they would have been lost without them. However, only a fool would dismiss Mannobans as mere provincials. Locals declared that although they might indeed reside in a village, it was a village with town aspirations.

The straight, planned roads from nearby towns either dwindled or came to a complete halt once they met the copper-coloured earth of Mannobe, but every local knew where they were going. Once upon a time, directions were given by a series of orders: follow the bumpy road until you see the bush with yellow flowers – not the red, spiky ones, that's right – then turn left and walk as far as the three gigantic potholes in a row, take a left after the burnt tree stump, and the Harbens' compound is to the east . . . But civilisation has a way of corrupting even the most basic of existences, and if street names were good enough for nearby towns that actually *had* streets, then despite its lack of them, their names, certainly, were most welcome in Mannobe. Many people had already claimed rivers and hills by giving them their names, along with whatever stretches of pathway their conscience would allow them to declare a road, and nobody ever really complained. Besides, there was more than enough land in the village for everybody's name to hold some *importance*.

Mannobe's latest triviality brought a smile to Allegory's face. He didn't see the problem with Anis Point, the stretch of land newly inherited by Hamid after his uncle's death. It was only natural the man wanted to honour the deceased's memory in some way, but the land's new name had caused much talk amongst the villagers, for they knew how their lazy accents could sully the most innocent of things.

One of the things Allegory had grown to cherish about the village was its predictability. One could never second-guess life, but there were certain things that could be counted on as anchors in an otherwise capricious existence. For example, you could guarantee that water from the Belago was as pure as a child's smile and that the Azevo dog would have left his waste in the square despite all attempts to encourage him to make him go elsewhere. Finally, you could bet that Le Papillon would have a generous number of customers, and that on Roast Sundays the line of roast pork pleasure seekers could almost reach the edge of his dwelling.

Every two months or so, the Codón sisters let meat marinate in large buckets almost to the point of spoiling before throwing the delightful slabs on grills blackened by recurrent use. That aroma, pungent, spicy, sweet, was siren song to any red-blooded male in the village and most women, who understood that no Sunday meal they had intended to make would match the smell wafting through Mannobe. Although Allegory had trained himself to ignore the luscious scents that drifted from the café to his abode, he accepted that Roast Sunday was his undoing, just like many others. He scratched at his scalp through the jumble of salt and pepper dreadlocks matted into a single gnarled knot atop his head. Ignoring his greying string vest, he adjusted his royal blue neckerchief and headed for his place in the queue.

By the time Allegory made it to the front of the line his

stomach was proclaiming his hunger heavily. M'elle Codón caught sight of him and waved, but before he could make it over to her, her sister directed him to an empty seat on a nearby bench with a commanding point. He sat willingly, anxious to quench his hunger as quickly as possible. Hamid entered and positioned himself at a table in front of him. It was the closest one to the door so he could keep watch over the tyres he'd deposited outside. Magdalena Codón wiped his table from the previous customer and put a glass of water in front of him. Allegory watched Mabel move over to greet Hamid with a squeeze of the shoulder. He took in their conversation as he braced himself for the chicken thigh on his plate.

'*Eh*, beauty runs in your family, Mabel. Your daughter looks more like you every time I come in.'

'*Tanka*, Hamid. What of your Somaya? So much like her mother, give thanks. Her husband will be coming, I'm sure . . .'

Hamid's dramatic exhale was synchronised with that of Allegory as he moved the spicy chicken from one side of his mouth to the other.

'I know, Mabel.' Hamid patted at the muscles underneath his shirt. 'Then what will I do? Who will feed me?'

'You won't have to worry about that, I'm sure,' she laughed. '*Pues*, for now we can help you.' She took the plate her daughter brought from the kitchen and placed it in front of him. 'Here you are. Eat. Breast is still your favourite, *non?*'

Allegory took his time with the remainder of his semolina pudding, watching the changing clientele as if they were animals at a watering hole. The creamy dessert was a refreshing salve for the pepper-rich main course but the ginger was a tingly throwback on his tongue.

He listened to a group a few tables away. The occupants

15

made up a large part of the village's fundraising committee and they were trying to determine the recipient of this year's collections while fighting for the yam chip scraps resting in their communal bowl. Driver, a local vendor, rescued a piece of meat that fell on the floor with a sneaky palm movement. His nickname was formed at four because the first time he'd laid his eyes on a moving vehicle he'd thought he was being chased and had run as fast as his terrified legs could carry him. Unfortunately, they weren't as swift as they'd been in his mind's eye, and he fell, splitting his top lip. It healed, leaving a mark like a cleft palate scar, but it lent character to an otherwise uncomplicated visage.

When Magdalena walked by Driver's table he offered up a sheepish smile. Allegory saw her foot mash the tips of his fingers but Driver just blinked rapidly in her direction, his silly grin still in place. Allegory hoped the man's rescued meat would be consolation for her blatant lack of interest.

He peered at the sky, trying to work out the time. Late afternoon was receding; before long the musician would arrive. He smiled to himself. The impromptu meetings had turned into a small ritual between them over the years. He'd grown increasingly fond of him. Babylon would come to his place having eaten at the café and they would chat until the early hours of the morning. After an adulthood spent in quasi-solitude, he looked forward to their candid interaction.

He was still scraping the side of his bowl when Babylon entered. It was as if the café received a boost of energy: the man was incapable of passing through unnoticed.

'Prophet!' Babylon boomed with an arm outstretched in his direction. Allegory heard the titters of customers as he raised his head. Babylon headed towards him, stopping at various tables to nod at people or to touch someone's elbow, shaking hands tricky with barbecue-greasy fingers.

The musician paused by Driver long enough to swipe a rib off his plate before moving on.

'*Bon dia*. You've eaten well?'

'The Lord stills the hunger of those he cherishes. I have had plenty.'

'That's good, Prophet,' Babylon replied before nudging the smirking, eavesdropping man next to Allegory. 'You can laugh but I tell you,' Babylon's voice rose theatrically, 'as true as I taste this pork, this man has a gift. He can see the future.'

'Tell us what you see, Prophet,' an anonymous voice cut through the dining room, drawing much laughter.

Allegory pushed his bowl aside to observe the clientele. Everyone was belly-drunk on food.

'I see nothing that others who love the Creator cannot see,' he said. 'That when times are good, be happy. But when times are bad consider this – that the Creator has made one as well as the other. Therefore a man cannot discover anything about his future.' He eyeballed them sternly, causing one man to drop the bone he gnawed, in alarm. 'It is better to go to a house of mourning than a house of feasting,' he continued, sweeping his arm across the café. 'Death is the destiny of every man. The living should take this to heart. Those who have eyes to see . . .'

'Yes, Prophet. Tell them,' Babylon encouraged cheekily.

'*Pues*, my stomach is paining me from my feasting,' a large man said, raising his half-mutilated drumstick in the air. 'Now that I'm mourning, I can stay . . .'

'Me too,' another teased. 'Let me mourn some more. Bring meat please!'

Allegory shook his head at his useless congregation and rose, ignoring the peals of laughter echoing at his exit. Babylon squeezed his shoulder as he passed. They would catch up properly later, away from the noisy jovialities of the other customers. As Allegory walked the short distance home, he was extremely grateful for his proximity to Le Papillon. It pained him to admit it, but his belly ached from overeating.

Mabel brandished a long barbecue fork in her hand like a weapon. The singing that had led to a chant had forced her from the relative sanctity of the kitchen.

'Music man,' she scolded, seeing the configuration of diners around Babylon. 'You and your sharp tongue done bring trouble into my restaurant.'

'Apologies, Madam, for my trouble.' He laughed gently, his eyelids dimming in reflex flirtation. 'You know there is only one thing that can silence my tongue,' he added before raising an eyebrow suggestively.

Mabel wiped imaginary sweat away from the back of her neck, suddenly flustered. A crash from the kitchen brought her back to her senses.

'What nonsense are you talking?'

'Your barbecue, Madam! What did you think I meant?' he replied smoothly.

Mabel kissed her teeth but a knowing smile hijacked her face. She waved the fork at him threateningly as she left, and resumed her labour in the kitchen while her sister M'elle took a welcome break. Coughing a path clear above the grill, she flung a huge side of beef over the flame and flattened it with the force of her spatula satisfyingly – imagining it was Babylon – the beef's sizzle as it cooked, music to her ears.

Three

Man confident enough not to swagger
Cock left limb
Loose right
With bravado worthy of the most reputable
Pamplonian bullfights
Sucked gut in tight
Like a balloon exhaling its lifeblood
And began his journey

Babylon was black
With deep indigo hues
Gyrating under latticed skin
Rivers of Congo rhythms pulsing
Created contours of such precision
You could cut diamonds
With his cheekbones

A gleam permanent in both eyes
Belied his age
For Babylon had walked this earth
Four minus forty years

But still retained the optimism of youth
Had savoured the sweetbreads
Of the truth tree
Moved unencumbered through life
Swiftly like the Duchemgba breeze
Lifting the skirts of ironed ladies . . .

Babylon was lazy
A privilege bestowed
On certain Mannoban indigents
A quiet form of indulgence
Like basking in the three p.m. sun
No mouths to feed except his own
He combed the streets
For pearls of wisdom

With Guitar swinging gently
From dancing hips
And on his breath
The faintest kiss of a lullaby –
He always caught the ladies' eye
Causing gasps to become
A little more shallow
Their soprano voices
Developing raspier undertones

They stole furtive glances
Through shuttered lids
Slackened loving grips
And took chances
Hoping dirty thoughts lay hid
Then bolder gazes with shameless pauses
And licking of lips
Had women fiending for a hit from the tips
That strummed that guitar

And laughter would mark the end of a song
No one knew was playing
Ladies placed their betraying bodies
Closer to their partners
Needing to be touched by someone
By Anyone
By Babylon . . .

Introduction done, for a man whose reputation precedes him requires little in the way of fanfare! Besides, in Mannobe, with its average population of nine hundred and falling, everybody's story was written on the tongues of everyone else and gossip and innuendo carried more value than the currency. Babylon was as notorious in Mannobe as one of the last remaining vestiges of the old: the sundial in the square. The ornate dial supposedly imported by Mr Dorique, one of the founding fathers of Mannobe, and as its pride-filled people claimed 'where the "O" in the village's name came from'.

As it was told, Dorique had been embroiled in a decade-long affair with his mistress in Peddie until a weak heart took her to the Creator one summer. Grief-stricken, he was rumoured to have uprooted the sundial from the garden where they had spent endless moments cloud-gazing and carried it all the way on the arduous boat journey back to his beloved home town. By the time he returned to Mannobe, his once black pompadour was white and his eyes held a melancholy that weighed the lower portion of his face down. Nevertheless, setting the sundial down in the square, he'd declared boldly in front of the welcoming party that his heart was rightly back where it belonged. And leaving the spectacular monument in the centre, he returned his significantly less swollen organ to his wife.

Depending on who recounted this tale, Babylon had been present at this occasion even though it had occurred

21

before most grandmothers' memories began. Some even claimed the B in the village's name was attributed to him – if you'd believe it! The musician cast such a big shadow that it short-circuited their memories. To them, he was their son. As Mannobans would say: he was welcome.

The truth was that no one remembered *exactly* when Babylon first arrived in the village, nor could they remember a time that he wasn't there; it was as if such a time never existed. Mabel Codón loved to recall the day she'd been shelling corn and noticed the faint smell of sulphur in the air. Looking skyward, she saw a grey, bird-shaped cloud. It had rained continuously for five nights and after that a man appeared by the river with a guitar.

However, her twin sister refuted this story completely. She was convinced his tale was linked to a pregnant woman who'd passed through the village unaccompanied. M'elle would cast her eyes heavenward slowly as if she were trying to piece the event together in her mind. Then she would clasp her hands together and begin.

'Cleo came across a bundle in the long grass after the woman gone. A baby – can you imagine! She looked after him carefully at home in her orphanage of unwanted things, nursing the boy on a diet of goat's milk and mango pulp. Things were smooth until the day the Great Fire passed through Lugobiville, singeing the outskirts of Mannobe and devastating all in its path. Cleo followed the charred fields back to emptiness, ash and debris choking her throat. The fire had ripped through the place, stealing souls as it saw fit.

'She shuffled through the rubble, roll-calling her creatures by the order in which she'd rescued them, but when she came to the boy's mattress in the corner – empty! *Eh*, they found her by her stove three days later, the child's blanket over her rickety frame, rocking herself gently. She put on her never worn wedding dress – her rippled back exposed for all the world to see, the concerto of buttons too much for old woman's fingers to master. You know, she never wed because all the men had been too afraid to court her! Anyway . . . Babylon is that boy returned.'

M'elle loved to tell Cleo's story, moving the words around her wide mouth like honeyed almonds, her eyes deep with memory. Finally, when Mabel could bear her sister's reportage no more, she would cut through the quietness with a loud cackle.

'*Eh-heh*, M'elle done inhale too many fumes from her years in the kitchen! But she can tell a good story . . .'

Most of the adults in Mannobe had heard and told Babylon's story in one form or another. Still, it was occasionally necessary for the younger generation to go straight to the source; they seemed to realise instinctively that one could drink water from a gourd, but only fresh water from the Belago could quench a thirst.

Babylon would catch sight of a little one after his performance had ended and descending from his towering height, he would focus his gaze on his challenger and draw out the question without moving his lips. Then the youngster would raise watery eyes towards him and beg his tale.

He'd make a grand show of settling his lithe frame on the ground, giving his interrogator and wary friends time to arrange themselves in a circle of wonder around him, and deliver the following story:

> '*Eso es mi cancion*
> *Eso es mi historica*
> *I am going to tell you a tale*
> *De una mujer, Gloria . . .*'

'My mother was a woman of enormous beauty. When we were little we wouldn't look her in the eyes for fear we

23

would be struck blind – like from staring right at the sun, or looking directly into the face of God. She had an individual song for each of us children. You know, we had to dream in shifts? There were so many of us, we took turns in sharing the beds.

'In time, some of my older siblings were beckoned by wandering spirits to new towns and some of my sisters married and sang songs of their own to their young. But I always remember us as a family, one pulsing organism with a dazzling mother for its head, and a wriggling body – forty strong of brothers and sisters – Titus, Joshua, Sonny, Nwadi, Rafael, Luis, Adaobi, Francisco, Chika, Theresa, Chi-Chi, Ngozi, Bilbao, Mazi, Joyce, Andrew, Bo-Bo, Eunice, Francesca, Mali, Stephen, Amaka, Salome, Milicent, Yanda, Marina, Eve, Emmanuel, Annabelle, Daisy, Ema, Raymond, Adam, Patience, Gloria, Lupe, Cheo, Pepe, Ramón and I, the youngest.

'Pepe was six lunar eclipses older than I, but still it was near impossible for anyone to tell us apart. Ramón, who came between us, was extremely jealous of this closeness when we were small. He would always hide my writing-slate so that I would have to spend time looking for it and he could play with Pepe alone. Once, he even fed me strawberries, knowing that my head would swell up like a blowfish and my throat scratch like mosquito spit if I even looked at the fruit.

'When Gloriama found out what happened, she slapped him hard across the cheek with an iron fist but quickly kissed the pain away, drowning his tears inside her floured apron. Three days later when I was better, Ramón had wrapped his larger, much cherished slate for me by way of an apology. My pain had been too horrible for even *his* jealous heart. From then on the three of us were inseparable.

'Every summer, *le Cirque d'Orgeuille* would come to

Borone. It wasn't a real circus – more a band of gypsies, clothed in such vivid colours: saffron, vermilion and guava pink. They smelt of distant, unnamed places shrouded in mystery, of aniseed and hickory smoke. The women would dance, their chestnut hair flowing behind them like the manes of wild mustangs, clutching gigantic balloons of skirts in their palms. The men sat on three-legged wooden stools with various hand-crafted instruments between their thick legs. They created the most beautiful of music without stopping for breath or break as the sun turned to moon and back again.

'We would sneak out to spy on the foreigners, staying out as long as we could before Gloriama's mystical power called us back to the sanctity of home.

'On my eighth birthday, Ramón, Pepe and I parted the trees to catch a glimpse at our dry-land mermaids before Gloriama's traditional feast of warm cassava bread and guava jam. We were watching the gypsy women shaking themselves into a collective frenzy when I felt a stern grip on my shoulder. Behind me was a man as fearsome as a wildebeest! Huge swirls of smoke chuffed out of his nostrils from a cigar tucked in the corner of his mouth. Locked in his grey-eyed gaze, I was temporarily paralysed with fear, I could only stare. In weathered hands the size of bear claws, he held a knobbly flute out to me and motioned for me to play.

'I held the flute to my lips and blew, but it snorted wickedly. Ramón and Pepe pointed at me and laughed until the giant looked sternly at them. Pepe snatched the flute from me, pursed his lips and whispered softly into its shaft. Suddenly, the air around his mouth was littered with magical flute food, his fingers kneading the wooden pipe as if it was fresh dough. Seeing his talent, I bowed my head in shame. I was removing phantom dust from between my toes when the man ruffled my hair and whispered softly,

"That is not your instrument. I have just the thing for you. Come."

'We followed him through the leafy shelter, finally in close proximity with the carnival. Conversations erupted around us, we saw the sweat dripping from the women's skin like caramelised onions in apple-buttered skillets. Pungent odours of cinnamon and cardamom paraded arrogantly around the makeshift compound. We became a six-eyed monster, suckling greedily on the vision of those gyrating beauties, enjoying the free concert.

'The giant prodded me again and I dragged my gaze from the sirens to see what would become my future: a perfect figure of eight body carved out of the smoothest of rosewoods – varnished the exact consistency and colour of tupelo honey, followed by a lean shaft with strings of varying thickness dancing through its veins. It looked even more masterful than the hollow tube Pepe had tamed earlier, and the man laughed at my amazement.

'"I told you. *This* is your instrument. *Play.*"

'I balanced the heavenly creature on my tender knees like I had seen the travelling men do for days. My left hand held the shaft – its main artery – and I caressed its veins. The guitar sighed with pleasure. I closed my eyes and played. The giant instinctively mimicked my mother's lull-aby to send me to dreams, it was almost as if her voice filled the entire arena. My music moved those grown gypsy men to tears. The sirens stopped twirling to listen to me, small as I was, unravelling a tale as old as the universe through my inexperienced fingers. In that moment, *la musica* and I became one, being united by the hand of the Creator.

'I spent every free moment I could with the foreigner, known to me by then as Gogoa, and he taught me how to hone my gift. One afternoon as we practised scales and spit melon seeds on to the ground before us, I asked him how he could spend his whole life travelling. He chased a pip around his pink gums pensively and replied after what seemed like a long time.

'"You see the sky? That is my roof. And this earth is my bed. That is all that I require in this life. Travelling is for people who want to experience another place. We are searchers, Babylon, scouring these magical lands. Because out here . . ." and he stretched his meaty arm across the whole horizon before stabbing at my chest with his fingers. ". . . this is where the music comes from. *Eso es la musica.*"

'Spitting the pip at my feet, he handed the guitar to me with a smile.

'"This is yours now. I have shown you all I can. The rest is up to you. We are leaving tonight, Babylon. But you have been called. Whether you choose to answer, it is not for me to tell you."

'I returned home that day with a heart filled with sand. I was so perturbed I couldn't even settle the argument between Ramón and Pepe about whose feet were the biggest. I fought my mother's haunting song as she crooned her magic words to me. In that final moment between dreams and lucidity, she kissed me softly and whispered, "*I understand my darling, go see for yourself.*" With her permission I slipped off to sleep.

'I woke up to that unmistakable smoky scent. Gogoa's ugly face smiled down on me and I swung around to inspect my surroundings. We were travelling in a wagon across the back of Borone over the mountains to Monte Rosso. As the ground disappeared under the carriage before my eyes, I reached beside me and felt for the guitar. My mother had tied a lock of her hair around its wrist. Gogoa ruffled my hair affectionately, chuffed his putrid smoke and laughed at me.

'"Now you are a searcher too."

> '*Eso es mi cancion*
> *Eso es mi historica*
> *Eso es la verita*
> *Eso es mi testimonia* . . .'

After the last gangly child ran home, lips repeating the story so as never to forget, Babylon would dust off his backside before stroking Guitar gently as they composed lazy melodies together.

Once, Guitar had asked him if he would ever reveal the real story of his childhood.

'Are you saying I'm lying?' Babylon had challenged with a knowing smirk.

'*Pues*, embellishing the truth is more—'

'But that's the definition of an artist!' Babylon's eyes flashed as he laughed his '*ha-ha*' laugh ferociously, releasing tiny saliva pearls from his lips that looked like scattered gems on the roadside. The breeze behind him, he'd continued his stroll, humming quietly under his breath while Guitar winked in the setting sun like a restless cowboy.

Four

Mabel had dreamed of owning a café ever since she was a little girl and her mother had shown her how to make groundnut stew, adding two spoons of brown sugar to the mixture to give it some punch. Mama Codón had refused to cut down her sugar intake, despite her diabetic condition, reasoning that if her life was destined to be short then it was also predestined to be sweet. Even though she'd been taken to The Eternal Compound at just fifty-three years old, having choked on a bone from her renowned honeyed catfish, that didn't stop Mabel from procuring her childhood dream. The way she saw it, a café was just like having a very big kitchen.

Le Papillon was situated on the Eastern Shore in Halome, where the scent of cherry blossom was blown over by the Belago River. When a cool breeze hit, the trees would rain pink petals so that the river looked as if it had been decorated with sequins.

The land by the river had been vacant for years, until Mabel brought the documentation back with her from Joucous, along with a lorry loaded with bags of cement. While clearing her newly acquired property she'd stumbled across Allegory, then a middle-aged man with wiry arms and legs, preceded by a stomach as round as a football. All attempts to move him and his ramshackle tent had been fruitless, even with her big-city documentation. The self-appointed preacher had remained as steadfast as a man his size could (the growth spurt all young men awaited had abandoned him decades earlier at five foot four inches, preferring to concentrate on his hair instead). As he claimed that she couldn't own what the Lord had given him and pointed at the earth beneath his ashen feet, Mabel had grown tired of his fight and built around him, which was the reason for her café's irregular shape, that of a painter's palette, or – as she saw it – a butterfly.

The old man's discomfort had actually drawn people when she first opened the café. Food was always sweeter accompanied with some entertainment, even at Allegory's expense. Beloved by the village, he'd been given his prestigious name because everybody thought he spoke in riddles.

Only Babylon called him something different: Prophet. The musician was convinced that the old man was capable of seeing things beyond the eye and when villagers cackled at his belief, he'd tell them of how the old man had saved him from a puff adder when he'd first come to the village. In some ways, Allegory had shaped all of their lives, for if his garbled wisdoms hadn't managed to help, then the laughter his rambling elicited was medicine enough for their recoveries.

Where or how Mabel had acquired her sizeable fortune was one of life's mysteries. Even M'elle hadn't procured the truth after all these years. Mabel had left Mannobe an innocent, wide-eyed beauty, and returned, determined and distinguished, with a little daughter in tow and the fragrance of money encircling her hand-finished clothing.

M'elle never understood why she'd wanted to leave the village; she herself had never heard the call of distant spirits. She couldn't imagine waking up without the smell of palm leaves or flan clinging to her skin, but Mabel had acquired an insatiable appetite for travel at an early age. An avid day-dreamer, she'd always longed to feel stranger soil underfoot. And so one day she took off amidst kisses and tears, and later returned in true prodigal daughter fashion. The whole village became her mother when Mama Codón – who died a year before her return – left an opening.

M'elle had never left the idyllic cocoon, she'd had the pleasure of watching the village grow and evolve like the offspring she never had – from an awkward youngster to a fully fledged adult that could make the adjacent districts blush, embarrassed by their own inadequacy. She'd watched many people leave their home town to come back older and much more disillusioned than when they'd set out. She'd lived vicariously through others' loves and losses, and mostly through her twin who'd managed to grow heavy with a child when she couldn't. All her life, she'd secretly wished that she had been born second of the two – convinced that the extra thirteen minutes Mabel had remained in their mother's womb without her were when the angels had conveyed the secrets of motherhood to her sibling.

Her name had changed from Eloise to M'elle over the years as she'd aged. It wasn't exactly clear whether the 'M' stood for 'Madame' or 'Mama', even though – strictly speaking – she wasn't anyone's mother, in that her belly had never experienced the weight of a child. But her unique moniker conveyed the village's affection for her; she was relation to few but a friend to all, which was plenty because, she reminded herself time and again, friends are the family you choose, not the people tied to you without your say-so.

M'elle wore her sadness like a second scent, a salty residue that coated her skin, but she never breathed a word to anyone, particularly her sister. And her inability to share her deficiency with her twin was the thing that began to separate them as they grew older. She weighed her secret down with food until it lay buried in the pit of her stomach. Her circumference widened, erasing the contours of her former shape. They had once been identical life-size groundnut shells: now only Mabel was.

M'elle had always considered her sister to be the more beautiful of them. It was difficult to explain, but her sister's face offered something hers did not, and that thing made her the more alluring twin. Perhaps it was the dimples that ran across her features like naughty schoolchildren whenever she told a joke, or the arch of her eyebrows that hypnotised men into doing her bidding.

People were always more drawn to Mabel. And that, combined with her capacity to bear children, made M'elle feel less like a woman.

Jericho hugged her knees to her chest as she sat on the bank of the river, observing the clementine shade of the sky. She liked the nip of the dawn chill against her cheekbones. It would only be a matter of time before the sun turned on the dry heat of the day. At least she could enjoy the morning with very little disturbance; the gentle breeze and the leopard-coloured spider that crawled off the edge of her dress and over her toes didn't count.

Her nocturnal return had been more subdued than it would have been if she'd come home in the day, yet despite the late hour of her arrival that night, her mother had been able to summon a respectable amount of people to stand around and stare at her. Luckily the dark had hidden her features as she feigned excitement at meeting people she hadn't even thought about since her departure. Penny had been her first genuine greeting; she'd missed her best friend dearly.

The neighbour's cockerel had roused her from her confused dreams too early. Its incessant cry made sleeping an impossibility but gave her the opportunity to collect her thoughts away from her mother's scrutiny. She was grateful for the peace.

She was pleased about her mother's delight at her homecoming, but almost instantly, the suffocation had set in. It wasn't just that she missed Angel, but it seemed as if her mother had stored all the things she wanted to tell her in her absence down a well and now was constantly drawing up buckets of information that threatened to drown her. Plus, she was used to looking after herself now, and there was something about the way her mother issued orders, no matter how simple, that made her skin prickle.

Words replayed themselves in her mind; the comment her mother had made after hugging her forcefully and turning her head from side to side to inspect the new lines in her face and other changes to her appearance. '*Eh-eh*, you look like your father.' She'd felt happy because her mother had rarely mentioned her father since his departure, but then she'd noticed her mother's lips curling downward and realised that the statement hadn't exactly been meant as a compliment.

Watching the tranquil waters of the Belago trickle by, its indigo ink ripples in the light, the city seemed far away. She closed her eyes tightly and resurrected those sounds in her memory: the quiet of the city that was never as quiet as life in the village, the clanking of horns and the buzzing of industry a constant noise in the back of everything. As she flicked through stored images, a face sprang to the front of her thoughts and she felt her lips spreading into a smile.

*

33

Driver took his legs off the pedals as his wagon rounded the corner quickly, enjoying that feeling of almost flight. If he weren't a grown man he would have squealed with delight. As a boy riding his bicycle, he had liked squealing as he raised the handlebars in the air and rode on just the back wheel. He'd been convinced that yelling like a baby mouse was the key to maintaining his balance for such a long distance.

He adored his barrow, fashioned from a bicycle with a large receptacle on the back to deliver goods throughout Mannobe. As he was still emotionally scarred from his early memory, everyone knew that getting him to go anywhere near a vehicle with an engine would be like trying to make Allegory drink alcohol: impossible.

Early morning was his favourite time of day. The roads were clearer, without impediments, like other riders or the obstructions of market workers and their ever-expanding stalls, the cold wind whipping at his face until the afternoon sun warmed his throbbing limbs. In the morning he felt like a king. The whole village was his dominion as he pedalled, selling his wares. He enjoyed the feel of his carriage; the way it got lighter throughout the course of the day as he made his deliveries comforted him.

He inspected his battered legs briefly before transferring his attention back to the road. His legs could tell his whole story, each bruise and dent housing a cherished memory. He knew that they didn't look like the legs of a man, that his daily exercise of pulling the wagon behind him toned his legs extensively. Combined with a metabolism that seemed determined not to affix fat on his frame, his physique was youthful, but this realisation annoyed him at times. Of course, because he was thinking about his inadequacy, his thoughts flew to Babylon. They had been friends for a long time but sometimes their pairing seemed as unnatural to him as a mongoose walking through Waranga arm in fin with a monkfish. It was their sense of humour that united them, the comedy they created from the villagers' lives. His friend could move him to laughter quicker than the servers at Borrow's bar could ignite his loins with a twitch of their eyelashes.

Driver relished the titbits of information he gleaned from people as he persuaded them to buy his goods. His job gave him an open window into the lives of others – not that he was a gossip! He never left anyone's house without a smile, a snack or a story; he would have felt cheated otherwise. Then he and Babylon would pore over the truths he'd discovered later, loosening their jaws with home brew so that their laughter slid freely out of their mouths as they chuckled at others' expense.

It had been a long time since his morning journey had been interrupted by such an arresting distraction. Rounding the narrow street that led from the bakery into the centre, he was stunned by the woman in the long brown dress. She must have been a newcomer to Mannobe because he hadn't seen her before on his rounds.

He observed her greedily, her sparkly eyes and royal features, the remarkable symmetry of her lips that were now pursing in disdain. He heard the sound fall from her mouth, the sound of air being pushed out between her closed teeth – like air leaking from a tyre – and realised that he must have been staring at her. Driver laughed and allowed his feet to touch the ground either side of his wagon wheel. He pretended to clean the invisible spectacles he wore but she didn't find it at all amusing. He was mildly disappointed. He knew he was no charmer like his musician friend, but his glasses skit usually softened whomever he was admiring.

'Hello? *Hello?*' he called out but she cut her eyes at him and began to walk off. 'Everything good with you?'

She hesitated and threw a polite nod in his direction. He watched her open her mouth as if to say something but almost instantly she decided against it and continued walking. Driver felt his shoulder muscles tighten and found that he was standing with his hands on his hips. It dawned on him that he must have looked a little idiotic but at least the position he'd adopted kept his hands still. When she'd moved away from him, he rested his feet on the pedals and accelerated to catch up with her.

'*Bon dia*. I said hello!' He displayed his best smile when she turned to face him. 'Would you like to buy something?'

'What are you selling?'

'A bit of everything. I have nice things for someone like you.'

'I don't have money.' She waved empty hands at him.

'That's okay. If you tell me where you live, I'm sure we can arrange something?'

Now that he was nearer to her, Driver saw that the young woman was even more attractive than he'd imagined. There was something distinctive about her features. She looked as if she was from the village yet she had an air of refinement that only came from outside, as though her good looks had been magnified by somewhere more vibrant, making her seem less provincial. He was out of his league and he knew it.

He gawped at the smoothness of her skin and the gentle swell of her breasts that peeked out of the top of the dress's neckline. Honing his gaze, he saw minuscule beads of sweat that made her body glow and he felt as if someone had dropped a plate of Mabel's fiery red beans down his shorts. His previous comment had been entirely innocent but inexplicably her eyes had dropped downwards. She noticed the telltale swelling and kicked the back of his wagon sharply with the heel of her sandal.

'*Disgusting*,' she hissed, moving away from him.

'Sorry,' he offered, covering himself quickly. 'Can I help it if I'm a man?'

'A fool is what you are. Now carry your load and go.'

When she'd escaped down a side road, he pushed off with more force than necessary. He was hoping the brisk exercise would cool the fire and shame stinging his loins. It was then that recognition struck: she was Edith Lwembe's daughter, newly returned. With each rotation of his wheel he was further away from her rejection and conjuring up the horror on her face as she caught sight of the secret between his legs. He wanted to laugh. He imagined replaying the incident for his friend later on, the musician's voice like the bray of a donkey as he wiped tears from his eyes at Driver's failed flirting. Ordinarily, he would have been nonplussed by a woman's lack of interest and would have happily scattered the carcass of his rebuff for Babylon to interpret its bones; it was the rising sweet potato in his shorts on this occasion that made him feel the most stupid.

Sliding his legs off the pedals again, he leaned his back against the wind he'd managed to gather around him by speeding and turned his face to the sun. Golden light wiped the woman's features from his memory and he sighed, deciding that this was one anecdote he would keep for himself alone.

Five

'You know when you have an itch, high *so*, that your left hand or your right hand can't reach it?'

Babylon scowled to accentuate the power of his question. He'd been trying to describe the woman in his dream to his friend, but was struggling to find the words to attach to her. Already her features had faded from his memory, but not the memory of looking on them: that feeling still remained.

The dream had been so vivid that he'd awoken grudgingly, trying to hold on to the fading seconds of his reverie. When he was lucid, she was the song on the tip of his tongue that he was trying desperately to recall but was adamant he knew.

It had been a while since anyone in the village had captured Babylon's attention and he'd grown lazy as a bear in a salmon-filled stream. He was happy to eat freely, but there was very little pleasure in it. It was as if Mannobe's fish had resigned themselves to their fate, impaling themselves readily on his jagged claws. But it was in a bear's nature to hunt.

Luckily he had his imagination to fall back on. Unlike

the bear, he could at least draw on his artistry, his music, and season each fish accordingly – more bass here, a high chord there, and so on. That creative pastime confused his palate temporarily although he was always aware of his dissatisfaction once the meal reached his belly. But he knew that many men in the village were starving, his friend included, while he was fortunate enough to have a steady diet. This always consoled him when his taste buds protested their lack of variety. Still he couldn't help thinking that perhaps the time had come for him to venture elsewhere. It wasn't as if he'd intended to stay in the village for ever, even if it had served him well. Babylon tried to recall the last place he'd stayed in for so long. Whenever he settled, it was as if an uneasiness called him from within, urging him ever onward.

'What you do?' Driver asked of Babylon's earlier question.

'*Ewo*, find someone else to scratch it,' he replied philosophically.

Magdalena could easily recall the first time she'd seen the musician up close. She'd been rushing through Le Papillon balancing a platter of fish curry when she knocked his fork to the floor with her protruding behind. Apologising, she lost herself in the depths of his gaze and was held hostage to a beautiful smile, his teeth a dazzling array of stalactites. When she returned to the kitchen a minute later, her aunt M'elle looked at her asking,

'What's wrong with you? You look like you lost your head.'

M'elle had laughed, the sound like dry bread escaping through her dark lips, and Magdalena busied herself washing plates, all the while slipping furtive glances through the beaded curtain that separated the dining area from the kitchen.

*

39

Babylon would wander into Le Papillon sporadically after meeting Allegory in his tent for a meat pie or a slice of her mother's honey cake. He would relax in the café her mother had decorated with the artefacts she'd accumulated on her travels: metal cooking pots and elaborate tribal masks that lined the burnt orange walls. He and the other customers would eat and listen to the twins' harmonies as they finished each other's melodies behind the curtain, the pans and wooden spoons providing percussion.

At first, they didn't speak, but Magdalena would feel her body temperature rising under the intrusion of his watch and so hid behind her thick lashes and made sure to limit their conversation to *'yes, tanka, and bon dia.'* Whenever he smiled on his exit, she noticed her body softening in anticipation.

She loved observing him teasing his guitar affectionately while he took large bites of his meal. Sometimes he sang a little as he sipped his drink and the Adam's apple in his throat tinkled like a bell only she could hear. He'd caught her staring at him on several occasions, but he just grinned knowingly, while she fell deeper.

One day, as she walked past the square on her way to the meat market, Magdalena saw a small congregation of people gathered by the sundial. Even though she was pressed for time, she squeezed her body in with the onlookers. She saw Babylon, the beads of sweat glistening in his wild locks, his voice as powerful as a thousand choirs, delivering his melodies.

The crowd were transfixed by him and his song of liquid velvet, recalling tales of purple mountains, of queens, of love lost and rekindled in the afterlife. When he swung his head back to remove the tangle of hair that obstructed his vision she swore that he'd focused on her alone. She observed him whispering deep into his guitar conspiratorially while his right foot pounded out a rhythm. It wasn't her imagination: she distinctly heard him weaving her name in and out of his song like a mantra, a prayer, a caress. The guitar preened as Babylon began to sing gently behind his crystalline teeth, 'Magdalena, Magdalena, como una promesa . . .' before a knowing smile teased the corners of his mouth.

Magdalena felt her heart quickstep. It swelled up so much inside her chest that she welcomed the weight of the two men either side of her keeping her upright. She intercepted the look that Babylon offered to her, wrapped it tightly in her small fist and sprinted to Manuel's before it closed.

She'd almost fainted the following day when he'd strolled into Le Papillon humming his, or rather her, song. She'd blushed, embarrassed by his boldness, and escaped behind the curtains. She returned, hiding behind a fortress of ginger cake for her waiting customers. Her back towards him, Magdalena arranged plates around a table for her clientele. As she picked up the heavy jug of her mother's spiced tea she felt a tingle climbing up her legs. She turned her eyes downward in time to catch his long fingers tracing the exposed shaft of her calf. It was a wonder she didn't scald the customers as she fought to retain her composure and contain the excitement that was causing her heart to beat like a djembe drum.

Jericho watched her mother straining to fasten her sandals with a hint of amusement. She knelt to help her with the clasp, marvelling at its longevity even though her mother only wore the sandals once a year, before her birthday, in preparation for their walk.

Jericho had loved celebrating her mother's birthday as a child, not only because birthdays meant peppered goat and, if she was really lucky, cake, but also because of the long walk she and her mother would take, their combined steps winding around the village like an intricate tapestry while her mother unravelled countless tales and offloaded any secrets light enough for her childish frame to carry.

Her mother always started the walk at Mannobe's lowest point, a fact that Jericho could never comprehend as they would invariably get more tired as their journey progressed to its culmination at the Crescent, before they made their way back round to Costa Lina, their preferred rest spot so that they could pick the wild flowers that grew on the bend before stopping to ogle the Dorique mansion.

Jericho loved threading her fingers through the cold bars of the Dorique gate before pressing her face up against the iron barrier. The house itself was too far from the gate to peek inside, but counting the windows had been enough to convey its scale. The delicate carvings about the main front door had illustrated an attention to detail and even the grass that circled their house had been intimidated into growing evenly.

As a child she'd often imagined what it must be like to grow up wanting for nothing. Of course she realised that the Doriques must have had their own private desires, but it wasn't really the indulgences she'd considered then but more practical things like being able to go to school in a new uniform. She knew Penny's family helped to pay for her schoolbooks after her father had gone and she'd been grateful and secretly embarrassed at the same time. She loved her mother's wrappers but had longed for one that had been bought solely for her, green with butterscotch giraffes laughing all across the fabric. Not that she would ever say it aloud, but while she'd fingered the gates of the mansion and looked at the house, she wondered what it would be like to live inside that beautiful space, where they didn't have to choose between butter and milk, in a household that used a different fork for each season.

When she was in her teens, her mother had revealed that she had once interviewed for a position in the Dorique mansion. Jericho's eyes had widened in admiration of her mother, who had been witness to the splendour of the mansion's interior and had waited so long to impart this information. She'd revelled greedily in her mother's account of the Doriques' lavish furniture, the sofas with legs like tiger paws, lamps with enough arms to rival any weeping willow, the sweeping rooms that took longer than rivers to cross. Her mother had been offered a position as a fill-in cook. She'd visited the house and was shown the kitchen in great detail, which, she'd emphasised, was bigger than the entire bakery she opted to work for instead after turning down the coveted position with the Doriques. Jericho had reprimanded her mother for her choice as her mother pulled her away from the gate, explaining that as wonderful as the job had seemed, she wouldn't have been able to handle the responsibility of breaking a plate she knew would probably be worth a month's salary.

Their walk had much more resonance for her now she was a woman in her own right. She'd wanted to tell her mother about Daniel as they'd looked at the house that was still magnificent but a little worn with age, but the words hadn't come. She'd felt guilty, particularly as age seemed to be loosening its clutch around the truth where her mother was concerned. Her mother had mentioned a trip she'd taken with her father very nonchalantly, which was a complete reversal from her childhood, when she'd always had to make do with incomplete stories.

The birthday strolls had started after he left, as if her mother wanted to erase the memory of his footsteps by creating new ones with her daughter, and over time it had worked. All Jericho's attempts to reference him had been greeted with a meaningful silence, except she hadn't known what that meant and so allowed her child's imagination to fill it in. She knew plenty of other children who had done the same, the adults of Mannobe seemingly less than

43

forthcoming when it entailed matters of their own heart, even though they could pontificate for days over what went on in other households. Gradually, she'd learned not to ask questions, knowing that ignorance was preferable to the withholding of truth and in those moments where the weight of uncertainty felt ominous, she dug deep and pushed through the pain. The Mannobe way.

Jericho looked from the frangipani tree to her sketch. She'd drawn musical notes hanging from some of its branches instead of flowers. A muted aria sounded in the distance; one of the village's musicians was playing a guitar nearby and she made out a horn of some kind.

She laughed in spite of her picture's unconscious error, relenting because much of life's beauty had resulted from some of nature's greatest mistakes.

The flirtation between Babylon and Magdalena went unnoticed throughout the village mostly because the musician's conquests were overlooked as one would overlook a stutter or the nervous twitch that Driver, Babylon's dear friend, had.

Driver had tried to warn his friend against playing with Magdalena's affections, knowing first hand the kind of effect his compatriot had on the female population. He could see straight away what Babylon's smouldering looks were doing to Mabel's daughter and it was beginning to cause him concern. Even more seriously, however, he was tired of receiving the smaller portion of food whenever she served them – a matter that troubled his stomach a great deal more than Magdalena's romantic well-being. For although she lovingly heaped spoonfuls of peppermint rice on his friend's plate along with succulent cuts of meat, he had to make do with a wing or whatever chance piece strayed out of the pot.

Driver knew that Magdalena Codón couldn't occupy

Babylon's wandering attentions. The musician's sweet tooth ached for exotic women and while Magdalena was attractive in a retiring kind of fashion, she was rather homely, to say the least.

She was one of those women that had stood on the crossroads of beauty and mediocrity in their puberty. Most assumed she would take after her mother as she'd appeared to in her early infancy, but somehow the hormones coursing through her body, fusing cells, locked her features into that of another relative; in other words, she'd taken the wrong turn. Her mediocre features were salvaged, however, by her hair, one small blessing from her maternal line, and she kept it tied in a long silky braid, whose tail reached the small of her back.

Yet, despite her simplicity, the young woman possessed a gentleness that was alluring, although Driver suspected her cloyingness would be her undoing. He'd wished briefly that she burned with a passion for him, but he was used to losing women. It was clear that Babylon secreted some hypnotic scent that drove damsels crazy. Babylon could do no wrong in the eyes of the sexier sex.

Driver observed him as they sat, devouring a large chicken breast and smacking his lips in delight. Suddenly Driver felt a crimson fire burning the back of his throat. He gulped down water to quench his unexplainable anger with Babylon, who continued his idle chatter, clearly oblivious to the struggle within him, even casually reaching across the table to scoop up the wishbone that rested on Driver's plate.

The commotion caused M'elle to remove her head from the oven, and she listened like an animal seeking out danger before rushing through the café. She found Babylon's hair decorated with rice grains and gravy splatter. Driver had puffed himself up to his full height but he still fell short of the musician's stature. Nevertheless, he looked as if he'd been possessed by the devil. She watched Babylon reach out to Driver, who brushed his hand away as if his touch was infectious. She knew he was now so high up on his moral cross that he was afraid to climb back down.

'You always get what you want. Why is that, *eh*? You get everything and then you want to take the small I have. Leave me in peace!'

'*Tranquilo*, Driver. I was only . . .'

'You were only! Can't you take responsibility for your actions? Can't you just say sorry?'

M'elle stood in between the two men, providing a no man's land with her veritable size. Placing dough-like palms against each man's chest, she tried to massage their battered egos to a peaceful resolution as her customers looked on greedily at the show included with their meal.

'Please, stop this nonsense, now – *now*! Not even children fight over a piece of meat.'

'Auntie, stay out of this, *abeg*. This is not about meat, this is about him!'

'What has he done today that is different from what he does every day?'

'He does anything he likes and everybody says, leave him; *ah ah*! Babylon, here are the slippers we sewed for you, Babylon, take these mangoes we picked for you. All the women—'

'I thought you said this wasn't about meat?'

Babylon's glib statement cut through his soliloquy like a sickle through long grass and, distracted from his train of thought, Driver wavered.

M'elle watched Driver's features rearranging themselves, as if he was battling with some extraordinary emotion. Deep dimples appeared either side of his mouth and he began to laugh involuntarily.

'You're so stupid. Very stupid indeed. You see what

46

I'm talking about?' He moved past her and swiped half-heartedly at his friend's shoulder but Babylon caught his hand mid-flight and pulled him into a bear hug, planting a kiss on his cheek.

'But you love me, *non*?'

They settled themselves down at the uprighted table, chuckling while Magdalena busied herself cleaning up the discarded food on the floor. Shaking her head at the ways of men, M'elle returned to the kitchen, pontificating loudly about how they could waste the perfectly good food she'd so lovingly prepared.

Magdalena approached his table keeping her eyes averted, staring only at the calico cloth as if it were fashioned from spun gold. She held her breath as she wiped down the table, aware of Babylon's stare searing a hole through her blouse. She'd counted up to seven when she felt his warm hand stroking the side of her face.

'You have some rice in your hair,' he whispered as his fingers worked the rebel grain loose.

Her cheeks burned under his gaze and she scuttled through the curtain. It was only when she'd placed the dishes on the counter that she realised she was still holding her breath. Risking a glance through the curtain, her eyes met instantly with his. He raised his glass to her in a silent toast before emptying the entire contents down his throat and Magdalena grabbed the stacked dishes sharply.

M'elle noticed that her niece was becoming clumsier of late. That was the second plate she had broken in a week.

As Jericho neared her compound, her nostrils twitched in recognition. She'd been expecting the tickle of scotch bonnets to assault her as she returned from gathering flowers for her mother's birthday, the mouthwatering aroma of goat meat massaged laboriously with heavy spices, but what she detected was something far more exciting. Jericho heard her mother's spoon clicking savagely against the side of the pot and winced at the two-pronged attack on her senses.

She'd perfected the art of eating soup at a tender age. She'd been perplexed to learn that some people ate theirs with utensils; everyone knew that soup didn't taste the same unless it was eaten with the hands.

As a child, she liked to break off small sections of her pounded yam and roll them into little balls. She loved the sensation of the cooling dome against her fingertips, the tug of the yam as it threatened to stick to them for ever like glue. She would assemble the little balls around the edge of her bowl. The first ball would be dunked into the soup until her knuckles almost disappeared into the broth her mother had prepared, the heat of the soup searing her skin and softening the yam ball so that she could barely grip it. Chewing was entirely optional, depending on what the soup contained. Her favourite then had been bitter leaf soup, which was curiously the opposite of what its name suggested. The yam would slide down her throat easily like an oyster; all that remained to bite on was the meat or pieces of dried fish in the soup.

'Mama, why is your soup so good?' she would ask every time, fanning her fingers out so that they made a soupy web between them for her mother to see.

'Because of my special ingredient, *bona*.'

'What's your special ingredient?'

'I can't tell you! Okay, only if you promise to be a good girl,' her mother would respond, wrinkling her nose.

'I'll be a good girl, Mama.'

'All right. You have to cook the soup with love.'

Jericho loved begging her mother for the soup until she became annoyed and tried to sweep her out of the room with the tired, wooden broom she used to clean their floors. Then she'd leave, pouting and grumbling under her breath quietly in case her mother heard her and refused to make the soup ever again.

Some days when she came back from school, from delivering one of her mother's parcels, or from playing with children in the nearby compounds, her nostrils would pick up that familiar smoky scent of the leaves as they boiled down in their mossy green concoction, the thick smell of palm oil and meat percolating through the soup, causing her mouth to water. She would skip the rest of the way home and hug her mother tightly from behind; her mother would welcome her, holding her briefly against her wrapper until Jericho's warmth along with the rising temperature of the kitchen would prove too much and she would dislodge her with a lift of her bottom.

Evenings couldn't come quickly enough then. She would hover between the kitchen and the front room, watching flies resting on surfaces for a millisecond before their bodies grew hot and they searched for shade elsewhere. To alleviate her frustration she peered outside longingly, waiting for her father to return home from work, his handkerchief flapping in his left hand as he mopped the beads of sweat that congregated on his forehead while he climbed the bumpy road to their house. If she saw him, Jericho would run outside and dance around him like a dog whose master had returned. On days when her mother was making bitter leaf soup, she would sing as well, circling and circling him until he had no choice but to place his handkerchief against her small forehead as though it were a banknote, to praise her for her excellent performance.

By the time they came back to the house, her mother would be serving up the hot soup. Once her father had washed his face in the bowl her mother had brought to him, they would sit on the floor to eat and her yam-rolling would begin.

Jericho retreated to her private world, muting her mother's disapproving scold and her father's quiet laughter as she began her ritual. All that remained was her and her fingers, the different textures that played with them before teasing her mouth in an explosion of taste, everything else leading up to that moment forgotten.

The first day her father didn't come home her mother didn't speak. Nor did she summon her voice the following day. Her eyes had been wide with tears that she refused to release, that welled up dangerously in her lower lids. It reminded Jericho of the time she'd tried to keep her eyes open when her friend Penny had attempted to teach her to swim. Every time she closed her eyes later on, it had felt as if her eyeballs were being scratched by a fish's tail.

Three days after her father's disappearance, her mother had made her favourite soup. Jericho smelt the distinct herbs and habit caused her to run from outside and dance up to her mother's waist until the soup was cooked. She leaned her body as far out of the window as she could, trying to divine her father's shape from the shadows the trees cast in the darkening sky. As she'd tried to go outside to look for him, her mother raised her voice, and so she'd cowered behind the wooden bench in the front room as her mother cleared her throat three times, her action that signalled the meal was ready.

Jericho had sat cross-legged on the floor while she waited for her mother to fill her bowl. If her father was here, their toes would have touched under the table and she would have wriggled wildly as he tickled her arch with his big toe-nail until her knee banged against the edge of the table causing her mother to frown. Now, her toes had room to wriggle without restriction and they felt abandoned.

A wave of fragrant steam fanned her face as her mother placed a bowl in front of her and Jericho looked into her favourite dark soup. Silence filled the room, apart from her mother's slurps as the soup passed her lips and they smacked together briefly. Jericho lined up her loyal balls of yam ready for their dive, surprised that she'd been able to inhabit her sacred space without her sadness calling her out of her trance prematurely. She'd dipped her fingers into the waxy mixture, closed her eyes and placed the soup-glazed yam into her mouth.

'Did you forget the secret ingredient?'

Her mother looked up, confused.

'It tastes strange,' Jericho had revealed, pulling a face, as she forced the unyielding yam grudgingly down her throat.

'Eat your soup.' Her mother's voice was stern and she'd obeyed, sending each of her circular divers on their half-hearted mission, wondering why she'd never noticed the sour aftertaste that coated her tongue before.

Later that night as she settled into the rhythms of the dark, the scuttling of insect life and the sighing of leaves caressed by bird wings, she discovered a new sound. It was one that was determined not to be unmasked, a moan strangled between teeth and a pillow. She imagined the stinging tears leaking from her mother's eyes a few feet away, and she turned to face the wall, giving her mother the only privacy she could.

As she waited impatiently for sleep to come and chased mosquitoes away with her foot, Jericho rubbed the bloat of the food she'd eaten earlier on. She understood then that all food prepared without love is bitter, and that no matter what she ate from now on, she would never escape the feeling of hunger.

*

51

Most villagers cut across Silas's land to save time when returning from the market. Today's short cut was born out of necessity rather than pleasure, as the Creator rained drops of water the size of mangoes from the skies. Its usual pearly colour was now opaque, blackened by the universe's less than cordial mood.

Magdalena had left for the market later than usual, owing to M'elle's accident with her tiger prawns that had cost them two hours in the kitchen trying to salvage the intricate dish. But she'd been glad of her market task because it allowed her the time alone to pore over the musician's coded advances.

Things like this simply didn't happen to people like her. Then again, she argued to herself, many a plain woman had managed to find a husband in the village. Even six-toed Patience Okido who walked with her eyes downcast, as if her neck was the problem, not her feet, had found comfort in the arms of a nightwatchman and proceeded to have a steady brood of rightly footed children.

As she approached the fork in the path, she was about to veer right when she heard a faint melody coming from the other side at the start of the route to Costa Lina. Drawn by an inexplicable force, her feet took her down the other lane where the music grew louder. The breeze pooled under her skirt so that it plumped up around her like a bell. Magdalena caught Babylon's distinctive baritone along with the strains of his guitar. She stole a glance through the parting leaves and saw him sitting on the stump of an old tree, singing to the clouds.

Magdalena was riveted by the movement of his right hand, his fingers jerking and twitching as if they were possessed while the other hand moved gracefully, slowly, as if he was stroking the guitar's lean calf. His chest seemed to be connected closely to his instrument and she imagined it was his heart magnified. His eyes closed as if the weight of his melody had pulled them shut, his lips pressed together in a half-smile. She couldn't understand how he was doing it, but it sounded as if he was drumming and playing the guitar at the same time.

What mystery, what sorcery was it that made his guitar mimic her own heartbeat so vividly? How was his voice able to reveal the secrets of her soul? That strange voice that split itself into various permutations of spirit: sometimes heavy with promise; at times as gentle as an infant's kiss; and in the moments in between, as empty as an abandoned well.

His eyes focused on her and her entire being began to pulse. She pictured those very same hands moving at lightning speed across her body. Imagining the feeling of his warm palms and the determined pressure of his fingers as they subtly responded to her movements, she fought to keep her spirit within the confines of her earthly body.

She found herself sitting at his feet as his song ended, with his eyes fixed firmly upon her. He smiled like a snake about to devour his prey and the sky around them mirrored the colours of the smoke that danced around her mother's pots as it fled the kitchen. The trees in the distance appeared to stand closer together, making their location more intimate than when she'd begun her journey through the fields alone. Babylon sank to his knees alongside her and buried large hands inside her hair, freeing it from its constriction. Finally, he placed his mouth against her head. Volcanic heat permeated Magdalena's temples and she moaned like a frightened animal. He captured her fluttering hands in his own and placed them against his chest and she felt his heart beating through the thinness of his shirt. It reminded her of the time a butterfly had wandered into the café and lost its way. It had knocked frantically against the wall, looking for an opening, until it fell, exhausted, on to the table beside her. She'd picked it up with the utmost of care, willing it to live. When she'd opened her hands, the beautiful creature flew to freedom, but not before effecting a dance of thanks above her head.

The musician's lips brushed across her own and for a moment she acquiesced, angling her neck to receive more. But when the full realisation that she was actually kissing him hit her, she recoiled.

Magdalena pushed him away and rose sharply. She bolted, fleeing her own desire into the leafy throng. She heard him come after her, one of his strides amounting to three of her own. She continued her frantic getaway but her weighty behind proved her downfall. Her long skirt snagged on a branch and made her lose her footing. She fell to the ground and he quickly reached the spot where she lay. Placing both hands on his hips, he laughed like a precocious child. He extended his hand to lift her up but the guitar on his back slid, almost as if it wanted to get a better view of her legs, which she suddenly realised were exposed. Babylon, in turn, stumbled and fell; foot over ass, over Magdalena.

Chuckling, he checked his breathing and made sure that his beloved instrument was unharmed from the fall, before looking over at her. He said nothing as he steadied his breath, perplexed as she tried to hide her flushed features in his shirt and push him off her at the same time.

'Why are you fighting? Are you afraid?'

'Leave me, please! I have to get home before dark.'

'*Ewo*, let me help you.'

He trailed his hand up the flank of her leg, easing the upper part of his body away from hers. Although she was partly free, she stayed where she was, afraid to move and reluctant to untangle herself from the heat of his body.

'My dear, it's getting dark,' he whispered ominously.

Magdalena remained silent. Babylon's hands disappeared under her skirt, riffling through intricate folds and pleats, and she gasped as his fingers made contact with her flesh. She watched as his head bridged the gap between them in slow motion. He observed her closely, looking for any signs of retreat from his catch. Sighing, she wrapped her arms around his neck with a strength that alarmed her, sinking her fingers into the forest of his locks.

The aroma of oranges and Babylon on her skin, Magdalena tiptoed into the Le Papillon. Gently easing the door closed, she beseeched her guardian angels to prevent its hinges from creaking and rousing her sharp-eared aunt. She stifled her giggles, remembering those frenetic moments that had changed her for ever. She became more conscious of her body as she bent to put away the food she'd bought at the market.

The musician, her music man, had awakened her insides. She could still feel his hand moving over her as she'd undulated beneath his touch like an eel. A quick glance at her waist and she saw her skin darkening slightly where he'd fastened his teeth around her flesh and begun to suck on her skin, a form of pleasure so exquisite that the memory made her buckle, and she knocked over a tumbler someone had left on the counter. She dived for the glass but failed to catch it. It rolled around noisily like the steel drums the children played with while running around the square, but it didn't break. She froze, hoping her mother had consumed copious amounts of Sting that night and that her aunt was entranced by the lavender and hyssop she kept under her pillow.

M'elle's hoarse voice was first. Thick with sleep-stained dreams, she coughed heavily, a sound that certainly roused her twin. They shouted in unison, 'Magdalena, is that you?'

'Yes, Mama, Auntie. I was making something to drink – I'm thirsty.'

'Where have you been?' Her aunt's voice grew more lucid.

'With Tebo, Auntie. We went to her house after the market. Sorry. Go to sleep, everything is fine.'

'I hope Oscar brought you home,' her mother chimed in.

'Yes, Mama,' she lied, making a mental note to remind her friend to corroborate her story.

'Good,' M'elle added. 'Women alone at this time of night are up to no good.'

Magdalena spent what remained of Springtemps with Babylon in her arms. Using the cunning afforded to every woman and even more learned from watching the Mannobe men, she whittled away moments to share with him, blooming in his attention. She braided her hair for the café, but as soon as she neared his house she let her angelic tresses fall about her shoulders, softening her average features. The other her. The milkiness of her eyes developed a depth suggesting intrigue, and her behind rose ever so slightly, a surefire indicator of the secret pleasures she was now privy to.

She loved falling asleep on the island of his bed, fragrances of eucalyptus and musk baptising her while the sound of the guitar choreographed her slumber. She would turn to him in sleep, her body locked tightly around his, and their two bodies would remain pushed together until first light. Then she would scuttle through the drowsy roads to Le Papillon and remove the sacks of rice from under her blanket before M'elle commenced her day's work. She talked to him endlessly of venturing outside the safe haven of her home town and he sang to her songs of foreign lands, of women who wore trousers like men, of houses seven storeys high.

When the crispness left the air and the colours of Mannobe began to deepen ever so slightly, she didn't notice him slipping away, so consumed was she by his flame. Dutifully scrubbing the pots with vinegar in the kitchen, she hummed quietly while her mother coated her pies with eggs before placing them into the oven. But she was remembering hours earlier, when she'd been feasting on the nectar of Babylon's lips.

'I wish we could stay like this for ever,' she'd whispered into his open mouth as he played with her waterfall of hair.

'We can, *preciosa*,' he'd mumbled before nuzzling her earlobe.

'*Really?* You promise?' She'd looked longingly into his opaque pupils.

'For ever is as long as you remember it, Magdalena. As long as you remember it.'

Six

In Mannobe, gossip travelled faster than the Creator's wrath and was much more damaging to the individual whose affairs were the subject of discussion. The tale spread like wildfire, tripping up on its own importance along the way. No one could point their finger at the originator of the gospel, but the women mulled over the information like the sweetest of all chewing sticks. Accustomed to a diet of villager news, when one of the prominent families was involved it was as if a visiting chef had arrived in town with a free banquet.

Why the Doriques had chosen Mannobe to settle in many many years ago was still the subject of endless disputes, but their stature lent the village some prestige. Everybody knew of the family. Although they crept into the village – extending their stay in the summers until Mannobe became a permanent residence – their manor did not. Nobody could recall a house going up quicker in Mannobe's history. One minute there'd been sticks marking out a generous foundation and before young women – who were now great-great-grandmothers – could bundle their weekend washing for the Belago, a huge edifice had appeared, blocking out the sky and even the sun, to boot.

The family kept to themselves and others of similar social standing nearby, but very occasionally a sense of community overtook them. Then, they gifted money or their expertise for a variety of functions but usually at a price. For example, Mrs Dorique had generously gifted a specially commissioned gazebo to the village, but it had come with the proviso that the Senoritas Ball move to Costa Lina as opposed to the square, its original location.

The ball was another Mannoban tradition that had been infected by overstatement. It was a dance, at best, but it boasted inappropriate amounts of food, an elaborate stage, and even fancy costumes. Therefore 'ball' was a much more fitting term for the festivity held for the village's single women. Besides, while most villagers could find an excuse almost every day to shimmy to the music of their own making, there were very few occasions one had to don an *outfit*.

But it was the Doriques' very isolation that created the air of mystique. The Doriques had more businesses than extended relatives but had never seen fit to create any industry in their beautiful backwater. Perhaps it was a haven for them too, potholes and all. All these things contributed to the villagers' conflicting feelings about them – complimentary in one instance and derogatory the next, but always with a tinge of admiration at their arrogance, of course. After all, that spectacular mansion was easily ten times the size of the village's spirit house.

People were elated that they'd fallen off their perch temporarily. André Dorique, one of the youngest sons, had reportedly developed an understandable crush on – *can you imagine?* – a local girl, Hamid's daughter. Every Mannoban knew Hamid too, not just because he was the owner of the only junkyard in the village but because he looked like a bull on two legs. The taxing work he undertook honed his upper body to fearful proportions and even though he was known to be a mild-mannered man, no one dared bait him in case the truth was different.

Hamid's daughter eventually confessed a love so great that her body alone couldn't contain it. The surplus was growing inside her. However, André had rebuked her in front of his family, the Creator and anyone who would listen. So the Doriques, well aware of their son's predilection for pretty young things, offered Hamid a sizeable sum for his complicity and silence. André promptly married a beefy, available girl of standing overseas while Somaya was mysteriously sent to Odin to visit distant relatives.

Still, the tale lingered on, like the smell of fish long eaten.

Mabel reflected on the latest piece of gossip as she cleaned and de-seeded the bell peppers for tomorrow's dish. She sighed as a piece of pepper fell to the ground. Bending to pick it up, her knees cracked so loudly that she immediately stopped her descent and kicked the sliver across the floor in annoyance. When the pepper stopped shy of its destination, she let out an automatic yell. Daughters were so handy in situations like this. Besides, where bending was concerned, Magdalena could definitely use the exercise.

The news about Hamid's daughter had unsettled her and forced her to dig up bones she had buried a long time ago. She didn't visit the grave of that particular memory very often but the flowers that grew through the once disturbed soil gave her small comfort.

She warmed some milk, Sting and cinnamon and allowed the memory to engulf her like a huge wave. Embracing its peaceful surrender, she drowned sweetly in her past and the event that had occurred many years earlier.

She hadn't meant for it to happen, but the familiar scent of home in a place full of strangers had been as intoxicating as the bottle of home brew he'd brandished while they'd dined.

Mabel had only been in Joucous for nine months after leaving Mwinbona, but the sheen of the new town had long since disappeared and had only been replaced by hard work. She'd managed to stave off her boredom with the married mayor who was unofficially romancing her, his young cook, but she was tired of chewing unripe limes to remove the harshness of his breath after he left.

She'd been ecstatic to see the junkyard owner's face amongst the droves in the cobbled streets that swallowed her up every day in Joucous. His wife was still alive then; he was yet to experience the harem of women who would audition for the role of his future once she passed.

That night, the drink had turned her bones to mercury. As the warmth spread through her, his gentle face reminded her of Mannobe. Suddenly, she'd realised how much she wanted to go home even if it was through another.

Neither spoke out loud of his wife; it was as if the words would choke both their throats, but they held tightly on to one another as if the spirit of conspiracy fused them together.

Believing that the child was his own, Mayor Belen had been all too happy to pay Mabel a huge sum of money to make her disappear. Shuffling expenses from Joucous's welfare fund and the money raised to re-tar the main road, he'd sent her away before her belly became a talking drum.

She returned years later, smelling the distinctive fragrance of Mannobe air long before the dusty roads took on the pomegranate hue of her village. Her heart had somer-saulted in recognition of its home. In true Mannobe style, everyone had been rendered temporarily insane as they ran out to greet her. She'd offered no explanations about the father of her child and no questions had been asked. Even Hamid was none the wiser about his unplanned fatherhood. To them, she'd conceived her daughter immaculately. They were willing to accept anything from her, so glad were they of her return.

Over the years, she looked upon Hamid only as a clandestine tryst, never a co-conspirator in her child's conception. In some ways, Magdalena wasn't Hamid's child but hers alone; her free spirit in infant form. Her union with him had merely allowed her seed to be fertilised in Mannobe soil.

As she thought of her past and his daughter's current situation she felt sad that Hamid's news was being exploited, although she was relieved that her story was still firmly underground. Everybody tried to keep secrets in the village but sooner or later they always came to light. Her mother used to say that keeping a secret in Mannobe was like trying to feed a rabid dog vegetables: sure, it was possible, but hardly worth the effort.

During the Festival of Lights each household placed two candles outside their home, one representing the past and the other the future. Mannobe never looked more beautiful than at this time, when fireflies serenaded the golden flames at twilight and tiger moths warmed their wings in the glow.

It took place every year during the first four days of summer and had become such an acclaimed occasion that all the neighbouring townships flocked to its vicinity to witness the changing of the village's scenery as the season took shape, like a child growing into its adult features. The senior council spent the entire year planning the festivities for the event, with each council leader trying to outdo his predecessor. Last year's celebrations were still firmly in the minds of everyone for they had been cut short by the sheer might of the Phutse wind that had sent stalls flying across the square in an ear-splitting squall, while the rain beat the happiness out of the fleeing onlookers.

Jericho groaned as her dream evaporated against her will. She raised her head a fraction to gauge the time from the light coming through the window. One of the candles her mother had placed outside had burned down but the other had fallen overnight. Jericho imagined her mother's horror on discovering that her forward or backward movement in life had been compromised.

The Festival of Lights had been her favourite time of year ever since she was a little girl. She would fight sleep with the force of the juju men – the masquerade dancers that shuddered like aggrieved spirits – to watch candlewicks contorting in the dusk. Eagerly she would anticipate the final moments when the candle would spit and gasp for life before the wind put the waning wick out of its misery, followed by the thick cover of darkness. Then she would sigh contentedly into the opaque black and slip happily off to sleep.

The magic of this occasion must have dwindled with age. The candles were beautiful, but they could no more safeguard her future than the vials of blessed water older villagers toted around with them. Everything in the village had grown much smaller in her absence. The city had expanded her view of the world so that all the local customs seemed constricting in the cramped quarters of her home. But the house hadn't shrunk; it was just that she'd never noticed how close together everything was. She could catalogue every one of her mother's movements during the night and her mother could probably do the same with Jericho's. That knowledge made her feel invaded.

63

She thought back over her last few months in Angel, her excitement at the escalation of her relationship and her growing connection to the city, her trepidation when they announced the closing of the hospital and thereby the end of her job. At least she'd managed to procure a general medical certificate during her time there, but the thought of searching for another position had tired her until coming back seemed the most obvious choice. Fate had interceded by sending Daniel away too, to Ologo state, to oversee the management of his family's drilling company. She'd hoped he would ask her to accompany him, kept her wish tightly bound to her chest, hoping he would uncover it each time he peeled off her clothes, but the question never came. Instead they'd made tentative plans for the time that remained, fantasised about their reunion, and he'd promised to come for her ball.

In some ways she liked the fact that they'd left one after the other. It wasn't as if Ologo was renowned for having the most alluring women, if indeed there were any women at all. An old army district, it had transformed itself into one of the most industrious manufacturing sectors of the Northern Delta, and she didn't imagine that would leave him much time for dancing girls. Had he remained in the city, she couldn't be sure if she would have returned to Mannobe so readily, knowing first hand how delightful the distractions of Angel could be.

Yet she'd come home. Her mother's out-of-date letter had managed to issue enough guilt, swaying or cementing her decision. It was only when she received it that she became aware how long she'd been away from home. There was no way she could miss another ball; the only woman on record to have missed three in a row was Miss Cleo. Although some said it had been her choice not to marry, most locals considered it a curse for renouncing those balls. When Jericho was growing up, the Señoritas

64

ball had seemed the stuff of fairy tales. From the city, however, it looked like such archaic, traditional nonsense that she'd made excuses of work, much to her mother's disappointment. She didn't need to dance around a gazebo; every night in Angel was a ball. But on threat of disownment she'd acceded to her elder's plea grudgingly, although the fact that she'd be on the arm of a Dorique helped. Maybe this had been the best time to return to find out how much she'd changed. The only way she could really know was by coming back.

When she'd first seen Penny, it was as if no time had passed. They had been small again. Close as water can be without being blood. Home had felt so comforting, so familiar. Now it pinched her like a pair of shoes she'd outgrown and she wondered if she'd be polite enough to say nothing. She thought of the life she'd left behind, poring greedily over the images she'd treasured safely inside her. That was her real future, she told herself.

Jericho heard a slow cough and knew that her mother was stirring. She closed her eyes but suddenly remembered the fallen candle outside. Wrestling with laziness, she tore the covers off to force herself out of bed and tiptoed outside. She righted and lit the candle before her mother discovered it. Her good deed done, she smiled to herself at the realisation that, however grown she'd become, she was still somebody's daughter.

Observing a milky sky, Allegory concluded that this year's celebrations were going to be decidedly untampered with by the forces of nature. As the dwindling candlewicks flirted with the dawn, he watched the village slowly awakening with loving familiarity: Kinu sweeping the dirt that had crept surreptitiously into her house during the night back outside where it belonged, the chickens from her yard squabbling over crumbs; Hamid clanging all things metal on his way to work; and finally M'elle and Mabel Codón with their aromatic concoctions that danced from their stove all the way to his nostrils. He licked his lips and his belly rumbled like a disgruntled volcano as he began his walk to Widow's Creek for his daily bath.

He lay belly up in the stream with the ice-cold water sliding over his onyx skin. He allowed thoughts to wash over him like the minuscule diamond-backed fish that swam underfoot and shuffled through memory folders in the back of his mind. He paused as his brain tried to resurrect a flashback and chastised himself as he fought to maintain his balance in the water. He'd become adept at burying the past, had successfully wiped the images of his parents' faces and those of his sisters from his cerebellum. Before he'd been plagued with graphic images, so brutal were their slayings as brotherly tribes turned against one another – from his teenage perspective – overnight. He still couldn't understand the arbitrariness of life, why he'd been sent to deliver a message that morning to the next village, and the horror of what he'd discovered when he'd returned.

How he had run. He'd never thought it possible to run through the red fire that scorched his lungs and past the pain in his calves, to ignore his heart pounding so loudly in his eardrums, to flee the imagined machetes aimed at the back of his head. If it was possible he'd run for years. It was only when he'd reached Mannobe that his feet had stilled and his heart released its vice-like grip on all the muscles in his body. How young he'd been ... barely a man. The forest had been his only friend then, offering anonymity and shelter when he needed it most, before he became a man. It was a debt he'd been certain that he could never repay and so had turned it over to the Creator, a deserving second best as nature's maker.

His thoughts rested on the progress of Mannobe and he

reflected on how this sleepy hollow had gradually awoken and begun to stir. The village was very much like a baby in its infancy; it relied on the neighbouring dwellings for sustenance and nurturing. But as it evolved it began to create its own movements, its personality was emerging. And with the gradual influx of younger generations it was apparent that Mannobe was veering towards the future.

This realisation did not sit well with Allegory. A lump of grief formed in his throat that so unsettled him, he lost the careful balance that had kept him horizontal, and the creek flowed over him. He spluttered frantically like a drowning bear. He hated the feel of water on his face. It always reminded him that he couldn't really swim.

Driver woke up with a growling headache, a keepsake from the night before, and tasted his sour breath on his tongue. They'd been playing cards and drinking at Borrow's until the early hours of the morning. No matter how hard he tried, he'd never been able to hold his drink against his compatriot Babylon.

Borrow owned the only real bar in Mannobe and his impressive physique ensured that there was no one around to object. He was also the one that had introduced the infamous Sting to the village, the liquor he made from old banana skins and coconut water. Leaving the concoction to ferment for several weeks, he then distilled it in petrol cans and rubber tubing. The result was almost pure alcohol, which scorched the throat with velvet fire – hence its name.

Driver shook the blanket off his shoulders. He was still sitting in the chair he'd occupied during their game the night before. He prised a matchstick off his cheekbone – he'd been reduced to playing with them after the coins had long left his pocket yesterday – and blinked repeatedly while his eyes focused on his surroundings. There was no sign of Babylon. Driver tipped his head to chase back the remainder of the liquid in the glass by his side, and the memory of last night washed over him like the cool bath he was no doubt in need of.

They were completely immersed in their game of cards and the waitress, Corál, had settled herself behind Babylon and toyed with his locks until he pulled her on to his lap. Driver had been momentarily lost in his cards when he saw a flurry of skirts whirling off his friend's lap in exit. Dragging his attention to the door, he noticed Magdalena Codón billowing in front of them, an unguarded fire. Huge veins popped out of her neck the same way the junk-yard owner's did when he walked through the square grasping enormous tyres under each arm, and the kohl under her eyes was smeared from obvious tears shed. Even though her mouth had been moving at a lightning pace as it hurled a mountain of abuse at Babylon, her voice was so quiet that no one could hear what she was actually saying, and everyone had been too embarrassed to interrupt her diatribe.

Babylon tried to appease her, as if one could contain an erupting volcano by merely placing one's hands over its mouth, but in her fury she'd grabbed the first thing within her reach, a stool, and flung it with her full force. They were all so engrossed in watching the stool's parabola through the air – eager to know its ultimate destination due to her misguided aim – that no one even noticed her pick up the bottle and launch that as well.

Nobody heard it smash, but there was a communal hush when Babylon's vest turned crimson from the inside out. He looked down at the flesh wound on his right shoulder before looking at the banshee, rendered dumb by the success of her endeavour. For a split second she held his scowl; then uncertainty crept in. Babylon seized his moment and leapt for her with the speed of a big cat. He'd lifted her over his good shoulder like a sack of grain and bundled her out of the bar.

The shock inside Borrow's was palpable. People had been frozen in amazement until Corál restored the stool to its original place and sat down beside Driver. Picking up Babylon's hand, she'd thrown a card on to the pile in the middle, resurrecting the game. The players had scrambled back to their original positions – their minds firmly back on the bounty.

Driver felt nervous as he meandered along the narrow path leading to Babylon's compound. Normally when he walked down it he was welcomed by his friend's voice harmonising with his instrument, followed closely by the smell of canela tea on the brew. Today, however, the air was charged with a strange energy. The closer he got to his friend's house the more he felt like crying.

He was greeted by quiet. He made his way around the house slowly before stopping at the back door. Reaching through the sheet behind the open window, he unlatched the door expertly from the inside, then entered. He knew by now that his friend was not home, the musician's energy clearly not present in the house. He turned his back on the bedroom and was about to retrace his steps to the back door when he heard a whimpering sound. He followed it, pushing aside the heavy velour curtain that separated a living room from the makeshift bedroom. Magdalena lay crumpled on the floor like a heap of soiled bedclothes. It was clear she hadn't heard him enter. After several minutes she turned in his direction, when she realised she was being watched.

Driver placed his arms over Magdalena's shoulders comfortingly and brushed her hair off her face while she rocked wildly like a malcontent cooking pot.

'How far, Magdalena? What happened?'

As she dried her tears on his shirt and he breathed quickly and deeply, he could feel her breath escaping through her nostrils and curling into the hairs on his chest.

'Where Babylon?' he tried another question but at the mention of her tormentor's name, Magdalena wriggled out of his grasp.

'Where is he? *Abeg*, no worry me. Is he all you're concerned about? All of you! Everybody loves him, but no one more than himself.' She kissed her teeth in anger.

'*Eh* Magdalena, of course I care. Would I still be here if I didn't? I just wanted to find out what happened after Borrow's. Are you hurt?'

'Am I hurt?' She chased back a laugh, smearing the kohl from her eyes as she tried to brush her hair aside. 'Yes, your friend hurt me,' she continued, pounding her hand against her chest dramatically. 'Not just yesterday when he dragged me back here, but every day since we first met. Every day he threw my love back in my face like it was rotten stew, he hurt me. Every time he lie in bed next to me smelling of another woman he hurt me, Driver. Every time, every time, *every time*!'

It was the first thing that came to his mind, the only thing he could think to say. '*Va passar*. It will pass.' The phrase that was as common as hello and goodbye in Mannobe. The answer to everything.

'No it won't,' she protested. 'Why am I even bothering you? You can't understand. Do you know what it's like to not be enough? If your friend only felt one quarter of how I feel about him, he would die a happy man. But he doesn't feel anything. He has no respect.

'I see the way everybody looks at me, especially the women. For once I had their respect. I wasn't just poor Magdalena who couldn't get a man. I had the one they wanted. *Eh*, when he sang to me they would all hide their heads in shame so I didn't see the jealousy in their eyes. *Ha!* If only they knew there was no reason to be jealous so.'

'What happened last night?'

'He was in pain from where the bottle cut him but as I went to put some salve on his wound he wouldn't let me. He looked at me as if from very far away and said "This is the last time you will touch me." He said, "Our journey is over, Magdalena. All we have now is memory."'

She looked over at Driver but he could only stare at her blankly. His heart felt heavy, and he could not think of any words to say that would lessen her pain; couldn't translate any of his thoughts into rafts to float her hopes upon.

'Nothing to say? That's not like you. No *"va passar"*? I didn't think so. He said that when love has died, it is disrespectful to try and raise it from its resting place. So, I don't know where your Babylon is. Maybe he has gone to another's bed or to find his precious guitar – as wooden as *he* is. He can bleed to death in a gutter for all I care, but all I know is he has broken me.'

She sat on Babylon's makeshift bed and began to clean her face in the pane of glass the musician used as a mirror. As she fought her hair and tried to restrain it in a long plait, Driver's eyes caught hers in her reflection for a brief moment. Then she was lost in the glass, searching for some veil of recognition.

Excusing himself, he left for the kitchen to the sound of shattering glass. He wondered fleetingly whether it was her heart and not the mirror that had just smashed into tiny pieces.

Allegory heard the familiar sound of M'elle's footsteps beating a path in his direction as he was cleaning out his home. She was in high spirits; he could hear her melodic voice floating on the fresh breeze, absorbed in a song. But long before the first wave of her music flooded over him his senses were aroused by an overpowering odour and his mouth watered greedily. He couldn't remember when he'd eaten last.

'Hello? Allegory?'

'*Bon matin*, M'elle. What's good with you?'

'Will you try this for me? Mabel and I have been experimenting in the kitchen for the day's celebration. She thinks there may be too much saffron in the dish but I told her that her ageing palate is getting tired.'

She chuckled as she thrust the platter forward but he hesitated suspiciously. He didn't tolerate pity, and he'd noticed that lately she'd been approaching him with some very bizarre requests.

He glanced at his ribs through the holes of his string vest and puffed his chest out as best he could without drawing attention to the action. He licked the corner of his mouth but was still hesitant to accept her outpouring of charity.

'If it was prepared by your God-fearing hands, then it must be perfect,' he replied, shaking his head.

'You won't try any?'

'I've just eaten,' he lied. With comic timing, his stomach rumbled like an angry wasp and the aching chasm of his empty insides echoed, compounding his embarrassment.

M'elle's cheeks deepened in colour and she coughed weakly.

'Well, if you don't want any, I'll take it away.'

'If you really need me to try it, then I am sure I can squeeze a little in. *Tanka*, M'elle.' He took the platter from her plump hands and inhaled its perfume deeply.

'You're welcome, Allegory, you're welcome.'

He didn't even wait for her to retreat before dipping back into his tent and ripping a leg off her chicken like a starving animal.

The festival was in full swing when Driver arrived with Magdalena a few paces behind him. How he'd persuaded her to come to the gathering, he didn't know, but he'd felt a certain obligation towards her.

It seemed as if the whole of Mannobe was out on display. The park buzzed with activity, the hubbub of people's conversations blending with the sound of different meats crackling on open grills, the cacophony of musicians jamming, the unmistakable melody of children darting through the legs of grown-ups, eyes laughter-filled.

'Where do you want to go first?'

He turned to face her but she didn't respond.

'Are you hungry? No? *Pues*, I could eat. Let's go.'

He resorted to talking to himself and made his way through the crowd, stopping to greet people on the way. He saw Corál immediately, decked out in all her finery, and he eyed the temptress longingly. She'd tied her brocade skirt expertly.

'*Bon dia*, Driver. How are you?'

'Well, Corál. How beautiful you look.'

'I believe it is *you* who are looking, but I am beautiful, *sha*?'

Corál laughed in her unladylike fashion and her bronze dress caught the sun once more, so that she twinkled like a star. She gazed over his shoulders and he noticed her glassy eyes widen in recognition of his companion. She stepped back instinctively and, sensing her discomfort, he turned to usher Miss Codón between them.

'You know Magdalena?'

'Of course. Hello.'

'*Bon dia*,' Magdalena said curtly, turning and weaving her way through the throng of people.

'Where are you going?' he shouted after her.

'Home.'

He started to follow her but Corál grabbed his hand and cooed. 'Leave her. Come and dance with me.'

Driver was flummoxed for only an instant, straddling

the worlds of responsibility and impulsiveness. In the breeze circulating the park, her camomile perfume hit him and he succumbed to the latter.

Magdalena was determined to go back to Le Papillon and marinate in a brew of self-pity, when a familiar scent beckoned her. The crowd separated and she saw her matriarchs standing over a huge grill with gigantic slabs of meat choking in the black smoke that gushed skyward in the shape of a mammoth mushroom. She spied the glossy lips of greedy children sitting on the ground, their stomachs swollen with food as they gawped at their peers who were still fully mobile and tearing around the park like angry flies. Her mother caught her eye and beckoned her over by waving the skewer fork she held.

Magdalena pushed her way through the people lining up to fill their plates with food, to stand behind the grill. Her mother planted a wet kiss on her cheek while M'elle stopped fanning the fire long enough to hug her niece from behind.

'Where have you been?'

Mabel held her by the shoulders. 'Are you sick?' she asked, taking in her drawn features.

'No, Mama,' she sighed, 'I was up all night helping Tebo sew her gown for the ball. I'm just tired.'

'Fine. Have something to eat then you can take over from your auntie. She has to go back to Le Papillon.'

Before she could protest M'elle thrust a huge plate filled with pig-chicken, fry pork, blackened corn cakes and wild rice in her hand and began to remove her apron. Resigned to her fate, Magdalena perched on the stool behind the grill and began to pick at her meal. But even the sumptuous harmony of flavours of her family's cooking couldn't comfort her. The food danced down her throat well enough, but burst into tears in her stomach.

*

Magdalena glanced behind her several times to see whether her mother was still looking around, trying to account for her whereabouts. After accomplishing her good deed of delivering a platter of riches to Mama Abandela, she'd stolen through the pocket of partygoers and disappeared down the trail.

She stopped to sample a competing vendor's banana and almond flan . . . the flaky pastry melted away on her tongue and managed to console her a little. Mama Abandela had been pontificating about the troublesome hips that might preclude her from future festivals, her mouth moving at the speed of an over-zealous sewing machine. Finally, she shuffled down the road with her food, a huge ochre beacon against the red clay horizon.

Magdalena knew she ought to be grateful for the simple things like her youth or her agility, but she just couldn't. She remembered how she and Tebo would climb the banana trees behind the Dorique compound when they were small. Her friend had been much more adept at it, shimmying up the tree like a small monkey, her arches glued to the side of the trunk. She would shake off some ripe bananas while Magdalena, standing underneath in her shadow, caught the fruit as it rained from above. Then they would sit in the high grass and feast on their bounty, fantasising about boys. They longed for the kind of attention that Tebo's older sister received from the generous mangoes that rode underneath her blouse.

The remainder of the flan flew out of her hand as a whirl of children barged past her, arms and legs akimbo. They flung a casual apology behind them in the wake of their departure, which lay unclaimed at her feet like discarded, stale bread. No – she would never command the kind of attention she yearned for. And Babylon would never see her properly, she reasoned, wiping her hands on her skirt. After all, the children had clearly proven that she was invisible.

She gave up on her task of trying to make a sound from putting two blades of grass to her lips. She'd positioned herself well in the shade of the little brook that ran alongside the park on the outskirts of the activities. Her mother would have given up looking for her by now, long resigned to serving the unrelenting masses by herself. Magdalena felt a little guilty but she pushed the feelings down to the pit of her stomach. She didn't want to entertain any other feelings today except pain; there was no room for remorse.

She traced imaginary patterns in the sky, joining clouds with ornate birds that fluttered by, before taking in the tops of the tents villagers had erected for the fête that were decorated in iridescent colours along with banners and streamers. One particular tent drew her: she was hypnotised by the way its sides billowed in the semi-breeze, its dark pink hue like that of a lung contracting and filling with air. The knot of anger in her belly began to subside. All the locals recognised the tent; it belonged to Venus Oracene, the obeah woman. Many adults had grown up believing they would perish simply by calling on Venus's name, she yielded that great a fear in their hearts. M'elle called her the 'wayo woman', turning her nose up at her trickeries while admiring her skill, but Magdalena had always held the woman in high regard.

Over the years, the obeah had been called upon to perform many tasks, from exorcisms to curing sick cattle; even delivering babies contorted in weird positions in the womb. But when people remembered the medicine woman it was always for the stranger episodes, the ones most likely to instil terror in the eyes of others. Mannobe's young, privy to no more than little snatches of adult conversations and gossip gatherings, preferred to think of the woman as crazy, and so her mystique lived on in the frantic whisperings and half-truths that only children can tell so well.

Magdalena was contemplating going to the tent for the first time when she saw a young woman part its flaps. The stranger held her head high and swayed as she walked, almost as if her body was making an involuntary figure of eight as she put one foot in front of the other.

She knew the woman was beautiful by the way she carried herself. Almost as quickly as it had ebbed, the knot in her stomach tightened and she felt her mouth moving into a scowl. She was thinking of changing her position to get a better look when she saw Driver approaching the brook, the bar's waitress in hot pursuit. Lowering herself deeper in the grass, Magdalena rolled to salvation, all thoughts of the woman gone from her mind.

The breeze blew soft through Mannobe, lounging casually among the day's celebrations and providing a welcome relief from the over-eager sunshine. Children, having gorged on sumptuous delights, waned on wide pockets of grass. Only some diehard energetics twirled like butterflies in the wind. Driver moved towards the shelter of the tree under which Babylon was resting, watching as his friend opened his eyes from his daydream.

' 'Lon.'

'D. What's good with you?'

Driver sat down beside him heavily, just outside the shade. He rubbed his eyes, looking scornfully at the sun, but his friend pretended not to notice. Not even the Creator himself could make Babylon shift his position in the cool spot.

'Magdalena is here.'

'I know.'

'She very upset.'

'I know.'

They sat in silence for several moments, the only sound disturbing their quiet coming from the musician's soft belches as the snapper he'd eaten battled with his system. The Codóns made the best red snapper in Mannobe, but looking at the discarded wrapping Driver knew his friend had settled for another's offerings.

Driver had known Babylon too long to give him a lecture. He knew the musician was set in his ways and would do nothing about the way Magdalena was feeling.

It was funny but while he was seated beside Babylon he felt nothing about her plight. The huge knot of guilt weighing him down earlier had completely dissipated. But he knew that if he returned to her side he would begin to feel bad, as if the despair she felt on account of his friend unwittingly penetrated him as well.

He sighed again and looked over at Babylon, who had closed his eyes. He watched his eyelashes dancing against his flesh. Babylon touched the wound in his shoulder and scowled briefly, then his features relaxed again. From this angle, he seemed almost childlike. Driver wondered if he was aware of just how much anguish he'd brought to the women in Mannobe. And as if Babylon had read his thoughts, a half-smile ran across his lips before they reverted to their original position.

Allegory was sucking on a chicken bone when M'elle caught him unawares. He coughed to mask his embarrassment and mild disappointment. He'd wanted to crush the bone with his teeth before scooping the marrow out with his tongue.

'*Aha*, the dish was good?' she commented eagerly, taking his smile for approval. 'I took it to the festival anyway, in case we ran out of food . . .' she stammered. 'I think we'll add it to the menu.'

'Yes,' he replied, handing over the dish and steering her away from his tent opening.

'Eh, everyone is in the park, you should come down! I can't wait to see the girls at the ball. Every year, it gets me *so* . . .' M'elle sighed longingly. 'I wore Mama's dress for our first ball, hundreds of white daisies stitched across the hem. Mabel got the only new one we could afford, not that I cared. On Hamid's arm I knew I was a princess.' As her eyes clouded over with remembrance, he averted his gaze, partly out of discomfort but also because his sixth sense had alerted him to the danger before his nostrils latched on to the smoke. He pushed M'elle aside, breaking her reverie, for a clear view of her café.

'*O-ho!*' he called out, pointing to the smoke escaping Le Papillon's interior.

'Quick!' M'elle was a surprisingly swift sprinter. 'Help me with the door.'

Allegory sprang into action, shouldering the flimsy door open and looking for the source of the smoke. He located the oven and opened it to free the torrent of fumes. Cinnamon fritters that were now the colour of the oven's insides were revealed.

M'elle grabbed one from the tray with her asbestos-like fingers and bit into it, shuffling the remainder from palm to palm to handle the heat. She chewed on the morsel thoughtfully as he watched her amidst the smoky kitchen.

'If we scrape off the top no one will know,' she said and winked.

He walked through the café opening all the shutters and the door at the front. When he was satisfied that air was circulating through the premises and unsettling the smoke that was threatening to take root in the restaurant, he moved back into the kitchen. He stood awkwardly beside

M'elle and scraped the black coating off the fritters with a small knife.

The sound of a vehicle backfiring caught Babylon's attention. Opening his eyes, he watched the fumes escaping the back of a truck and saw some bodies jumping into the back of the moving vehicle. His body felt hot despite the fact that he'd fallen asleep in the shade and he got up grudgingly. The fête was showing no signs of abating as the day elapsed and his stomach growled as newer food smells permeated his nostrils. The twinge in his shoulder had lessened but he already knew that he would decline the other musicians' request that he play again in the evening. There had been such a din from the morning's audience that no one had noticed when he lost a few notes to the wind.

Luckily he hadn't come across Magdalena in the festivities. He'd scoured the crowds painstakingly, glad that he'd even been able to avoid the Codón matriarchs as well, even though he'd had to forsake their incredible fritters.

He'd felt awful last night, first because of the depth of Magdalena's pain when he'd declared the end of their union, but also because he'd spent an uncomfortable night under a large tree in the square. But at least he'd managed to escape her wrath and tears. The bruises on his body had been worth it.

The time had come, he realised, to widen the net for game, even outside the neighbouring villages. Driver had been right about Magdalena and *he* was only partly responsible, Babylon reassured himself. Yes, he might have initiated the kiss, but she had manipulated his body with the strength of a bull.

Perhaps the time had come to leave the village, to stretch his legs and devote more time to his music. He'd been a bona fide travelling musician once; it was Prophet's kindness that initially made him stop to gather his breath. That pause had allowed roots to anchor him in Mannobe.

A chill came over Babylon whenever he reflected on how close to death he'd unwittingly been that day, reclining readily in a mound of soft bushes in the grassland at the village's entrance. He'd slept deeply and had been so recharged after seasons of touring that he'd felt compelled to play. Neither Guitar nor he had seen the snake. Instead, what he recalled was the stick-thin man who had hurried towards him brandishing Guitar's case like a weapon. Babylon jumped aside just as the camouflaged adder sank its long fangs into the soft leather case. How Prophet had spotted that snake in the dark he never knew.

That moment had bonded him to Allegory and consequently tied him to the village. He'd been in scrapes before but that odd little visionary had saved his life. As a Borone man, he was bound to him until he repaid that debt. But Allegory had asked for nothing in return, regardless of how many times Babylon had besieged his tent. His feet stilled for the first time in years and Mannobe spirit seeped in, bonding him to the red clay. Truth be told, after a lifetime of travelling, he'd enjoyed the respite. They'd embraced him readily as a relative and he'd been reminded of Gloriama, of receiving that feeling of security. After so long, he had a home.

He didn't want to question how long or whether it would last. Far better to press on before their affection dimmed. His roots in Mannobe soil were already twitching.

As he walked towards the colourful tents he decided that the woman frequenting his dreams was a sign. He knew he liked the idea of her because he couldn't picture her. Whenever he was especially taken with a woman, he could never recall her face. Perhaps she'd been sent to rouse him from his lazy ways. Her wide smile and penetrating eyes that were the shape of almonds set on their

81

sides. Her black hair that resembled a silk scarf wrapped around her small, delicate ears. The red, blue and yellow criss-cross pattern of her dress that exposed her angular shoulders.

The woman he described walked right by him before he realised that she was real. As she sauntered past, he stared at the thick skirt swaying under the force of her stride. Her name bubbled up into his brain, opening his mouth with the weight of it.

He saw Driver eye her approvingly as he walked towards him. His friend smiled and Babylon wanted to return it, but he was as confused as a cockroach in a pool of water.

'Your gum flapping like Oracene's tent.' Driver laughed and pointed.

'What?' he said finally, when his vocal cords resumed working.

'You want to see the winch?'

Babylon looked in the direction his friend was pointing, to the largest tent a few minutes away from where they stood.

'I don't need to see that crazy woman, friend,' he replied happily as the figure moved further into the distance. 'I already seen my future.'

Seven

Jericho held her sides in agony as she watched her friend flying round the compound, trying to restrain Dungu who was making a nuisance of himself, engrossed in his daily pastime of disturbing chickens. They'd watched him soaking up the afternoon sun until his stomach reached boiling point, when he rose, panting heavily. This always fooled the chickens, who assumed he was too tired to torment them. Dungu would stroll leisurely, stopping to mark a tree or to smell the neighbourhood competition. When he noticed the chickens were unperturbed by his presence he struck, darting about at an alarming pace. The squawking was incredible as the chickens ran for safety, their wings horizontal in fright.

Penny was occupied in the task of trying to catch a chicken but the dog's assistance was providing more of a hindrance, much to her amusement.

'Why don't you help me instead of laughing?' Penny moaned as another speeding hen slipped through her fingers.

'And ruin this dress? I don't think so,' Jericho had replied seriously.

She laughed as Penny shook her head and immersed herself in the hunt, shouting at her pet along the way. Having successfully cornered a chicken by the water tank, Penny swung her agile frame from side to side like a goalie trying to protect his patch. Her movement temporarily foxed the stupid animal and she skilfully made her approach, imprisoned the quivering bird in her arms with a small but firm grip and carried it in a medieval headlock over to the step where Jericho sat watching.

Jericho moved away. Penny was now brandishing a knife. She'd no desire to see blood splattered all over the orange dress she'd treated herself to before leaving Angel. She knew that with its intricate beadwork, and the new sandals she wore, she was overdressed for visiting her friend, but she was reluctant to relinquish that city feeling.

Penny's knife was sharp and swift: one clean slice separated the chicken's head from its body. Despite her petite size, Penny was strong. But even she couldn't control the life that spilled from the bird after she gripped its detached head in her hands. They watched as the chicken's spirit danced frantically. Penny leapt up from the step as the chicken headed for its murderer and bolted in her friend's direction for help but Jericho squealed and took off in a sprint, her own escape paramount. The poor chicken gyrated to its own tune for well over five minutes before coming to rest by the head that Penny had dropped in her getaway. Exhausted, they returned to the step, Penny clutching the chicken's lifeless form in her hands. Jericho rested her arms on her head to prevent herself from sweating all over her new dress. She stared at the blood spattered on the ground of the Azevo compound as Penny went inside the house briefly and returned with a pail of hot water. She positioned it between her legs and dunked the bird inside.

'So, we still in your blood or are you still fixed on running back to the city?' Penny teased, and Jericho didn't respond. 'What will you do there?'

'What will I do here?' she countered swiftly. 'It's the same . . .'

'You know, there are walls in the village too? It's painting you want to do, but it's not only city people that buy artwork. There are other places.'

'Yes, Woolustown, Griffin . . . Is that a living? If I'm lucky, I can sell one piece a year—'

'Then you paint portraits of yourself! They will sell as fast as Mercelline's hot cakes,' Penny laughed at her own joke.

'How can I come back with a medical certificate and tell my mother I want to paint?' Jericho demanded.

'*Eh-eh*, but it's to tell her that you want to leave for good? That one is easier?' Penny rolled her eyes. 'You should give one of your paintings to the Manna sale. They're raising money to change the benches in the park.'

'Maybe,' Jericho replied pensively, thinking about the village's fundraising effort each autumn.

'Look at you. Not maybe. Do it,' Penny encouraged slowly before her impatience overtook her. '*Pues*, aren't you going to tell me about Angel?'

'How can you stand to do that? *Ay*, look at all the blood.'

Jericho wrinkled her nose as her friend removed the bird from the steaming water to pluck the feathers off its pruning corpse.

'Mama says if you're not brave enough to kill it, you shouldn't bring your mouth to eat it. Now tell me!' Her friend's eyes flashed like the blade of the knife she'd used to vanquish the chicken.

'It's so beautiful. I wish you'd come to visit me like you planned.' Jericho stared, mesmerised by how Penny's nimble fingers were successfully removing all of the chicken's feathers, including the tougher, stubbier ones on its wings. Naked, the bird looked even sadder than it had done after its beheading, making her – witness to its execution – feel a little guilty. Penny took the chicken indoors but returned quickly. The memory of her earlier murder seemed to be completely wiped from her face. She cleaned her hands on a cloth that looked like the remnant of an old wrapper. Holding its end, she flicked the cloth in Jericho's direction.

'Tell me about *him*. Properly,' Penny ordered, excitedly.

Jericho avoided the dirty cloth with a quick movement and placed her hands between her knees.

'Him?' Jericho teased, grimacing before winking at her friend. 'I wouldn't even know where to begin.'

She'd chosen La Ciudad d'Angel from the name alone. She didn't know a soul, nor did she have any idea what such a place would have to offer, but despite her mother's objections she'd surrendered to the name, allowing herself to be led by fate.

It had even begun to work for her before she left the village. One of her mother's friends had a second cousin who worked in the city hospital and had promised to help her find work when she arrived. She'd listened to her mother repeatedly updating her neighbours and friends on her child's impending travels, embellishing the truth, declaring that her daughter had gone to study in the city. She couldn't understand why her mother was so embarrassed that her daughter simply wanted to explore life outside the village, why a young woman couldn't venture out on her own, why school or marriage were the only acceptable markers of success but she refused to let her mother's words dishearten her or taint her vision of Angel. She'd fallen for the idea of a city full of angels trying to fulfil the destinies of their charges.

The contrast to her village had been staggering. Angel was humid, not like the dry heat of Mannobe, and its wind – when it came – left a sticky residue that reminded her of being licked by Penny's dog. Except unlike Dungu's breath, the air in Angel was sweet and inviting. She felt her heart expand in her chest as she surveyed her new sur-roundings. She would like it here a lot.

Dot had eyed her suspiciously when she collected her from the bus stop. Jericho imagined she'd looked ragged after her travels, squashed up against a man in the aisle whose acrid sweat assaulted her every time a faint breeze perco-lated through the overpopulated bus. For the entire journey, the woman in front of her had talked so loudly that it prevented her from sleeping. She'd cleared the back of her throat savagely at the end of each statement so that Jericho had spent most of the bus ride with her knees tucked under her arms in order not to get her exposed feet baptised with the stranger's disgusting outpourings.

Her eyes were dried-out wells by the time she went to greet Dot, her mother's friend's cousin. Dot had the face of a woman who had been pretty once, but life had steadily worn down its softness so that only a bitter edge remained. She was a good ten years older than Jericho, and her feet were so aged they looked as though they should have belonged to a turtle. The soles were as thick and cracked as the once-black slippers that smacked angrily against them as she walked. Her feet reminded Jericho of the ground back home, how the red clay cracked during the dry season until the rain moisturised the soil.

She'd caught the way Dot had looked over her sandals, the long straps that she'd tied several times above her ankle, the black and brown leather seamlessly intertwined.

'You want to be careful. They may not last long on your feet here.' Dot's frown creased her forehead.

'We have a long way to walk?' she'd asked, naïvely.

'Not so,' Dot had replied. 'But there are thieves every-where in Angel. You may want to hide your nice things. Though with the way you look,' she waved her hands over Jericho's face, 'there's not much you can do about that.'

Dot's place was a large room with a kitchen at the back, cordoned off with a dark brown curtain. Outside the kitchen there was a corrugated iron overhang which had been blocked off with pieces of wood, and she'd turned this into her bathroom. Dot had already cleared some space for Jericho in the corner where she normally placed her shoes and books. A blanket had been folded on top of three cushions rescued from a discarded sofa. As payment for Dot's kindness, she would sweep the house, occasion-ally fetch water from the well and collect the firewood for Dot's traditional stove.

The hardness of the stone floor hadn't bothered her in the beginning, nor the cold that seeped into her spine in the mornings, making it feel as rigid as a rusty pipe. What had incensed her most was Dot's snoring. The woman lay on her back in an elevated position, her mattress set on blocks of wood, so that the sound floated over Jericho's head and rested there like grey storm clouds. Dot's sleeping mouth was a drawbridge that threatened to close but never did.

She'd pulled her braids over her ears tightly to drown out the din and thought of the quietness of nights back in Mannobe; a bird's midnight seduction of its lover, fruit sliding through leaves and landing with soft thumps, the wind that sometimes sounded like the end notes on a sitar.

The sounds in Angel had been different, foreign to her novice ears. There were horns at odd hours of the night, a *pa-paaaa* sound that woke her up thinking an animal was in danger; metal and glass clanged and broke intermit-tently – prickly sounds splintering her dreams; and voices, even when they sang, seemed raised and full of tension. Even Dot, who slept noisily and peacefully, always woke up irritated.

Dot had taken her to the hospital where she worked in the mornings before going to clean the houses of several businessmen who lived across the river. She'd shared Dot's workload, sweeping out the rooms in the mornings, making the beds and sorting out the dirty linen into different bags for the cleaning woman who arrived at eight.

She worked efficiently, allowing her mind to wander while her hands carried out the same rituals, hardly noticing when her duties increased and the supervisor determined that she was now able to take on a position on her own.

One morning as she knelt on all fours, scrubbing the floors she'd swept with a soapy cloth, a doctor had come in early. Alarmed, she banged her head against the table and he'd taken pity on her. It was then he learned that it was she who'd arranged the scanty instruments on his shelves and the papers on his desk. Two days later, the supervisor pulled her aside as she went to the closet to pick up her broom at the start of her shift and told her that her work had changed: Jericho would now work as a doctor's aid.

The news had astounded her because until then she'd thought her work had gone unnoticed. Dot had instructed her not to draw attention to herself so that if there were cutbacks, which the hospital regularly suffered from, she would not be in anyone's mind.

Her new position gave her more money, and from the way Dot cut her eyes at her as she passed her by in her hall, Jericho in her brown uniform while Dot swept the floors in her work wrapper, she knew that she had to find a new place to live soon. A woman had come into the hospital when her sewing machine had fallen on her foot and broken her toe. She told her of the room above her shop, and Jericho had eagerly accepted it, reasoning the woman would not sew at night, and even if she did the steady chatter of the machine would be easier to bear than the rattle in Dot's mouth.

The living quarters over Yalla's shop were almost the same size as Dot's room. Even though Yalla stored the overspill of her sewing materials in her room, Jericho didn't mind. It was still a place of her very own. She used the first bit of the money she'd saved to buy some paint and transformed it into a bright yellow space.

One weekend when the rain would not allow her to leave the bedroom, she looked through Yalla's materials and discovered bits of broken wood and some canvas. She ran down to Yalla, who was happy for her to use what she'd considered junk, and by the afternoon Jericho had made herself an easel. Every time she received her pay, she would buy herself a new colour. The man who sold her supplies seemed glad of her visits and even poured the paint into small jars so that she didn't have to buy more than she could afford. She gave him her second painting, which was really a replica of the first one she'd done but couldn't bear to part with.

Almost eight months after she'd arrived in Angel, a woman had stopped one day to watch Jericho painting.

'*Si preciosa!* You have a good touch,' the woman exclaimed, remarking on L'Eglise, the magnificent church she captured.

'Thank you, Madam.'

'Claudia, please. Wait, try holding it like *this*. See how your stroke is smoother.'

The young woman demonstrated other techniques, and the two of them remained there until the church was bathed in darkness. Claudia told her that she'd lived in

Angel all her life and was finally realising her dream of being recognised as an artist thanks to her father's financing: he was a politician. Claudia invited her for dinner and informed her of her latest idea over the guineafowl.

'I shall adopt you, Jericho Lwembe. I always wished for a sister. I'll take you under my wing and introduce you to absolutely everybody in Angel. We'll have so much fun!'

It had taken Jericho a long time to make real friends in the new city. Work at the hospital kept her busy during the week and the stories of strange lands her mother had beleaguered her with during her childhood, that had terrified and enthralled her, had made her reticent about adopting new acquaintances. But something about Claudia's infectious enthusiasm had reminded her of her best friend back home, so far away. She'd never met someone with that much unspoken pedigree before. It didn't seem to matter to Claudia that Jericho's wrapper was faded and worn, or that she only wore earrings on special occasions. Claudia embraced her as if the two of them were the same, as if they'd both hitched their skirts about their heads and splashed about in Dodo's swamp – back in the village – on a hot day.

She'd been wary of city people when she first arrived: seeing imaginary thieves in every corner; cheating husbands in every wink; and disapproving looks with every female glance. But after a few months she saw certain similarities with her birthplace, only Angel's people were more refined, more 'worldly', even if they were less welcoming than in her home town.

Jericho played with her hair nervously at the bar, as if smoothing her locks would quell the anxiety she felt at being in such a place. She wished that Penny had been there for support.

Her friend's absence had saddened her momentarily but

as the rhythm of the music began to work through the floorboards into her body, the melancholy that pierced her breast was short-lived. Claudia was clearly in her element. She wore a red dress created from a whisper of lace and Jericho watched her lithe figure bisecting the crowd that parted eagerly in her wake as she headed directly for the bar. Claudia leaned provocatively over the surface that was covered entirely with glass and planted a kiss on the lips of the man behind.

'Your finest cocktail for my newest friend.'

She'd beckoned her forward with a gloved hand and Jericho squeezed herself apologetically through the gyrating bodies to stand next to her new friend.

'He's good-looking, *non*?' Claudia whispered. 'He has the fastest hips in town.'

Jericho had managed to rearrange her face before he returned with their drinks. Claudia's glass was opaque with a long stem, reminding Jericho of a flower. She'd never seen anything like it before in her life. Although hers was a regular tumbler, its rim had been fringed with sugar. She'd been mystified at how the bartender had managed to sculpt the sugar so that it clung to the glass's edge but she hid her praise.

'Drink slow,' Claudia advised.

She'd taken a cautious sip. The amber concoction was a snakebite to the back of her throat. It may have been more refined than Mannobe's Sting but it was potent all the same.

Claudia led her to a table in the corner near the band. Jericho felt a pair of eyes watching her, boring a hole in her back. Her scalp grew hot, loosening the soft curl of her hair. They sat down and sipped their drinks, taking in the atmosphere. Her friend's voice was steeped in excitement as she went around the bar telling her gossip about the revellers.

She'd wanted to ask Claudia, but couldn't bring her

mouth to form the words to enquire about the gentleman with the copper eyes. So she dipped her head lower as Claudia's body undulated to the jerky rhythm of the house band, her foot tapping against Jericho's under the table. Claudia's movements became more pronounced until she finally jumped off her seat and on to the makeshift dance floor.

It was the bartender's cue. He leapt over the bar and swept her up in his arms, and they began twirling like churning butter. Alone at the table, Jericho painted a frosty smile on her face, hoping that would keep all potential suitors at bay, and quietly watched her friend's gyrations. She'd hardly noticed when someone sat down next to her. Quickly she turned to face the man with the eyes she'd already memorised. As he smiled at her lazily like an animal that had just been fed, she'd felt her face open like a window.

'Allow me to present myself. My name is Daniel.'

'Jericho. I'm Jericho Lwembe.'

They shook hands and when he kept hold of hers a little longer than was necessary she'd pretended not to notice but masked her delight behind thick lashes.

'You're not dancing?' he asked with a curious expression.

'No. I prefer to watch.'

'Liar.' He laughed and sat back in his chair, allowing his head to rest against the wall.

'You know me five seconds and you call me a liar?' she replied but felt her treacherous lips parting into a smile.

'It's not a judgement, more of an observation. Look at the way you're watching your friend. I'm amazed she can dance with four feet in her shoes instead of two!'

Jericho pinched herself under the table to stop herself from giggling, but it was obvious he could see that he was amusing her.

'You're not from La Ciudad?'

'No, I'm from Mannobe. You won't have heard of it but—'

'Me too!'

'You're lying.'

Her eyes held his but he didn't look away.

'You only know me fifty seconds and you call me a liar?' he laughed. '*Da vero*. Okay, I wasn't born in the village but some of my family is from there.'

'What's your father's name?'

'Dorique.'

'Oh!'

Jericho smiled faintly but felt a window close shut as his family name sank in and she knew he'd sensed her retreat.

'There is something wrong?'

'No, I'm just tired,' she answered.

'But . . .'

Whatever he'd been planning to say was lost when Claudia returned to their table.

Daniel excused himself politely and returned to his companions.

'My, my, Jericho, you are a sly one. I've been coming here for months and he has never spoken to a strange woman, and he likes pretty girls. You know who that is? The Doriques have so much money even my own father is envious. And that one.' She pointed in Daniel's direction. 'Family obligation yet all the signs of classic rebellion. He likes to pretend but everyone knows he'll take over from his father one day. You know I tried for his older brother, but I was unlucky. Not that I could have endured that overbite for the rest of my life . . .'

Jericho allowed Claudia's voice to wash over her. She wanted to tell her that she knew the Doriques' history even in more detail than her own; that she had been raised on his family's story, the customary diet of all growing

Mannobans. As much as she enjoyed the brightness of Claudia's excitement, fear formed clouds over her head at the thought of how unlikely their union would be.

'Yes,' she replied heavily. 'I know who he is.'

Jericho ran her hands down the plain brown blouse and skirt she wore for her work at the hospital, scowling at the uniform. Luckily she would only have to wear it for the rest of the year. She could hardly believe that only a few days earlier she'd been wearing exquisite sandals and a lovely gown. She heard the sharp tinkle of the bell outside and knew that Mr Paul was delivering the newspaper to the shop over which she lived. Hopping into her sandals, she took the stairs two at a time, knowing she'd have to hurry to make it to the hospital on time.

Outside the protective cocoon of Mannobe, initially she'd been oblivious to how striking she was in the city, favouring the poised women she saw moving about town. But she'd soon grown accustomed to heads turning. Maybe they weren't used to her colouring; they didn't seem to worship the sun here like she'd done in the village. As her confidence grew, she challenged the old fools that honked or whistled brazenly as she passed them. 'Do you have a daughter?' she would ask, delighted when they looked down, disgraced. '*Pues*, I am somebody's daughter,' she would declare, knowing they imagined a father standing beside her for protection. She would imagine alongside them.

Jericho yawned like a tired lion after her shift was finished. She made her way back home slowly, enjoying her surroundings as she walked. The buildings never ceased to amaze her. Back in the village she could walk for stretches of time before encountering another human being, let alone a house, but the buildings in Angel seemed to sprout up out of any piece of land. Houses and factories in abundance. She'd been so grateful that she could see trees from her small window over the seamstress's shop that she'd sent a small thank-you to Venus Oracene who she'd visited before making the monumental journey to Angel, who'd predicted her little dwelling.

A figure was seated on the shop's green steps. Her gut told her instantly that it was him. Daniel Dorique stood awkwardly as she approached. He removed his hands from behind his back, brandishing a bouquet of wild flowers.

'I thought they would remind you of home.'

She'd covered the distance between them, her eyes narrowing at the large bunch. She tried to fight the smile that spread over her lips, and failed.

'*Tanka*,' she breathed shyly before sneaking a look inside the doorway to see if Yalla was watching.

'Your friend told me you were staying here,' he'd confessed. 'I don't know what I said to offend you the other night but I would like to make up for it.'

She fixed her eyes on her sandalled feet as warmth fanned throughout her centre. She realised then that she was afraid. She felt like a fusion of cells pulsing, and fought to keep herself together.

'Mr Dorique—'

'Daniel. Please.'

'Daniel,' she repeated shyly. 'I don't think this is such a good idea. I don't know what you want, but I am here to study.'

'And who am I to stand in the way of your schooling?' he'd countered.

'There is no future for us.'

'If you already know the future, what more need do you have of an education?'

She was silent, unable to win this battle of words and fast losing it against her will.

'I simply thought you could use a friend in a foreign place. One that knows where you are from. There is no harm in that, surely?' His eyes rested on her face.

'I suppose.'

'Then at least afford me the pleasure of your company for one evening. If after that you no longer wish to know me, I will not disturb you.'

Suddenly exhausted by her struggle with instant attraction after a difficult work shift, with a nod of her head she accepted his invitation.

That evening had been enough to unravel her reserve. His charm and intellect captured her and she fell willingly into his seduction. He'd swept the hair off her face and looked down at her seriously, his voice breaking with passion.

'You truly are the most beautiful thing I have ever seen.'

In the semi-darkness, she'd seen her skin glowing in the moonlight. Daniel planted a succession of kisses in a path down from her third eye, stopping at the tip of her small nose.

'I don't want to sleep tonight, in case my dreams take me away from you,' he'd whispered against her earlobe.

She laughed and pushed his wandering hand off her ribcage.

'That nonsense may work in Angel, Daniel. But you forget: I'm a Mannobe girl.'

'Deus,' Penny sighed heavily as they strolled slowly through the square.

Jericho continued the story, revelling in the way her best friend digested each word eagerly, embellishing the worldliness and mystery that had attracted her to him. She exaggerated his determined pursuit, cataloguing the gifts he had bought her and highlighting his audacity when he took over paying her board to Yalla without consulting her.

She replayed every one of his ear-scorching endearments that she could remember for her friend to unpick. Her voice was heavy by the time she arrived at the agony of their separation, with Daniel in Ologo state; thankfully, all that would cease with the ball.

The sun was in the middle of the sky as they walked, looking for shadows to seek solace in. Jericho stopped at the young boy selling ice on the corner and called her friend over. They both took a piece and Penny removed two small coins from her skirt to pay him.

Although Penny sucked greedily on the ice as it expired in the scorching heat, Jericho ran hers down the back of her neck, allowing rivulets of cool water to run down her dark skin. She sighed then bent down to grab the bottom of her dress. Lifting up the hem, she rubbed the ice up her legs. She caught Penny looking at the boy, whose eyes were now the size of small planets, then back at her. It was only then that she became aware of the people around her and the effect she was having. Almost simultaneously, the chunk of ice between her fingers evaporated. The small boy immediately handed her another piece, trying to initiate an encore. Jericho pulled Penny away, laughing, oblivious to the slap the boy received from his returning mother for the unwise sale.

Babylon's eyes followed Jericho intently as she strolled from the square with her friend and a while later his feet gave chase accordingly. He felt Guitar's weight bobbing up and down on his back, his strings singing his happiness at being in the sunshine and at their reconciliation. They'd fallen out earlier that day over a disputed A minor.

The musician watched the girls stop under the shade of the large tree near Borrow's while Jericho bent to dislodge a stone from her sandal. By the time she stood up alongside her friend, he was standing beside them.

'*Bon dia, señoritas,*' he said, doffing his imaginary head-gear.

'*Bon dia,*' he heard Penny reply while Jericho echoed a vague response, dismissing him with a knowing look.

'It's a beautiful day we are having, *non?*' he enquired, looking directly at Jericho but she quickly averted her eyes.

She didn't respond but gave a smile, although it didn't quite reach the corners of her mouth. She looked over at her friend with a raise of her eyebrows and he sensed that they were ready to continue their amble. As they turned to move away, he blocked their path, retrieving Guitar from his perch in one smooth movement, who spluttered in surprise.

'I was wondering, Miss Lwembe, if I could play a song for you?' he asked, flashing his teeth at her.

'No!'

Her rejection took Guitar aback even more than himself, judging from his audible gasp. Jericho grabbed her friend's elbow, sidestepping him and his advance, and he watched them walk away. Try as he might he couldn't draw his gaze from her. She sashayed slowly, almost as if she suspected his eyes were still on her, and Babylon fell like a tree in Waranga forest. Silently, stoically, leaving the vista forever changed.

Eight

Allegory sensed the trouble brewing before his fears were confirmed in words and voices. Although nothing in particular alerted him to the unrest, an unhappiness had settled in his centre and he couldn't shift it, so he knew instinctively that something was amiss. At times like this, his mind wandered to his previous existence, severed prematurely by the evisceration of his entire family. He wondered what his life would have been had he remained in Kodo, whether he would be dead or maimed, or married with a family of his own. It was difficult for him to conceive of an attachment again to people, who could be swept away so easily in life. Nature was more tangible, it was much harder to imagine being abandoned by land.

Wading into the creek, he watched the dirt coming off his feet in cinnamon swirls. He recalled when Mabel had offered him an old basin next to his tent. It had been a peace offering for disturbing the stillness of his settlement with her new business. He'd refused easily, his body long since acclimatised to his baths in the stream. Besides, there was nothing quite like washing one's feet in fresh water. The motion of the water relaxed him and he lay back and allowed his eyes to close, enjoying the feel of the sun as it lapped softly against his lids. Suddenly he opened his eyes and looked around, taking in the complete view. When he was satisfied that his daily ritual was not being spied on by someone he couldn't see, he closed his eyes. But slowly a feeling of apprehension flooded him again, weighing him down in the translucent water. When the water level reached his nostrils, he prised his eyes open and inspected the horizon painstakingly. Taking even breaths, he emptied his mind; he knew that the answer would come to him eventually.

The water's surface was calm apart from the occasional fish that bubbled to the surface in search of something edible. Even the flies seemed suspended mid-air as opposed to their normal bothersome selves. As for the trees nearby . . .

His mind sprang to attention then, and he scoured the lines of greenery with narrowed eyes. He watched the leaves catching the breeze, but there was none of the usual flirtation that accompanied their dance, there was only a perfunctory shuffling motion. Gradually his ears attached themselves to the collective groan resonating from within the gnarled tree trunks that shadowed him. Something had disturbed them greatly.

Mannobans have been known to argue long and hard with neighbouring villages about the attributes of their place of birth. Those who ventured over the borderlines would inevitably have to endure a competition that called their cherished landmarks into question, and what started as a mild quibble would inevitably escalate as busybody strangers were pulled in to settle the dispute. Villagers from Ankara were loath to think that any other village west of Woolustown had a better butterfly trail, whilst the people of Begum claimed that their monkeys actually helped the farmers harvest their bananas, for which they were paid a small sum. Most Mannobans tolerated the small, misguided boasts and whims of their neighbours. They understood that it was hard to live so close to perfection and not actually *be* from it, so they allowed these injustices to slide by. But there was one area where Mannoban pride would not allow a foreigner a careless tongue on their mouth, and that area was their beloved forest.

Waranga Forest Reserve was a large block of moist semi-deciduous trees occupying Mannobe's beautiful undulating land. The thick region was a winding tapestry of wide, shallow valleys and flat-top hills rich in animal and plant life. Locals loved to boast that their forest held the largest primate collection anyone had ever known. Strictly speaking, Waranga didn't belong solely to Mannobans, but they had argued rather successfully, a long time ago, that because the forest territory started on their land they had superior claim.

Allegory loved to wander through the forest, unearthing a new trail on each voyage. He happened to prefer their own butterfly trail to that of Griffin, not that he'd ever be called into an argument over it. Now, as he strolled in perfect harmony with the elements, he watched the pale blue sky interrupted by flashes of coloured light from the butterfly wings overhead that rippled through the air, attracted by the pink and yellow petals of the flowering plants. He watched a blue kingfisher with green markings perched on a slim branch, its eyes darting around feverishly as it sought its mate. When it sensed it was being observed, it took off with a call that sounded to him like a rattle.

The forest had changed greatly over the years, right in front of his eyes. He remembered it best when it was simply a mass of green, almost jungle, almost not. The dips and swells of the land would suddenly open up to display papyrus swamps, and trails suddenly closed up as if Waranga had swallowed you whole, only its teeth – the trees – were so far apart that they were incapable of causing much damage. Then he'd frequented the forest to commune with nature; the land had been heavy with the competing conversations of plant and animal life. White-throated bee eaters had argued daily with dusky long-tailed cuckoos who abhorred the monkey tribes and their incessant chattering high above the forest canopy; vervets that despised short-tailed fruit bats and the sting of hornets, but loved to use them in their parlour games.

At that time, the forest was largely uninhabited as folklore and far-fetched tales elevated it to superstitious levels that wouldn't allow any villager with a soul to try and live there; but it had always been a source to live *from*, providing everything those villagers with less than others could use, and it was essential to their survival. Expert farmers weaned edible fruit, yams and dioscorea tubers from the soil, then sold them in the village, using what remained to feed their families. Wild coffee was harvested and the waterfalls and rivers provided fresh water. The forest also helped to catch the rain that was a long-lost relative in Mannobe, and fill up thirsty rivers. It was a vital source of firewood, charcoal and timber, and for those who built their houses in the old-fashioned way, particularly when mud and cement were hard to come by.

Commercial use had crept up on the forest slowly, slyly, almost as if it were trying not to alert and anger the animals that made the territory their home. And where local farmers had at one time siphoned off small quantities of wood, eventually their greed and the greed of others had been awakened, and larger parts of Waranga were harvested for timber. But there had been enough forest to go round. Nature was forgiving.

It pained Allegory to see how much of the beautiful forest was being exploited and indeed lost for the sake of money, as larger areas were encroached upon for vast banana and coffee plantations. 'Nothing good ever lasts,' he lamented, watching two monkeys cavorting a few feet ahead of him in a clearing. They were Mangabeys, and their grey cheeks and slick fur were eye-catching. This species of monkey was particularly mischievous and often raided villagers' gardens on the forest boundaries.

One of them was intent on mounting the other's back even though it was the larger of the pair, and the other, refusing, would throw it off, dealing heavy blows with a slender but mighty wrist before escaping a few feet away. Their foolery was peppered with yelps and frantic breaths yet Allegory sensed that this was more play than a fight. These animals were safe here, for the time being.

He felt his heart clench and freeze in his chest as if someone had placed their hand inside and hampered its beat. A time was coming when all of this would cease to exist. They had rested for many decades in their safe haven but the dangers of the city that were as fantastical as the places of their nightmares were now a living reality. His walks took him closer and closer to people and workers. Once he would go days before encountering a face that resembled his own or another creature that had two legs, or if it did, at the very least one didn't fly.

Magdalena broke from her dream bathed in sweat. She'd been in hot pursuit of Babylon but he was always outside her grasp. She could hear his distinctive voice taunting her as she ran: 'for ever is as long as you remember.'

Sweeping aside the hair covering her face in damp trails, she patted her body down to check that she was still intact. Outside, the village was quiet in the dawn light. The air was still, the crickets long since sleeping. She looked out of the window to clear her thoughts and saw a crimson-tailed lizard darting hysterically across the earth like the tongue of an inexperienced kisser. The rising sun crept slowly towards Le Papillon, bathing it in a warm glow, its bright iridescence rendering her vision blurry. She squinted at the light before heading back to bed. Pulling her blanket over her head, Magdalena wished she could run from Venus Oracene's reading at the festival as easily as she escaped the sunlight. At the thought of the obeah woman she shivered, recalling the woman's features as she'd delivered her prognosis.

She stretched a hand out and poked under her mattress for the parcel that Venus had given to her. Retrieving the small item, she sat upright in bed. She toyed with the packet idly between her fingers before opening it to reveal a fine yellow powder.

She sniffed the substance tentatively. Immediately the scent of rotten eggs assaulted her nostrils and her eyes watered at the shock. At the sound of her mother's footsteps, she refolded the packet and slid it underneath her pillow. She lay still as she heard her mother looking in on her. She knew she should have been up and carrying out her chores but a defeat had weighed down her bones, and emptiness filled the place where passion once was.

The slow heat of the morning began to make her drowsy, but she couldn't summon the will to move her body out of the glare of the sun. She sought out patterns in the sun's rays as it webbed her vision and listened to her matriachs' quiet morning conversation that sounded like a pot coming to the boil. They always began their day by exchanging words, which inevitably led to one of them recalling a tune from a phrase that her sister had mentioned, followed by them humming in unison. The melody finished, one would retreat to draw a bath or pray while the other prepared the menu for the café's day.

Magdalena yawned and followed the hypnotic sound of their song and the quiet pressure of the sun back to the land of dreams, and into the arms of Venus Oracene.

Venus was standing above Magdalena waving a raffia fan when she came to. It had taken her eyes a few moments to focus. It was only then that she realised that she'd passed out. Venus's brows were knitted into a pronounced W in the middle of her forehead. The albino woman observed her patiently, and seeing that Magdalena was gaining her faculties once again, attempted to lift her.

'*Eh* Magdalena, it's not that bad. All I said is that everything makes sense!'

She let Venus coax her on to the stool and propped her head against the tabletop before pouring a glass of water. Magdalena held the glass with both hands and drank small sips, her frightened eyes glazed above the rim as she gazed at the spiritualist.

'*Tome*. This will help you.' Venus offered her a handful of leaves.

Magdalena chewed them warily. The warm sensation that originated in her mouth slowly seeped through her body.

'If you're better perhaps we can continue, yes?'

She nodded sternly, turning a brighter gaze towards the obeah, who'd commenced her transformation. She'd watched, transfixed, as Venus's features grew tight and her pupils shrank to the size of black peppercorns.

'Now you may call me Oracene. *Ewo*; let us begin.'

Oracene centred the bowl on the table and pointed to a cluster of black crystals that had congregated on its left side.

'You see that? That is your heart. Black because you are starved of love. And who doesn't want love? But you must not put yourself in the wrong hands in order to get it.

106

Growing up without a father is always difficult. Even more so when you have no knowledge of whom he might be. Hmm, it's no small thing to raise a child alone, but some of your parents . . .' The obeah made a face. 'Mannobe women – they think they are protecting the children from their own shame. If only they knew. . . A child would rather feel the pain of the truth than suffer a heart full of questions, *non*? But do not blame your mother. She raised you well and taught you about love, even if it was only rudimentary. You must believe that you are beautiful, where it counts. This is why you chase him, yes? Because you think he is the only one who could ever want you? Continue to think such things and that is what will occur. You must not underestimate your power, *bona*. You must learn to embrace the light instead of surrendering to the darkness. *Pues*, I can barely make out your essence.'

Oracene pointed demonstratively as she spoke, stabbing the air to run home her statement.

'See? Nothing. You need to bring out your life force. Why are you so fearful?'

Magdalena opened her mouth but no words came out. She'd closed it swiftly on noticing a bluebottle that had penetrated the heavy flaps of the tent and was venturing perilously close. Oracene clapped her hands together majestically and pulled them apart to reveal the lifeless body of the fly. She blew the corpse harshly away from her palm.

'You have a long lifeline. You'll be around to be one of the elders – if you stay here that long. And there is travel, but the journey is more spiritual than physical. Watch out for your kidneys: apart from that you are in good health. But don't leave it too long or you will be unable to bear children like your auntie. There *is* a ring around your heart, which means you will be married. But you must learn to let go, Magdalena. Do not be afraid to try and fail.

107

And do not walk in anyone else's shadow. You must not allow anyone else's sadness to permeate your spirit. That is the trouble with woman energy – it is very intrusive.'

Oracene's smile smoothed out the frown in her forehead. Her eyes were smoky and her pupils danced madly, chasing the whites to the very far corners.

'Every house needs a little male energy. And every woman needs a little male, *non*?'

The spiritualist had wiggled her little finger suggestively at Magdalena in a way that was both comical and repulsive. She'd blushed, a beetroot colour flooding her cheeks so that she looked like a child experimenting with too much of her mother's rouge.

'I don't normally start with this but your case is rather unusual so we'll just have to accommodate you, won't we?' Oracene smiled, baring surprisingly small teeth.

'Ask me a question. Wait – not out loud. Close your eyes, *venga*.' Magdalena obeyed, not wishing to question ways she was not accustomed to.

'*Ewo*, count to ten. Okay, now shape the question in your mind's eye. Let your biggest worry come to the forefront of your brain, the issue that is troubling you. What is it that you wish to know?'

The tent was silent as the woman awaited Magdalena's query. Through the crack in her eyes where a little orange light peeped through, she saw Oracene's finger disappearing up her nostril as she tried to dislodge a troublesome object. Magdalena clamped her eyes firmly shut and tried to conjure up her question. She already knew what she wanted to ask, but she didn't know how long she was supposed to stay in that pensive position. She wasn't sure if Oracene was using her for entertainment value or whether having her eyes shut was an integral part of the woman's psychic process. Erring on the side of caution, she kept her eyes closed for fifteen more seconds and then opened them slowly. Oracene motioned for her to take her hands and she complied, reminding herself to wash them later on, remembering what the other woman's fingers had just been doing.

The obeah's voice was very low when she spoke. It seemed to come directly from her throat, not requiring the regular passage through the mouth to deliver its message.

'He's coming but you must be patient. It will be like nothing you have ever felt before. For even the hottest fire burns itself out quickly, Magdalena. But if you stoke the fire carefully, packing the wood tightly together and low, then you will have warmth throughout the night. Music comes in all forms; you just have to be quiet enough to hear it. But you are not still; you are too consumed with other matters. In order for you to experience love, you are going to have to experience pain. And the pain you are enduring now is not real pain, Magdalena. It's denial. You know, I once knew a woman who came to me in Chignono. She had travelled through four villages to find me. After using her last strength to knock on my door she collapsed.

'As I lifted her to my bed, I noticed her clothes were damp so I removed her dress and saw that her body was riddled with tiny cuts. It took her seventy days to heal. I looked after her and in that time no man ever came calling to claim her. When she was finally able to talk, I asked her who had done this; who was to blame. She replied that she had cut herself the exact amount of times her husband had professed his love before leaving her for another. She had done it for him, as a reminder of what love feels like. That is pain, Magdalena. And it is through pain that love will appear to you. This is not what you want to hear, *da vero*? You want me to tell you that the musician is yours for ever but I cannot do that. The truth is, there is no right person, only a right time. And this is not your time yet. You have so much to learn, my child.'

Oracene had released Magdalena's damp hands and reached up to hold her chin between her strong fingers. She'd wanted to cry out in pain but stopped herself. It was the first time Magdalena noticed the intricate henna marking that adorned each of the obeah's digits as Oracene's nails cut into her flesh.

'Tell me,' the obeah asked in a tone that sounded very much like affection, 'what do you desire in a man?'

'Umm . . .'

'Come on, speak up! If you don't know, how will you recognise it when it comes?' the woman scolded her.

Magdalena willed herself to find her voice. 'I want . . . I would like a good man, whose attention is fixed on only me. A man who is kind, gentle but tough, who works with his hands and who people like. I want a man who has travelled, who has lived a life beyond this village—'

'I hope you're not describing the musician to me?' Oracene interrupted quickly.

'No, Madam,' Magdalena answered politely. 'I was just—'

The obeah stood up and turned her back on Magdalena. She pulled two bottles off a shelf and poured the liquids into a short glass. The concoction – even from where Magdalena sat – had a slight aroma and was thick as molasses. The older woman downed the drink in one gulp and released a series of hacking coughs. Magdalena was convinced the obeah was trying to frighten her, and her sweaty armpits told her that the woman was succeeding.

'You know they call me a winch?' Oracene fixed her gaze on her. Her extended palm indicated she awaited a response but Magdalena had been too occupied with regulating her breathing, which had suddenly tripled. 'They say I'm a witch and, worse still, that I *know* everything . . . What do you think?'

110

Magdalena made a face as she pondered the woman's question. She couldn't think how knowing everything was worse than being called a witch, but she assumed Venus had her reasons.

'Perhaps . . . Perhaps the mysteries of the world are at your command . . . I don't know,' she'd admitted then in honesty. 'I think you are a strong woman. Maybe you do have powers beyond our eyes but they're not necessarily rooted in evil. People in the village are afraid, I think, when some women demonstrate the strength, the power, of a man. They think those women have something to be feared.'

Oracene was quiet for a long time. Magdalena watched the woman running her tongue over her lips for a full minute.

'Good answer.' Oracene took her chair once again, a satisfied smile softening her harsh features. 'As it happens, I *can* bring you such a man, but you must trust me. And you must be willing to endure a little *discomfort*. Can you do that?'

'*Si*,' Magdalena gushed. 'I'm ready.'

'So, if I asked you to endure what that woman in Chignono did, you could do it?' The obeah watched her eyes expand and laughed wildly at her. 'You must not be afraid. Your pain will be very quick. But most importantly before then, you must not lose heart.' Her hand came up and covered Magdalena's left breast as she spoke. Magdalena felt her heart rise up to meet the woman's penetrating touch.

'Or there will be nothing to give to him when he arrives. Take this. Find a nice spot outside and pour out the water. Don't rinse it out; just bring it back to me.'

Magdelena had clasped the proffered bowl carefully between her hands and parted the tent flaps. She walked for a few moments until she saw a small sapling peeking

111

through the grass. She carefully poured the water around its tiny trunk. When she returned, Oracene took the bowl and ran her finger around the inside. Scooping the residue into a pouch, she'd handed it to Magdalena.

'Bury this in a safe place. This is so your future can rest peaceful.'

Magdalena took the packet and slipped it between the folds of her skirt. Oracene held out her hand and instinctively she'd grasped it.

'I meant my fee,' the obeah elucidated, releasing her palm.

'Ah, yes.'

Magdalena scrambled for her coins and placed them into the hands of her advisor. The woman deposited them in the huge valley between her breasts and patted gently. She turned back to her table and picked up another small packet, which she held out to her.

'You young girls, you like to dream of your *nonnos*, isn't that so? Well, this should help you sleep. It's a potent sedative, one of my specialities,' Venus explained with a wink. 'Some tribes believe sleep is a kind of death. *You*, my dear, will be very happy to be reborn. None of the medicines in the village, except mine, can rival this.

'Your mothers will have to look further for help,' the woman mumbled to herself. 'Yes, I *do* know everything, Magdalena,' Venus continued, raising her voice, which at once adopted an ominous edge. 'You must take it the night of Biko's Eve, not a moment before, you hear me?'

Magdalena's mind fleetingly conjured up the autumnal occasion. Biko's Eve was also known as Wishing Day or the Day of Miracles. Throughout the day, most of the villagers made their way to the old well to deliver their wishes before an evening of prayer. Some scribbled their wishes on scraps of paper and dropped them into the dry well, but for the majority it was more of a ceremonial gesture. They

112

whispered their secret desires into a cupped palm before throwing them down to the angel below.

Magdalena snatched the packet from Venus's hand, a shy grimace ruffling otherwise perturbed features.

'*Tanka*, Madam.'

'What are you thanking me for? It's *your* future.'

Then Venus turned her back, rearranging her potions while Magdalena escaped through the tent, back into the light.

Babylon couldn't remember the last time a bout of insomnia had affected him so. Unable to feign sleep any longer, he decided to stretch his legs, hoping the soft dawn air would ease the tension between his shoulder blades. The village was just stirring as he strolled and he enjoyed each new sound and smell that greeted him. He bent to pluck a small flower from a nearby bush and winced at the new twinge in his arm. They were coming harder and faster now and he wondered whether to attribute the pain to Magdalena. Not the day she'd wounded him, but his guilt at casting her aside so easily. He'd known even before he became involved with her that she wasn't like his other conquests. Someone like Corál would have overcome her disappointment much quicker than the softly spoken Codón.

He massaged his right arm, noticing that the painful tingle had now eased to a prickle of excitement. It was almost the same feeling he'd experienced when he'd seen that woman by the winch's tent. All this time he'd occupied himself with lesser things when she'd been in the village, within his reach. If he hadn't seen it with his own eyes, he wouldn't have believed it for a moment.

He blinked as he focused on the silhouette in the square, suddenly grateful to the sleep that had eluded him and allowed for an opportune meeting this morning. Jericho hadn't noticed him yet but was consumed in her sketching. She shook her head fiercely and held the charcoal away from her drawing, in the direction of the tree she was capturing on the paper, before adjusting her skirt under her bottom.

Babylon slid Guitar from his back round to his front and began to play gently. He saw her head lift as she caught his music but she didn't turn around. Babylon practised his scales before slipping into an easy rhythm. He moved closer to her, aware that the more he played, the less she drew, as if she was more fixated on his music than on her work. Finally, when he stood right behind her, he tripled the pace of his piece before breaking off his flourishing so abruptly that she was forced to look at him.

'*Bon matin,*' he greeted her warmly, tipping his invisible cap at her.

'Good morning.'

Up close he noticed that she had laughing eyes, the kind that look as though they are still considering an amusement long after it should have passed. Even though she was trying to remain aloof, they were still littered with diamonds and he found himself calculating what it would take to tease her lips into a smile. He inspected her drawing up close, half expecting her to cover it and secretly pleased when she didn't.

'Is your work for sale?' he asked, watching her hand still over her sketch.

'Why? You have shillings to spend?'

'Depends. I mean, it's *good*. I like it, but your lines are wrong,' he offered cheekily.

'As if you know about art,' she replied, cutting her eyes at him. Inside he smiled but outwardly attempted to look offended. In response he held up Guitar to her.

'*Pues*, what is music but art itself?'

114

'Please . . .' she kissed her teeth. 'You call what you do *art*? Making sweet sounds to chase women?'

'You've seen me play?' he questioned, smiling even when she didn't respond. 'Do I look like someone who has to chase women? Maybe they chase me?'

'What do you expect – this is a village of scraps. If the men aren't married or someone's *nonno*, who else is left?'

'And what is it that makes a man eligible, in your opinion?'

'His breeding, his job, intelligence, his grace—'

'But wouldn't you say our conversation demonstrates that I am indeed a man of breeding?' he interrupted her again, enjoying her look of annoyance.

'No, because you're irritating me and distracting me from doing my work.'

'*Eh*, so you find me distracting?'

'I believe I said irritating first . . .' She fought a smile and won. 'You know I'm spoken for.'

'Is that so? You seem very capable of speaking for yourself,' he deliberately misinterpreted her. 'So *that's* why you're resisting my charms?' he continued, chuckling at her horrified expression. 'All right then, let me not disturb you. I'll leave you to paint.'

He moved away from her, dropping the flower he'd plucked earlier by her side. He saw her body relax visibly as he increased his distance but when he was just a few feet away he stopped.

'What are you doing?' she shouted to him.

'I'm concentrating on my art.'

Babylon ignored the look she gave him and began to play Guitar noisily, catching her shifting the angle of her body so that she didn't have to look at him. That was when he decided to circle her. He'd heard once that a zebra mother circled its newborn for hours until her stripes were imprinted in its memory. He tried to hypnotise Jericho in the same fashion. She kept her face fixed on her paper, but on his third lap around her she threw her charcoal down on the ground and looked up at him.

'See anything you like?' he asked innocently, still playing.

'No. Nothing,' she replied, her eyes suddenly dull ink pools.

He plucked one string exaggeratedly, spun Guitar rapidly and caught him before plucking another. She looked at him blankly. Even if she was impressed with his dramatics, he sensed that she wouldn't show it. Then an idea struck him; he stumbled, pretending to drop Guitar. She gasped and covered her mouth with her hands before he heard her quiet laughter.

'*Eh-eh*, at last she smiles. You mean I only have to play the fool to part your lips?'

'That can't be right,' she countered evenly. 'After all, this isn't the first time you've seen me smile?'

Babylon caught her insult swiftly and clutched his chest as if he'd been shot. 'You *eh*, you have pepper in your blood.'

'That's correct. I'm too spicy for you.' She stood up, gathering her things. He noticed that she didn't retrieve his flower. Their eyes met and he saw that her face had softened considerably.

'It's okay. I can take heat.'

She laughed dismissively and began to walk away from him.

'You should be careful,' she said, turning back towards him briefly. 'Too much pepper can kill.'

Nine

The annual rudón championship was always a bone of contention among many Mannobe indigents. The ancient game had been passed down through generations affectionately like dimples or a gap tooth. Traditionally, it was played only by the elders, but the energy that playing aroused in the competitors had spread to the younger inhabitants so that a warlike mentality pervaded all Mannobans whenever the competition began.

Out of season it was played in the square by the Kissing Trees, two majestic banyans standing about ten yards apart. Their outstretched branches were so huge that they met in the middle, which is why the villagers had coined the phrase that they were kissing.

Every year a pitch was whittled in the wild grass near the river because the championship demanded a more auspicious location. After the ground was burnt, lines were painted on the surface, and a white star stood in the centre with concentric circles around it. The game involved getting the appropriate sized ball into the correlating ring, the winner being whoever got the smallest ball to the heart of the star. The atmosphere the competition generated was a great precursor to the Señoritas ball that followed it later in the season.

Mabel dusted off her balls with the hem of her skirt. She could hear M'elle in the kitchen, frying huge batches of plantain to take down to the field that afternoon. This year she would surely beat her. Despite M'elle's size, she was surprisingly adept when it came to tossing her balls inside the circles. She, on the other hand, was always defeated when it came to the last ball. But this year, she had the edge – having taken clandestine lessons from last year's champion.

Neither of the Codón sisters had ever won the huge crate of palm wine that was bestowed upon the victor, but as long as her sister didn't beat her again, Mabel didn't care two figs who the winner was. She wondered if she'd be able to get her daughter involved in the event. Magdalena appeared to have sunk deeper inside herself and nothing, not even her favourite dish of tilapia chowder, could draw her out. The dress she started preparing in the spring for the ball hung off the wall peg like a deflated ghost. Strictly speaking, Magdalena was getting too old for the Señoritas ball. But she was still unattached in the eyes of the Creator and thus permitted to attend, according to village custom.

Mabel glanced over the abandoned gown. One sleeve lay unattached and flapped idly in the breeze as if it was trying in vain to engage its maker's attention. Mabel sighed heavily at the sight of her daughter staring into space on the edge of her mattress. She eased the door closed and returned to the kitchen. She stood beside M'elle, who rolled the sleeves of her white caftan up before she threw handfuls of plantain into the vat of hot oil. The heat was so intense that there was a luminous sheen to her nut-brown skin. Her sister smiled at the sound of her knife as it struck the wooden counter while slicing the vegetable

118

and the oil bubbled to its own six-eight beat as the knife sang in its soprano tune. *Fizz tap, fizz tap, tap tap fizz.*

Simultaneously they began to hum a song only they knew, M'elle instinctively taking the harmony. Mabel only stopped humming when the last bubble of oil popped as it settled, inert in its metal volcano.

'She's getting worse,' her sister spoke ominously.

'I know, but what can I do?' Mabel replied gravely.

They sighed in unison and wrapped the platters of food in cloth while tutting to one another. Then M'elle went outside to retrieve her balls.

Guitar's voice sounded raspy and tight in his chest. Babylon sighed twice: once in exasperation, and then finally in defeat. He settled his friend into his carry case then padded through his home, searching for some activity to occupy his one-track mind. But his task was fruitless: she was painted on the backs of his eyelids.

He prepared some tea carefully, letting the steam from the cup soothe his pulsing temples. His locks felt heavy on his head. He assembled them in a makeshift French braid but shook them loose after a few minutes, glad Guitar wasn't around to see him so perturbed. Lifting the tea to his lips he felt a twinge from his left shoulder all the way to the tips of his fingers. His tongue bit back a curse but his shocked hand had already sent the cup flying to the floor. As he knelt to mop up the strewn mess, Gloriama's words came to his mind. Whenever something fell in her presence she would comment in her gentle manner, '*Tranquilo*. It means someone is thinking about you.'

He wondered optimistically whether Jericho was the one with him in her thoughts. Strolling through the village, she seemed no more aware of him than she was of her own breath. His comments to her were always rebuffed in her quiet but clipped tone, and as much as he'd reprimanded himself for attempting to engage her in conversation or asking to spend time with her at each opportunity, he reasoned it was like telling the sun not to shine or the moon not to glow. She'd elevated the word 'no' to a new height until it became a sound he took pleasure in hearing issuing from her. A bittersweet tease. It had been a long time since he'd encountered a woman whose smell lingered in his nostrils long after she'd departed. Her inadvertent graze at their last encounter had set every hair on the back of his arm alight.

That intrigued him as much as her abrasiveness, but he dismissed her prickly persona as a mask of some kind. There was something paradoxical about her that was extremely beguiling. After all, the woman that rebuked him was the same one he'd seen hugging the Okavango boy with the ringworm patches right before she bought a piece of ice. She was also the woman he'd witnessed chasing after two teenagers who'd stolen a shoe belonging to the pretty mixed-race girl with golden curls. Even last week, after his performance for a group of visitors, he'd caught sight of her out of the corner of his eye, helping Mama Abandela and carrying her shopping.

All these occasions hinted at someone more complex than the rude exterior she exhibited in his presence, and so he could only deduce that he forced that reaction from her. This conclusion was enough to sustain his interest and he savoured the possibility that her disdain was rooted in attraction rather than extreme dislike. His competition didn't bother him, if indeed another man existed. He was half convinced she'd made it up. If there was someone, he wasn't in Mannobe – that much he knew.

He conjured up her parting expression the other day for the tenth time, smiling to himself. He'd caught her off guard by trying to procure her assistance during his performance for a group of elders. He'd softened her with his shameful plea in front of them, watching acquiescence work its way through her grudgingly as she took in the anxious faces of the village's elderly who'd clapped as she came forward. Excitement washed over him, but it was short-lived. As soon as her eyes fell on the cord he withdrew from his pocket, he knew he was going to fail.

He'd hoped to reproduce one of his old *Orgeuille* tricks for his audience, which involved tying his hand to a volunteer so that they only had two free hands between them to play Guitar. His laughter had been triggered by the terror in her eyes as she pulled out of his grip.

'*Tranquila*, I've done this a hundred times—' he assured her.

'I'm sure you have!'

'With the circus,' he grinned naughtily. 'It was part of my act.'

'Hmm . . .' she sniffed, suspiciously. 'Don't you have other ideas that don't involve *that*?'

'*Pues*, you could always sit on my lap while I play you a song?'

Her refusal had drawn titters from his audience, and her subsequent exit, even more. Babylon heard Mama Abandela's signature cough-laugh.

'Na how the youth of today do?' she asked, wiping her streaming eyes. 'Even with rope, they can't control woman, *oh*!'

Babylon shook his head more forcefully, so much so that the Lwembe girl's image was momentarily dislodged and replaced with that of Magdalena Codón. Perhaps this was how she had felt about him – the sudden realisation hatched boldly in the back of his mind.

'Eh, so now I'm a woman!'

He snorted as he tried to stifle a laugh and knocked his head against the table corner. His booming shout echoed

121

around the silent house so voluminously that even Guitar's strings sang in response. He rubbed tenderly at the swelling lump on his scalp, grateful that, temporarily at least, he had something else to think about.

He'd taken a fresh cup of tea to his favourite spot outside where his hammock swung low from the only two trees in his backyard, that were so slender they looked almost naked. But they'd proved alarmingly adept at supporting him. In times of turmoil he liked to let the woven twine accept his weight and allow the rocking motion to appease his frazzled nerves. Although his backyard was relatively bare, it still looked untidy. The grass grew haphazardly, and remnants of a bench he'd taken from Hamid's to restore rested quietly in the corner, waiting to be attended to.

He watched flies flirting in the sunshine and red ants making their treacherous journey up the trunk of his tree. He kicked sand at an approaching gecko with the leg that hung lazily out of the hammock. The sweeping motion pleased him so much that he repeated the action. He felt the thicker locks at the back of his head tighten as he concentrated. Inspiration came to the music man from the most extraordinary of places. *La musica* seemed to drip from the ends of his fingers into whatever he came into contact with, whether it was instrument or woman. Melody flooded his brain, transforming his features, and it seemed as if the ants halted their passage to watch the male medusa being transported. He wanted desperately to run inside and get Guitar to share this new music with him, but was afraid of losing his connection with this rhythm. His legs straddled the hammock now and his feet stenographed the beat he was channelling from the sky back into the earth, completing the chain. Words quickly began to stitch themselves to the intricate melody his legs wove and he covered the compound in a carpet of song.

'*Remember when we rode over the backs of Tigris?*'
'The night was like charcoal, exactly like this.'
'*Gogoa choked on a chicken bone,*'
'I chased Rafaela with a heart like a stone.'
'*The people of Madeenka welcomed us in.*'
'They wouldn't let us play; they said it was a sin—'
'*You almost lost me in a bar bet,*'
'There isn't a card game I haven't won yet!'
'*Tell me – when will the music end?*'
'Never.'
'*Never?*'
'Never, my friend.'
'*Tell me – when will we stop our play?*'
'Never.'
'*Never?*'
'Never I say!'
'*You are the music man.*'
'You are Guitar.'
'*You are the Alpha—*'
'And you Omega . . .'
'*I am the music,*'
'I am the song,'
'*Together we'll go on and on . . .*'

Driver arrived at Babylon's compound and found his friend's legs astride the hammock like one of the rafts the fishermen waded on patiently as they waited to hook their livelihoods. He approached the musician slowly, waiting for him to become aware of his presence.

' 'Lon,'

'D . . .'

Babylon's voice was low, as if it was coming from a faraway

place and had to catch up with the rest of the man present. They both reached out to touch knuckles while Babylon's eyes appeared to reacquaint themselves with the universe. Driver stooped to retrieve his friend's cold tea and drained it, smacking lips together loudly once he'd finished.

'There more inside? I feel like my forefathers have a thirst.'

The musician nodded before adding, 'Bring my shirt and Guitar.'

'Sure, I'll bring out your lover,' Driver teased.

He returned with the tea and some bread he'd found in the kitchen, then looking over at Babylon, he winked knowingly.

'Me fathers are hungry too.'

They both ate and drank quietly, watching the day unfold. Babylon cradled Guitar in the hammock next to him and Driver felt his body soaking up the burning sun overhead.

'That's five shillings you owe me . . .' he said after a while.

'For what?'

'I told you I was right about Essé.'

'She sleep with Hamid?'

'Pearl tell me so when I drop off her yam. In fact, I heard it from Essé herself!'

Babylon reached into his pocket, pulled out a coin and tossed it to Driver. 'I only charged you four shillings for your tea,' he replied smoothly.

'You ever think about settling?' Babylon asked when their laughter subsided.

'You mean taking a wife and children?' Driver squawked as his friend's question fell awkwardly into their conversation like a beetle in the water leaf soup he'd eaten the night before. 'The sky must be falling, for I never thought I hear you say such a thing.' He chuckled and some bread-

124

crumbs dropped from his stubble to the dirt at their toes. 'You serious?'

'Yes.'

'*Ewo*, I don't know. Sometimes I wonder what it like,' he disclosed gently. 'When I go and see Maurice.'

Driver's thoughts went to his son then, the young boy he'd made that was becoming a man with very little of his input. He sighed heavily and fell silent.

The two of them sat speechless, deep in their own thoughts, and only the wind singing through the leafy trees made conversation. Driver watched as Babylon set his guitar on the ground. Placing his hands behind his head, he seemed to inspect the clouds, looking for the answer to the question he was afraid to voice until Driver called him from his reverie in the mottled sky.

' 'Lon?'

'Yes?'

'How many children you think you have that you don't know about?'

He waited as Babylon pondered the question for a full minute before responding.

'If I don't know about them, how can they be my children?'

Allegory was on form by the time M'elle left Le Papillon, balancing her balls in a sack over her shoulder along with a big platter of plantain. As she made her way to the river she saw a small crowd clustering around the wise man, obsidian eyes ablaze as words tumbled down from his flapping gums.

'Then shall he give the rain of thy seed; that thou shalt sow the ground withal; and bread of the increase of the earth, and it shall be fat and plenteous: in that day shall thy cattle feed in large pastures. Those who have eyes to see . . .'

She watched his eyes roll around in the back of his head like miniature rudón balls. The crowd stood, immobilised by his energy as he thrust a skinny hand skyward, casting out imaginary spirits. He stilled as he saw her approaching, his frantic movements slowing before coming to an abrupt halt. She smiled as the throng parted for her, partly because the Codóns commanded such respect, but most probably so as not to upset the tray of delights she so lovingly cradled to her bosom. Once she'd exchanged pleasantries with him they fell into step together.

'You're not joining in the championships this year?' she asked, even though she knew he had never – as far as she remembered – participated in any of Mannobe's competitions.

'My work does not permit me to do so.'

'And I can't persuade you? Oh.'

Her face fell as he shook his head, followed by the plantain until his swift reflexes halted their descent.

'Would you like me to walk with you?' he asked, still holding on to the tray. She nodded in agreement, unable to control the huge light beaming from behind her eyes.

'Is that you, Coco?'

'Yes, Mama.'

Edith Lwembe floated into the kitchen. Her eyes lit up when she saw Penny was also in there. They both rushed over to greet her.

'Did you have fun outside?'

Her mother always spoke to them as if they were still little children, as if she'd frozen them in her mind and was reluctant to undo the spell. Before they could answer, she ushered them to the other side of the house. Jericho moaned as she felt her tepid body heating up again when they approached the eastern side of the house.

'*Ah-ah,* Mama. We were just—'

'Hush. I have something to show you.'

Edith disappeared while Jericho pulled faces at Penny, and they made each other laugh in ways no one else could. When her mother returned, she was holding something folded delicately in her arms.

'I wasn't sure I would finish it in time, so I didn't tell you before.' She winked at Penny and unravelled the garment in front of her daughter. The robe fell to the floor, a pale yellow gown in the thinnest of fabrics. Jericho recognised it instantly, she'd run baby fingers over it many a time in her youth when her mother wasn't looking.

'I altered it for your dance,' her mother uttered, pride choking her voice.

Jericho placed the sleeves up against her shoulders and looked down to see the dress resting halfway down her calves. Disappointment suddenly gripped her, but she held it from her mother.

'Thank you, Mama. Are you sure it will fit?'

'There's only one way to tell. Put it on.'

She turned to undo her skirt, throwing a look to Penny who stared back, flummoxed. A loud voice called for her mother's attention outside in the compound and she left the room.

'What's the matter?' Penny whispered.

Jericho wrinkled her nose at the dress. What had seemed like the most precious garment in the whole world when she was a little girl now looked like a simple tunic, especially after the dresses she'd seen in Angel; even compared with Claudia's dazzling outfits. She knew Mannobe women sometimes handed down their dresses to their daughters and what that meant, but she didn't know how to tell her mother that she had another garment in mind for the ball.

'Daniel bought me a dress.'

127

'But Coco! Your mother . . .' Penny's words trailed off in shock.

'Quick. Close the door.'

Jericho dived under her bed to retrieve an old wrapper and Penny glanced outside into the small doorway before easing the door shut. Jericho unfolded the wrapper carefully to reveal a sheer dress hidden inside it.

'*Bona!*' Penny gasped with pupils bigger than a full moon.

Jericho held the dress against her and swung round in delight. Gold satin caressed her body, a beautiful strapless gown with a feathered bodice, that dropped all the way to the floor. While Penny eyed the dress greedily, she knelt to retrieve some gold sandals so exquisite that her friend relinquished her watchman's post for a closer inspection, fingering them gingerly.

'I already know how I'm going to wear my hair,' Jericho whispered.

They giggled together like schoolchildren before Penny composed herself, guilt-ridden.

'But what are you going to do about the other dress?'

'I don't know . . .' Jericho hesitated before an idea formed in her mind. 'Suppose it accidentally tore?'

'It's your mother's *wedding* dress. Eh, Coco, you only have one mama,' Penny gasped.

'And there is only one *first* ball,' she replied petulantly. 'He bought it for me, Penny. How can I not wear it?'

They glared at each other, separated by both mattress and manners. It was only her mother's steps in the corridor that united them as they scrambled to dispose of the evidence while Jericho jumped out of the remainder of her clothing.

'Well? Does it fit?' Edith Lwembe queried, entering the room.

'I'm just trying it, Mama.'

'*Eh* girls, you must be quicker than that. There's only one first ball, you know.'

Mabel collapsed on the bench, exhausted. The air was so still, she prayed for a dragonfly to speed by and ripple the atmosphere. Even a lizard's fart would be welcome, providing a temporary current from the heat that enveloped her. She swept her hair off her face and surveyed the landscape with an eagle's gaze. In front of her M'elle was deep in conversation with Hamid. Their heads bobbed towards each other as they spoke. In the heat, the subtle movement had been slowly lulling her to sleep until her sister's quiet laughter, like wind chimes, caught a slow breeze and drifted out over the field.

The competition had been well under way for an hour and Mabel had been making a valiant attempt to stay in the running. She stole a quick glance at Magdalena, who she'd dragged along on pain of disownment, but her child seemed decidedly uninterested in the event. Although the field was awash with most of Mannobe out in attendance, she kept her eyes downward, as if the patterns on her burgundy wrapper held the answer to the meaning of life.

Mabel's nutmeg eyes flashed angry flecks of gold. She wanted to go over and dislodge the melancholy from her child as if it were a bone stuck in her throat. She wanted to grab her by the shoulders and shake her until her head wiggled dangerously on her neck, but she fought to keep herself restrained. She spat on the ground and fiddled with the folds of her expertly tied sari. She'd chosen the tie-dye outfit specifically in the hope of dazzling the other competitors so much that they'd lose focus on their game, plus the roomy skirt also gave her space to manoeuvre her fleshy thighs in order to send her ball thundering down the pitch.

Her concentration was broken by her sister's euphoric

cry at a successful turn. She was still grinning when she flopped down on the bench next to her twin.

'Did you see that? The Creator is on my side, *abi*?'

'*Hmmph*.'

M'elle's playful punch caught her by surprise.

'Why you want to beat me so?'

'Because it's my turn,' Mabel replied haughtily.

'It's always your turn.' M'elle's smile was strained as she stepped aside for her twin to pass.

'I told you she wouldn't be here.'

Babylon ignored his friend's whining and combed the field with his eyes. He didn't want to admit it, but Driver was right. Jericho Lwembe wasn't watching the festivities. He kicked the ground angrily, unearthing a clump of grass. In one fluid movement, he tucked it neatly back in and searched for a prime position to watch the game. Sensing a gaze on him, he avoided looking in its direction but instinctively knew that Magdalena was somewhere close by. He chided himself for wanting to see his prickly princess so much that he'd inadvertently placed himself in Miss Codón's presence, but at least he had Driver as a buffer. He noticed that Mabel had sensed the shift in her daughter's persona at his appearance and had drawn her away under the guise of re-tying her robe.

The air was peppered with heavy clunks from rudón balls as they made contact with each other followed by the whimpering of grass as it was being flattened. By the time Mabel returned alone, her sister was well in the lead. M'elle appeared to have perfected a flick of the wrist that sent her balls soaring, as if their route had been mapped out by the Creator himself. Mabel pushed her way through the supporters to get a better look. She was annoyed at Mr Bauba, the reigning champion, who'd obviously been weakened by the case of palm wine that was last year's prize. His throw was so askew, it seemed to her as if he was aiming at a field thirty degrees to the right of the allotted one.

She grasped her last ball determinedly. Spitting on her fingers for good luck, she accustomed her hand to the weight of the smallest sphere. She'd painted it bright orange and fantasised that she held the sun in her palm. Mabel surveyed the playing field and swung her arm long and low. She held her breath as the little ball meandered its way through the other balls that had taken up residence on the pitch and stopped two blades of grass shy of the star at the pitch's centre. She quickly held on to her exclamation before it left the harbour of her lips. Although she was in premium position, there were still a few more players to go, and her sister's final throw.

The heightened competition had awakened Babylon's appetite. He left Driver who was busy observing a dung beetle crawling over a young woman's shoulder, and trudged round the crowd, stopping to buy some fried meat from a vendor. After paying, he turned around and found himself facing his adversary. Babylon looked behind her hoping to find her mother, anyone to usher her away before she made a scene, but no one came to his rescue.

'*Bon dia*,' she breathed, with a confidence false as her expression.

'Magdalena, how . . . *well* you look,' he lied smoothly.

She flushed and smiled nervously.

'Can we talk, just for a second?'

He hesitated, not wanting to be drawn into a lengthy dialogue with this woman; internally reprimanding himself for not being more prudent in his choice of lover. If he'd known she would have taken their ending this hard, he would never have blessed her with his body in the first place. However, the plea that lurked behind her features softened his reticence. Now on the losing end of unrequited love, he recognised the alien feeling as empathy pervading his bones, making him nod in acquiescence.

They walked together and reached the far end of the field, having left the frenetic energy of the game behind them. Babylon pointed at the ground and offered her his hand as she sat down. She shivered as she took it and a tiny part of him felt flattered that she was so affected by his touch. Still, he hardened his gaze and decided to let her speak her piece before moving on.

'It's beautiful weather, *non*? It should be even better for the ball. I thought—'

'No, Magdalena,' he interrupted her speech as soon as he plotted its course, watching her flinch in anguish.

'But we agreed before ... that we would go together ...'

'I said perhaps we would go. But I think it is best if you go with someone else.'

'Who will I find to dance with me now? How can you do this to me?'

He couldn't find any words to comfort her with. He was used to telling women what they wanted to hear, but now he found himself struggling. He didn't know whether it was Jericho's effect on him; whether his puzzling feelings were weakening him, or indeed if he did truly feel sorry for simple Magdalena. He knew that anything he said would fuel her false hope or anger her further so he reached out to still her agitated hands, but she swatted him away like a bothersome child.

'I don't understand you. Did I mean nothing to you?' she continued when he offered no reply.

'Of course not, but that was then ...'

'What did I do?' Her voice rose in desperation. 'Was it something I did? Is there someone else?'

The question hung in the air precariously. He knew that he couldn't answer it either way, that to answer would force him to face revelations he was not yet prepared for. He smiled warmly at her and covered her hands with his.

'Dear Magdalena,' he drawled earnestly, disclaimers dripping off his tongue, 'I care about you too much to saddle you with someone as unworthy as myself. You deserve so much more than I can give . . .'

'I don't care, I want you!' she cried, grabbing him to her. Winded by the force of her embrace, Babylon was even more surprised when she connected her lips to his. He leaned into her kiss instinctively, momentarily comforted by the familiarity of her lips. She looked into his eyes and although he knew she wanted him to mirror her gaze, something else occupied his attention. She followed his line of sight towards Penny Azevo making her way towards the field with her friend. Magdalena broke away from him and ran. Although he called after her half-heartedly, his eyes chased the horizon for his future, completely oblivious to his past.

The Codóns were gathered in the kitchen of Le Papillon but M'elle was having a very hard time staying seated.

'You should have seen it, *bona*.' She swung her arm, mimicking her movement from the competition, the stroke that had made her the victor.

'It was a lucky shot,' Mabel muttered sulkily.

'Yes it was. Lucky I was a better player than you and pushed your ball aside as easily as blowing away an eyelash.'

She laughed, and noticed that her niece was caught off guard by the sound. Mabel shrugged her shoulders, but the skeleton of a smile formed on her lips and she laughed.

'You only won because I lost my concentration. I was busy looking after my child.' Mabel reached over the table and pulled her daughter to her bosom.

133

'*Ewo*, Mama,' Magdalena whined half-heartedly, snuggling into her mother's softness.

'*Da vero*, but all your secret lessons with Bauba should have accommodated for that.' M'elle arched an eyebrow at her sister, who spluttered like a dying fish before surrendering to the truth.

'I admit he may have given me some tips, but the skill was all mine.'

At this they both burst into a fit of giggles. Magdalena tried to excuse herself from the room but Mabel detained her.

'And where are you going?'

'To bed, I'm tired.'

'You cannot mend a broken heart with sleep, *bona*. Have you finished your dress?'

'No, Mama. I'm not going.'

'Yes you are. You think a man is going to come for you in your bedroom? Tebo is coming for you in two hours to take you to trim your hair. Meanwhile, we will finish stitching the dress you started. Now you can go.'

Mabel rose, closing the discussion like a book. M'elle watched Magdalena looking at her for support, but stuck resolutely with her twin, mirroring her sister's expression. Defeated, Magdalena left the room with her head down. When they heard her enter her room – her bottom creaking the springs of her mattress noisily – the sisters risked a sneaky chuckle.

'*Coco I can't*,' Jericho listened to the pleas of her friend since birth.

'Do it.'

They eyed each other but Jericho knew Penny could never rival her glare.

'*Please*, Penny. I know it's bad, but if *you* do it, then truthfully I won't have damaged my mother's wedding dress.'

134

'But *I* would!'

'Yes, but it's not *your* mother's dress.'

'Please, I don't want any *wahala, abeg*.'

'*Ewo*, if you won't do it!' Jericho shouted impatiently.

She picked up the dress and held it by each sleeve, pulling at it dramatically. Her friend's eyes shrank to the size of slits in horror and she rose, defeated.

'Okay, okay. Give it to me.'

Jericho kissed her as she handed it over.

'Something small,' she instructed guiltily. 'Not so it's completely ruined, just so I can't wear it. Meantime, I'll find something else to wear.' She winked as she rifled underneath the mattress for Daniel's dress.

The sound of the dress ripping caught her attention as much as Penny's gasp. Jericho saw the gash that started on the seam but had worked its way against the grain of the fabric. She let out a desperate laugh, in shock, and Penny let it fall from her hands. Her mother called loudly from the other room and she had mere seconds to compose herself. Casting Penny a sideways glance, she left her alone in her bedroom with a guilty conscience big enough for the both of them.

Babylon couldn't believe his luck when he saw Jericho coming out of the salon or rather the annexe of Mama Nabokei's house. He'd strolled into the centre to look for another E string. Guitar was proving very troublesome lately. He was anxious to return home to finish penning the tune he'd been haunted by since his last interaction with Magdalena. It had sneaked into his head some time after he'd seen Jericho and her friend walking together. Days had passed quickly as the music overtook him, forcing him to string complicated notes together even when he was sleeping. But at last, the song was finally coming through him and his thoughts were his own again.

He watched Jericho exiting the salon unhurriedly. Her hair was expertly woven above her head in a threaded crown garnished with tiny gold beads. She turned the heads of both men and women as she walked but seemed oblivious to the stares as if it was second nature to her. She smiled to herself and touched the back of her neck, and although the action wasn't provocative, the muscles in his groin twitched. He wondered what it would be like to trace her pulse with the tip of his tongue.

She stopped outside the general store and was talking to the house-girl of the Dorique manor when he caught up with her. He watched her slip the envelope the house-girl had handed her up her sleeve before she acknowledged him.

'*Bon matin*, Miss Lwembe.'

'*Bon matin*,' she replied as she moved away from him with an expression that suggested he either smelt or carried an infectious disease.

'I have a song for you,' he continued, following behind her.

'No thank you.'

'Every time I ask you, you say the same thing—'

'A smart person would stop asking . . .'

'Is it music you don't like or musicians?'

'Both.'

'I beg your pardon?'

'Annoying musicians.' She rubbed the back of her neck awkwardly.

'You don't like musicians?' He raised his eyebrows.

'My father was a musician,' she offered noncommittally and cocked her head.

'Was he annoying?'

'I wouldn't know,' she muttered quietly. She continued walking but he fell into step alongside her. He hummed gently beside her, content to say nothing, and pretended they were having an intense, albeit unspoken, conversation. She watched him from the corner of her eye, and a small smile flitted across her lips. Instantly it dawned on him that she was amused by his pursuit.

'It's a shame. My song is very sweet.' Babylon kissed his fingers for emphasis before winking at her.

'I'm sure,' she replied. 'Like the ones about you? Your amazing prowess, or your endless siblings.'

'You like those?'

She shrugged.

'You know, it flatters me that you study my lyrics so carefully,' he said and squeezed her arm playfully but she scoffed at his comment and quickened her pace.

'Will you be attending the ball tomorrow?' he continued, unperturbed.

'Yes.'

'May I be permitted to grace the floor with the most beautiful woman in the southern hemisphere?'

'I don't know. When you find her, you can ask her to dance.' She blushed.

He laughed inwardly at her sass, but speedily attempted a different approach.

'Why is it that I unnerve you, *señorita*?'

'Do I look unnerved?' She faced him head-on and he found himself fighting to maintain eye contact. His pupils burned with the intensity of her glare and he felt rivers of water beginning to pool in the back of his eye sockets.

'Not at all. You . . . you look amazing.'

An expression he recognised as disappointment skated across her features. He racked his mind to figure out what he'd said that had aroused the sentiment.

'You seem upset.'

'No, you haven't upset me,' she sighed, feigning a yawn. 'But you are boring me small.'

'Really? I've never been accused of that before. And

137

what may I do to alleviate your *boredom*?' He accentuated the word playfully.

'*Pues*, why not try something more original?'

'Original?'

'Yes, original, or is that your best offer? You men are all the same. You're so beautiful – *preciosa, señorita, bébé* . . .' She mimicked his rich drawl to perfection. He stared at her for a moment before laughing in spite of himself. 'It's true. Every time you see me . . .' She rolled her eyes. 'Do you think that does anything for a woman? Does it really work on your conquests?' she said acidly.

'What do you know of my conquests? You've been asking after me?'

'No,' she replied hastily. 'It's common knowledge.'

'Then it should also be common knowledge that I don't chase after women like you think. I am the hunted rather than the hunter.'

'So what are you doing with me? Why do you even like me?' She placed a hand on her hip as she eyeballed him.

'You're different, this is different. *E destino*,' he answered earnestly.

'I don't believe in destiny,' she countered after a pause.

'*Pues*, what do you believe in?'

'I don't know,' she shrugged. 'Science. Fact—'

'Ah yes, I heard you are a lady with education.'

'Yes . . .'

'For someone with an education you show a distinct lack of politeness.'

'Perhaps my education taught me that if people dismiss you as beautiful, the last thing they see are your manners,' she retorted swiftly. 'I'm sure you are familiar with that. Or will the women of the village tell me otherwise?'

'I can tell you anything you wish to know.'

'That would be nothing,' she delivered smoothly.

'I think you're scared.'

'Scared? Of you?' She giggled.

'Maybe,' he replied softly. 'Only you can answer that.'

'Wait. I do have one question.'

'Please.' He smiled.

'When do you intend to end this conversation so I can go about my business?'

'Far be it from me to stand in beauty's way.' He extended his arm as if allowing her to pass. 'But be warned, I'll continue this at another time. I want you, Jericho Lwembe.'

She laughed openly at him before covering her mouth with her hand. He felt his face spreading out into an uncontrollable grin as he contemplated her transformation during her outburst. It was the first time during their exchange that her features had seemed completely engaged. He looked down at her mouth and, realising her lips were moving, he instructed himself to listen.

'If we all got what we wanted, Babylon, I would be living in the Dorique manor.'

'Really? Will your boyfriend live there too?' he quipped and saw her smirk. 'All things are possible, *señorita*. Although I must warn you, I never fail. One day, you will come for me . . .'

She paused when they got to the end of the path. Raising her eyes slowly to meet his, she approached his lips deliberately. Babylon felt his heart somersault, making its presence known in his chest. Mustering up all his willpower, he kept his head still and battled against his desire to steal her lips inside his own.

'As you say, all things are possible,' she whispered slowly, inches away from him, and her words formed tiny clouds he inhaled. 'Equally with failure, there's a first time for everything.' She pulled back her head sharply and sashayed down her road without a goodbye or even a backward glance.

*

139

Caramel flan was one of the things that appeared simple to make but was actually very easy to get wrong. The lightness of the pastry, the texture of the filling, all these things were delicate as brush strokes. When they were ill conceived, which they occasionally were, what should have been a masterpiece on the tongue, sadly became a hot mess.

Jericho tossed the piece of flan she'd saved to appreciate at home to one side, finding its flavour less than satisfactory. She compared it to the flan she'd tasted in Angel and felt her cheeks flood with heat. In the first few months that Daniel had courted her she'd found herself inexplicably holding her breath. But that day with the flan marked the first moment that she'd actually released that air in utter surprise. He'd taken her to a restaurant so lavish that melting the tiniest spoon on their table would surely have financed a child's school fees for one year.

She'd thought the night couldn't be surpassed but then he'd led her through the maze of rough-looking streets that were so different from the places he normally took her to. Finally the road they walked down ended in front of an old store with no sign. He pushed open the door and stood aside for her to enter. Once inside the poorly lit interior, she realised they were in an eating establishment. After where he'd first taken her, it would have been unfair to call it a restaurant. They were seated at a table so close to its neighbour that she had to position herself carefully to stop her legs from rubbing against the man's oily overalls next to her. Daniel whispered quickly to the woman that served them and she returned promptly with a carafe of plum wine along with a covered plate. He motioned for her to uncover it and when she did, Jericho saw the delicate pastry.

It had been so long since she'd been moved by food, but as soon as she spooned a piece into her mouth, its taste was washed away by the saltiness of the tears that rushed to her eyes. It had been an overload of recognition and pleasure all at once, a taste of her home town tripping on her tongue and suddenly she and Daniel were connected and she could see the Mannobe inside him.

It was one of her most favourite moments to replay. She remembered everything so vividly, which made her feel better on days when Daniel's profile was hazy and she was unable to recall him exactly. She told herself it was only natural as their time apart elapsed that certain things would become muted, but poring over her memories helped stoke her fire whenever it threatened extinction.

As the Señoritas ball approached, her fear escalated in direct correlation to her excitement. She envisaged the expressions of people's faces as they watched her dancing with a Dorique, their eyes aflame with the intrigue of it. But she was also aware that there would be repercussions she needed to prepare for. She would be the subject of much discussion and expectation. While they were in Angel they had been above it all, suspended on a cloud of fantasy, but the reality of the acknowledgement of their relationship in the village would ground them.

Mannobans were so old-fashioned in their thinking. In larger cities, there was the inevitable forward movement of ideas and the metamorphosis of ideas that meant that while situations like hers might be momentary fodder, they weren't the headline on the local agenda. Even though gossip was a favourite Mannoban pastime, she was sure people's lips would flap much less if she attended the ball with Penny's brother, with a donkey or, even worse, that pestering musician.

Jericho stretched out on her mattress and pressed her face into the pillow. She pondered Babylon and his silly attempts to dazzle her with his musical prowess. She'd interpreted enough of the looks he threw to females in his audience to know that he was trouble in human form. Undoubtedly he thought she was like those other women, the ones who drooped like tired flowers at the caress of his voice as they admired him, wishing it was them lying across his lap. Their envy of that treacherous, hollow instrument for its proximity to his body was laughable. Even the men . . . she'd seen some men wiping beads of sweat from their brows in awe of the wizardry of his fingertips.

As much as it pained her, she had to admit that there was something entertaining about him. She'd begun to look forward to his pestering. At the very least, his flirtation provided some spark amidst the languid village days that rolled into one, and temporary compensation for the lack of affection from her absent *nonno*. She particularly enjoyed him tipping his imaginary hat at her, and sometimes a faraway look overtook his eyes if she accidentally scowled at him for too long.

He was good-looking and talented enough to approach a woman normally. She couldn't understand his exaggerated flirtation or why it proved so successful. Maybe there was nothing underneath his attractive shell, hence the grand masquerade.

But as fatigue began to weigh down her eyelids, her thoughts rested on the one time she'd seen him when he hadn't been aware, and how different he'd seemed then. She'd gone to pick her mother up from her late shift at the bakery and they'd struggled home with their sacks of provisions.

His lean silhouette was highlighted by the bright moon on the other side of the square, casting an elongated shadow. Jericho had increased her pace instinctively but when her mother put down her shopping to watch him play, she'd had no choice but to join her.

'Papa used to sing that song badly,' her mother had whispered in a sorrow-filled voice, temporarily immersed in the past. Jericho had admired the tautness of his shoulders in silence, contemplating the harsh line of his jaw as he concentrated. He looked almost boy-like, his pleasure captivating because it was obvious that he was playing for his own enjoyment. She couldn't even describe his actions as showing off for he was alone.

She was about to pull her mother along when she saw a woman walking close to the musician. Even from a distance, she caught the gauntness of the woman's cheeks and her hunched form, that rendered her the shape of a bow. She was probably one of the women that walked around the village begging for food.

Jericho squinted and made out the shape in the woman's arms before she heard the escalating tone of the child's cry. Babylon stopped playing and approached the woman. Jericho watched him removing something from his pocket. She knew from the pitch of the woman's voice and the way she clasped her hand tightly that it was money.

'Bless you! *Tanka, tanka* . . . May my son grow up to be just like you!'

Babylon moved closer and stroked the boy's head, then reached into his other pocket. 'In that case,' he'd replied warmly, 'he'll need more shillings.'

Jericho had dragged her mother away, feeling her body grow hot. She told herself it was because of their trek and his music, those cloying harmonies that followed them until they were far away. But deep down she knew that it was the witnessing of his act of kindness that had struck a chord in her.

'You look like I did at my ball.' Mabel's voice choked with emotion as she spoke.

She and her sister gazed at Magdalena as she stood in the kitchen of Le Papillon. Mama Nabokei had curled her mane of hair so that it hung freely in a lavish curtain of

143

auburn ringlets down the length of her back. She wore a pale blue dress with three-quarter-length sleeves, and the huge bow at the back hid the size of her behind as opposed to accentuating it. Mabel praised her twin who'd fashioned it quickly from the fabric they'd cut off the dress's hem so that her daughter's delicate ankles were now exposed for the world to see. She shifted from her seat and went to stand by Magdalena who was still blushing gently. Rooting around inside her cleavage, Mabel unearthed a pair of carnelian earrings, which she placed on her daughter's small lobes.

'Do you know how beautiful you are, *bona*? No, don't cry, you'll ruin your dress.'

The trees in Costa Lina were robed with lanterns, banishing the austere nature of the place and bathing it in a warm iridescence. The gazebo that had been donated by the Doriques, decorated with winding leaves and jasmine flowers, waited patiently for the dancing to begin. All the village's musicians were in full swing by the time people started to arrive. Mabel hadn't intended to come this year but Magdalena needed her support. She coerced M'elle, who grudgingly accompanied her to the outskirts of Costa Lina. The music that greeted them was almost as heady as the aroma of the mountains of food erupting from the erected tables and the drinks flowing were more bountiful than the Ten Rivers themselves.

Magdalena tried to commit her surroundings to memory. The necks strained to catch a glimpse of their beloved. Smiles and tears refracting against candlelight, creating delicate patterns on fabrics of the dresses the girls wore. As each couple passed, a hundred eyes flicked over them before fixing their attention on the next in line and she was next. Magdalena had never felt so beautiful in her life and

144

she beamed as she passed her mother and auntie, accepting their proud waves.

She tipped her head to get a good look at the adoring crowd but found that their eyes were not focused on her. Instinctively, she knew that a late arrival was walking behind her.

Turning her head, Magdalena chased down the jealousy that flooded her throat as she took in the golden dress that skimmed the other woman's slender physique. Jericho held the train of her skirt up slightly as she walked so that the onlookers could admire her fine sandals. Even though Magdalena knew the onlookers were congratulating the girls collectively, she read the longing in some of those eyes as they rested on the latecomer, and felt her shoulders drop. Jericho smiled briefly at her before inching in between her and Penny and she couldn't summon her voice in protest.

'Where were you?' Magdalena heard Penny hiss to her friend.

'I was sick. The dress is tight! Then I fought with Mama,' Jericho whispered, her smile still in place.

'About the dress or Daniel?'

'Of course the dress. I still haven't told her about him. Don't look at me like that. I'll have to after tonight, *non*? *Pues, maybe.*'

'Have you seen him?' Penny whispered.

'Not yet. But once we finish this dance, I can have a good look.'

M'elle surreptitiously popped some nuts into her mouth as she watched the girls taking their position for the performance. The sequence that followed was as engrained in Mannoban girls as the village's inaugural dance. They'd witnessed it every year when the single ladies performed it. But every year, it seemed, nerves would sabotage some

145

poor girl, leaving those watching in fits of giggles as she fought to move her legs in time. This time, the poor woman in question was their own.

She looked on, horrified, as her niece fumbled through the steps. It was as if Magdalena couldn't tear her eyes away from the movements of the girl next to her, which were consequently impairing her own.

As the band played its lively tune, M'elle cringed as Magdalena became more and more lost in the music. It was as if she was dancing to her own private song. Then something incredible happened. The girls either side of Magdalena began to ape her movements. M'elle watched them latch on to Magdalena's routine without a hint of comedy in their expression. They persevered, unperturbed, until one by one the other waltzers began to parody the steps. Eventually, all the dancers were moving in synchronicity, albeit in an unknown dance. When the music ended, the young women halted with a small curtsy and the onlookers burst into unbridled applause spiced with appreciative roars.

M'elle heard herself and her twin whooping like prepubescent boys. She waited impatiently as other girls made their way off the makeshift platform and dispersed, entering the outstretched arms of their families.

'We didn't know you could shake so,' she teased her niece lightly and slapped her shoulders.

'Was I bad?' Magdalena asked sheepishly.

'My dear, you just create a new dance! How bad can that be?'

Magdalena sank into the bosoms of her matriarchs readily, breathing in their familiar smells, drawing comfort from the simplest of things. As they led her over to the tables stacked with food, she stole a glance at Babylon who was tuning his guitar amongst the other musicians. He was wearing a pair of leather trousers and his shirt hung open lazily at the neck and the crucifix he wore around his neck glinted in the light. A beacon calling her home.

She watched as his long dreadlocks fell, masking his face as he leaned over his beloved instrument, and felt a pang rip through her centre as she recalled his thick hair trailing the length of her body. She felt her cheeks flushing and bowed her head, embarrassed.

Magdalena gasped as Jericho breezed by her, leaving the unmistakable scents of mandaflower and sandalwood in her wake. She stopped briefly to appease her admirers; a group of young men that waylaid her begging for a dance. She cast glossy smiles as she made idle conversation, but she seemed removed from the situation. Her eyes moved beyond the men she enchanted; no doubt searching for the Daniel she'd spoken of. Excusing herself, Magdalena made her way to the table for some liquid sustenance.

Over the rim of her cup, she saw Babylon approaching. Gulping down her drink, she ran her tongue over her teeth. His eyes were searing a hole right through her clothing, she realised excitedly, and her scalp prickled in anticipation. Perhaps her dancing had jolted something inside him. Or maybe it was the dress, after all: it was his favourite colour. She squared her sloping shoulders and fixed a half-smile on her face, wondering what his opening line would be.

'Magdalena.'

'Babylon.'

'You look divine.'

'*Tanka*. It's blue,' she replied, swinging her skirt casually for his inspection. His eyes softened and his lips curled into a smile. She couldn't fathom what had caused this transformation from the abrupt man she'd encountered earlier, but she was thankful for it.

'Your dress is beautiful . . . Excuse me.'

He touched her shoulder gently as he moved past. She followed him with her eyes and found him heading towards Jericho. She wanted to go after him but her feet were rooted to the spot. She felt the cup leaving her hands and looked up to see her aunt. M'elle poured out her wine – or devil's brew, as she referred to anything alcoholic – and looked disapproving.

'You'll thank me for this later, *bona*,' M'elle said wisely.

'Thank you, Auntie,' she replied quietly.

'Now come.' Her aunt pulled on her sleeve, ushering her into the party. 'You think I sew this dress so you could remain alone?'

'Allow me,' Babylon offered, easing the ladle from Jericho's hands and pouring her a drink. Their fingers touched for a moment and he felt a frisson of electricity course through his arm.

'We meet again.'

'*Ewo*, if one sees an angel, does one run and hide or approach for a closer look?' he crooned.

'Now I'm an angel?' Jericho arched her eyebrows in amusement but touched the delicate ivory comb tucked behind her hair in a sign of nervousness. '*Tanka*,' she added shyly.

'In truth, there are no words to describe you. They haven't been born yet. I could only attempt to do so through music.'

She seemed temporarily thrown by his words and he was surprised by his own candid tone. Suddenly aware that their fingers were still touching after he placed the glass in her hand, she moved away, fluttering her eyelashes rapidly. A bolt of recognition registered on her features as she caught sight of someone through the shadow of spectators.

'I'm sorry, did you say something?' she asked, distractedly.

'I have written a song for you, *señorita*.' She shook her head, exasperated.

'You think that will change the way I see you?' She flashed doe eyes at him in a latent challenge.

'I think that has already happened,' he replied enigmatically.

'*Fine*,' she sighed.

'Can I play for you?'

'*Si, si*, now let me go . . .'

She smiled fleetingly and floated off into the crowd like a lily on the Belago. Babylon smiled to himself and went back to Guitar to prepare for his, or rather, her song.

Jericho followed her *nonno*'s back as it wove through the thronging crowd with difficulty. Her expanding heart made the dress she wore feel tighter, affecting her pace. She was just closing the distance when Penny grabbed her.

'Is he here?' she asked, excited.

'Yes! And I was just going to get him.' She scowled. 'What do you want?'

'Which one is he?' Penny craned her neck, scouring the crowd for Daniel.

'He's . . . oh, I lost him!' she shouted in frustration. She heard Babylon completing the first four bars of 'Troubadour', one of his routine songs, aware of the hush gradually spreading amongst the nearby spectators. The sound of the guitar floated along the magnetised air, as sweet, as familiar as a lover's perfume.

Jericho dragged her eyes from him and scanned the crowd. She looked down at her dress quickly, satisfied that she looked exactly as she'd hoped.

'Never mind. You'll soon find your *nonno*.' Penny interrupted her thoughts. '*Eh-eh*, what song is this?'

Jericho turned to face the gazebo and found Babylon standing in the centre. His face was turned downward as if he sought salvation in his strings while his fingers bled sweet music that filled the whole of Costa Lina.

A rush of melancholy caused her to stumble backwards. A flock of birds stirred in her ribcage as she watched him commanding his onlookers, the guitar he played no longer an instrument but a living, breathing entity. She stood, captivated as he teased it mercilessly, holding it at the final point of ecstasy until its voice erupted in unabashed release. The speed of his fingers became impossible to follow: it was as if he performed and shook the blood back into his fingertips simultaneously. She latched on to his words then, when he reached the crescendo and the baritone burst from his throat, as guttural as a Muslim prayer.

'He's singing about you!' Penny screeched the obvious before she hushed her to silence. 'It's about you.'

Jericho smiled widely at her friend, but had already instructed herself to stop listening. The corners of her lips curled up as she beamed, blocking her ears from his musical magic. She told herself that she was merely basking in the glow of his public adulation. Secretly, Jericho was taken aback by the musician's brazenness, but she refused to allow herself the compliment of his lyrics and forced her attention back to Daniel. She wanted to locate him while she was still fresh, before the creases in her dress became sharp lines or the pressure of the event caused her to perspire.

Through a gap in the crowd she momentarily saw the figure she'd been searching for and squealed in delight.

'There he is, Penny! Look.'

She pointed but soon the smile disappeared from her lips like a solar eclipse. She'd assumed that the woman next to him was just another bystander until she saw the scrawny hand curling itself around his bicep. Daniel's eyes connected with hers for a brief moment before a blank expression overtook his face. She caught him removing the woman's grasp before he began to move towards Jericho.

150

Jericho turned on her heel, catching the last strains of Babylon's song as she ran. She'd envisioned such a different ending for the night of her first ball. She would have danced with her big-city boyfriend. Everyone would have encircled them to watch in wonder. As she fled Costa Lina it was her final thought that made the tears fall.

She should have worn her mother's dress, she lamented. After all, as she strode off like an infuriated bull it hardly had the same effect, knowing that she was in the dress that he'd paid for; that wasn't really hers.

Babylon watched the woman he sang about, performed for even, fleeing the scene. A lightning pain shot through his arm. Guitar's string snapped abruptly, pulling everybody out of the trance his melody had sunk them into, and they looked up to him for guidance.

Spurred into action, he mumbled a polished apology and removed the broken string in one fluid movement. He played a fast-paced song then threw Guitar in the air and caught him behind his back with his good arm. Babylon bowed theatrically and waited for the thunder of applause. But he knew, and he knew Guitar knew too, that his heart wasn't in it. It had left earlier, along with his departing angel.

Ten

The village settled into a collected quietness after the festivities, like the relaxation that follows a good feeding. Even though many volunteers had helped to clean up as the ball played out, evidence of the feast still remained the morning after, with the inevitable chicken bone trail. Clouds of flies circled pockets of rice that had spilled off plates, along with plantain cubes and other bits of strayed foodstuff that the dark of night hadn't allowed them to discover.

Allegory frowned as he sidestepped the hardened mounds. He was aware of the hunger growing in his belly as his mind wove the discards together into a meal. Suddenly he longed for M'elle. Her chicken curry would balance very nicely in the hole that emitted an angry rumble as he walked. He rubbed his stomach as thoughts of her came into his mind. That she occupied more and more of his thoughts of late would be a fair statement, but he couldn't quite conclude in what manner she rested there. Images of her, although they stirred his curiosity, didn't tighten his loins or cause his heart to skip from its normal rhythm. Perhaps there was something more spiritual to it, he reasoned. Maybe he was supposed to take charge of her, as he'd done with others like the musician. Yes, perhaps if he watched her more closely, his divine purpose might appear in his mind and push her out of the frame.

He shook his head to affirm his resolve, satisfied that his hunger pangs had been fleeting. It was not good to fill one's belly so readily, one might not truly be hungry and might be substituting food when really another factor was lacking. This was one of the teachings that had stuck with him all these years later and one reason he relished his slim physique. As he bathed in the waters each morning, he liked to catch sight of his reflection as it disappeared in distorted waves. Sometimes he would run his hand carefully over his ribs, feeling their angles under a taut layer of skin. He imagined that were he to strike them, they would sound similar to the xylophones Sheriff made out of bamboo stems and tried to hawk to the foreigners that occasionally passed through the village.

The furtiveness of their profiles – bent as if one of the men were about to anoint the other's crown with oil as the priest, Moses Lovewell, did at the spirit house – was what called Allegory's attention from his mental physical inspection. He watched the two men, recognising one of them as a member of council. Allegory didn't concern himself much with local politics; after all, he was privy to a much higher government – that of the Creator. Still, it was important to be abreast of things. Even small matters that seem inconsequential in the daytime might take on a very different shape during the twilight hours.

The men stood apart from each other but they waved their arms around frequently. The council member even rubbed his hands together: that is, after turning his face to the side and releasing a ball of saliva that shot from his lips like a bullet. Allegory watched as the strange man removed

153

a fat envelope from his trouser pocket and handed it to the councillor. The councillor's smile was a sickle. All these things added up to something bad, Allegory thought fearfully, feeling the bottomless cavern open up in his belly again. The men shook hands; the stranger took off on foot while the councillor went back to recline in the shade, at the table of the diner where he and his colleagues were lunching.

Allegory was at a crossroads. He'd seen very little, yet he wanted to go closer to the table and see if he could sniff out something awry. At the same time, his feet wanted to pursue the man he didn't recognise, to find out if following him would uncover something more revelatory. He paused on the street, his hand unconsciously caressing his belly, perturbed about how best to proceed. A server came out to the councillor's table with a tray and a plate covering another one. She placed the tray on the table and removed the top plate, revealing a large steaming dish of beans buffered by a wall of meat. As Allegory felt himself growing faint his answer suddenly came to him. His crossroads quickly forgotten, his feet guided him to the only road that mattered, the one that led to Le Papillon.

Jericho's frustration tripled as the spray from the bus pulling away showered her skirt with dirt. She swore as the archaic automobile roared off into the distance, leaving behind a cloud of black gasoline as an added insult. She watched the travellers and packages that clung to its sides precariously. There were so many appendages flailing through the small windows, it reminded her of an upside-down centipede. She was annoyed enough already, but to make matters worse she would have to wait another two days for the next bus ride.

She brushed off her clothes and strode in the general direction of civilisation, hoping to hitch a lift from one of the passing vehicles. Many of the farmers and legitimate rides would have already left for the city at dawn. The people on the road now would be the sort she was reluctant to ride with, knowing all too well the stories about naive girls who wound up in ditches with torn wrappers and wounded innocence. She chastised herself for setting out late but she hadn't really intended to go at all until her impatience had packed her bag on her behalf.

Mannobans often referenced the Doriques when considering sensitivity, or rather, the lack of it. The swiftness at which Mr Dorique had chopped down the oldest tree in the Costa Lina area – probably at his wife's behest – had been so unbelievable at its time that it sat easier in some people's minds to claim the autumn wind had done it instead.

Lots of the village's trees had been responsible for untimely deaths, twisted limbs or, at best, skinned knees during their legendary residencies. Others were reprimanded for their paltry yield of fruit or shade. But as far as everyone could remember, that ancient laurel tree with its branches and leaves splayed out proud as a peacock display had only committed one crime: being born on what had become, through a series of transfers, Dorique land. But the Doriques didn't wait for the standard objections to percolate through the village until a general disharmony was reached that would result in a confrontation or discussion about what would become of the much-cherished piece of history. No. Quicker than you could say 'they wouldn't dare', they had! That laurel was whittled into what resembled a humungous pile of toothpicks and undoubtedly sold for a profit at one of the family's businesses elsewhere.

Jericho could now see that Daniel possessed that same insensitivity, even if he was capable of downplaying other of his family's personality deficits. Surely, it would have dawned on him that showing up to the ball with another woman, after weeks and more weeks apart, would convey some message to her? Why come at all, if not to wound her? In her birthplace, no less.

She'd been festering at Penny's house, replaying her shame until she decided to confront him. The maid at the Dorique manor had informed her that Daniel had returned to Angel in the waking hours of the morning.

Penny had beseeched her to be patient and to go to Angel in a few days' time, after she had reflected upon what she wanted to say to him. But Jericho had long stopped listening to reason; her spirit had been too possessed by feuding demons to absorb Penny's advice.

'You're not well enough to travel. You were sick a few minutes ago.'

'I don't care; I don't want to lose this feeling. Leave me, I have to go now.'

Jericho went home quickly, and told her mother that she would be spending a few days at Penny's home. Still wounded by her daughter's rejection of her wedding dress, Edith Lwembe did not object to the separation.

Going over the previous night's events as she walked, Jericho untangled the musician's song from the mess.

She'd half expected him to come after her. Not Babylon, she told herself, but Daniel. She thought she'd seen him break away from the meerkat he'd escorted to the ball before she'd turned and ran, yet she found that she made it all the way home without interruption. As if that wasn't bad enough, she'd lost her comb. She hadn't even noticed when it had dropped. Her hands had reached for the comb automatically, a treasure and an anchor rolled into one, but it wasn't there.

Three weeks before his vanishing, her father had brought

156

it home, removing it from his handkerchief in an elaborate magic trick. She'd been fascinated by the delicate comb, the miniature elephant on the painstaking carved rim, even down to its tusks. He'd placed it behind her ear, telling her to keep it safely otherwise a real elephant would come demanding its tooth back, which the smooth hair-pick had been made from. He'd spoken so sincerely that even after her mother revealed the truth she'd still believed him.

Jericho placed a hand on her stomach to quiet her tumbling nerves, and continued along by the road. Perhaps she'd been hasty when she refused the only ride she'd seen in almost an hour. The car had only one door instead of the two it had originally come with. She sank on to the grass to rest her feet. They were still throbbing from the sandals she'd worn at the dance. She thought of Claudia who'd introduced her to that kind of footwear and decided to seek her friend's counsel before facing Daniel. That way she would have more ammunition with which to cause his ultimate surrender.

She laughed quietly, re-energised by the passions coursing through her veins. She refused to think about why he hadn't pursued her at the dance. Instead she focused on the woman who'd wrapped herself around her lover, those thin lips that no doubt housed crooked teeth and the woman's blank eyes that clearly suggested a weak spirit. Squeezing her eyes shut, she imagined the woman's breastless body being pushed against Daniel's lean muscles, and frowned.

'He hates women like that,' she said out loud.

'Like what?'

Her head whipped round quickly. Babylon sat a few feet away from her in the grass.

'What are you doing?' Jericho spat out. She stood up quickly, downplaying her alarm by dusting off her skirt.

'Resting. Has it been forbidden?'

He smiled at her, exposing his perfect teeth.

'*Bon dia*. Are you all right? Is there anything I can get you?' she snapped at him.

'If *Señorita* knew me better, she wouldn't ask me such a question.'

Jericho lowered her eyes quickly from the intensity of his gaze. She'd no time to be sidetracked by the musician yet she was surprised to feel her body pooling with heat. Already she felt her former rancour dissipating and she would need it in order to challenge Daniel.

'All right then, I'll be on my way,' she responded as if she hadn't heard him.

'To where?'

'Angel.'

'*Señorita?*'

'What?' She shrank back as his voice tickled her ear canal, wondering how he could have crept alongside without her noticing him and, more importantly, why all the hairs on her neck were standing to attention.

'Angel is *that* way.' He raised his eyebrows innocently at her and the guitar on his back shifted, emitting a flat moan. 'You don't know where you're going, do you?' His eyebrows danced above his flashing pupils.

'I do,' she replied tartly, moving off in the direction he pointed.

'Well, perhaps if you'll allow me to escort you?'

'In exchange for what?' she asked cautiously.

'*Pues*, at the ball, I would have asked for a dance,' he continued.

'Hmm,' she replied noncommittally. 'I hadn't intended on walking.' Her tone sounded like a challenge.

'I should hope not. Such pretty feet should never have to endure such discomfort,' he replied, looking down at her bare feet and she curled her toes into the ground to hide them.

'Does that turn into a carriage?' Her voice was laced with sarcasm as she pointed at his guitar.

'Of sorts,' he replied cryptically, 'but I can arrange transport if you give me a moment.'

They faced each other in silence and she cast a snide glance at the gaping desert the road had become, resigning herself to her fate.

'Okay. Well, *venga*! Before I change my mind!'

Babylon could only smile at his spectacular good fortune. Not only had he won the game of cards at Borrow's but he'd also stumbled across his princess on his morning walk after he'd left the bar. He'd been surprised at how deeply her abrupt exit had affected him at the ball. He was crestfallen following her desertion, and Guitar had provided little consolation. He'd been convinced that his song would have softened her up enough to accept a dance, and he knew that his hips pressed up against her body would certainly have done the rest, had they had the chance.

He'd gone back to the venue after his bar win, if only to relive the pain of her departure in its rightful place. As he walked he felt something snap underfoot and looked down to see what he'd broken. It was only the wishbone of a chicken; but then his eyes spotted something a few feet away. He moved closer to the splinter of ivory, recognition lightening his step. He bent to pick up the comb that had glinted behind Jericho's ear the night before. He dusted it off on his leg before placing it against his mouth and playing it like a harmonica. Its return would provide another opportunity to see her again. Yes, luck was undoubtedly with him.

He smiled to himself, remembering a few moments earlier when she'd folded her arms across her chest in defeat. With her bottom lip jutting out slightly she'd looked like a child trapped in woman form. He'd wanted to laugh out loud but found his voice constrained. He couldn't decide whether she was spoilt or pretending to be, but he liked it. Besides, wasn't fruit on the point of being spoiled often the sweetest?

He should have taken her by surprise and kissed her, he told himself as she faced him with a puzzled look. But he'd settled for squeezing her arm and had retreated quickly, praying that Driver was back from his first round of errands.

'Can't you move any faster?'

'*Tranquila, señorita*, we'll soon be there.'

'Fine, but will I still be alive? That's my only concern.'

She settled in the back of Driver's wagon while Babylon pedalled with all his might, wondering if he was up to the Herculean task he'd undertaken. He knew he would be pedalling hard all day, and even well after night came down. His friend had been reluctant to part with his motor, wondering what scheme he was so eager to participate in without him, but once he'd left Guitar as collateral, Driver had been suitably appeased.

As his feet struck the pedals, he started to make a list of all the things he should be thankful for: that he'd had the good sense to leave Guitar behind, that his passenger weighed little more than two sacks of rice, that all his travelling years with Gogoa had prepared him for their impromptu journey. He cycled the dry red road with his pricey cargo, navigating the tiresome journey partly by memory, partly intuition, hypnotised by the subtle rhythm of the poorly built road. Its bends and dips like sheet music, the colour of the road changed by time, use and improperly mixed materials.

At times, bored by her futility, she made general conversation or offered him water, but he replied in monosyllables, his energy focused on keeping both of them mobile. When he picked up speed travelling down the sloping road, he sur-

160

rendered to the wind whipping at his locks. He welcomed the cold breeze through his tangled mane, pretending that she was the one massaging the ache in his temples away.

After some time Babylon came to a halt near a roadside vendor. He parked the barrow and dismounted from the bicycle, holding his hand out to her. She refused it and exited the vehicle unaided. He would have been insulted if she hadn't inadvertently flashed an expanse of upper thigh.

'This is as good a place as any to stop. I have to rest a while.'

Jericho studied him carefully from the road. She looked as if she was forming an objection but had been distracted by the motion as he stretched his legs, observing the material of his trousers tightening as he moved. He felt his body grow warm under her inspection. She declared herself hungry but he had anticipated her and walked towards a vendor, the old woman whose exposed breasts looked like raisins.

The woman fanned the corn on her makeshift grill and then periodically fanned herself from the smoke it was creating. Babylon bent down to pick up two cobs of roasted corn wrapped in newspaper and headed back to Jericho. He watched her bite into it greedily, gorging herself on its rich, succulent flavour. His eyes were fixed on her over his cob, as he munched the corn row by row.

'Why did you choose Angel?' He broached a topic from earlier.

'The name,' she smiled softly. 'La Ciudad d'Angel . . . Like being away from Mannobe, but home at the same time.'

'Without all the greenery,' he added slowly.

'I guess.'

His attack on the corn complete, he approached the orange seller. The little girl balanced a wide aluminium tray on top of a piece of coiled material on her head. A perfect pyramid of oranges was assembled on the tray. She lowered it deftly and he accepted two, holding one up to Jericho, but she shook her head and so he took them for himself. He sat back down beside her and they watched the girl peel them swiftly, her rhythm hypnotic as she moved the fruit around her knife, using her thumb as a buffer against the blade's sharpness as slices of the peel dropped on to her feet. Her task completed, she reassembled her pyramid, lifted the tray and continued her walking trade.

They finished the makeshift meal and retired under the shade of a palm to recover before making the final stretch of their journey. He could sense her agitation as she toyed with the corn wrapping while watching him sucking the juice from the whittled cob, having grown bored with the oranges.

'So, who hates women like what?'

'None of your business. I mean, it doesn't matter.' She'd been startled by his question and he knew she'd softened her tone, thinking it best to refrain from tongue-lashing the man ferrying her to her destination.

'It must matter, or are you in the habit of talking to yourself in the grass?'

'Fine,' she sighed heavily as if deciding whether to take him into her confidence. 'My *nonno*. In Angel.'

'I see. What's his name?' He tried to keep his voice bright.

'Daniel,' she revealed defiantly.

'*Daniel*.' He rolled the name around his tongue. 'What a pretty name, for a boy.'

She rolled her eyes in response. Smiling, she folded the newspaper wrapping into a shaky crane. When she was finished, she held it out for his inspection.

'Beautiful,' he praised her. 'Did Daniel show you how to make those?'

'Don't be ridiculous,' she scolded, placing it delicately on the ground next to her. He picked it up gingerly and played with its edges, careful not to damage her creation.

'Does he like women who make birds?'

'You know, you ask many questions but you don't say anything in return,' she accused him gently.

'What do you want to know?'

'It's not about that . . . It's clear you don't reveal anything about yourself. Nothing real, at least. Why?'

'A bad habit. I guess it never occurred to me that anyone really cared.' He pulled a face and pretended to wipe away a tear. He winced when she punched his arm playfully.

'Don't you take anything seriously?'

'*Señorita*, life is serious enough already.'

'You're saying no one ever cared for you?' She looked at him intently.

'I believe we were talking about you and Daniel,' he replied smoothly, pushing a stone through the dirt.

'*Now* who's afraid?' she whispered. He couldn't decipher her expression as she moved further away from him.

'So, what sort of women doesn't he like?'

She hesitated before responding. 'Simple women; with lanky hair. And stupid eyes. *Ugly*.' Her lips curled over her last statement.

'The opposite of you, then.'

He sprang to his feet in one swift movement, casting her a loaded look before moving several feet away. He couldn't refuse to take her the rest of the way now he knew the reason for her journey, but disappointment unsettled the corn in his stomach. He looked at the nearby foliage and chose a tree suitable for him to relieve himself upon. He placed one hand on the trunk of the palm tree and struck a pose, imagining her busying herself with her paper creation to avoid looking in his direction. He saw her retrieving his discarded newspaper wrapping to create a mate for her bird, but she began to read the page intently, using her finger to trace each word.

He was observing the graceful arc his piss was making as he tried to hit a passing lizard when he heard her shriek. He turned to face her, missing his sandals by a narrow margin, and saw her talking loudly to an invisible foe, ripping the newspaper as she paced. Abruptly, she took off running towards Driver's wagon. Hitching up her skirt expertly, she hopped on to the bicycle and began a wobbly pedal, trying to acclimatise to the cumbersome vehicle. Babylon finished in double time and took off after her as she was beginning to get to grips with the bike. He just had time to snatch the torn paper and hurl himself into the barrow before she continued at a lighting pace towards Angel.

When they finally arrived, intermittent city lights illuminated the darkness around them. Jericho was sleeping deeply, curled on the wagon seat, exhausted by her pedalling. Babylon slowed as they approached L'Eglise and came to a stop instinctively. He didn't have the heart to wake her. All at once, he lamented Guitar's absence. He would have liked to capture this moment in song, not just in memory, which would no doubt fade over time. The stillness of the vehicle roused her and she opened her eyes slowly as if they were sealed with honey, batting her thick eyelashes at him. Realising where she was, she shot up quickly and glared at him.

'We here?' she asked, reaching her hand out to smooth her dishevelled hair.

'Yes, *Señorita*. Welcome to La Ciudad d'Angel. Where are you going?' He watched as she got out of the wagon and began striding off. He pulled the barrow with him.

'Please don't drag that beside me.'

'What, the wagon?'

'Yes.'

She shot him a quick look, hoping he would interpret what she was trying to say without her having to vocalise her prejudice. He was dumbfounded for a moment, then realisation penetrated and he felt as if a thousand bees had stung him in the face.

'There's no one around to see us. Besides, if you just let me take you to your door, we can get you out of the public eye as soon as possible.'

Jericho had imagined facing Daniel a hundred times after his rebuke. Each time she attacked the pedals, a new scenario hatched in her mind until Babylon took control of the bike again. She remembered the newspaper headline in bold lettering, *'The announcement of Mr Dorique's engagement to Mlle. Lara Inodu . . .'* and another wave of humiliation washed over her. Now, as if that wasn't enough, she'd ridden into town on a rickety chariot.

The quickest way to end her humiliation would be not to protest so she crouched down in the wagon, praying that no one she recognised would see her in the back of the claptrap vehicle. Trust Babylon to be somehow affiliated with that strange peddler of goods back home! She'd almost refused to enter it when she saw him heading towards her, by the roadside, in that unmistakable transport many, many hours earlier, but there'd been no alternative.

She whispered directions to Babylon, hiding her face inside her blouse as they cut through the sharp city streets until they arrived at Yalla's storefront. Once they'd dismounted from the barrow, she wheeled it out of sight and hid it around the back of the seamstress's house before ushering him up the steps and into her room. There was no way she would meet Daniel now, at least not without making herself presentable first. Not if she wanted to make him appreciate what he was sacrificing for Mademoiselle Inodu.

She watched Babylon drinking in his surroundings, pleased that he'd been allowed inside her lair. She was sure he'd half expected her to forget her flagging manners and leave him outside. Something about him irritated her, making her straddle the frontier between petulant child and rational woman, not knowing what form to adopt for good.

She was surprised at how much she'd missed her small, bright room. Daniel had been paying for it – and still was – but it was her home. Her canvases everywhere sprouted colour in the otherwise neutral setting of her white bed sheets, table and chair. The mauve curtain she'd attached to the window leaked blue light, tingeing her dolphinesque skin with an iridescent glow.

'You want something to drink?' she offered, as her hostess role now dictated.

'Please.'

She went downstairs, and came back up with a jug of water. She'd tucked two of Yalla's lemons into the waist of her skirt and turned away from him to remove them. She sliced them roughly, feeling his gaze on her activity before he busied himself studying each of her paintings. She added some honey to her lemonade along with a sprig of mint from a pot outside her window, and brought the jug over to the table next to him.

As he refilled cup after cup, sating his thirst from the ride, her surroundings, normally her sanctuary, felt small in his presence. His shirt clung to his skin after hours of strenuous cycling. His nipples were two alert eyes on his chest. His head almost grazed her ceiling and he seemed to slouch slightly in her room like a giant trapped in a cage. Jericho touched her stomach; apart from the corn, she hadn't eaten all day. Gripping the chair to balance herself, she wondered how quickly she could dismiss him so she could execute what she'd returned to the city for.

'*Pues*, Babylon.' She pulled the chair out for him and motioned for him to sit down. 'I can't thank you enough for bringing me here but—'

'Shh. What's that?' he interrupted.

They listened to the sound of small stones against her window. She knew only two people who threw pebbles for her attention and her heart soared as she pictured Daniel below outside. Jericho flew to the open window and looked down. She swallowed her disappointment when she saw Claudia.

'Coco!' she cried. 'Daniel said you would come into town. Let me in.'

'Wait, I'll come down.'

She saw Claudia scrabbling at her feet and unearthing a rock. She waved it up at Jericho threateningly.

'Do you know how many times I've come here today? If you don't let me in, I'll send up this little present.'

'Okay, okay. Come up,' she capitulated, reluctantly throwing down the key.

She scanned her small room for somewhere to stash Babylon, who was grinning foolishly, clearly enjoying her predicament. She dragged him into a corner, wondering momentarily if she could cover him with a sheet. Her friend seemed tipsy; she could probably convince her she was working on a new piece of art. She was reaching for a spare wrapper when Claudia burst through the door in mid-conversation.

'. . . when Daniel told me this afternoon that he'd missed you at your dance I knew you wouldn't be long behind – *hello*?'

Claudia paused, sighting Babylon in the corner. She looked from him to Jericho and then back at him again longingly.

167

'Claudia,' she introduced herself, reaching her hand out to him.

'Claudia. It sounds like the song a bell would sing,' he said smoothly. 'What a precious name for such a lovely woman. I'm Babylon.' He dropped his head from the ceiling to graze her hands with his lips and Jericho rolled her eyes as Claudia blinked her blurry pupils at him.

'He gave me a lift home,' Jericho elucidated. 'He was travelling from Mannobe.'

'Mannobe? Coco, your home town does have spectacular men, *non*?'

'Thank you but our local charm pales in comparison to the women of Angel,' Babylon continued softly and Jericho rolled her eyes again in disgust.

'Claudia,' she said, shouldering her way between the two of them, 'Babylon was just leaving. We can talk—'

'But you just got here, *non*?' Claudia looked at Babylon as she spoke. 'I can't allow you to leave before you've enjoyed some of our city's hospitality. Hani Nomawetutu is throwing a party in Khisa. *Pues*, he has been since . . .' A hiccup stole her final words. 'Anyway, the city doesn't sleep. You must come with us.' She waved Jericho off like a servant and dropped on to her mattress.

'Babylon is tired, I'm sure—'

'I'm sure Babylon can think for himself.'

Claudia kicked off her shoes and swayed over to the music man in a seductive manner. Jericho watched, stunned, as she trailed a perfect fingernail down his neck, stopping on his Adam's apple. 'You tired, Babylon?'

'If I was, that surely woke me up.'

'*Pues*, that's settled then.' She bent to retrieve her strewn shoes with much effort and handed them to Babylon, who accepted them willingly as she curled herself around his arm.

168

'You come with me while Coco changes. Wear the tangerine.'

Claudia threw the last comment over her shoulder as the two of them moved down the steps, already bonded. Jericho heard her friend's laughter hanging high-pitched in the air like a birdcall. It sounded forced, the way it always did when she was clearly trying to gain a man's attention; not that they could tell the difference, or cared either way. She sighed angrily and rifled through her city clothes for the instructed dress.

On the way to Khisa, Jericho remained mute as her two companions threw comments back and forth between them. Her mind was torn between Daniel and the foreign sensation she experienced every time Claudia stroked the inside of Babylon's arm. She felt her jawbone harden and knew she must be frowning.

Jericho pasted a smile on her lips that masked her confusion as they entered the party. She wasn't afraid of Babylon accompanying them to Hani's, knowing the mixed bag of people he consorted with. Claudia liked to disguise the wealth her family possessed by befriending the wealthy and locals alike, and Hani was the same.

As they immersed themselves in the throng of revellers Jericho slipped away, anxious to comb the crowd for Daniel. It was hardly his kind of affair, but he sometimes played cards with Hani and his crew, so anything was possible. She circled the fiesta and when she returned to where she'd started she exhaled heavily, finally accepting that he wasn't there. Frustration wiped the artificial expression off her features and fatigue took over. She wanted to curl up in the bed against the softness of Daniel's chest, the rhythm of his heartbeat sending her to sleep.

A bold man broke away from the group he was with and headed in her direction. She looked quickly for rescue but found Claudia's face an inch away from Babylon's. He felt Jericho's gaze on him and turned to look at her but she eyed him before looking away. Seconds later, she heard Claudia's laugh and saw her shining her teeth towards the ceiling while Babylon whispered something in her ear. Wounded, Jericho turned her full attention to the approaching beau, beaming like the sun in retaliation.

Babylon removed himself from Claudia's embrace momentarily to refresh his drink but yawned as soon as his back was turned. He winced noticeably as he stretched. The ride to Angel had exhausted him. It was obvious Jericho was unnerved by all the attention that her friend was bestowing upon him, but still she pretended to be unfazed. Ordinarily, he would continue the game until she surrendered to him regardless of any third-party casualties, but he'd warmed to Claudia's personality and couldn't bring himself to use her in the process. Perhaps fatigue was affecting his judgement. Claudia was using him to quench her desire for a tradesman as opposed to the pathetic moneyed individuals she'd grown up with. He'd encountered many women like her, their eyes twinkling as they gazed upon him, imagining what music fell from his lips in the midst of lovemaking. Women excited by his coarse hands, who moaned as he placed his fingers inside the moist cocoons of their mouths.

As thoughts ran through his mind his resolve returned and he glanced over at Jericho. He could peel that dress off her quicker than the fruit of its colour. She was clearly bored in the company of the young man trying so desperately to impress her. Babylon approached them, fixing his ears on their conversation. When the drink the boy extended spilled dangerously close to her dress, she shouted at him. Babylon laughed. He passed the dejected boy on his way towards her and threw him a look of commiseration. She was stifling a yawn when he arrived.

'You're tired. Why don't you go home?'

'I'm surprised you're concerned. I thought you only had eyes for Claudia,' she answered.

'Does that upset you, Coco?' he enquired, pasting an innocent expression on his face while she scowled at his use of her nickname.

'*Ewo*, there's no accounting for taste. But no, I'm not upset. In fact, I'm glad.'

She thrust her face up to meet his gaze and her nostrils flared wildly.

'Glad?' he asked, eager for her response.

'Yes,' she snapped angrily. 'Now your attention's elsewhere I can finally get a moment of peace.'

'But I was just about to ask for my dance,' he continued optimistically.

'Come and take,' Jericho snapped, kissing her teeth.

They glared at each other but Claudia came over, breaking the mood. Every drink she'd consumed rendered her more sober, so when she stood between them she'd regained most of her womanly composure.

'That's where you've got to. Goodness, people are starting to look as unattractive as they really are. Quick, Babylon, give me a drink.'

Babylon handed Claudia the glass he was holding, an intimate enough gesture in itself but then their hands skimmed each other's during the exchange. Claudia left her fingers there a fraction too long and even in the darkness of the room Jericho caught it. Suddenly the weight of the evening took its toll on her tired body. The proximity of bodies, the music, the melange of perfumes, along with the stench of boiling tar from the neighbouring factories in Angel's thriving industrial district, made her light-headed. She excused herself rudely and searched for somewhere quiet to settle herself. She hadn't anticipated that Claudia would follow.

171

'*Venga*, let's get some fresh air,' Claudia offered gently, pulling her elbow.

'No, it smells worse outside.'

She allowed Claudia to usher her into the empty kitchen and sat down, while her friend soaked a cloth in water. Claudia placed it over the back of her neck and blew cool air around her head while Jericho rested.

'You can go if you want, I'm sure you'd rather be somewhere else.'

'What are you talking about?'

'Don't let me keep you. If you want to go back to Babylon . . .'

Claudia laughed at her and flicked the cloth against her ear. 'Please.'

'What were you talking so intently about anyway?' she asked, glad that her expression was hidden.

'All sorts of things; art, mostly. Can you believe he *knows* Messina Ado? He's my all-time favourite. I wonder if "Man of Music" is about him . . .'

'Indeed,' Jericho snapped. 'Ado is at least thirty years older than Babylon, and as if he would really paint his portrait, like he doesn't have more important things to do with his oils.'

'You know, sometimes you're so rude. Why couldn't Ado have painted him?'

'Because he's hardly the—'

'You're a *snob*,' Claudia said accusingly. 'If someone's not your Daniel, you can't see.'

'And how long have you known Babylon, that you're so quick to judge?'

'I'm not the one judging him, that's you . . . And if you heard him talking about you, you wouldn't be wicked.'

'What did he say?'

'Huh, like I'll tell you now?' Claudia raised an eyebrow. 'Okay, when I asked him what his favourite painting was,

172

he said there was a woman in his village that could rival the greatest works of art.'

Jericho battled a wave of nausea. She wasn't sure if it was her stomach or the jumble of thoughts inside her head. She hadn't meant to question Claudia about Babylon but her friend's closeness with him had been unnerving. It wasn't that she was envious, but her sense of ownership over his public affection had waned in Claudia's presence, making her confused. There was nothing wrong with liking being liked, so she wasn't ashamed, but tonight had alerted her to territorial stirrings where the musician was concerned. That, combined with her oscillating feelings for Daniel, was proving too much to bear.

'I didn't mean . . .'

'I know you're just upset because Daniel's not here. I saw you looking.'

'Looking at who?' Jericho asked quickly.

'For Daniel.'

'Oh. Yes, well maybe he's too occupied with his future wife.'

'His wife? What are you talking about?'

'He's engaged! It was announced. Didn't you see the paper?'

'*Bona*, you know I don't read anything unless Papa requires it . . . Daniel didn't say anything to me.' Jericho returned Claudia's smile weakly. 'Who's he marrying?'

Jericho raised her head feebly and croaked out the name.

'Lara? I don't believe it. I know her family. They've been circling the Doriques for years but I would never have thought Daniel . . . She's so . . .' Claudia trawled her vocabulary for a fitting word.

'Plain? Ugly?' offered Jericho.

'Irrelevant.' Claudia fingered the word as she released it.

'Well she is very relevant, because she's marrying *my nonno*.'

Claudia kneaded her shoulders consolingly and Jericho welcomed her touch readily. 'It will never happen. Anyway he loves *you*; blind-man Bantu can see that. It's probably – no – it's definitely his family making him announce the engagement,' Claudia continued with deductive reasoning. 'Her family has all that property in Sogodo, you know? It's just a business agreement – a merger of money. I mean, can you imagine the two of them being together *por vero*?'

Jericho had been comforted by her friend's words but felt her stomach lurch at the last comment. Leaping off the chair, she vomited in the corner by the pantry door. Behind her, Claudia squealed with delight, gripped by such a manifestation of emotion.

'*Eh-eh*, you *have* got it bad, haven't you? I haven't seen projectiles like that since Marema had her baby . . . *Banju*, you're not pregnant, are you?' Claudia's giggling stopped abruptly when Jericho's smile took too long to scramble to the edges of her mouth. '*Ewo!* You are, aren't you?'

'Not for much longer,' Jericho replied, decorating Hani's pantry floor with more regurgitated corn.

She woke up swaddled in a blanket on the kitchen table. There were no other signs of life in the kitchen. Jericho unravelled herself from her cover and felt her stomach dip angrily. She remembered last night's dry heaving once all the corn had left her system. She'd longed for her mother's loving hands to rub away her troubles the way she used to do when she was a child and was suffering a bellyache.

She crept through Hani's house, surveying sleeping bodies that were strewn around like elaborate pieces of furniture. Claudia and Babylon were intertwined on a divan in a secluded corner of the front room. She peered over them cautiously, surprised to find him already awake.

'*Bon dia, Señorita*,' he whispered so as not to rouse his sleeping partner. 'Was the table too uncomfortable?'

'How do you know where I slept?' she asked suspiciously.

'You're welcome to the blanket,' he winked.

She kissed her teeth loudly. The sound caused Claudia to stir. Babylon cuddled her gently, and Jericho felt her anger rise at his display of tenderness. Claudia's hands came up to stroke his chest while the rest of her body fought sleep. Grudgingly, she opened both eyes and met Jericho's, dagger-blazing.

'How are you feeling this morning?' Claudia enquired in a concerned but sleepy voice.

'Fine,' Jericho snapped. 'I'm going home. I have things to do.' She got up to leave and noticed Babylon unwinding himself from her friend to follow her but Claudia pressed his arm firmly with her hand, subduing him.

'Go slow. You haven't paid me my fee for last night's festivities yet,' she drawled, using her free hand to pull him towards her.

'Your fee?' he repeated.

Lifting her head and laughing, Claudia placed her lips on his. Jericho watched them briefly but didn't wait for them to disconnect. She marched home with the sound of Claudia's joy resounding loudly in her ears.

Eleven

News about the forest filtered through the village like water through sponge. The council was proposing the sale of Waranga, or at least a sizeable portion. Some whispered it to each other like they were passing on news of family illnesses or illegitimate children. Some shouted it in their brash village manner as they sought to be the bearer of bad tidings before another villager could steal their glory. 'Can you imagine?' 'If you can believe it!' 'How can you sell a forest?' 'The very audacity!'

To Allegory, it was a knife in his heart; a slap in his face, a snakebite on his ankle. Yet somehow, the news had been unsurprising when it finally dropped. As the story came to light amongst the villagers, stitching their piecemeal nuggets of information into cloth they could all wear, he too sewed little incidents together in his mind. The councillor he'd seen with the envelope was being paid off by someone, maybe another official, or a contractor that stood to gain from the impending development of the reserve land. Possibly a sugar-caner. He remembered that he'd seen that same councillor before, on the night of the ball. He'd walked the *scatter-scatter* roads, as the locals called them, the ones so poorly built that they were only used in an absolute emergency. Many vehicles had met their death on those roads, parts of exhaust pipes and undercarriages impaled on deep ridges of earth, scarred by potholes that would never be filled, that were simply waiting for all the other intermittent potholes to connect and make a smoother road, albeit it a foot and a half lower than intended.

Visitors to Mannobe always wondered how locals managed to navigate the roads at night without the aid of lighting. Even when a car passed, which wasn't often, there were no disastrous accidents, as if Mannobans had developed the same abilities nocturnal animals used to see in pitch black.

Allegory had committed those raw roads to memory; even in the darkness he hadn't lost his footing. He'd been approaching Medusa Avenue – the smooth section of road that led down from the Medusa compound – where the rocky road began to right itself again and the strains of music from the ball had cut through the village's night sounds; the darkness that seemed to emit a subtle sound as it throbbed in the invisible heat, lizards scratching their low bellies over stones, crickets, cockroaches and other animals one could only imagine in the dark because they were unseen. As he'd neared the music and people, he'd been surprised to find a gathering of men on the fringes that seemed more interested in their discussions than in the women of the village dressed as magnificently as princesses. He'd only managed to secure snatches from their conversation, but they'd been extremely animated in their business talks. He'd recognised the councillor's booming voice, which contradicted his high laughter that sounded like a handsaw scratching away against a piece of wood. The other men had joined in so the melody of voices had sounded like a brief musical intermission, and then they'd reverted to their heated discussion. At the time it had meant very little; it wasn't peculiar to see men of business scheming. Even in the village, business was business, politics was business, and money was everything, for some people.

Now as scenes arranged themselves in his mind he came to the realisation that he'd already sensed what was going on, even though the prophecy hadn't written itself boldly in his brain. Even the trees had tried to warn him during his daily bath.

He'd heard many locals' concerns. Their anxiety was valid but most of them had no real attachment to the land. That forest had been his home. But their anger rivalled his – anger at being unheard; superseded by profit-hungry men who wouldn't be the ones to carry out the back-breaking work, to trek for miles before the labour began and then stand under the blazing heat of the sun, exercising muscles that became as unyielding as iron rods.

M'elle waved at him as he crossed by the café on the way to his tent. He stopped at the opening and returned her wave. He was filled with a sudden tiredness, and wanted to be alone. The villagers were riled up about the forest and there needed to be a solution.

'Mabel has a new dish,' she offered, coming to stand in the doorway. Her hand was on one hip and the other she placed against her eyebrows, making a visor against the sun.

'Thank you, but I'm not hungry.'

'Come on, a small man like you? You always say that. But a man needs to eat. You need fuel for your thoughts.'

Allegory nodded and followed her in.

'I'll go and bring you a plate,' she said, cupping his shoulder.

He watched her scuttle off and settled himself on the bench closest to the kitchen. If he had to eat in company then he'd be as inconspicuous as possible. He heard Mabel leading a conversation with a group of men in the middle of the room. He knew they were the men that were involved with rebuilding the school's roof. Part of it had fallen off but luckily it had happened when the teachers were on strike, there had been no children on the premises that day. The council had taken so long to allocate money for the replacement that some parents had covered the gaping hole with pink tarpaulin that made ghostly noises to rival corrugated iron during heavy winds.

'Yes, it may bring jobs,' Mabel argued loudly, 'but they will be paying these people rubbish. The whole thing is a nonsense.' She kissed her teeth in disgust.

M'elle brought out his plate just as her sister was moving past his table back to the kitchen.

'Thank you,' he said gently. 'The whole town is angry.'

'Yes. This forest business is giving people plenty stress.'

'Uh-hum. What do you think about it?' He looked up into her eyes and saw her look away quickly.

'I don't know. Mabel is the politician in our family.'

'Who's calling me?' Her sister poked her head out of the kitchen.

'Allegory was talking about the forest.'

'Please, no worry me, *abeg*!' Mabel waved a large spoon threateningly. 'Don't get me upset again.'

She returned to the kitchen and he heard her banging heavy pots against surfaces and talking to herself. Before he had time to register amusement or alarm, she came out again.

'Somebody needs to stop these people. They cannot just do whatever they like and say it is a law. What is a law? What makes them think they can just give away the forest? What makes it theirs to give away?'

M'elle stared at her sister, and Allegory assumed that she was trying to establish whether her twin was waiting for an answer from her.

'What the Lord has—'

He began to speak but Mabel cut him off.

'Don't bring your gibberish in here, philosopher. I am trying to talk and here you are taxing my mind with something I can't follow.'

'I was agreeing with you.'

'Oh. Then there's sense in your head after all.'

Nobody paid attention to their discourse but M'elle blushed and he didn't know if it was because she was embarrassed by her sister's outburst or if she was simply reacting to his proximity.

'I feel like going to that council quarters and giving them a piece of my mind. But sometimes this village is so backward. They will probably throw me out because I am a woman.'

He watched her face contorting with conflicting expressions and found that he was suddenly unable to swallow the dollop of yam he'd put in his mouth.

'*Abeg*, M'elle, go and take the soup off the fire. I'm so tired,' Mabel ordered her sister gently and sat down on the bench next to him.

Allegory pushed the food down his throat while she fanned herself with a cloth beside him as if he wasn't there. He could smell her in the waves that came off her body, the kitchen ingredients that clung to her skin as she cooked before he detected her subtle scent, wet clay. His crotch spasmed.

'Maybe I could go to the council,' he heard himself say.

'I don't know,' she sighed, defeated. 'But we must do something. It's the principle.'

'I will go.'

'Please,' she chided him with a raise of her hand. 'They will laugh at you. Even if you go with the weight of the village behind you, these businessmen, *sha*. Even then they will dismiss you, old man.'

180

She rose slowly and he heard her knees cracking as she stood upright. She wiped the edges of his table absent-mindedly and he knew instinctively that she was wishing she could clean up the other, more pressing, situation as easily.

'Nevertheless, I will go,' he resolved out loud, surprised by his insistence.

'How courageous,' she laughed him down. 'But one man cannot save the forest. It takes many farmers to pick a crop,' she said, turning away.

'It only takes one ox to plough a field,' he replied and watched her swivel around to face him.

'Doesn't that depend on the size of the field?'

Allegory shook his head. 'No. On the ox's determination.'

As Babylon waited patiently outside the large oat-coloured house, he tried to imagine living in the city but couldn't. Cities bored him – their noise, their infrastructure. He'd been to Angel several times but had never developed a taste for its charms. He much preferred the smaller communities that villages offered; undeveloped roads that were time-consuming to manoeuvre.

He'd watched Jericho slip through the front door, squaring her shoulders as if preparing for battle. She'd tried fiercely to shake him, but he'd remained as steadfast as a shadow. It wasn't just that he'd assumed the unofficial duty of chaperon seriously, but the only other option remaining to him was that of accompanying Claudia around town. Only who would be escorting whom, he was still unclear about.

He shivered in remembrance but quietly acknowledged that he'd liked her sleeping in his arms. He'd missed the sensation of another person against his skin, of exchanging dreams in twilight hours. Still, he couldn't help wishing it

181

had been someone else he'd cradled, the person who was coming down the steps now with a frown on her exquisite features.

He waited for her acknowledgement as she walked towards him. But she strode past him, muttering loudly to herself. He let the comb in his palm drop back into his pocket and reached out for her arm. He held it firmly, which stopped her forward movement, but she continued to pace in the same position.

'What happened?' he asked softly.

'He's not home. I have come all this way and . . .'

'Why don't we just wait until he returns?'

'Who knows when that will be?'

She stamped her foot impetuously, sending dry sand all over his trouser leg, and he felt his stomach knot in arousal. They both looked down at the mess on his trousers. He glanced at her but she didn't apologise; not that he expected her to. He coaxed her towards the drinking fountain at the end of the road and sat her down on the low wall.

'Relax, you are upset. There is no point meeting him like this. No—' He silenced her words of protest before they came. 'I am a man, at least give me *that*. If I was your *nonno*, I know how I would react, you confronting me like this. Besides, it is not right for someone so beautiful to hold their face in anger.'

She opened her mouth as if to speak, but again he silenced her, this time with a stern look. '*E vero*, you know I am right. Go slow. Let's go to the places he normally goes or where you have been to together and we will find him. I'm sure by that time your thoughts will be much clearer.'

He lifted her head up with his fingers and held it as he waited for her agreement. She nodded, blinking back invisible tears. She let him lift her off the wall and they began to walk side by side. As they walked he remembered how hostile she'd originally been to his presence. Now she didn't even notice when he slid his arm through hers as they moved about town. It felt like the most natural thing in the world.

The day unfolded itself slowly as a tortoise revealing its head from its shell and Babylon was grateful to the universe for acting in his favour. He was glad that he was able to spend the day with Jericho. Even her subdued temperament couldn't depress the butterflies in his stomach.

After spending hours chasing her elusive *nonno*, they went to Moma's for some food. It was almost as if they'd picked the wrong city: Daniel was nowhere to be seen. Babylon was surprised that she knew places like this. It felt very similar to some of the eating-houses in Mannobe and other places he'd visited over the years. For all her supposed airs and graces, she'd evidently retained her villager's palate.

The small rest stop was crowded and the rich smells emanating from the kitchen made Babylon's stomach growl loudly. They settled at a table at the back and he distracted her with small talk until the server brought out their food. She'd ordered a small omelette but eyed his plate longingly while she ate the eggs in front of her, pathetic in comparison. Naturally, he offered her a taste and she refused. But when he held out his spoon to her she took a few mouthfuls before returning it.

'Too much *masala*,' she said, wrinkling her nose.

Their eyes met and unexpectedly she laughed until the chilli moving through her system caused her to gasp for air. She downed her cup of water before reaching for his.

'Is nothing ever to your liking?' he teased gently.

'I don't know,' she replied, her face a stone statue. 'If this day would end . . . I'd like that very much.'

*

Babylon's emotions were a seesaw. The Lwembe girl's unnerving beauty was what had first attracted him but what drew him now was far more puzzling. Something about her stirred him deeply, calling him up from inside himself and twisting his brain into questions. He suspected it was this very thing that had triggered his strange behaviour moments earlier when words had issued from him as if he were under some type of possession and he'd been unable to recall them, but saw himself from a great distance coercing her into submission. Her mouth had formed a delicious pout as she repeatedly declined his request, but he'd refused to be swayed by her petulance.

'I don't want to go anywhere.'

'Come *on*. I promise you, we won't take long. And after I cycled all this way to Angel with you, it's one small thing you can do for me,' he argued rationally before rubbing at his thigh suggestively. 'Unless you'd prefer to massage—'

'Where are we going?' she ceded rapidly and he laughed at her immediate dismissal of his alternative action plan.

'It's not far. Follow me.'

'Fine, but hustle. I still have to—'

'Yes, I know . . .' He cut in smoothly. 'You have to find Daniel.'

He walked in front of her pondering the mixture of nerves, tension and excitement moving quietly through him. During their silences earlier in the day he'd thought over what she had said on their ride to the city and tried to remember the last person that had questioned his façade. With the exception of Gogoa, he couldn't. Her unwitting accusation had rendered him real, but it also made him feel exposed, which disturbed him. He was always so confident when he played; with Guitar over his heart he was invincible. Even alone, his gilded tongue could charm a mother from her newborn, but suddenly he felt vulnerable at the thought of revealing another side

184

of himself, with her especially, and he wondered briefly whether it was too late to change his mind.

She caught up with him just before he turned into their destination. It was a long street, populated by very few houses with stretches of empty land in between. The houses appeared to deteriorate the further down they walked, and he stopped in front of a small cement building that was charred as if a brush fire had tried to violate it but failed, leaving a dirty imprint on the building's paintwork nonetheless. He knew the place must have looked pitiful to her but he was comforted by the fact that the rate of dilapidation had plateaued. To him, the place hadn't changed at all since his last visit.

He banged loudly against the gate, ignoring the sidelong look she gave him, and waited for the watchman to open it. Babylon stood aside to let her pass through first. Then he strode up to the house purposefully, gesturing for her to follow. He decided to walk hurriedly through the building and not allow her much time to observe her surroundings. Soon, they reached the back door, which opened into a large courtyard leading off into several darkened rooms. It was there that they came across the first child and Babylon inched in front of Jericho and knelt down to reach the boy's height.

'Hello, where's Sister?' he asked gently.

The boy used his chin to point out a direction and Babylon stood up, pulling Jericho's hand to follow. He heard more voices as they approached the classroom and he waited outside as a procession of children moved through the doorway. They eyed him as they passed and one or two of the older children greeted him.

'Why didn't you tell me it was a school?' Jericho hissed as the teacher left the classroom.

'*Eh* Babylon, what brings you here?' Sister Samadi reached up to hug him affectionately. He'd known her

185

husband well before he died and Sister had managed the children's home by herself ever since. More of her hair had turned grey since he last visited but she still looked very fit for her age. 'We weren't expecting you! What a blessing.'

Babylon laughed and introduced Jericho. 'I came to Angel by chance, Sister,' he explained. 'I thought I would check on my protégé while I was here. Where is he?'

Sister chortled and led them through the building. 'He's been torturing the others since you brought him that lute. We had to take the strings off at one point!'

She steered them to a large, bare room that was used for activities. Some children were absorbed in a game of Awari on an ancient-looking board while another group appeared to be doing homework; one child was even asleep on a chair. Babylon saw little Nkomo over by the windowless window and went across to him, taking in his recent growth spurt. The boy was still painfully thin and his stomach was the exact shape of a soccer ball. He bent to hug the boy, feeling his runny nose against his shoulder.

'Komo, look how you've grown! What is it? You're trying to catch me, *eh*?'

The boy laughed and then stopped abruptly, pulling at Babylon's elbow. 'I can play Kokorow now!'

'It's a lie,' Babylon teased playfully.

'No. I can, I can,' Nkomo insisted. 'I'm going to show you.'

As the boy raced off to collect his instrument, Babylon turned to look for Jericho, who was talking to Sister. He noticed the room had filled with more children since their arrival, and Jericho's expression wavered between discomfort and concern as she observed each of the abandoned kids. It was sad to see but he knew each one of them was lucky for having been taken in by Sister, and however unhealthy some of them looked, Jericho was viewing them

186

on the road to wellness. She probably couldn't have endured the sight of them at their worst.

Nkomo returned, clutching his lute in one hand, and with the other trying to pull up his shorts that had slipped to reveal his naked backside. His tongue peeked out to catch the run-off from his nose before he shouted excitedly, 'Okay, Kokorow!'

Babylon sat next to him and watched the boy trying to get to grips with the song. He'd decided not to dishearten his young friend by telling him the song was in fact called 'Cock Crow', but watched him attentively, adjusting Nkomo's fingers as he worked his way slowly but effectively through his piece. He made the boy play the song over a few times, satisfied at the child's growing confidence with the instrument and his conversion from the subdued boy he'd encountered three years earlier. The other children crept closer but Nkomo seemed to thrive with his audience, his tongue slipping out of the corner of his mouth in concentration.

Babylon caught Jericho's eye mid-performance and winked at her. The smile she returned was genuine and suddenly he felt embarrassed. He looked over the audience to right himself and spotted Anya, one of his admirers, near the front, partially hidden behind another child. He extended his foot to tickle her leg. The little girl's face broke out into a huge grin and she covered it with the older girl's skirt. Nkomo finished his piece and waited for the other children to clap. An older boy requested a song from Babylon so he asked Nkomo politely for his lute. As Babylon played he made faces at the children and added ridiculous mistakes so that they convulsed with laughter at his expense. He took a couple more requests before protesting loudly about fatigue and returning the instrument to its proprietor.

He entertained the children for another half-hour, giving

the smaller children rides on his back and letting the ones that asked touch his hair. It was as if they were thirsty for human interaction. He didn't want Jericho to grow bored, but he felt bad about leaving the children. She'd been a spectator at the beginning but she'd gone willingly when some girls pulled her aside for a game of ball-chase, and gradually her group had gravitated towards his.

They'd been winding down to leave but the children were reluctant to let them go, making demands or asking questions in attempts to draw out their stay.

'Babylon, is she your girlfriend?' One of the older boys braved the question before the group burst out in shrieks and catcalls.

Babylon dodged the query smoothly. 'How can you ask me that in front of my future wife?' he replied, holding his hands out towards Anya who screamed and ran, waiting for him to catch her. The children squealed as they spread out, giving him room to grab her and ruffle her hair, divided into three jagged Afro puffs. He span around the room with her, and when he finally put her down, he chuckled at her wobbling legs as she tried to steady herself. He saw Anya kick Jericho's ankle as she moved towards the child she liked to hide behind. Babylon fought to control his laughter and lost. He'd played for enough women in his life to spot a jealous rival when he saw one, even one that was knee-height.

For the rest of the day, Babylon saw Angel through fresh eyes. Jericho had been subdued before lunch, as if she'd resigned herself to not finding Daniel, but the children had changed that. Their conversation, which had issued in temperamental spurts earlier, like water from an old outside tap, began to flow freely, then in abundance.

He thought back to the morning when they'd started off their search, targeting areas where they expected to find him: the factory, Dasuka, another bar they sometimes spent time in, even scouring the customers' faces at Moma's. But after visiting the home, she seemed less driven and began to take him to places she liked to frequent. Even if it was in a meagre attempt to lighten her spirits, he was happy that, at the very least, her agenda had changed.

They strolled by Siete, a small estuary that contributed to the Ten Rivers, and he eventually managed to cajole her into a game of skipping stones: he noticed that it took him less time to persuade her into acceding. She appeared to enjoy herself until her fluke winning streak vanished and he brought the game to a timely close. They'd wandered steadily to view the Camel, two hills rising from flat plains. It was one of the few small areas of land in Angel that had not been butchered by development. Even though he'd travelled far and wide, Babylon's breath caught in his throat as he took in the impressive mounds sitting next to each other.

Suddenly, an impulse overtook him and he grabbed her hand tightly, excited when she didn't pull away from his touch.

'Why don't you climb one and I the other?' he challenged, a twinkle lighting up his eyes.

His competitiveness triggered something in her and before he knew it she'd gathered the hem of her skirt and begun racing up the incline. He allowed her a few yards' grace before breaking into a leisurely sprint, each stride he took doubling her own. She kept turning to observe his progress as he ran, which almost cost him his footing. She was fast but pretty soon she was walking with both arms at her sides and panting heavily.

Unable to stop himself, he ran to the peak of his hill like a child, whooping as he arrived at his destination. He performed a little jig of joy and in spite of her setback she laughed along with him. When at last she arrived at the top of hers, she threw both hands in the air.

'*Dance, dance!*' he shouted across the small divide.

She curtsied and he bowed in return and they began to dance on top of the camel's humps, two free spirits in perfect time. She mimicked his dance exactly and laughter spilled out of her.

Babylon's world stopped spinning. He watched her, twirling around the top of the hill like the gypsy sirens from his youth, like the planets around the sun, like the heart inside his chest. He collapsed on the ground heavily and waited for the universe to steady itself. She did the same on the other hill. By the time they climbed down, the sky was beginning to change colour, signalling that night had come.

When she'd complained of tiredness, he'd swept her up from behind and placed her clumsily on his back. She'd pounded his shoulders in shock but she didn't climb down. Her arms relaxed around his neck and he tightened his grip under her legs, beaming as she let him carry her for a good ten minutes.

They stopped outside L'Eglise, the magnificent church with ornate, tinted windows, and admired the large edifice. Its age was evident from sections of stone eaten away over time, its endurance humbling. The sound of singing hummed through the walls of the building bathed in night-blue light as the sun fell, warming their bones. Drunk on their childish exploits, he'd let her lead him closer to the building, where they stopped to savour the voices leaking from the church. She was accustomed to the services there and knew that this particular one had started several hours earlier. Babylon listened intently to the church's attendees. The congregation seemed to gain more strength with every passing minute in the celestial space, their voices growing louder with spirit. As he strained his ears to catch their melody, storing it in his memory for Guitar later on, he caught the smile softening her bottom lip. He realised that she was completely at peace in his company for the very first time.

'Come,' she spoke suddenly, pulling on his arm. 'I'll show you something.'

He followed as she led him around the church. The noise inside grew louder as the hymn reached a crescendo and then faded. Then, they could only hear the priest's voice faintly. They reached a small wooden shack annexed to the church and he watched her pull aside a pane of wood that served as a door and enter inside. He followed her into the enclosure and saw little tables and chairs. Sitting next to her, he looked up at the latticed corrugated tin roof.

'How do you know about that place?' she asked him softly.

Her question took him by surprise: not the enquiry itself but her tone. It sounded as if she'd been thinking about it ever since he'd taken her to Samadi's.

'What? You're shocked I don't use my powers just to pick up desperate women?'

'I'm serious.'

'*Pues*, seriously . . .' He thought for a moment. 'Music takes me places. Not all of them as happy as I would like, but at least I can bring them a little joy, a little comedy,' he answered earnestly before stamping his feet out in a rhythm, the clap of his hand echoing inside the tinny shack. 'Not everyone can have the breeding or education you so admire,' he added, regretting the words in the tense silence that ensued afterwards.

Moving to the far table, he retrieved a scrap of paper from the desk and twisted it into a tight coil before handing it to her.

'What's this?'

'A paper snake,' he replied gently. It had the desired effect. She laughed.

'I love it in here,' she revealed shyly. 'The church uses it for small classes. Sometimes when it's empty I hide in here and listen to the singing.'

'Do you come here with Daniel?'

'Daniel in here?' she replied with a laugh, unravelling the snake. 'He wouldn't come here if the Creator himself sent him a personal invitation . . . No; you're my first guest . . .' she said with a giggle.

'I'm flattered you brought me.' He spoke gently, with a small tilt of his imaginary cap, and realised that he genuinely meant what he'd said. It was as if his admission changed the alchemy of the small room. They both became aware of the heightened level of tension.

'We should go,' she replied quickly and began making for the door, and he knew that she was embarrassed. But as soon as she'd stuck her head out of the gap, the heavens opened. The dark canopy of sky exploded, releasing a downfall of rain, and she pulled her sodden head back in sharply and repositioned the wood. She waved her finger threateningly in his direction as she turned to face him.

'Don't you laugh,' she warned.

'Me? I wouldn't dare,' he replied with a huge smile that displayed all his teeth.

She ran her fingers through her hair, trying to salvage the style, and he fought to keep a straight face. Together they listened to the rain beating the rippled, metal roof smooth. It sounded sharp as it ran off the church's higher roof and struck theirs head on, adopting a hollow resonance as it dropped off the sides of the building. Inside the room, she tried to dodge the runnels of water that permeated the scanty roof and pushed herself up close to him. She cast him a knowing look that seemed to suggest he'd conspired with the elements to bring about such a turn of events and he raised his eyebrows innocently.

'So what instrument did your papa play?'

'More interrogation,' she said and eyed him suspiciously. 'Why do you ask?'

He paused for a beat before continuing. 'Was he a guitarist?'

'No. He played the horn . . .'

The relentless rain had wiped all conversation from their minds. Babylon began to hum quietly to the rhythm of the rain running off the sides of the roof and splashing on the ground. Outside, a discarded container struck by the water sounded like a tabla drum and his humming grew louder, rivalling the shower. He tapped his feet along to his composition.

'Do you hear music everywhere?' she probed, hesitantly.

'Everywhere.' He picked up his rhythm as if they'd never spoken.

'What, in anything?' she interrupted again, intrigued by his concentration.

'*Anything,*' he repeated.

Desperate to dispute his statement, she looked around the bare room for something to assist her experiment but found nothing. She raised her arm in exasperation and he caught it with his right hand.

'Here, let me show you.'

He fashioned a violin from her extended arm and began to play with an imaginary bow. His ear grazed her biceps as he mapped out his invisible tune, humming so she wouldn't feel excluded from his concert. When he finished his song, he turned to look at her, their faces a breath apart. Noises from the city fell away as they stared at each other. He asked her to dance and she nodded.

Babylon approached quickly, in case she changed her mind. Lacing his fingers through hers, his other hand cupped her tailbone, drawing their bodies closer even though neither of them moved their feet. Looking down at her, he realised that she was willing him to kiss her, yet praying for him not to. Sensing a change in her demeanour, he brought his head towards her lips to seal them with his, but at the last moment she pulled back.

'*Listen*, I think it's stopped.'

She got up and pushed the wood aside before escaping through the opening.

'But it's still raining,' he called after her.

'It's only a drizzle,' she shouted, '*venga*.'

His stomach grew heavy with disappointment. He watched her sleek profile dissolve into the gentle rain before following.

Jericho was lamenting her speedy acceptance of Daniel's apology as she walked back home. He had finally made an appearance after they returned from the church. Luckily for her, Babylon was hidden away upstairs in her room while she'd gone down to meet him.

Jericho saw Claudia and Babylon outside: Babylon was checking the wheels of Driver's wagon. She settled herself in her seat, wishing she'd returned sooner so they weren't leaving for Mannobe so late in the afternoon, and waited for the two of them to finish their conversation. As Claudia squeezed Babylon to her bosom as if he was her dearest child, Jericho scowled but managed to paste a smile on her face when Claudia approached and reached for her hand.

'When will you be back?' She heard the hope in her friend's question.

'I don't know yet. I have to spend some time with Mama. She doesn't even know about Daniel,' she replied truthfully. They both watched Babylon stretching his long legs over each side of the cycle.

'And when will *you* be back?' Claudia gushed to the musician. He didn't answer, but laughed and kissed her hand slowly. Claudia studied the back of her hand, as if she was expecting to find a burn mark where his mouth had been.

'No *importa*. If they are all like you,' she gazed at him hotly, 'Coco, maybe I'll visit you in Mannobe some time.'

Jericho surrendered to the rhythm of the wagon and thought of the events of the past few days. She watched his back as he rode, the muscles in his sinewy arms tensing and relaxing as he flung his hair from side to side to escape its heat.

As they left the city, the conversation had jumped from memories to religion, to ambitions and art, before silence. He plagued her with questions and challenges until she'd argued or laughed. Then suddenly she'd clammed up with the knowledge that she was genuinely enjoying herself. She had been ever since she'd tried concentrating on skipping a stone across the water's emerald surface in the way he'd shown her the day before.

Jericho couldn't decide whether this realisation made her happy or sad. She thought of the children back at the home. Before, she'd only been concerned with Daniel, but seeing what real struggles others much younger than her had to endure, she'd felt stupid. She remembered the kindness Babylon had shown in amusing them; it had affected her more because of the child within her. She placed her hand protectively on her belly.

She'd taken Babylon to the church impulsively, oblivious to the intimacy of its setting. That place for her had been a shelter when she yearned for her village's warmth so far away. The voices caught in song always reminded her of the comforting lilt of her home-town dialect. But then, in that enclosed space, it had seemed that the two of them were sharing the same coffin: she'd even felt intuitively that they were breathing in tandem.

195

She felt her arm tingle in remembrance of when he'd played it as an instrument. Questioning him about his music, she'd been surprised at his response. She wondered why she'd been so quick to dismiss him as a mere musician when she could see the superior skill behind his ability. Maybe the crudeness of the city had rendered her more critical of the majesty of the Creator's simple gifts.

Jericho opened her eyes and scrutinised her clothes. The wrapper she wore now was her favourite: indigo blue with large red hibiscus flowers that had become pink as the material softened with its many washes. Now she was a far cry from Claudia's dresses, from Daniel's fine suppers and presents. She observed the dust on the edge of her sandals that rimmed her dry feet and the sweat erupting from Babylon's exhausted body that made him look as if he'd been subjected to ten thousand pinpricks. Her stomach lurched as unfamiliar feelings crept in, stirring the being growing inside.

'Don't you want to do anything else, anything more?'

Jericho had been unable to recall the words once they'd formed in her brain and slipped from her mouth.

'Why are the aspirations of a musician less than that of a businessman?' he'd countered calmly. 'Surely mine aren't any less valuable because they are less rewarding financially?'

She felt queasy but didn't call out to Babylon so that she could quell her churning stomach. Stopping him would prolong their time together, and she needed space to think. But it was hard to focus her thoughts while she could smell him in front of her; the steady waves of musk coming off his body as they rode. His body a tight coil of energy.

The longer she spent in his company, the larger he seemed to grow. She tried faithfully to conjure up Daniel's image but the bubble burst whenever it reached the top of her head. Babylon caught a rock under the wheel and the wagon jolted dangerously. He threw an apology over his shoulder and she accepted it in silence, wondering why she was so filled with sorrow.

They rode quietly for most of the way home. The return journey weighed more heavily on Babylon's legs because of the tension between him and his passenger.

He wanted desperately to know what had happened between Jericho and Daniel but the expression on her face had given nothing away. He wasn't sure if the ground he'd gained the day before had been stolen from him and berated himself for not kissing her in the church. Even if she'd slapped him afterwards, at least he would have had more to think over when they parted ways on their arrival home. He'd hoped for the perfect opportunity to give back the comb he'd recovered, but he found himself dismissing every moment that arose, reluctant to lose the small piece of her in his pocket. He felt a little childish, but it wasn't as if there was any hurry to give it back, and so he hadn't.

Hour upon hour passed until finally the tapestry of landscape grew more familiar as they approached the out-skirts of Mannobe. He sighed, tasting the tang of salt on his breath. He'd hoped to make it all the way back without stopping for too long but his strength was waning with each wheel rotation. The hypnotic scent of Silas's fields called to him and he licked his lips as he rode, the heady scent of those wanton oranges intoxicating. He slowed down the bike and, surprisingly, received no objection from his cargo.

Babylon stretched his aching thighs dramatically while she sat firm in the wagon. Heading towards a nearby clus-ter of trees, he plucked some tender oranges from the lower branches and tore one apart greedily and popped a piece into his mouth. He went over to the barrow and extended an orange towards Jericho. She took it without looking at him. She peeled the fruit slowly, toying with each segment before consuming it. He sat down beside her and the wooden seat creaked.

'*Ewo*, it was a successful trip, *non*?' he offered by way of conversation.

'I guess so,' she muttered in a low voice.

'You are not convinced, *Señorita*?'

'Well maybe for *you* it was, and please stop calling me that,' she replied harshly, climbing out of the barrow.

'Where are you going?' he called to her. 'It's getting dark.'

She ignored him and marched off into the distance. He remained where he was, suddenly exhausted from shadowing an ungrateful shrew. Yet when he could barely make out her outline, he sprinted into the tangle of trees after her. She took off at the sound of his footsteps. He pursued her and felt the tightness lifting inside him with each stride.

'What's the matter with you? Are you mad?' He shook her forcefully but she slapped his hands away.

'Take your hands off me. I'm not Claudia,' she said and glared at him.

Babylon stared at the young woman transformed by anger and the truth struck him.

'You're jealous!' He belted out the words.

'Don't be ridiculous.'

'*Ewo* . . . You're jealous of your friend. What? Did she tell you something happened between us?'

Her loud slap reverberated around the nearby trees. Even she looked shocked at the force with which she'd struck him.

'You'd better apologise,' he said in a low voice.

'No.' She jutted her chin out at him in defiance.

'Say sorry or I'll kiss you,' he warned.

'Try it! Maybe you want another blow to clear your mind.'

He lunged at her and although she raised her hand to strike he caught it easily. He grabbed the other instinctively and pinned them down against her sides. She wrestled him half-heartedly before surrendering, a limp creature in his grip.

'Finished?' he asked sarcastically and didn't wait for her response.

He lowered his head to hers and kissed her with all the remaining strength in his body. When he freed her arms, he half expected her to box his face but she sighed and pulled him to the ground, rolling on top of him. She imprisoned him between her thighs and asked breathily, 'What did happen with Claudia?'

He laughed underneath her and shook his head incredulously. He dreamed up a quick tale to spin before deciding, alarmingly, that the truth was the best way to proceed.

'I told her that I done met my match,' he replied, rolling her beneath him, to her rightful position. Trailing a path of hot, orangey kisses down her forehead and across her neck, he baptised her with her name over and over again. His hands tried to explore her body eagerly but when they came to rest on her stomach she pulled away.

'Your eyes could make the stars jealous,' he whispered sincerely, but she was oblivious.

'Wait! Do you hear something?' He groaned in protest as she pushed him off.

They pitched their ears to the wind simultaneously, animals on the alert. A twig snapped and Babylon rose swiftly and moved in the direction of the noise. In the darkness, he couldn't make out the features of a person, only a profile, but still he recognised it instantly. Only one person possessed a behind that big in Mannobe: Magdalena Codón.

Twelve

'*Tell me again!*' Guitar sang as Babylon caressed his flank.

Babylon's laugh sprayed its wooden curves as he relayed the incident with Jericho earlier in Silas's field. He recalled the overpowering beauty of the orange groves, the way her lips had trembled, and then, finally – when Guitar refused to comply until he spilled the goods – he confessed to their kiss. She'd tasted of mandaflower and vanilla and every fragrance he'd committed to his memory as being pleasurable.

His hands worked a delicate rhythm from Guitar. His eyes rolled to the back of his head until it no longer looked as though he was the person playing but as if some spirit was moving him and he was merely a puppet that thrashed at another's will. Commanded by those invisible hands, bewitching, echoing sounds issued from Guitar, his own voice a river of unspilt tears at the back of his throat.

As Babylon's rich baritone filled his home, Guitar listened intently to the story over again. Babylon had heard about Waranga before he'd reached his house but Jericho was still the most pressing issue on his mind. He stopped playing abruptly and rubbed his arm while flexing his long fingers in an attempt to bring more dexterity to his joints. It felt as though years had passed since he'd last spoken to Guitar, not the few days that it truly was. It was as if someone had poured cement into his veins overnight, making his hands impossible to control.

Something was affecting his ability to play but Babylon pushed the nagging concern away forcefully. He massaged one hand with the other and plucked at Guitar's strings with his feet. He'd perfected this act as a child, knowing how much secret enjoyment the other derived from it. Guitar yelped as Babylon grasped each string between his flexed toes, pulling Guitar's G string repeatedly. He laughed as the instrument trembled with delight.

'*Again, again,*' Guitar cried.

'I can't. I'm getting drowsy.'

'*Please? Just one more time.*'

'Okay,' Babylon conceded hesitantly. 'One more time and then *basta!*'

He plucked the C string with all his might before picking Guitar up and strumming a quick *chacona*. He was preparing to put him down in his velvet-lined case when he heard a small voice asking,

'*Did you miss me as much as you love her?*'

'How could you even ask me such a question?' Babylon answered his beloved quickly, his eyebrows taut with horror.

He heard Guitar's smug sigh as he cradled him to his chest.

Jericho applauded Penny's constitution as her friend held her hair away while she expelled her breakfast. She'd gone to the Azevo compound the morning after the trip to Angel, eager to recount the episode to her dearest ally. The two of them had crept to the backyard for some privacy.

She watched Penny pounding some eddo yam for the

evening's soup. The plunging motion of the pestle her friend lifted high in the air before crushing the defenceless root with its weight caused her stomach to empty its contents.

Penny handed her some ginger water and then moved her wordlessly between her legs. Jericho offered no protest as Penny began braiding her untidy hair unasked.

'Why didn't you tell me?' Penny whispered after a while.

'I don't know,' Jericho admitted slowly. 'I guess I didn't want to tell myself.'

'Well, you're not big at all.'

'Thank goodness . . .'

They sat quietly as Penny painstakingly shaped her hair into identical cornrows. When she finished, Jericho moved on to Penny's step and hugged her tightly.

'What are you going to do?'

'I don't know yet,' she replied, avoiding Penny's gaze.

'You could tell him,' Penny offered gently.

'What? And live happily ever after, another villager romance gone wrong . . . Who's the latest – Hamid's daughter?' She shook her head vigorously, aware of the lightness of her new hairdo.

'Finish telling me what happened,' Penny soothed, shifting the mortar back between her legs. Lifting the pestle to resume pounding, she looked over at her cautiously. Then she wedged the pestle into the mash in the bowl and sat back down on the step. The yam could wait until after.

Jericho had climbed into Daniel's car with mixed emotions. She dug her nails into her palms, finding the pain comforting as the vehicle shunted effortlessly down the streets. Although the car hadn't been moving at an alarming rate, her frayed nerves coupled with her pregnancy made her feel queasy. She hoped that her pallor didn't give her away, or worse, remind him of his vapid fiancée.

She sneaked glances at him, looking for changes in his appearance since their separation. His face had thinned and deep lines were beginning to form above his eyebrows. There was also a more pronounced roundness to his stomach, and subconsciously she'd reached out to cover her own. He hadn't hugged her on their greeting and at first Jericho assumed that he feared her controlled wrath. But as they rode along, shuffling strained monosyllables back and forth, she realised that the tension in the car was emanating from her and not him. By the way he leaned into the corners as he steered proudly, her *nonno* didn't seem to have a worry on his mind.

The drive ended when they reached Daniel's house. He came around to open the car door and helped her out. He still kept hold of her hand as they climbed the steep steps. She wanted to let go, to brush his fingers aside angrily, but she didn't. He wanted to keep hold of her, she'd told herself with a sense of relief.

As soon as they sat down on his crushed velvet divan, the mountain of tension resurfaced. Daniel inched closer and she took this as her cue, flying off the chair dramatically as if the cushions had stung her.

'So I hear you're to be married? Congratulations,' she spat at him angrily, her mouth curling in disgust.

'The announcement in the paper . . .'

'Yes, Daniel. The announcement! Who's Lara?' Her lips pursed around the other woman's name.

'*Ah*, you know her; she's a family friend. My father and hers have known each other for years. She's like a cousin. Surely I've mentioned her before, haven't I?'

'I think I would have remembered that,' she replied, ransacking her mind for the memory and hoping it was there.

'*Pues*, I don't know, but you know she's not even my . . . *Please*, it was not my doing. My parents made that announcement, *cara*.'

'So it's not true?' she asked, still on the attack.

'*Ma non!* I am with *you*, Jericho.'

'Then why did you bring her to Mannobe?' she shouted.

'It was for appearances, *carissima*. My father has invested a lot in her parents' business. I told him I was going down to the village and he thought it would be a nice gesture for her to see Mannobe. I could hardly say no! The only choice would have been not to go. At least I got to be near you. Isn't that what matters? *Ewo*, all this is boring. Come here now, it's been so long since I've seen you . . . Let's talk about something much more interesting: how beautiful you looked at the ball.'

He moved behind her smoothly and enveloped her in his arms. She bristled like a wounded bird before turning to receive him but the fight had been in her head, not in her body. She knew the nervousness she felt was really shame at her own weakness.

'After those months in Ologo,' he shuddered exaggeratedly, 'you blinded me . . . I couldn't take my eyes off you in that dress, *da vero*. No one could,' he whispered into her hair.

'Stop it.' Jericho pushed down her guilt as she recalled the other dress she'd rejected in order to be seen in his.

'It's true. Hey, I was so jealous. They were all looking at you and I wanted you all to myself. It's a pity nobody tried to dance with you in front of me. I wanted to practise my high kick!'

He looked at her seriously and she felt her face softening as she laughed in spite of herself. Allowing his arms to come around her, curling deeper into his embrace.

'Anyway, I have a surprise for you. Come.'

She followed him grudgingly into the dining room, taking in the lean metal chairs and the matching table that belonged to his parents. She wondered if Daniel's bottom had ever met the ground to enjoy a traditional meal. She couldn't imagine his toes dancing with the child's she was carrying as they waited to be fed, while the smell of whatever she was cooking permeated the living room. As soon as the thought surfaced, she pictured Babylon with the little girl in the home, trying to tease her with his foot. The ferocity of the child's grin had set the room aglow.

'What do you see?' Daniel asked with his arms spread, refocusing her attention.

She scanned the room but there were no obvious signs of gifts.

'Daniel, why don't you just tell me—'

'Come on, Coco. *Pues*, what *don't* you see?'

As her eyes moved around the room again, they were drawn to the rectangle of blank space above the head of the table.

'My painting. Where is it?'

'I sold it.' His voice was triumphant as he waited for her praise.

'You did what?'

'Are you angry? I thought . . .'

'But it was for you!' She could picture the painting clearly. The church she'd toiled so painstakingly over, the piece she'd prided herself on because it had taken so much from her to really finish.

'One of the ministers from Ologo. He came for dinner. *Eh*, Coco, you should have seen his face when he saw it. He would have smuggled it off the wall in his caftan if he could, I swear to you! He couldn't understand why I wouldn't give it away and so I decided to charge him. I told him an impossible price and the next day his assistant came with the money. Can you imagine? I kept it for you somewhere.'

He came to stand beside her and placed his arm around her. 'Don't you see? It's a good thing. Look how much people like your work.'

'I know but . . . I gave it to you . . .'

'Don't be annoyed. I understand, but you know they would have asked questions if I refused. Besides, I have *you*. You are more special than any painting. But to sell it, I mean, it shows just how much I believe in you, *creu non*? Your art will be famous one day.'

He kissed her shoulder and when she didn't object, he inched his way towards her earlobe.

'Okay, but . . . when will you tell your family about us?' she whined softly into his armpit.

'Soon, Coco, I *promise*. Now you look very uncomfortable to me. Quickly, let's get you out of this dress . . .'

Jericho strolled through the village later, eavesdropping on bits of conversations. Many farmers and local business owners were assembled in pacing huddles, adamant that they would have their say. One man was giving an impassioned speech.

As she listened to his protest, his anger welled up inside her like a volcano and she found herself attaching his contempt to Daniel, or rather his society. What those with money and power could do.

She nodded her head in agreement as she saw others doing at his outrage. For him it spelled the beginning of the village's demise. A farmer like most of the others, he knew the loss of the trees would affect the fertility of his land. Their agricultural environment was at the Creator's whim as it was, sometimes favourable but mostly lessons in hardship. Most farmers would inevitably be forced to move on, many people would be displaced. He was equally right about the work itself – the rich wouldn't be the ones to break their backs with cutlasses and axes clearing the trees, or risk limbs and lives with archaic machinery they didn't understand; dodgy tanks that leaked gasoline and fires that erupted and melted off the skin as easily as polythene. The

206

poor would carry out the work, the rich would see the rewards, and the land would be stripped of life.

Something in his manner reminded her of the musician. She wondered why she'd edited the role Babylon had played in their trip to Angel, in her account for Penny. She touched her lips absent-mindedly and instantly resurrected the orange grove, the smell of the grass underneath her as his weight pressed her into the earth, and the saltiness of his lips. The gentle pressure of his tongue. The unexpected bliss of their brief kiss, so different from the way Daniel took possession of her lips. Babylon had been surprisingly tender.

She enjoyed the reverie until the musician's dark face ran together with Daniel's image, plucking her sharply from her daydreams. As she swayed dangerously with the weight of her guilty conscience, strong hands righted her from either side.

'Are you all right, my dear?'

The familiar inflection of Venus Oracene's voice greeted her momentarily before Jericho surrendered to the wave of nausea.

The first time Jericho entered the spiritualist's house she'd been so terrified of the strange objects she'd seen that she'd almost run out screaming. But as she'd sat in the woman's home, the objects began to normalise in her mind. Although it was peculiar to find a bowl full of feathers, glass jars filled with different-sized bones, grotesque wooden dolls and the skeletal heads of what looked like monkeys in someone's house, her weird interior decoration somehow lost its demonic edge because the obeah had seemed as womanly as Jericho herself.

'It was a good thing I found you. You were about to take a nasty fall.' Venus's voice startled Jericho and she wondered if she was merely imagining the concerned inflection.

'*Tanka*,' she whispered.

'You've been having quite a time, not so?'

Venus approached her chair and lifted up her face with one finger under her jaw. For a split second, Babylon's face flashed before her. She held her breath as the spiritualist peered into the depths of her pupils before commanding her to stick out her tongue. Jericho complied, spellbound as Venus prodded the fleshiness of her tongue with a strong finger before releasing it.

'I suppose now you're here you want a reading? Come.'

Without waiting for her response, Venus ushered her towards the table and pointed to a chair. Although she'd intended to visit the obeah, the coincidence of the situation now made her hesitant. She knew she didn't have the courage to refuse the spiritualist. Her purported powers were so revered and feared and – as far as Jericho knew – her only challenger had been spirited away from Mannobe soil.

She sat down tentatively and waited for the obeah to join her at the table. Venus rifled through her shelves as though looking for a misplaced item. When at last she located the pack of cards, she sat down opposite Jericho. She blew on the cards but Jericho imagined this was more to remove the dust that had collected on them than for any particular spiritual flair.

'Why don't we try something different?' Venus enquired with a raised eyebrow before handing the deck to Jericho. She took the large cards and shuffled with great concentration. Occasionally, one fell from the deck and floated to the ground like a feather. Each time it happened Venus said nothing but her deep-set eyes took note of the dropout.

'Cut them into three piles – no, with your left hand, that's it – now put them back together. Good.'

Venus took the cards and placed them out on the table in an upside-down cross.

208

'Let's get started.' She smiled enigmatically and Jericho watched her peculiar transformation into Oracene.

Mabel laid all her ingredients in front of her in a long line: onions, tomatoes, garlic, scotch bonnets. Something was missing. Oh yes, she remembered. She went to the pantry and removed four red peppers from the bowl. She placed the chopping board on the counter and brought her swiftest knife out, the one with the bone handle. She started with the onions, immersing herself in the rhythm of the knife tip slicing through the vegetable, the translucent slivers as fine as moths' wings. Thick tears pricked her eyes as she chopped. She worked her way steadily through the ingredients, taking her aggression out in particular on the red peppers that had to be diced just so, small enough to melt away as soon as they hit boiling hot oil.

It had been a while since she'd been this stirred up. There were lots of petty squabbles that heated her blood every now and then – such was life in a small place – but it had been a long time since she'd been so affected. It reminded her of those days in Joucous, where the tensions of city living seeped into her bones, making her features scowl constantly. Every day had blessed her with something that had really annoyed her, which had been capable of changing her mood in an instant.

Perhaps it was because all thoughts of business, politics and councillors reminded her of Mayor Belen – that relationship she tried never to think of because it was so closely linked to her union with Hamid, to her betrayal with her sister's crush.

They'd never spoken about it. Yet when Magdalena was growing up, Mabel had harboured fears in her heart that she only looked at when she was alone in bed at night after a long day's toil in the restaurant. She'd willed every spirit that watched over her to ensure that her daughter inherited *her* features; that she didn't adopt Hamid's tight shoulders, or the curve of his lips that drooped downwards as if they were determined to jump off his chin. She'd wished on falling stars and red egg yolks that Magdalena wouldn't develop his flaring temper. And she'd been blessed. Still, Mabel couldn't help thinking now that her daughter's eternal sadness was somehow punishment for her deception all those years ago. Maybe Magdalena was paying for her own mistake, her sister's stolen happiness, with a lifetime of anguish.

Magdalena was frantically uprooting the contents of her bedroom like a farmer tilling soil during harvest time. She searched for the obeah's sleep serum but the tiny packet eluded her. She'd taken to hiding it in secluded places every few days to combat her mother's new pastime of spot-checking her mental state.

No matter how much she tried, it was impossible to focus on where she'd deposited the packet. Whenever she stood still, the scent of oranges rolled over her, rapidly followed by the image that had assaulted her many times over – the one of Babylon locked in an embrace with Jericho.

Her chest ached. She placed her hand against her breast to feel the dull throb of her heart and let out a sound like a wounded animal. She recalled a time back in the musician's bed, when he'd rested his heavy head against her naked skin and created a song from her heart rhythm. Hot tears wet her cheeks as she remembered him turning his head and attaching his lips to her exposed breast. She shifted her hand upwards unconsciously as she pored over her memories, covering her lonely flesh in a pathetic caress. She was standing like this when M'elle surprised her.

'Ah, you're here. *Bon*, I wondered if I could hang this up in here.'

Her aunt entered the dark room unhurriedly even though she was grasping a large painting in her fat arms, and Magdalena knew that M'elle was giving her time to compose herself. She held the painting up for her to view: it was of a young woman sitting on a chair next to a window. Half of the painting was so dark the woman's features could barely be seen, yet she'd captured the despair and melancholy of her with deft brush strokes. An identical woman overlapped the darker one in a lighter colour so it looked as if the woman's spirit was trying to escape through the window. The woman's face radiated beauty and peace as she rose from the other's lap, reaching for the light. Magdalena's hands traced the edges of the painting as she observed it carefully. It was only when M'elle's hands, tired from holding up the canvas, faltered, that her concentration was broken.

'It's beautiful, Auntie.'

'Can you imagine? A young woman did this. I'll leave it here for now.'

Her aunt rested the painting on the floor, and after stopping to draw the blinds, sat next to her on the mattress, which strained under the weight of their two bodies. Magdalena felt herself being sucked into M'elle's fleshy frame and instinctively she put her arm around her. Her aunt clung back, fused by sadness. She knew M'elle was willing her to speak but she remained speechless. They stayed there, seated on the bed together like distant cousins forced to bond, while Magdalena tried to magic herself into the painting.

M'elle was reminded of the first time she saw her niece, the day her twin had come back, princess style, to the safety of Mannobe. The tiny girl had worn an embroidered cape with a matching bonnet that hid the comets of her eyes and M'elle had bent down, with much more fluidity than

211

she did these days, and lifted the cap gently off her head, releasing a bevy of curls.

The little Magdalena had been drawn by the familiar eyes that mirrored her mother's, and lulled by her auntie's warm smell. She'd come freely into the outstretched open arms, snuggling into the body that followed. M'elle had inhaled the scent from the top of her niece's head and felt her sour ovaries throbbing in response. She connected with the child as if she'd experienced her own womb contracting in labour, as if the new life force had spilled from between her thighs in the shape of a daughter.

She recalled Magdalena's youthful curiosity and wondered when the light inside her had dimmed and, more importantly as her protectors, why they'd failed to notice.

She never thought that the love of two women would cast such a wide shadow, but maybe their shelter had been too much for the girl. Maybe she'd also needed the sun, the light only a man could give, to help her grow.

When Magdalena was about eight years old Mabel was airing the sheets outside while she'd been teaching Magdalena how to sew. The young girl had been determined to draw blood with her needle and repeatedly stitched her thumb to her dress.

'Auntie, how old are you?' Magdalena's question had startled her, but she realised the time she took in responding was because the answer had caused her a similar shock.

'I don't know,' M'elle confessed at last, snickering at her niece's incredulous expression.

'You don't know when you were born?' Magdalena had persisted.

'*Ah*, but that is a different question. I was born on a Sunday . . . it was market day then. Why are you eyeballing me like that? That was how we did it those days.'

She'd resumed her sewing but her answer hadn't

212

appeased Magdalena and she'd called out to her mother outside with the same line of questioning.

'The only way to tell is to cut off my neck!' Mabel had shouted. 'Cut it off and count the rings like you would a tree. Then you'll know my age!'

'You still be ancient as the mountain,' M'elle had teased her twin at the top of her voice.

'No matter, old woman,' her sister shouted back. 'However old I am, I'll always be younger than you.'

Now, as she sat in the adult Magdalena's room with her niece's head resting on her elderly shoulders, she bent to inhale that familiar scent once more.

'You know we have all lost in love, including me,' M'elle said heavily.

She tensed as her niece raised surprised eyes to her. She knew Magdalena was trying to imagine her with a man and she saw her niece smiling as she pictured her in a less maternal role, giddy with anticipation at the arrival of her lover.

'*Vero?*'

'Yes, *bona*. You think you're the only one with the capacity to love?' She squeezed Magdalena's shoulder gently. 'It was a long time ago but I will never forget it.' She rocked them both as she spoke.

'What happened?' Magdalena asked intently, inching closer. M'elle sat quietly collating her memories for a long time before she replied.

'My heart would jump every time I was in his presence. I genuinely felt it somersaulting in my chest; you know the way you throw dough in the air before making flan?' She chuckled softly to herself. 'Every time he came near me it was like so. He was so strong, so big yet so gentle when we were alone. He was very kind and sweet. Your mother – she always went for men with a lot of fire and talk. Me, I

213

preferred the more quiet ones whose beauty was perhaps less obvious, you know? Who burned with a passion behind closed doors.' She winked at Magdalena.

'What was his name?'

'*No importa*. Why, you know him?' She laughed out loud. '*Ewo*, his name isn't important, what matters is the way he made me feel. We would talk for hours, he knew so much about life instinctively. He had spent all his days here in the village yet knew so much about the whole world. Sometimes when we were feeling foolish, we talked about leaving and moving to Beleey to sell fish to the foreigners! Through his eyes it felt possible – you know – to leave here, Mama and your mother and go in search of the unknown. That was what it was like with him. I thought that anything was possible; I felt like the best M'elle I could be . . . I wanted to be a better person, you understand me?'

Her eyes became thick grey clouds as she spoke. Magdalena clung to each word, intrigued by the raw depths of her emotion.

'It's very difficult growing up as a twin. No one sees you, the *real* you, deep down inside. Your mother was wonderful as a sister; I don't want you to think otherwise. But it was hard when it came to men because, *pues*, I guess because we were very similar. Only women can really tell the difference between two mangoes that fall from a tree. To a man, a mango is a mango. But still I felt . . . Well, you know how beautiful your mother is . . .'

Her voice trailed off as if her memories were too painful for her to express. Still twined with her, she rocked her niece whose spirit seemed to awaken with each word of their one-sided conversation.

'But for the first time I felt as though someone actually recognised and acknowledged me, Eloise Amara Codón. It was wonderful. Out of all the girls in the village, even your mother, he wanted me.'

She pointed emphatically at her chest, at her own incredulity at being the chosen one, which drew a giggle from Magdalena. M'elle's heart softened at the sound. It had been a while since the Codón residence had heard her laughter.

'No one ever tells you that happiness is finite. When you're in love you imagine that feeling will last till you reach the Eternal Compound, you never anticipate it running out for someone else.

'I can't remember if he met someone before our happiness ran out. Maybe it had faded for him before he started looking to another, I don't know. But I remember I was devastated that my emotions weren't being returned. *Hmm*, I felt so cheated that I was led to believe all of that was mine, and then it was snatched from me. Still, I loved him and I wanted him to be happy. But it pained more knowing that I was not the one to make or to keep him feeling that way.'

She looked down at her niece whose features had hardened at her suddenly remembered heartache. '*Ewo*, as you grow older you learn to let go of things and to simply cherish the memory. I'm glad I got the opportunity to feel—'

'So I should thank him?' Magdalena interrupted. 'How can you say that? I'd wish she were dead if some woman had taken him from me! *Vero*, Auntie, I wish I was dead so I would never have to feel again.'

'Bite your tongue,' M'elle hissed before making a sign of the cross in remembrance of Hamid's wife Soma who'd passed over many years ago. 'You can't steal a person, Magdalena. He belongs no more to you than all the trees in Mannobe. They belong to the earth and to themselves; they are free to grow where they please. We should be content simply to be blessed by their beauty and shade.'

Magdalena kept her eyes to the ground. M'elle knew she was ashamed of her outburst. She suspected that her

215

niece wanted privacy to wallow in her misery but she was reluctant to leave her. Magdalena wasn't ready to face reality.

'To hold on to this feeling is arrogant, *bona*.' She felt her anger rise but continued in a gentler voice. 'It shows you have no faith in the universe. Everything is as it should be. Your time will come.'

'And what of you? When will your time come?' Magdalena countered petulantly.

'*Now* is my time, I think.' She squeezed her niece's shoulder tenderly before easing her weight off the mattress with some difficulty. On her way out she paused to gather up a plant wilting in a dark corner of the room.

'You can't keep this here. Look, all the leaves are reaching for the window.'

M'elle picked up the small pot and deposited it on the window ledge in the sunlight. She kissed Magdalena's temple before leaving.

She felt Magdalena's eyes following her exit but she didn't turn around. Had she done so, she would have seen her niece waiting for her to advance far enough down the corridor before retrieving the packet that had been disclosed when she'd moved the pot. Magdalena slipped it into the folds of her skirt and placed the plant back in the corner before drawing the blinds shut on the afternoon.

Jericho stared at the spread on the table. The first time she'd had a reading, it had taken some time to realise that Oracene wasn't observing the cards alone. The obeah had repeatedly demanded seven at a time and Jericho had selected them slowly, much to the other's annoyance. Oracene kept ordering her to move her hand away from her mouth as she contemplated her choices. It was then it struck her that she, not the deck, was conveying the messages to the shaman.

Jericho inspected the cards she'd drawn, her pupils dilating in fear, and Oracene smiled knowingly.

'Don't be frightened, my child, we'll get to that later.' Oracene pointed to the first card Jericho had drawn, the queen of wands, and began to unleash her wisdom to a captive audience of one.

'Your biggest pleasure comes from leading and attracting others. But you knew that already, didn't you? They gravitate towards your spirit. You have truly been blessed.'

Jericho watched Oracene looking at the ceiling as if she was waiting for a confirmation from someone her novice eyes couldn't see.

'Your creativity, your light draw people to you. But you have a tendency to daydreaming, *bona*, which can lead you into dangerous territory. It is very important to go through life with your eyes open.' The obeah widened her own eyes for emphasis and Jericho noticed that most of the whites had disappeared. 'You see this card here, it's pretty, *non*?'

She looked at the card Oracene's hennaed finger was directing her attention to. It was a picture of the moon. At first she only noticed the full yellow body with its jagged edges but then other things came into view. Canine animals with satanic features and a scorpion rose from the sea at the bottom edge of the card, to howl wickedly at the moon. Jericho looked pleadingly at Oracene for clarification.

'Appearances can be deceptive, *da vero*?' The obeah wiggled finely drawn eyebrows at her. 'That is what I mean about having your eyes open. This card marks your environment, the external influences around you. The moon signifies illusion; sometimes even fraud and insincerity. You, Jericho, are so busy chasing a dream that you are missing the truth right before your eyes. Yet this card is an indicator of darkness. You know the person around you is not being entirely honest but you don't want to accept the truth. You are no longer a child, *bona*, where if you didn't pay attention your mother would be around to avert the dangers. Now, if you don't tread carefully you will pay the price. But do not be afraid. As they say, it is always black before morning comes but everybody knows nothing can harm you in the dawn.'

Jericho's eyes swept over the cryptic spread and Oracene addressed the card that had invoked the most terror in her, holding it up for her to fully appreciate. Almost entirely black, the card's picture was barely decipherable. She had to strain to see the totality of the drawing on Oracene's well-thumbed card. A horse looked as if it had only just managed to escape the jaws of hell. Bulging grey eyes, and muscles that popped out of its lean legs, all four of which were off the ground. The horse's rider had a body clothed in a brown jacket and a skull for a head. Jericho gazed fearfully into the emptiness that formed the skeleton's eye sockets, chewing her tongue to stop herself from fainting on the obeah's floor.

'Settle. This is truly not a bad card. Death is a symbol for transformation, for change. You must make room for the new. Your life is going to change, *bona*. Be prepared to undergo some reconstruction, for a new era is about to begin. But that is the essence of life, *non*? It is filled with mystery and intrigue so rich you can taste it.'

Jericho caught the sparkling whites of Oracene's eyes twinkling like fool's gold. She wished she could echo the sentiments the woman was expressing, but all she felt was terror. She escaped into her mind, half listening to the remainder of Oracene's prophecy, allowing only the positive messages to penetrate. She returned at the mention of her future husband.

'With the blues in his eyes . . . Are you listening to me?'

'Where will I find a man like that?' she interrupted.

She'd only seen pupils in variations of chocolate, not blue – apart from Oracene's alarming grey ones.

The obeah woman shifted her seat so that she faced her directly. Reaching over, she placed her hands on either side of Jericho's belly as if trying to cover the ears of the child residing there and whispered, 'It's not about looking . . . Sometimes the loss of something is essential for a new beginning.' Oracene smiled. 'You didn't really come for a reading, did you?'

'No.' The quietness of her own voice astounded her.

The obeah's hands pressing against her stomach made her skin tingle and feel alive. She longed for the woman to remove them, yet the moment she withdrew her hands, Jericho felt abandoned. She covered her belly with her own hands but the sensation was gone.

'*Bon*, let's finish then we can get on to other things.'

Oracene's voice was businesslike, leaving no room for dissent. Although Jericho pretended to listen to the rest of her reading, the woman's words and her gravelly voice washed over her. Jericho fixed her gaze on the only card that seemed favourable on the table: that of a naked woman bathing in a small pool of water surrounded by thousands of little stars, with a huge one shining above her head.

'This is your realisation and your destination. The star is a sign of hope, of faith,' Oracene declared.

The tension in between Jericho's shoulder blades subsided. The hope that one card inspired dispelled her fear of the less promising ones.

'It is an indicator of inspiration and unexpected help, a good symbol to have on your side. It points to perfect balance, a place where everything is in unity: desire and work, hope and effort, love and expression. Energy and desire are essential in the pursuit of happiness, *bona*. In your heart you know your *nonno* is not the one. You have always known it was the case; you just don't want to wake up from the dream. But how stupid you would be to stay sleeping, to miss all the stars.'

Jericho watched as Venus swept up her cards and fondled the deck absent-mindedly. The reading was over.

'Is there anything in particular you would like to ask me, dear?'

Jericho bit the flesh on the inside of her cheek, willing herself to speak. She knew why she'd wanted to see Venus, but she couldn't bring herself to utter the truth. The words were fine inside her head, but to put her request into words seemed grotesque. The spiritualist could cover her unborn child's ears from the outside but there was no way she herself could whisper without alerting her child. Words came from the inside: they only took shape when they became airborne.

She willed the woman opposite her to understand and pleaded for compassion with eyes constricted by fear and shame. She watched Venus put away her cards and observe her intently.

'Very well, I think we have finished,' the spiritualist uttered after a time. 'Take this: it should help your condition.'

She handed her a small vial and Jericho resisted the temptation to open it immediately.

'What is it?' she whispered, watching the obeah's approach. Venus placed her hand against her womb for the second time.

'It will settle your stomach,' Venus said, the gravity of her words mirrored in the length of her gaze. 'It's pennyroyal, mostly,' she elucidated with a slow wink. Her opaque grey eyes grew darker as she spoke, as if someone was stirring the ashes in them. 'Biko's Eve: they call it the Day of Miracles. People say any wish can be granted on its moon,' she explained in a gentle voice. 'This thing . . .' she

220

pointed at the vial in Jericho's hand, 'only drink it if you are completely decided about your fate, *bona*. And I assure you, if you are not awake before you take this, you will be after.'

Jericho was convinced she felt the growth in her belly somersault with the obeah's words and pulled away from her touch. She extracted some money to pay but Venus pushed her hand away forcefully.

'This is not something you pay me for. But leave money for the cards,' she added quickly.

Jericho turned to leave but faltered in the doorway.

'Madam?' she asked quietly.

'Yes, Jericho?'

'Why is the truth so heavy?'

Venus picked up her raffia fan. Unfolding it, she threw it in the air with her eyes closed and caught it expertly in her palm. 'Take heart, *bona*. Some say the heavier you are, the swifter your fall, *bona*.'

Confused, Jericho escaped into the brightness of the afternoon. She heard the obeah humming as she left. It was a song sumptuous as sorrel on a scorching day, a song that she vaguely remembered from that night at the ball. A song she knew only came from one source, one person: Babylon.

> '*Remember the rum we drank in Xanadu?*'
> 'And the women of Tome, dressed all in blue?'
> '*The foothills of Guam,*'
> 'The bread in Mofasso,'
> '*The rivers of lime,*'
> 'The mountains that snowed,'
> '*Orienne who refused to let you go,*'
> 'I had to escape when the moon was low . . .'
> '*But you don't feel that way about Jericho?*'
> 'No – *ow!*'

'*What's wrong?*'
'Nothing. My arm is paining me. It feels funny.'
'*Funny how?*'
'Heavy.'
'*Maybe your heart is weighting it down.*'
'Maybe, Guitar. Maybe.'

'Really? Tell me again.'

Babylon eyed Driver who was massaging his jaw with delight. He'd been pummelling him for information ever since he returned the wagon, but at the time Babylon had kept the details vague.

Babylon touched on what prompted his spontaneous journey briefly, and commented generally on the weather before enquiring about his beloved instrument. He then departed swiftly under the pretence of some pressing business but the incident had been too delicious for him to ingest alone. When Driver came by later that day, he'd eavesdropped on some conversation with Guitar. There was only one topic that interested them: Miss Lwembe.

Driver must have crept in so as not to disturb his confession, savouring the sweet melody of man and instrument as Babylon sang his secret to the heavens. After Babylon realised he wasn't alone, he deposited Guitar on the ground by his side and turned around. He recounted the journey to Angel and waited for Driver to pick the trip's carcass clean, relishing the kiss between himself and Jericho like it was his favourite food, cowfoot.

'There's nothing left to tell,' the musician assured him with a grin.

'I don't know how you do it.' Driver scratched his head in disbelief before cleaning his fingernails.

'She's really something, I tell you.' Babylon searched the air for the word to convey what he was feeling but found his vocabulary desperately limited. She'd stirred something in him that was dormant or ignited something that was never there, and he liked it. The way she made him feel. In Mannobe he was an entertainer, but she aroused a more sensitive side of him, extracting something deeper. He laughed foolishly as her image flashed before his eyes.

'*Deus*. You got it bad, eh?' Driver teased.

Babylon placed Guitar back on his lap and began tightening his strings expertly. He played with Guitar again, allowing the music to flow freely from his fingers wherever it saw fit like a butterfly shooting the breeze, waiting for the best wave of wind to ride. His friend stared in admiration, never tired of watching him play. Driver was envious of his command of wood and metal, and the knowledge filled Babylon with pleasure. He remembered when Driver had first described his playing, likening it to the Codóns' beef stew: it tasted different each time – a little more cilantro, a little less pimento – but it always made his taste buds orgasm.

'So what are you going to do now?' Driver asked at the end of the piece.

He searched for an answer but found none forthcoming. Surely he'd done all he could? They'd kissed, so clearly she was attracted to him. If she intended on staying with her Daniel she wouldn't have acquiesced so readily to his embrace. He recalled the expression on her face as she'd grilled him about Claudia and he'd become aware of her jealousy. There was no disputing the fact that she wanted him.

Happiness filled his chest and he banged Guitar with sheer euphoria.

'I don't know, but she's mine,' he answered with conviction.

'For how long?' Driver looked at his friend over a bottle of brew.

'What you say?' Babylon's voice was a low growl, a bear about to strike.

'C'mon 'Lon, how long will this last?' Driver cackled, taking the liquid down his throat in one practised movement.

'This is different. For ever. I'm serious.'

Driver came over to him and placed a dry hand against his forehead with a worried expression. 'You don't have a fever,' he commented, removing his hand after careful deliberation.

'*Jackass*,' Babylon hissed, dealing him a half-hearted blow to the chest. Driver laughed.

'But what makes you so sure? How do you know she doesn't love this Daniel? How you know she wants to be with you?'

'As sure as I have five fingers on each hand, that night follows day, and that yellow and blue make green. She is my music; she is music. I can't explain. I just know.'

Babylon watched his friend standing over him, his mouth a perfect circle of surprise.

'You feel all this from a kiss?' Driver asked.

Babylon laughed as his friend tried to wrap his mind around the possibility that one person's lips could yield that much power.

'Not from a kiss, no.' He smiled and tried to arrange his thoughts carefully. 'But the moment I laid eyes on her in the park I knew our stars were aligned, that my future was linked with her and my past because of her.' Babylon stood up and paced the compound. 'When I was small I remember asking Gogoa what love was. And you know what he told me? He said it's what love isn't; there are no limitations. There is nothing I wouldn't do for her, to win her. To have her.'

'Like cycle all the way from here to Angel?' Driver quipped.

'Exactly. What a journey.'

Driver moved towards the hammock and retrieved two

224

bottles from its shade. He handed one to Babylon and clicked the bottles in a salutation.

'Let's hope you never find out what you have to do for her hand.' Driver sighed and spat on the ground. 'To the end of an era,' he added, making a small bow.

'On the contrary,' the musician replied. 'To the beginning.'

Babylon lifted the bottle to his lips. He cursed loudly as he brought his hand down swiftly and a pain ripped through the length of his arm, causing him to drop the bottle. It fell to the ground, missing Guitar by a millimetre, and shattered. The two of them watched the pale liquid forming an intricate decoration against Babylon's bare legs.

'Uh-oh,' Driver said ominously.

'You think it's a sign?' He laughed, wiping froth from his toes.

'Definitely. You better go see Venus Oracene. You in love for two seconds and already you can't hold your drink.'

Guitar was riding shotgun on his back as they combed the roadside. Babylon pursed his lips and whistled a little ditty as they walked. He listened to Guitar's protests when he swung his arm around casually, quietly amused.

He'd decided impulsively to take a walk to Jericho's side of the village after Driver left. Usually, when he was involved with a woman, he would wait for his conquest to come for him; that way he could gauge how much she had been affected. But Jericho Lwembe was different. Reluctant to lose the footing he'd established in the orange groves, he wanted to talk with her before his smell left her clothing or his imprint was wiped from her curves until all that remained was the memory of her boyfriend.

He pictured the comb in his pocket, wrapped inside his sheet music. He extracted the small package and traced the page carefully, his eyes closing as the music came off his finger in gentle waves. Whether Jericho was a muse or a catalyst, she was responsible for his most poignant music in a long time and the realisation was humbling. She'd forced him to reach deeper inside himself, to stretch his musical muscles.

To pass time, he stopped to witness Hamid's dispute with the blacksmith over the council's plans for the forest. Hamid appeared to have aged overnight. The proposals for the forest threatened to ruin him and many others like him. Their worry was infectious, yet Babylon couldn't help feeling disconnected. Waranga wasn't in his blood like it was in theirs. He understood their upset but was giving up some land really that bad?

He'd been about to enter Borrow's for a small card game to fill his pockets when he found himself sandwiched between two women. Corál, heavily perfumed and made up, wound herself around his left arm and pushed her bosom up against his chest. The other, a woman as blue-black as the night sky with lips as inviting as honeysuckle, cornered him on his right. Guitar squealed with delight on his back even though neither woman took any notice of his presence.

'Hey sexy,' Corál crooned thickly before placing her lips against the vein on the inside of his neck.

'Corál,' he replied warmly, nodding to the other woman who was stroking the hairs on his arm.

'It's empty inside,' Corál whined with a pout on her delicate mouth. 'We're bored.'

'Yes, we're bored,' her accomplice echoed, batting velvety lashes at him. 'Won't you entertain us?'

Babylon marvelled at how effortlessly Corál's fingers had unravelled his shirt and were now weaving patterns in his scanty chest hair. Furtively, he tried to extricate himself from their touch. He'd developed an understanding with Corál over time, having spent many a heated night tossing and turning with her until dawn. In all his years he'd never met a woman whose voracious appetite superseded perhaps even his own, and the knowledge excited and repulsed him at the same time, making him forever wary of her.

'What's the matter?' she asked, sniffing at him like a tracker dog. 'You have a new woman?'

He took his time responding, sizing up the women circling him like professional matadors. He wondered if he was ready to confess his truth to the world.

'Maybe you two are too much woman for me,' he drawled, flashing ivory molars at them.

'*Eh*, there's no such thing . . .' Corál pressed her lips to his, depositing a feeble kiss on the corner of his mouth. Ordinarily, her foreplay would make his scalp prickle in anticipation but today he only felt anxious to escape. He accepted her kiss patiently, knowing the sooner she started the sooner she would finish, then he untangled both unwanted barnacles from his frame.

He slid Guitar off his back and assumed his musician's pose. The blue-black woman clapped her hands together excitedly and bundled her skirt up over her thighs in preparation for his performance. But Corál hissed and crossed her arms and he saw her bottom lip protruding at his subtle rejection.

'What? I thought you wanted me to entertain you?' He raised his eyebrows at her innocently.

'So play already!' she shouted, sinking down on the stairs next to her friend.

Babylon tuned Guitar, amused by the women in front of him. Corál started to yawn halfway through his performance, no doubt trying to wound his inflated ego, but he didn't care. His thoughts were fixed on making it to the Lwembe household in good time.

Allegory's footsteps were so gentle that Babylon didn't hear him approaching. When he looked up from Guitar, he saw the lean figure standing in front of him. The old man nodded in greeting and he promptly lowered Guitar, bowing to his elder and appointed guardian.

'Prophet.'

Allegory placed his hand on Babylon's damp crown as if bestowing a silent blessing.

'What brings you this side?' Babylon asked.

Although the wise man was known to walk the entire length of the village in periods of reflection, Allegory never ventured near Borrow's inn. He might have looked like a vagabond but Allegory was more pious than Father Lovewell, who engaged in many covert activities, believing firmly in the absolution that came with the next lifetime.

'You perplexing about Waranga?' Babylon queried.

'I came for you,' Allegory revealed ominously. 'And thou shalt be secure, because there is hope; yea, thou shalt dig about thee, and thou shalt take thy rest in safety.'

Babylon stared at his protector, bewildered. As hard as he tried he was never able to fully interpret his friend's garbled messages; he could never separate the real scriptures from the chaff. But he felt compelled to listen. His old friend had saved his life, and he would always be beholden. He nodded in what he hoped was a sincere fashion. Allegory took this action for implicit comprehension and gave him a satisfied look.

'And thou shalt lie down, and none shall make thee afraid; yea many shall make suit unto thee. You understand what I am saying?' Allegory pointed his index finger between Babylon's eyes.

228

'*Si*, Prophet, *si*,' he replied and shook his head knowingly in well-timed pauses during his friend's speech.

'Play me something.'

He eyed the old man suspiciously. In the years they had known each other, the spiritualist had never commissioned a song from him. He knew that the old man enjoyed listening to music, but most of the times he'd watched him Babylon had been attempting to serenade the undergarments off a female. He'd therefore assumed that Allegory had frowned upon his playing, considering it a dumbing down of his musical gift.

'Any requests?' he asked, suddenly eager to please.

'No,' Allegory replied. 'The first thing that inspires you will do.'

Babylon gripped Guitar tightly. He stilled his hands over his friend's veins as he thumbed through his mental files of music and offered a quick prayer to the clouds, hoping that today was a good day with his instrument. The new, involuntary tremor of his hand was utterly unpredictable and he didn't want to be shamed in front of his discerning audience of one. It was only then he noticed that the women had disappeared, probably into the darkness of the bar when Allegory appeared.

Guitar waited patiently, taut with anticipation of the fingering that was to follow. Babylon started gently, delicately plucking at each individual string. He held on to each note a fraction longer than necessary so that it sent vibrations through Guitar's centre on release and the resonating sound baptised Allegory. The old man listened passively, the expression on his face neither one of joy nor sorrow as he simply observed the artist at work.

Babylon played for a quarter of an hour with ease, allowing his eyes to close as he surrendered to the will of his fingers, automatically calling Guitar's fluid responses from an otherwise quiet afternoon, while his vocal gymnastics chaperoned them. As he started his final song, Babylon didn't know whether it was the ambivalence of his spectator or the excitement of the last few days, but he felt consumed by tiredness in his arm and a dull ache coursed through him each time he changed his positioning on Guitar's finger-board. The song he played – the one he'd penned for the mistress of his heart – which had started off so sweetly began to lose its momentum. Guitar bristled as he snagged his finger between two strings and the flat note echoed loudly in the empty evening, making the mistake more noticeable. He looked over at the old man: his countenance seemed more animated now than when Babylon had started playing. The fact that his mentor seemed to be deriving pleasure from his inadequacies further frustrated him and the throbbing in his shoulder tripled. Babylon halted his concert, exasperated.

'Apologies,' he offered in sporting spirit. 'I guess the music is not with me today.' He laughed sheepishly.

Allegory accepted his offering but didn't relinquish his penetrating gaze. He remained pensive for a few minutes and Babylon busied himself studying Guitar's tuning pegs, embarrassed.

'What if the music was not with you every day?'

Babylon pulled his eyes upwards as the voice steeped in wisdom finally spoke.

'Excuse me?'

'What if it was no longer there? If you could no longer play?'

Babylon looked confused, and then shook his head, dismissing the thought.

'Why would that be?' he hedged, aware of the trickle of fear that chilled his spine.

'The universe is a fickle creature,' the wise man told him. 'She gives and she takes away, not to punish but to challenge. Surely your mentor, Gogoa, must have taught you that?'

230

The old man looked at him deeply, searching for comprehension, but Babylon knew all he found was apprehension and fear. If Allegory was looking for a man, then all he discovered was a boy, because that was how Babylon felt as Allegory continued his sermon.

'The fruit of the Spirit is love, joy, peace, long-suffering, gentleness, goodness, faith. Now faith is the substance of things hoped for, the evidence of things not seen. What do you love, Babylon, besides *la musica*?'

An image of Jericho twirling on top of the hill flashed through his mind. He pushed it away and tried to stay in the moment, to get on top of the man's words so that he could see the horizon clearly. But he was still stuck on the craggy surface of the spiritualist's first comments. Allegory wiped the dust from the wall he had been resting against off his backside and moved towards him.

'Sometimes, what we think is lost has simply become something else. Those who have eyes to see . . .' Babylon knew he was waiting for him to finish his trademark sentence.

'Let them see,' he answered his mentor faintly.

'For the song.'

Babylon watched the old man bending to place what he assumed was money into Guitar's case and out of respect he bowed to him as he left. When the wise man had walked far away and he could barely make out the pineapple shape of his locks, he looked down into Guitar's case. Allegory had left him a tarot card.

He turned it over to reveal the five of swords, a huge, bleeding heart with five austere daggers thrust through its membrane. Babylon put the card in his breast pocket, puzzled as to its significance. But now was not the time to be concerned with such things. The day was closing and he still hadn't reached Jericho.

*

231

The evening was stained with flecks of night when he arrived at her compound. The normal sounds of life, sporadic chatter, the hissing of flies, and the rippling of running water, transformed into the subtle pulsing of plants as they prepared to rest, the singing of stones, overturned in haste, as villagers hurried home to make it in time for supper, and the animated chirping of crickets preparing for the night shift.

In the darkness, Babylon made out an object that looked foreign against the traditional backdrop of a Mannobe horizon. As he approached, he realised it was a very classy automobile. He'd only seen cars of that calibre in the city.

He knocked on the back door forcefully, wincing as a shooting pain lanced his shoulder. She opened it and he stiffened on seeing her. Her features were flushed and he closed his mind, trying not to think of what she could have been doing in the moment before she stood facing him. He kept quiet as she slipped between the crack of the door and held it shut behind her but all his nerve endings prickled with anger. He knew that there was someone inside her kitchen she was trying to hide.

'Babylon! This is not a good time,' she said somewhat cagily.

'I wanted to give you something,' he countered with a smile false as a black moon.

Despite the pain in his arm he reached into his pocket and pulled out the slip of paper with the enclosed comb and held it out to her.

'Look, I don't think it's—'

She froze as the door opened behind her and a tall man appeared. Her hand, that had been on the verge of grasping his gift, dropped it as if it were coal from a fire.

Babylon recognised the man's features instantly; he'd observed that telltale pinched nose on the statue in the square while he was playing, encountered the same beady eyes in the paintings and busts of Mr Dorique on display around Mannobe, had seen the same pale skin and rigid backbone of those born of position flouncing seasonally through the family mansion by way of visiting relatives.

'Who's this?' her Daniel asked frostily, before turning to inspect him with a look of utter condescension. 'What are you selling?'

'Go back inside, it's nobody. It's nothing,' Jericho quickly corrected, ushering him back into the kitchen. Daniel sneered over her head at him and grabbed Jericho's waist in a mark of possession. She was mouthing a weak 'I'm sorry' before the man slammed the door in his face.

Babylon stared at the closed door, waiting for the shock that immobilised him to dissipate. He couldn't hear precise words but the mumbling of voices in conversation leaked through the wooden barrier. When he heard her laugh, velvety and provocative, he felt a pain pierce his ribcage. He struggled for breath, telling himself that the sensation was connected to the one in his shoulder, and even though Guitar coughed knowingly from his back, he knew better than to air his opinion.

Magdalena yawned dramatically like a dog in the afternoon shade. When she stopped she realised that she was smiling, glad that the day had finally come to an end. She'd walked to Tebo's after her aunt's talk that morning.

She found it easier to think when she was away from Le Papillon. The blistering temperature of the day that warmed her cooling spirits, her aunt's counsel coupled with Tebo's encouraging words, had softened her melancholy.

Of course she'd thought of him, but the pain that had resembled a serrated knife plunged through her gut now felt more like a dull ache. Somehow, M'elle's newfound version of happiness was contagious. She suspected that her aunt was referring to Allegory when she spoke of her second chance at romance and the thought of the two of them pleased her. They were equally eccentric. She imagined their union would last for the foreseeable future; after all, they'd been in each other's past for almost as long: since the café was built.

She recalled the two of them in the park at the Sky Festival, tracing the border of the river in quiet conversation while she'd watched unnoticed. How she'd longed to walk openly with Babylon like them and not just be allowed to love him during the sleeping hours of the village. Not that it mattered now. Still, M'elle would help her believe again.

Magdalena entered the restaurant and walked to the kitchen in the back, but sensed some activity outside. She crept towards the window. Although she could scarcely see through the maze of trees and black, she made out Allegory's hovel illuminated by candlelight. Her curiosity piqued, she opened the door quietly and ventured into the night with the stealthy movements of a phantom. She stopped as she neared his tent, alarmed and excited at the sound of a duet of muffled voices intertwining in the thick darkness.

Kneeling down in her wrapper, she covered the remaining distance on all fours until she was a few yards in front of the opening, obscured by the trees. The old man wobbled into view, and the voices she could hear slowly separated and distinguished themselves in her mind. Allegory giggled – she would remember the sound for ever, not having heard it before – and then collapsed on to the ground. She attributed his fall to the strewn bottles of palm wine – M'elle's rudón win – that were in and outside the crate at his tent's opening, but Allegory's plummet was impeded by his guest, who caught him easily in her strong arms.

Magdalena gasped, first with pleasure, and then with horror, as she watched the spiritualist climbing on top of her mother who trembled as if she was receiving the Holy Ghost.

Thirteen

'Come with me.'

Mabel dragged her daughter out of bed, ignoring her muttered protests. Magdalena struggled and hissed while trying to stop her petticoat from falling down – its elastic waistband long retired – giving up her battle when she realised how serious her mother was.

'If you don't want to help yourself, then you can at least help others.'

She thrust some paper in front of Magdalena and pointed outside. 'Go and bring the paint. There are some cans out there.' Mabel pointed with her chin, watching her daughter hover on the spot in confusion. 'Outside by the shed, come on.'

Something had to bring Magdalena back to the living, and if they had to do it by force, then so be it.

She heard her sister shuffle into the kitchen. The backs of her thong sandals had been worn thin as M'elle refused to lift her heels off the ground. It made her approach unmissable; it always sounded as if she was sweeping the floor. Her head-tie had slipped some time during the night and from its lopsided angle it looked like she'd suffered a fall and had bandaged her scalp accordingly.

'What's all the commotion?' her twin probed.

'That girl is troublesome.'

M'elle shook her head. She watched her headscarf glide to the floor and stepped over it. Mabel knew that she wouldn't risk the bend to pick it up but would wait for Magdalena to come back into the kitchen. She watched M'elle put the pot of water on to the fire. She shuffled to the pantry and returned with a handful of leaves, which she threw into the small gourd. Then M'elle sat down on a chair with an audible grunt and rested her head on her hand.

'Where has she gone?'

'To go and bring paint,' Mabel explained. 'From outside oh, not from Griffin! That girl can take time these days.' She lifted the side of her own headscarf to scratch at her hair before covering it.

'We should take her to see—' M'elle paused when her niece re-entered the kitchen.

'This is all I could find,' Magdalena stammered.

'Isn't this paint? Then it's what I asked for,' Mabel quipped, annoyed. She snatched the can from her, throwing it down on the table loudly. She went to fetch a knife and tried to remove the lid, biting her bottom lip with the exertion it took. Eventually she prised the lid off with such force that it shot off and landed on the ground, leaving a black ring. 'Clean that thing off, *abeg*!' she commanded.

While Magdalena wiped the floor, Mabel laid out the wide sheet of paper on the table. Of course, her daughter had forgotten about the brushes, or had not even given any thought to what the paint would be used for. The brushes had probably hardened anyway, she reasoned, it would be like trying to paint with a stone. She retrieved a pastry brush from the pantry and handed it to her daughter.

237

'What's this?' Magdalena looked confused.

'Make a sign. A few. Then you're going to hang them around the village. And when you've finished, you can hang them in Ankara, Lugobiville, all our neighbour villages . . . Take Tebo with you, and ask Oscar and the other boys. First, we need people to know about Waranga. Then we need people to care and we need people to act. It's not enough for them to flap their gums, they must do something.'

'But what am I supposed to write?'

'Use your imagination, *abeg*. Or is it only reserved for daydreaming? You spend so much time in your thoughts, it should be easy.'

Mabel softened her tone at her child's pained expression. 'We need to drum up the people, to awaken their fire. It takes many feet to cause a stampede . . . The more people you reach the better, *bona*.'

'But Mama.'

'Don't Mama me,' Mabel scolded. 'Go, but first make your auntie some breakfast.'

M'elle chided herself quietly. If she'd known Allegory was coming to the café that day she'd have worn her other bubu, the one with the white lace trim. Instead she wore one of her regular plain ones. At least she'd had the sense to fix her hair. She hurried to him, ignoring Hamid whose plate she still held, despite the fact that she'd walked past the hungry man's table.

'*Bon dia.*'

Allegory smiled at her and returned her greeting.

'What brings you here today? Don't tell me you smelt our catfish? I seasoned it well well.'

'The whole village can smell your fish I'm sure, but no, I came to see Señorita Codón. Mabel.' He smiled warmly as he clarified himself.

238

'Oh. I'll go and fetch her. You want to take something?'

'Water is fine. Thank you.'

M'elle hoped the smile was still firmly affixed on her face as she shuffled towards the kitchen. She wondered what he could want with her sister and why he'd referred to her in such an official capacity. She was the owner of Le Papillon; maybe he was moving, packing up his tent once and for all and was now granting her permission to build on the land. She chased down the frisson of fear that ran through her at the thought. He couldn't leave the village. Not when she—

'Hello!' She heard an annoyed voice call out to her and turned.

'Yes?'

'Are those my beans?'

M'elle looked from her inquisitor to the plate in her hands.

'Sorry,' she said, lowering the plate.

'You've been holding that for a while,' Hamid grumbled. 'How can it still be hot?'

She raised it quickly. 'Sorry, sorry, Hamid. Please. You want me to bring you ano—'

'No,' he answered, snatching the plate from her. He spooned two heaps into his mouth hungrily. 'Just bring me one more meat,' she heard him say as she went to look for her twin. '*Compensation.*'

'Philosopher,' Mabel laughed, wiping her wet hand on her apron. 'What can I do for you?' She motioned to a bench for him to sit down.

'I went to see the elders council.'

'Eh-heh?'

She plopped down on the bench next to him and he wondered briefly why his thoughts suddenly rearranged themselves in his mind. He put them back in their right

239

order, coughing and drinking some of the water M'elle had brought out to him – along with some lemon cake, of course, to buy some time.

'*Abeg*, before I burn my stew, what did they say?' she asked him, impatiently.

'Mr Mbamba says that they've had these plans in mind for some time. They had spoken to the villagers extensively and nobody had voiced their concerns about the forest so they passed their motion.'

'Please! How many villagers did they ask? Did they ask you – or you, Hamid?' her voice boomed, drawing the junkyard owner's attention.

'I'm only conveying what he said,' Allegory explained. 'He said that they were considering the matter very seriously. There are many advantages of the partial sale of Waranga and it would bring some much needed capital to Mannobe.'

Mabel kissed her teeth so loudly that several customers on nearby tables turned around to look at her. She eyed them evilly.

'Those people are buffoons,' she said sadly and he nodded in agreement. 'Isn't there some way? I mean, can't we go over their heads?'

'We need to act, like they did in Sullivan . . .'

Mabel scoured her café for the interjector and located a heavyset man taking a mouthful of food.

'Eh, if I knew I was cooking for a stupid person I would have served you rat instead of chicken, how little you know. Eat your food and let the grown-ups talk politics, *abeg*! Those fools in Sullivan that acted quickly by setting fire to their own trees during their protest? Giving the caners free pass, vacation! That made their work easier for them? *Hmm* . . . Sullivan indeed. *Rubbish*.' She shrugged her shoulders angrily.

Allegory looked at Mabel quizzically. He was waiting

240

for the Creator's sign, for she must certainly have been referring to something higher than the council.

'*Pues*, if it's not *officially* official, then there is still time. These small protests people are doing only cause more trouble. The businessmen have no doubt paid off greedy pigs like Mbamba. We need to fight fire with fire.' She got up, excited all of a sudden. He could see a plan hatching behind her eyes. 'Allegory, give me some time to prepare. You and I are going travelling. We must do something.'

'I thought you said one man cannot save a forest.'

'That is true,' she replied. 'But maybe a woman can.'

Allegory viewed the entire village from the Crescent, the wonderful patchwork of reds, browns and yellows until the beginning of Waranga – the green mass that stretched further than he could see. Over the past few days, he'd learned a great deal. He'd often questioned if their forest would stand steadfast, as other villages had lost their greenery over time through the avarice of the gods, or the whims of men. Yet Waranga had flourished, threat-free – until now.

He cast his glance into the future, the only direction he allowed himself to contemplate. He wouldn't look backwards, now or ever again. After his family's slaughter, he'd vowed to always predict danger's onset, no matter how frightful that vision might be. It had taken years, but he cultivated the gift of foresight and had looked forward ever since.

He thought of all the displaced villagers, those who had made the forests their home and the ones that depended on it for their livelihood. He couldn't begin to imagine how much endless greenery would also be lost. He mourned the trees prematurely, thinking of them as friends. They'd provided for him long before he could depend on the temporal kindnesses of strangers and the fortitude of the Codóns. It wasn't just their beauty he admired; these trees and vegetation provided important health benefits too. Many villagers relied on the medicines produced from Waranga: the herbs from a certain tree that helped treat prostates, the bark of another used as an aphrodisiac for men with impotence, the leaves that were chewed as painkillers. Even the obeahs came to the forest to replenish their stores of potions. While he wasn't happy with the more questionable parts of their so-called powers, at least their cures were rooted in nature.

As he thought about the village and its people his mind rested on the sisters at Le Papillon. He'd never been aware of them as attractive beings before. He understood their likeability, M'elle's unassuming demeanour and Mabel's raucous one, but he'd never truly inspected their physical features. To him, they were perhaps more alluring now than they had been in their youth; age softened their curves and the wrinkles and folds that adorned their features were comforting. He liked the halo of grey at their temples that in a way mirrored his own. He imagined that undressed they must look like sausages – the plump juicy sausages M'elle made that were stuffed with sage and apple: only their clothing held them together in the shape they appeared. Naked, their masses would be unpredictable as mitoke.

Allegory battled a sudden dizzy spell. Maybe he was hungrier than he thought.

'Magdalena!'

Mabel heard the kitchen chair scraping against the floor and her daughter's quickened steps.

'Yes, Mama,' Magdalena replied, standing in the doorway.

'Please, bring my papers for me.'

Mabel's papers were all her business documents and any

other bit of paper that she deemed important enough not to throw out during her lifetime. She rarely went over the jumbled mass but added more and more to the growing pile that had moved from box to bigger box in its life, like a plant outgrowing its pot. She'd wrapped her papers in a polythene sack to protect them and put the box on the top of her wardrobe, pushed back against the wall. She doubted anyone knew where it was, or if they did, would be able to reach it. Even she couldn't, hence her cries for Magdalena's help. Magdalena struggled with the box's retrieval, eventually letting it fall on to Mabel's mattress with a thump. Ordinarily Mabel would have shouted about the dust her daughter had deposited on her bedding, but she kept quiet about the box landing on her bed. She was more concerned with going through its contents; there would surely be something in there that would help their cause. She'd been smart then when she worked for Mr Belen all those years ago, but she was smarter now to have kept all her papers, knowing that there would come a day when they would be useful.

The speed at which Belen had paid her to make her disappear when she'd been pregnant hadn't hurt her as it might have done most women but had caused her to question what else he'd spirited away with money. She hadn't been sure what she'd stolen, but whatever he took the trouble to hide, she'd made the effort to find.

Back in those days, he had so many contacts; he seemed to know everyone from Coppersfield to Griffin. She recalled the hot topic when she'd been in Joucous decades ago. People had been dumping their waste in a marsh area, which had devastated the water supply and infected many small children from the nearby dwellings. Belen had been so masterful with that matter, demarcating an official area for waste and creating patrols for the marshes to curtail illegal dumping. It took time, but people changed their ways.

243

He would surely have some political acumen they could draw on for their own local issue. Failing that, Mabel reasoned, he would have the scandal on some council members that could certainly put a crimp in their plans. After all, the best business deals were done by finding your opponents' weakness and holding it against them. Maybe she could coax more money out of Belen to line the pockets of a greedy link in the council chain. A council member was even a distant relation of Belen's through marriage. If there was one thing she knew, it was that money had a way of lining a man's belly and making him too full to do any real work.

Her newfound sense of power invigorated her. Somehow it was easier to get behind the forest campaign than to dislodge Magdalena's depression. Catching sight of her daughter's long face, she was thankful for Waranga's consuming distraction.

'Make some food we can carry. Plenty, I don't know how long it will take us,' Mabel barked.

'Aunti—'

'Your auntie has to rest. She's been cooking and cleaning all day. Don't you know we're old women?'

'Yes, Mama.'

'All your age-mates are working hard while you are sleeping. When I was your age I was . . .' She caught a glazed look creeping into her daughter's face and realised that this wasn't the time to deliver her well-used speech again. 'Well, you know,' she finished.

'Yes, Mama,' her daughter parroted behind her.

'*Ewo*, be quick. Allegory could be here any minute.'

Mabel sat quietly in the back with Allegory while the driver she'd hired steered his battered car as steadily as the road allowed. She was glad she'd rescued from the boot the food Magdalena had prepared. As long as the big bag laden with provisions sat between her and Allegory, she wasn't inclined to chat throughout the whole journey and could distract herself with food. She reached into the bag and took out a container of fried meat. She offered it to him but he refused with a smile and patted his thin belly. She wrinkled her nose at him, mildly disgusted by his boyish frame, and took two pieces of meat. She sampled the first one quickly to assess her daughter's cooking skills. The pepper hadn't quite permeated the meat so that it initially hot-stepped on her tongue, but the more she ate, the less the pain. It was all right; she hadn't given Magdalena much time to prepare their food so she relented. She chewed the second piece deep in thought.

There had been so much paper, too much to sort, so she'd resorted to throwing handfuls of it into the bag she was travelling with, anything with a classified mark or a big enough town to scare the Mannobe councillors when they got back. If she could successfully locate Mr Belen's information again in Joucous then they would have something. She remembered clearly how they had handled the road situation at the time. He'd received unthinkable amounts of money to build that major road yet, mysteriously, it was never completed past Fado, and eventually the locals pushed the affair to the back of their minds and forgot it was ever there. People like Belen had a way of making pressing matters disappear.

As they rode, Mabel's thoughts rested on her last conversation with Hamid. For all of them, the forest was a vital fuel source as people burned the trees and shrubs for charcoal. Compared to someone like Hamid, their consumption at the café was meagre. She recalled the fear she'd seen in him, that she'd never thought possible. If Hamid's trepidation was so tangible, how many others were afraid of being driven out of business, or, worse still, out of Mannobe? The village would collapse.

Thinking about their destination, Mabel hadn't been prepared for how much confronting her past would scare her. Even though Magdalena wasn't his, Mr Belen believed she was his daughter. What if he'd confessed all to his wife and his life had been irreparably altered? After all, things always had a way of coming out.

She knew her reception would not be as great as the one she'd received when she'd strode firmly back on to the red dust of home town clutching her baby. Once, she'd lusted after the unknown; it had been what caused her feet to itch and propelled her to journey out into the world. But she was old now. More importantly, she felt old, and venturing back to past cities filled her with trepidation.

Allegory was taken aback by Mabel's determination. He watched her surreptitiously as they rode, her features furrowed in concentration. If all the villagers had been as stricken by the Waranga situation as she was, the council would have to reconsider. He wondered what it was about it that had touched her so deeply. It had to be more than the café's proximity to the reserves. Yes, she owned land but who knew how long they had left to watch over it? Unless she was concerned for her child – or her child's future children, even. Wishfully thinking, of course. That one had all the makings of M'elle Codón.

As they left the village, he saw their horizon changing through the car window. Pockets of housing became more and more infrequent, broken up by mountains of green and jagged rocks, the crystal-white clouds against an azure sky that looked as artificial as a painting. They drove past a farm and the stench of manure and ditches flooded the car through the cracked windows and stayed there. They all pretended not to notice but Mabel brought the scarf around her neck up to cover her nostrils and rested her head against the door frame.

His bottom was tired against the thin leather seat that cushioned it. It had been a long time since he'd sat on such a soft surface. He could barely imagine what it would have felt like to sit on it when the car was new and the seating firm and even, as opposed to the archaic vinyl surface with bits of stuffing exposed. It reminded him strangely of some of the village children's haircuts after they'd suffered an outbreak of lice, their hair shorn haphazardly so that when it eventually grew back it was patchy and misshapen.

'We're going to stay with my cousin,' he heard her say suddenly. He'd thought she was asleep.

'Okay,' he agreed, and the car fell back into silence. He watched Mabel reach into the bag with her eyes closed. She opened the container skilfully with one hand and extracted a piece of meat. She put it into her mouth and chewed it slowly, and, as it seemed to him, all the way until they reached their destination.

Mabel's cousin's hoot mimicked that of a Scops owl that lived in the forest. As they exited the hot car, the woman came running out of the house as if someone was chasing her. She hitched the sides of her skirt up to allow her to run faster before holding both her hands above her head.

'Heyh, Mabel! You done reach oh!'

Mabel stretched quickly and wrapped her arms around the woman, but their greeting looked awkward as the other woman was trying to curtsy to her elder. When they'd finished embracing, the woman ran round the car towards Allegory. Before he could stop her, she pulled him against her bosom. He just had time to notice that he fit perfectly between her wide breasts when she pulled him away.

'You're welcome. *Welcome.*'

'That is Allegory,' Mabel pointed. 'Allegory, this is my cousin, Donna.'

247

Donna pulled Mabel into the house. He heard multiple whoops from inside and assumed rightly that she was receiving as fond a greeting as Donna had bestowed outside. He waited for the driver to finish stretching after his whole day's drive. The back of his white shirt clung to his back and his shoulder blades poked through. The man saw him hovering and moved to open the boot. Allegory helped him with Mabel's cumbersome bag. He carried it to the door but hesitated once he was close. It made sense for them to stop in Radebinma because it was on the way from their village to their destination, but he wasn't sure if he would be staying inside her cousin's house. He'd never shared a house with anyone and the prospect alarmed him. Suddenly Mabel opened the door.

'Come and meet my family.'

'I'm tired small. If there is somewhere I can rest . . .' He pointed outside.

'Your tent fit in your small bag, old man?' she asked him evenly.

'No.'

'Then you're staying inside. And to get to your room you have to pass my family.'

She turned around and he followed her nervously, sensing that she didn't care whether he was behind her or not. Her family greeted him loudly while eyeing him suspiciously; not evilly but with curiosity. She announced he was tired and wanted to lie down and he heard their voices rise in protest. Donna wagged her hand at him disapprovingly.

'You must eat first. Then you can sleep.'

'If you can through the noise,' another voice added. 'A birthday is a celebration.'

'A feast,' Donna confirmed.

Despite his initial reluctance, Allegory warmed to Mabel's family. Plate after plate of food was brought from the kitchen whose direction he sensed only from the scent of the dishes before they arrived. He'd eaten very little in the car although he'd been hungry then. But somehow he couldn't bring himself to put his hand inside Mabel's hamper or tear the flesh off chicken wings, flinging the bones out of the window the way she did during their ride. His eyes widened greedily when they brought out the moharo. Each time he refused an offer of seconds, they ignored it and heaped more food on his plate as if they hoped to get him to reach their size in the duration of a meal.

Everyone was excited to see Mabel. The atmosphere was light and they laughed loudly together, resurrecting stories from the past and updating each other with family news. In these surroundings Mabel seemed different, more feminine. He was used to her barking orders in Le Papillon, shouting at helpers or entertaining her customers in her brash manner. She seemed more relaxed in Radebinma, he realised as a flash of her twin overcame her. Perhaps she was only aware of those sides of herself when she was away from her sister. When the two were united they shared one personality. She looked over at him then, aware that she was being observed. It was a surprise to him too; he hadn't been conscious that he was looking at her. She smiled at him softly and for a brief moment the festivities were cast into silence before she looked away. He must be very tired, he thought.

He was unsure what sparked the dancing. One minute, voices had been raised trying to recall who was responsible for the fire that burned down the palm tree in the Dlaminis' garden, and the next thing he knew, most of the people who'd been crammed into the small living room were up. A couple of men sat in the corner, one with a drum and another with an instrument he'd never seen before, that sounded like a flute but looked like the horn the villagers used to convey urgent news.

He watched bodies weaving in and out of each other, mesmerised when the groups of bodies seamlessly formed into a circle as people were called into the centre. Mabel had joined the circle. He watched her swaying casually; he imagined her hips would move that way even if music hadn't been playing. She fanned herself lightly with the scarf she tied around her neck and watched the young ones thrashing wildly and pounding the floor. He heard her name being called and the circle broke temporarily to allow her to enter the middle. He'd half expected her to refuse – he'd most certainly have done so if he'd been called upon – but she entered the ring willingly, pulling a small handkerchief free from Donna's waist as she passed. Mabel shimmied in the circle, handkerchief in one hand and scarf in the other. She thrust the slivers of cloth towards the ceiling, then to the floor, as she bent slowly and righted herself again. A thin film of sweat glazed her forehead as she danced with the crowd's encouragement. Some men broke the ring to place money against her forehead. The bills stuck to the sheen as she twirled.

Allegory felt the breath catch in his throat as he watched her dance. Something was happening to him, something he couldn't explain. He'd started to believe that M'elle was his charge, that he'd been called to her in some way. But maybe her sister was his real concern.

'You like what you see?' A man beside him poked him in the ribs and cackled. 'And she can cook so! Hmm, if it wasn't for my two wives and their trouble, I would follow that one, *eh*?'

Allegory needed to sleep. Only then would the truth reveal itself. He escaped to his room, thankful for the first time in his adult life that he had a door to close.

Mabel found it hard to rest her eyes with Donna lying next to her. She remembered when they were small; they'd thought nothing of five of them cramming on to a mattress, three across its width and one at each end, rolling expertly in dreams so that none of them were lost to the floor. But now she was accustomed to sleeping alone. It was hard to relax, so she kept her body turned outwards so much that her shoulder ached.

She got up and went to get her bag. She wanted to sort the papers but decided it was easier to drag the whole bag into the living room. She lit a candle on the table and sat heavily down on a leather pouf. She opened the bag and saw the money she'd been blessed with for her dancing on top. This would help her to pay the driver for their trip.

Despite her initial reluctance, she'd enjoyed the snatches of conversation in the car with Allegory as the wind had blown against her face. Never in her life had she imagined sharing a back seat with the philosofool of the village. She suspected M'elle had developed a fondness for him so she tried not to abuse him in her presence, but to her he was still the stubborn man who had affected the building of her place of business. Yet in the car, and with her family, he seemed very normal.

She glossed over her papers absent-mindedly, relishing each yawn that worked its way through her body. Then her eyes stopped scanning. She read the paper again carefully, holding it closer to the candle flame. It was something to do with the Joucous road fund. Even if Belen had made new copies, it was enough to get their conversation under way. At the very least, she would have enough to command a proper meeting with him, where he would be forced to listen to her outpouring.

Mabel's joyful clap extinguished the candle.

Allegory hadn't expected to find her waiting for him by the car. She'd participated so readily in the festivities of the night before that he expected their start to be pushed back a few hours. Mabel seemed rested yet determined, and he saw that she'd resumed the persona she adopted to attend to her customers at the restaurant. She smiled as he approached her and then moved to her side of the car.

'They are still sleeping. If we don't go now, we won't get out of there at all.'

'Your family are nice,' he said, when they were nearing the outskirts of Radebinma.

'They're your family now too,' she replied with a pronounced snort. 'Everyone is convinced you're my secret *nonno*.'

The ride to Joucous was pleasant but interrupted briefly by a car that had upturned on the road and blocked the flow of traffic. They waited for enough people to come by to push the car out of the way before they could continue. Mabel rifled through her bag endlessly, sorting paper into different piles. She yelled at the driver each time he forgot and opened his windows, blowing her inventory back into confusion.

'Where are we going once we reach Joucous?' He'd risked a question to her profile.

'Straight to business. There will be plenty of places we can rest afterwards.'

'Who are we looking for?'

'An old councillor.'

'He can help us? Is he a friend of yours?'

'Not a friend exactly but I'm sure he can be convinced to help.' She smiled slyly.

'We cannot do anything illegal.'

'What is this we?' she asked.

'I serve the Lor—'

'And I am serving Mannobans,' she replied sharply. 'Besides, what makes you think we are going to do anything wrong?'

'I don't know. It's just a feeling.'

'Please,' Mabel kissed her teeth. 'Save your feelings for your Lord. After all, he was so very helpful with Mr Mbamba.'

He'd tried to spy on Mabel's paperwork but the angle made it impossible. The old council building she'd directed the driver to no longer existed, so she'd spent a lot of time trying to sew together the piecemeal information she received. He hung back, knowing he'd irritated her in the car with offers of assistance, and allowed her to bark commands at the driver. At last they found it and she sighed with relief as they drove up outside. From the look of approval on her face, the councillors had clearly up-scaled since she worked for them. She climbed out of the car with difficulty and dusted her skirt off before slamming the door. Each step up to the building seemed like an effort. He was walking up the steps behind her when he heard her shout and pound her fist against the door.

'How far?' he asked.

'They're closed for lunch. We have to wait for an hour.'

They turned back but the thought of resting in the car was too much for him. He thought of the bucket bath he'd had that morning, squatting with the small pail between his legs as he spooned water over his body with half a coconut shell. Immediately he longed for the velvet recliner of his creek, floating in the cool waters and washing away all his impurities. He opened his car door so that it created an arc of shade and sat on the ground. Mabel scoffed as she observed him but when she crossed over to her side of the car she did the same thing.

Their wait passed surprisingly quickly and when the hour had elapsed Mabel stood up. He stood as well and began to walk behind her but she stopped him.

253

'Wait here. It's better if I go alone. Don't worry, I dey come,' she added gently.

She went up to the building and spent the next ten minutes adjusting her clothing before a woman with a rumpled blue skirt opened the door. He saw her enter the building and watched her back through the window. He interpreted her head nods as refusals she was unwilling to accept. The woman behind the desk looked vague, then angry then confused. She called another woman to help her and then an old man came to stand by that woman's side. Allegory saw the three of them facing Mabel. When he saw two of them turn and leave, he knew she was about to come out of the building. Her mouth was a thin line.

She entered the car but didn't say anything. He slid into the seat next to her. Her arm covered her eyes. Allegory sat quietly and waited for her to say something.

'They think I am a fool,' she muttered. 'They tried to rubbish me but they told me where he is. Khofosano,' she added with a tilt of her chin to the driver, who started the engine. 'They said he is sick but they were just pretending. Hmm . . . he will have cause for sickness when we reach, I promise you.'

It was dark when they arrived in the nearby town. She'd recounted the conversation that took place inside the office and he'd laughed despite himself. She impersonated the girl behind the desk who'd been so afraid she'd called her supervisors for assistance. Mabel talked of some of her days working there, recalling how much more confident she'd been than the woman that served her.

'That is the problem with youth today. They have fallen standards.'

He agreed with her, but kept his words to himself. There was something about their upbringing that had instilled manners in them. Manners and traditions that

254

were being lost or watered down by children who didn't seem to care about anything at all. The youth had too much food, he thought. Children today didn't really suffer as people their age had done when they were growing up. It was from that hunger in their belly that their fire, their passion came.

The driver honked his horn sharply at the gates of a large house. A man ran up and took some time fumbling with a large padlock before he pulled the gates apart. As their car drove through, Mabel wound down her window to announce herself.

'We're here to see Mr Belen,' she spoke forcefully.

'Eh, he's expecting you,' the gatekeeper replied, waving them on.

'Are you sure? I'm Miss Codón.'

'Aren't you a family member?' he asked, grinning stupidly.

'No,' she admitted truthfully.

'Okay? I thought you were family,' he giggled before composing himself. 'They've been coming all day. Mr Belen say he's expecting more people. His papa don die this afternoon.'

The Sting was satisfying as it attacked her throat. Disappointed by her fruitless endeavour, she was glad that she'd brought the flask although she'd hoped to be drinking from it in celebration. Her Belen had died just shy of his eightieth year. Yes, it had been a long shot but it would have been a good starting point for their Waranga battle.

She allowed the sadness to settle in her body, wondering whether some of it was for the man who had died from weeks of illness or whether it was solely about the forest. Strange as it was, she'd been catapulted back to a time when she was young and strong and the world had been

255

malleable. Now things didn't seem as clear. She knew that her desire to protect Mannobe and her vehemence about stopping the intended deforestation were rooted in something deeper, and as the alcohol reached the extreme edges of her limbs, she saw her sister's face.

Mabel couldn't out-swim the wave of guilt that surged towards her. She'd turned her back on her home town once before, in search of a greater life, and had left her sister behind. As much as she'd learned in her time away, she'd missed so many things and that knowledge still weighed heavy in her mind. In some ways, M'elle was Mannobe personified. Everything that was good in the village – its warmth, loyalty, sense of family and beauty – they embodied her twin, and she couldn't sit still and watch it become endangered.

Sadness and guilt were accompanied by something else, powerlessness, and that was causing her more concern. At the news of Belen's death, she'd felt it invade her body. She'd been unable to stop it, it had caught her by surprise too quickly. Mabel felt *old*.

Seeing Joucous again had brought about a confrontation. It wasn't the one she'd been anticipating – with an old lover – but a more startling one: with age. Back home, she revelled in her role as one of the older matriarchs of the village, taking pride of place alongside her twin in their duty of feeding the masses. They were respected, cherished, held in high esteem. But it was only a matter of time before they became mumbling, incompetent fools that no one listened to. The best they could hope for would be a twin plot in the Eternal Compound.

She saw how ephemeral their moment really was and the realisation shook her. She wanted to be remembered as a battleaxe, not a baking spoon; to be honoured for her fight and passion as much as her extraordinary cooking.

She hadn't expected it but Allegory's presence throughout their journey had been comforting. Even though he seemed ill at ease, at least he was someone from home. Never had she imagined such a trip, with him no less. She'd tried to enlist Hamid's help but even though he was stirred up, the battle had long since left him – Hamid was now a large guard dog with no teeth. Not that she could blame him; she relented, thinking of his life blows. Maybe he'd aged even quicker than herself.

She remembered when they'd crossed paths in Joucous decades earlier, how heated their union had been, and what had resulted. Mannobe soil. She'd wanted to feel comforted then, had ached for the touch and taste of the familiar. Her extended family's welcome before had been nice, but she saw those people so infrequently. Suddenly, she missed the people she saw every day: her daughter, even in her sorrow; her twin, even with her propriety; even the old philosofool and his stupid tent.

Mabel slipped the flask under the bed sheet before answering the knock on her door. Allegory was standing outside the room of the only boarding house the driver knew of in the area. She rubbed her eyes vigorously. Either the old man was dancing in front of her or the Sting had successfully reached her bloodstream.

'I was checking if you are all right.' Allegory's voice was steeped in concern.

'Me? I'm fine. Am I the one who died?' She laughed a little hysterically.

'Okay,' he replied sheepishly.

'Enter.'

She'd meant it as a question but when he watched him march across her threshold, she knew that her tone had actually conveyed an order. Mabel perched on the bed gingerly, feeling the hardness of the flask squeezing against her thigh.

'All is not lost,' Allegory said. 'There is still plenty we can do.'

257

She nodded to clear her head, and to agree with him. He smelt of peppermint.

'I guess one man cannot save a forest,' he mumbled quietly, almost to himself.

'Are you surprised?' she giggled, squinting at him. 'Look at you, skinny ox.'

Maybe it was the tinge of alcohol on her lips, or perhaps it was her lips themselves, as tender and delicious as Amarula. But when she pressed herself against him, Allegory lost himself. He could no longer hear the call of his Creator.

He decided in those fleeting moments that his brain still functioned, that if he was to sin he would do so the only way he knew how – to the best of his ability. Knocking the flask to the floor as he pulled her fully on to the bed, Allegory sinned with all his heart, all his soul, and all his might.

Fourteen

Wrapping myself inside sky
I choked on a cloud
Soft as cotton
Bitter as blood
My heart floods
With sorrow

For me
There shall be no tomorrow
Blue
Is the colour of loss
Not white
Like most people believe

Magdalena removed the tiny package from her bosom and unwrapped it carefully in case her trembling fingers made her spill the obeah's cure. She observed the fine grains of the bright powder. Its smell was so offensive she didn't think she could take the medicine at all. She dabbed a finger into the powder and brought it up to her lips. Running her fingertip tentatively over the inside of her gums, she gagged as she absorbed it with an inquisitive swipe of her tongue.

She wriggled out of the hole she'd squirrelled away in Silas's grove. It had seemed a natural destination after visiting the old well late in the afternoon. She'd braved the scanty line of well-wishers, her note clenched tightly in a damp palm until her turn arrived. She'd peered into that ebony cavern dozens of times but it was always with a sense of scepticism as her pleas seemed to go unanswered year after year. But this autumn had felt different. She'd wished with all her might, only turning to leave once she'd heard a response from the well. Perhaps a beetle dwelling below was rolling pebbles around its home, but that tiny scratching sound had been evidence enough for her that her wish had landed safely on the voluminous pile waiting to be granted.

Magdalena plucked a small orange from the closest tree. Inside her burrow she peeled the fruit slowly, dividing the orange into equal quarters before keeping one aside. She sprinkled the powder over the remaining orange segments to mask the taste and sucked the juice from the fruit, sneezing when some powder rushed up her nose as she bit into its tart flesh.

Almost instantaneously, the fumes jackknifed the short path to her brain, which felt as if it had split down the centre to reveal a brilliant white light. Her hand hovered precariously over the last piece of fruit. It was the one she'd kept to remove the powder's sickly aftertaste. But before her hands could get a good grip on the segment, she collapsed face down in the earth, into a dream-filled sleep of the dead.

The whole of Mannobe had flocked to the square as news of the betrayal was carried on the wind. Magdalena saw people standing around in clusters, heads bobbing towards each other as they exchanged gossip fervently.

The council building was the customary location for resolving any disputes that arose among normally temperate Mannobans but it was too small to house the entire village. The fact that this reckoning was being held in the square didn't surprise her. Two circles – for the feuding parties to occupy – were clearly marked out by stones. Seven council members sat in front of them on an austere-looking bench while the villagers formed a wobbly circle around the spectacle. The council elder fanned himself with a horsetail, puffing out his pockmarked cheeks repeatedly in his impatience for the proceedings to get under way.

Magdalena heard drumming. It wasn't the type reserved for their local festivities but the kind rumoured to originate from deep inside the heart of Waranga, drumming that caused her heart to clench like an angry fist. It was so loud that it battled with the blood clogging her hot ears and she looked around to identify its source. Everyone she could see held no instrument.

As the bell tolled ominously from the spirit house in the distance, she waited while the parties took their positions inside the stone circles. She did a double-take as her mother and aunt stood before her. Magdalena tried desperately to call out but her jaws were foreigners to her. No matter how hard she willed it, no sound parted her lips. Her eyes cried out in frustration but they were unable to halt the proceedings. Eventually, it dawned on her that no one was aware of her presence in the square. She was as see-through as air.

Terror raced through her body as the crowd's chatter dulled to the hushed reverence reserved for burials and weddings. On the periphery of the gathering she used the only power available to her: prayer. She prayed that she would wake from this nightmare swiftly before the whole of Mannobe witnessed her family's shame, even though in her heart she knew she was powerless to affect the

261

inevitable. The council elder struck a blackened metal gong on the table then gave it to the person sitting next to him to hold. Everyone waited for the complaining party to speak.

Even though the audience was quiet, M'elle made a great show of clearing her throat. She was dressed in blood red. Magdalena leaned forward for a closer observation of the woman who'd helped to raise her and held her breath as her aunt turned to face her. Her eyes were completely white; her pupils were nowhere to be seen. From where Magdalena stood, it seemed as though M'elle addressed her solely, the old woman had turned her back on the council. Magdalena looked around her, frightened. The rest of the village had vanished.

'You see this?' she heard her aunt shout while pointing from her grotesque eye sockets towards her mother. 'She took them. Tell me, what has she not stolen from me?'

As her mother turned to face her twin, Magdalena noticed her incessant blinking. Mabel opened her eyes fully to display two sets of hazel pupils against the nonexistent whites of each eye socket. Magdalena recoiled in horror and watched her mother holding her hips and cackling at no one in particular. She felt her body slick with sweat observing her mother's twin eyes spinning crazily.

As her matriarchs eyeballed her, she felt the scream she'd wanted to release welling up in her nose instead of her throat. It worked its way to the tip before exiting in the form of a sneeze.

Magdalena kept her eyes firmly shut as she evaporated into the wind, a fusion of atoms exploding.

Jericho felt the sweat sliding down her spine. She'd wandered the outskirts of Mannobe all day until the red of roads and the green of trees blurred together in a brown haze. She wasn't sure when her feet had secretly piloted her to Silas's fields, to the quiet shelter of the leafy grove. Her belly growled angrily but she ignored it, unsure if it was from hunger or the other life inside her.

She settled on the ground and allowed the squashy grass to accept her weight, relishing its gentle coolness against her skin. Around her the groves were quiet. She listened intently, expecting to make out trees whispering to each other or the unmistakable sound of birds making love, but she could only hear her own agitated breathing as it struggled to right itself.

She willed the universe for a sound, anything to show her she wasn't alone, and heard something whipping through the leaves. Jericho opened her eyes just in time to effect a quick roll as two oranges fell out of the sky. They landed in the indentation her body had left on the grass. She laughed and tore into the fruit, sating herself greedily on its succulent flesh. She lapped up the juice as it ran through her fingers and down her arm, before nibbling at the bitter outer peel. The orange's perfume triggered her memories as she ate. She recalled Babylon, recalled thrashing around underneath him in these same fields.

A thunderbolt ricocheted through her body and lodged itself in her left temple. She tried to remove the image of their kiss with a vigorous head-shake, but in the dizzying heat the action only triggered her headache and nausea. She lay down on the grass and stretched her body out like a cat, too exhausted to move away from the piercing final ray of the sun that warmed the hair at her temple. She imagined it was a hand stroking her, the way her mother used to do when she was small; comforting strokes that slowed her heartbeat, that she lost herself in. She counted the seconds between each pulse of her temple as the sun beat down on her. When she felt her body unfolding, she surrendered to its song of slumber.

She'd woken up in Daniel's bed, agitated while he snuggled deeper into the soft mattress of his impressive wooden bed with his initials carved into the backboard. She ran her fingers over the groove in the wood as he snored gently. His insistent cajoling had driven her back to the Dorique manor for the night. She was still shaken after their interaction with him outside her house after Babylon had left. She'd wanted to stay around the familiarity of her own things at home but had given in to him surprisingly quickly. She was too tired to argue, it had been easier to acquiesce.

She surprised herself when she slid down in the passenger seat of his car, ashamed to be seen in the flamboyant vehicle in the village, almost more than she'd been when she'd travelled in a claptrap barrow to Angel. Next to her, Daniel seemed oblivious to her discomfort. He was far too occupied in his pastime of frightening the nightlife with the glare of his automobile lights and the loud tooting of his horn.

They'd barely made it to the confines of his bedroom before he began to unravel her clothing as if she were a present long overdue for unwrapping. She'd simmered under his touch like a docile cooking pot, making perfunctory sounds and moans in response. Truthfully, she floated across the ceiling over his head, chasing her questions around the room as he shuddered above her. Babylon's kiss must have altered her alchemy, or her irritation with Daniel was choking the desire she felt. She'd looked at Daniel then, as she slipped in and out of their lovemaking. For the first time she noticed how lacklustre he was, twitching over her. He'd seemed much larger in Angel; his gleam had easily outshone the sun and moon combined until all that remained on her retina was his image. Yet somehow, that picture had dwindled steadily during their time apart. Now that her normal eyesight was returning, she wondered what it was that had caused her to be so besotted. It couldn't have been his heritage, there had to have been something else. Perhaps the newness of him was what had been so attractive, the headiness of all those new possibilities on a foreign terrain.

Since she'd come back home to the village, as gradually as her tongue had reverted to its original accent, so had her body been stripping away the mannerisms she'd acquired in the city. She felt different, not just because of the other person in the room with them that Daniel was still oblivious to. The child in her belly wasn't the cause of her diminishing of heart: she had made that journey all by herself.

She moved away from him and covered herself with the blanket, wishing she could throw her new revelations across the room and far away from her. Once, not so long ago, this man had been her entire universe. But now she'd landed on his island to discover that while it wasn't exactly hostile, it simply didn't support any real life.

'We should remain like this for always,' he cooed, licking her shoulder as he raised himself from his pillows.

'What's to stop us?' she'd replied half-heartedly, pushing his face away.

'What are you humming?'

'Was I? Nothing . . .'

'Dearest . . .' His body stiffened as his voice turned serious for an instant. 'I have to tell you something but . . . Promise not to be mad.'

Jericho eyed him cautiously. She'd felt her hackles rising, although outwardly she remained composed.

'Papa and I were discussing business the other day, and the, er, Inodu situation.' He stumbled over the other woman's name, hiding most of it behind a cough.

'Yes?' she waved her hand, issuing him on.

'*Pues*, Mr Inodu feels it would be more beneficial, for business, if we were to have a small ceremony . . . Wait!'

But she'd already flown from the bed, sending a torrent of pillows and foul words flying. Daniel's words ripped a black curtain in her mind that magnificent sunlight poured through. She saw the hollowness of all his previous sentiments, the perfunctory nature of all his endearments that had at one time been as captivating as any foreign language to her ears. Claudia's first appraisal of him had been right. Even if his heart did possess some secret desire that ran contrary to his Dorique inheritance, Daniel's will, it seemed, refused to deviate from his family's course. His weakness was so evident now. Instantly she saw their involvement for the shallow fantasy that it was. The realisation stirred up so much anger inside her that her remaining emotions were starved of oxygen.

'I don't know why I listened to you! This was what you were planning all along.'

'Of course not, darling. You know there is only you! But my hands are tied, you know what Papa is like. Sit down and let's discuss small . . .'

'Discuss what?' She kissed her teeth angrily. 'I thought she was like a cousin?'

'Come again?'

'Daniel?' she beseeched, strangely calm. 'Tell me, do you have any intention of asking for my hand?'

'*Ah-ah*, but how can you even ask me that, Coco? I've tried to talk to my papa! It was a blessing I managed to postpone Lara's family this long! Can you imagine – his last son? Maybe if I talk to him again he will listen . . . It's just going to take a little time but you know I do.'

She'd waited half a beat before delivering her blow.

'What if time is the one thing we don't have?' she'd asked, stroking her belly territorially.

He caught sight of her action and asked cagily, 'What do you mean?'

'What do you think I mean?' she countered, her cheeks growing hotter with heightened emotion in the moment that had finally arrived.

'Stop this, Jericho. Just tell me what's on your mind,' he demanded.

'It's not what's up here, Daniel,' she said, pointing to her temple. 'It's what's in *here*.' She placed both hands over her abdomen as she spoke, pleased as his face contorted in a series of emotions, confused about which one to adopt following her newsflash.

'You're, you're . . .' His voice failed him with the gravity of her implication.

'Pregnant.'

As soon as the words had left her body, all that remained seemed anticlimactic. Still naked, he'd approached her and placed his hand gingerly against her hard belly. She didn't flinch from his touch. He'd gazed at her as his hand surfed the plains of her stomach trying to locate the new life underneath and she accepted his hand, relief flooding her body as she assumed the worst was over. Daniel lowered his head and she parted her lips in anticipation of his kiss. But he recoiled from her as if she'd burned him.

'What's wrong?' she'd asked softly.

She reached out to him but he moved away, his expression growing as sharp as the cruel wind during Hivierno.

'You village girls are all alike,' he spat at her. 'Did you honestly expect to trap me with that?'

She'd flinched at the harshness of his tone, stunned by the severity of his response. She didn't recognise the man standing in front of her. His features were so transformed that he looked ugly, a far cry from the fetching Dorique gene.

'How do I even know you're telling the truth?' he continued. 'Or . . . or if it's mine?'

His words shattered her. Inside, she'd actually felt her heart absorb the blow. Her mother's image flashed before her, her expression when she'd seen her torn wedding dress. The light in her eyes had flickered briefly before dimming. Jericho hadn't allowed herself to feel ashamed

267

about that moment until now. Somehow, she summoned the strength to speak.

'If it's born without a heart, Daniel, then you'll know it's yours.'

She'd retrieved her clothing and dressed quickly, willing her tears to wait. She longed for freedom yet some part of her was waiting for him to stop her exit and apologise for his cruelty. But he'd just watched her go, nonplussed. She'd fled his house into the emptiness of night, under a beaming moon.

In the orange grove the ground was wet underneath her head. Jericho realised she was crying. Thoughts buzzed in her mind like angry bees. When she first came home, her future had been clear. She'd enjoyed being back but had felt unsettled. Now she knew why. All that time – she'd been waiting for him, hoping he would come, imagining he would take her away. Now she didn't have one answer, about anything.

Angel had held many delights, most of them surrounding Daniel, but her home town equally possessed certain charms that were incomparable. The council's agenda for the forest had activated her protectiveness in a way she hadn't imagined, given how she'd extolled the virtues of commercialisation when she first escaped to the city. Mannobans' resistance to the plan was endearing; they were brave in a way she'd forgotten. She was suddenly aware of this absence now that she really needed it.

As more worries assailed her, she wiped from her cheeks the angry tears that had followed the sad ones. It was all too much to think about. Her mouth was dry and the sour residue of oranges on her tongue sickened her. She removed the small vial of pennyroyal mixture Oracene had given her from her pocket and pulled out the tiny cork. She brought the container to her nostrils and sniffed its minty fragrance as the shaman's words about being awake replayed themselves. Venus was right – she didn't want to sleep any longer, dreams only led her to Daniel. It was time she opened her eyes.

She hadn't been to the old well to dispatch her wish but she prayed it would be granted from her alternative location. She placed the vial to her mouth and wet her lips with the oily liquid. It didn't take her long to finish it; there weren't many drops in the small bottle. Then, flinging it into the aching silence of Silas's fields, she waited anxiously for something to happen.

Magdalena coughed repeatedly and came back into view. She ran her hands down her body, relieved to find herself wholly intact, albeit at the top of the Crescent. She gasped as her eyes fixed on the horror unfolding in front of her... her aunt held her mother over the edge of the precipice by her thick ankles. Her mother's face was hidden by her caftan as she hung upside down but her muffled screams chilled Magdalena's blood.

She ran to where M'elle stood but her aunt's demon grasp was so powerful she was unable to prise her mother free. Suddenly, Magdalena felt her limbs growing weaker. Her aunt subdued all her attempts to free her mother with a look. In a flash, she found herself at the bottom of the peak, light years away from her mother's rescue. Her mother's arms seemed to stretch out towards her from the peak's mouth, trying desperately to bridge the distance between them. The caftan floated around her exposed body as she pleaded with her sister for mercy.

'Give me one good reason why I shouldn't let go?' Magdalena heard M'elle scream to the abyss.

'Forgive me cora, I was weak! I am weak. You were always the stronger one.' Mabel's attempt to sound sincere was strangled by the onslaught of blood that rushed to her head from her ankles, clogging her speech.

'Pues, *what if I'm tired of being the strongest?*'
'*Please, Eloise.*'

Her mother called her sister's real name from her upside-down position but that wasn't what made it sound awkward, it was the fact that they all used it so rarely. Nevertheless, it had the desired effect. M'elle froze in her tracks.

Down below, Magdalena covered her eyes, trying to block out the inevitable. She pictured her mother falling through clotted cream clouds to land on her. She imagined what shape their combined imprint would make on the earth, but her feet wouldn't allow her to move from harm's way. When she opened her eyes again she saw her aunt pulling her mother up from the edge.

She sighed with relief. Even though she knew she'd wet herself, she didn't care. She felt her body floating up to the top of the peak and gave in to the weightless sensation. She was as light as a feather on the breeze until she came to where they lay, breathing in synchronicity, eyeing each other like cocks before the fight.

'*You deserved it,*' *her aunt said, still oblivious to Magdalena's presence.*

'*I know,*' *her mother agreed.*

'*But why must you take the one thing I have?*' *M'elle implored.*

Her mother raised fearful eyes to her sister.

'*Because it's the one thing I want.*'

Her aunt's expression was awash with incredulity as she glared at her twin with a mixture of jealousy and condescension.

'*People love you, M'elle; they only admire me. Yes, I am beautiful to look at – whatever that means – but when you look within, what is there?*' *Her mother beat her chest angrily.* '*Even Hamid,*' *she continued in a hollow voice.* '*All those years ago in Joucous? That night as he told me how he supposedly felt about me, he called out your name.*'

270

Magdalena had never seen her mother cry before. As the shallow tears fell on her mother's cheeks while she appealed to her older sister, she felt her eyes stinging. Her own tears surfaced but her aunt's expression was indecipherable.

'I always knew I'd lost him,' M'elle whispered more to herself than to Mabel who fought to hear her. 'Not to Soma – before then, even. He used to kiss me with his eyes open.' She laughed hollowly. 'Then one day I looked and they were closed. And when they opened I didn't see my reflection, cora, but yours. That was the last time my lips met his.'

Magdalena felt melancholy gnawing at her centre. She attributed it to the two women on the edge of the peak and their problems. She clutched her aching stomach, trying to remember when she'd eaten a handful of scotch bonnet peppers. She wanted to relieve herself but couldn't tear herself away from the women's conversations. Despite the pain, she straddled the borders of lucidity and uncon-sciousness. She used her last strength to stay in reality, the hallucination she knew was brought on by the obeah's con-coction.

'Why Allegory?'

'I don't know.' She heard her mother's earnest voice again. 'I wanted to matter. Don't you see? I'm only impor-tant in relation to you, in comparison to you.'

'That's ridiculous,' M'elle interrupted. 'How long have I had to shoulder the burden of the lesser twin, the second best? You might as well have stayed in Mannobe all those years you travelled for they spoke only about you. It was never, how are you M'elle, how good you look M'elle, only, have you heard from Mabel? Such a divine creature can only be doing well.' Her aunt curled her mouth around the words as if it caused her pain to dispatch them.

'I'm sorry, cora. I have never truly experienced love either. I wanted to be consumed, da vero.'

271

Her mother's words resonated so much in her that Magdalena's chest echoed in recognition. Her aunt rose slowly and wiped her mother's tears and the mucus on her robe. Magdalena watched the colour of M'elle's outfit fading until its usual whiteness was restored. The two women remained there on the peak's edge until the sky was surrounded by night and she could barely see. Finally a voice cut through the darkness: it belonged to her mother.

'So, what do we do now? Where do we go from here?'

'There is only one way to go.' Her aunt's voice tore through the flesh of Magdalena's stomach and she cried out as the pain rippled outwards. 'An eye for an eye, the death of one love for another. Only then will we be equal.'

Magdalena heard the words distinctly but in the darkness she'd failed to see her aunt pointing over at her. She struggled when the two matriarchs suddenly attacked her, but they grabbed hold of her easily. By the force of their grip, she knew that M'elle had her wrists and her mother was at her feet.

They held her like the sacks of flour they hurled off their kitchen step into the pantry and extended her over the gaping mouth of the Crescent. The more she battled for freedom, the stronger the acid sensation moved through her veins. Her mothers hummed as they heaved her over the edge, bursting into full song when she left their grip. Magdalena felt her body floating on their lullaby as she soared upwards into the sky before gravity took its course. Only the looming ground waited to greet her.

On the other side of the grove Jericho tried to touch the warmth building between her legs. When she withdrew her hand, she inspected it cautiously. Her fingers were tipped with blood the colour of garnet. She laughed nervously as her uterus contracted and an image of Daniel shot to the forefront of her brain.

Webs of woe
Weave despair around me

Silence is my only friend

Let the earth embrace my secret
Never to be born again

They were back at the Señoritas ball. The crowd had parted to reveal him in his full glory, only this time there were sparkling rubies where his pupils should have been. He smiled at her and his liquefied eyes dripped blood. Even though a good few metres kept them apart, she didn't go to him but looked down at her clothing. She wore her mother's wedding dress but its hem was tinged with blood that was working its way up through the grain of the fabric. The entire village were pointing and hooting at her disgrace but stubbornly, she persevered through the waltz. She turned to Penny for aid but she too was doubled up in laughter, as were the other girls on stage. Jericho fled into the maze of Costa Lina; chased away by the village's ridicule.

She wiped her mouth clean with snatches of grass. The stench of her own vomit was intolerable. With each womb contraction she imagined the damage being inflicted on her stomach. As another wave of pain approached, she blacked out prematurely, escaping its impact. She found herself back in the labyrinth of trees at Costa Lina, trying to find her way home.

Her fingers gripped tightly on to branches and she felt around pieces of wood for an exit. In the distance she saw a shape resembling a man when she squinted. She smiled at first, thinking it was her nonno until the face morphed into Babylon's. Confused, she approached the musician cau-

273

tiously, astounded when he split into two separate beings before her eyes. She was looking directly at her parents.

Jericho combed her father's face intently for the characteristics that embodied her own. He smiled at her but it wasn't a warm greeting; more like his facial muscles stretching themselves. She saw her mother then, hunched up in discomfort, her own belly swollen with life. She knew instantly that it was her inside her mother.

She observed her strangely youthful mother, riveted by the angle of her back. It triggered a memory of being carried when she was a baby. She was harnessed in a double-cloth while her mother and the other women had scrubbed their clothing against rocks in the creek. From her perch, Jericho would watch the water appearing and disappearing before her infantile eyes while her mother flexed her back in the laborious task of beating the dirt out of her washing. Eventually the rocking motion would send her to sleep and she would wake up back home, oblivious of the hard work her mother had carried out. An image of Babylon's back taking her weight after they'd left the Camel that evening in Angel came to her, but as she began to feel the warmth of the memory she pushed it forcefully aside.

The proximity of her father's voice startled her and as she gazed at him affectionately, thoughts of the musician evaporated.

'Do you know who I am?' her father asked in a voice she remembered remembering.

'Yes, Papa.' She was shocked at her childlike voice.

'Well then,' he said coldly. 'You summoned me here, what do you want?'

'Me? I didn't—'

'Pues, if you want I can go?'

'No, wait please,' she cried out. 'If you say I did then you must be right. But can't you stay a while?'

Her father shrugged and she recognised the impertinent gesture as one she'd made her own over the years. She looked anxiously at her mother.

'So, you want something?' Her father questioned her again.

'Yes,' Jericho stammered. 'Why did you leave us?'

He looked bored, as if she'd disappointed him with the banality of her question. Her heart quickened in anticipation of his departure but he casually inspected the lint under his fingernails, flicking away her query.

'Ewo, nothing lasts for ever, my dear. Surely if I taught you one thing, it was that?' He raised his thin eyebrows.

'I thought you didn't love me,' she offered pathetically to the ground.

'Love does not die. It only changes,' he replied in monotone.

'I thought I wasn't good enough for you,' she whispered to herself as if he'd never answered.

'Perhaps I wasn't good enough for you. You never considered it that way, did you?' He looked at her and laughed quietly. The sound was so familiar and inviting that she joined him. 'Is that why you've made the choices you have? Why you're so . . .? Silly bona,' he chided before holding his hand out to her.

She moved to take it but as soon as she did her mother screamed, tearing a perfect hole right through Costa Lina. Jericho's womb ruptured and she felt a thick liquid rush down her thighs. She studied her mother's face contorting with the labour of childbirth. Her blood froze as she watched the tiny life form working its way through her squatting frame, to rest on the ground between her quivering legs.

The three of them peered over the grass at the translucent foetus. Her mother used her foot to poke at it gently but it didn't cry or gurgle, or even move at all. Like all ani-

275

mals rejecting their disabled young, her mother sniffed and turned her back on her spawn and dissolved into the craggy darkness of Costa Lina.

Jericho couldn't tear herself away from that congealed thing lying in the bloody grass. To call it a child would have been incorrect. She was aware of her father next to her, but she was too scared to turn her head towards him in case he too disappeared into the night. She felt the comforting pressure of his hand on her back. As he touched her, she saw that she was riddled in agony and slick with sweat.

'You want me to take it?' he asked gently.

She wouldn't allow herself to speak. She nodded and watched him bend down and cradle the minuscule body in his arms. He gave her one final look before he evaporated, leaving behind the enduring scent of oranges.

'You won't leave me, will you?' she called out to Babylon over the huge gulf that separated the humps of the Camel as they twirled on the twin hilltops in Angel.

'Never' he replied seriously, his eyes clear as water.

'Good. Come here, music man,' she ordered, folding her arms around nothingness.

Fifteen

And the rain came: long shards of liquid mercury that covered the land with a silvery grey film and charged red sand into the weeping atmosphere. The ground swam with the onslaught from the heavens; souls and spirits dampened in the relentless downpour.

Mannobans were long accustomed to this weather. It was natural that the euphoric days of summer couldn't endure and so the inevitable downpour of tears fell from above in honour of the season's end. The gentle breeze, that had once ruffled the village's trees flirtatiously, pooled its strength until its mighty power forced the most unyielding foliage into submission, ripping tender leaves clean off their branches to cower on people's floors before they were swept back outside where they belonged.

Those Mannobans blessed with roofs huddled underneath them while the Creator rained his fury; content enough to be together, at least during the inexorable baptism. Others moved frantically through the village, looking for shelter amongst neighbours, those with a pillow or a dry corner to spare. Owing to Le Papillon's strong edifice the Codón sisters accepted many of Mannobe's waifs.

They welcomed them in with hot chicken broth and one condition. Guests could escape the watery hell outside if they promised to offer prayers to heaven with Magdalena's name stitched inside them, their poor beloved who lay in bed stricken with convulsions.

Magdalena's hair seemed shorter now, shrivelled with the intense heat that consumed her body. Her faint moustache was lined with tiny beads of sweat. She inhabited a world of her own; talking with entities neither M'elle nor her sister could see with their naked eyes. The young woman thrashed so uncontrollably in bed that most of the time their elderly limbs were unable to subdue her.

They'd pushed their mutual mistrust of medicine aside and grudgingly called for the aid of the local doctor to seek a cure. But not before trying to track down the local obeah woman who, they were informed, had gone to Griffin to deliver an upside-down baby. They'd also attempted to solicit another young woman's counsel, but their pleas for Miss Lwembe's assistance, owing to her widely rumoured medical diploma, proved fruitless. The girl was nowhere to be found.

Both Mabel and M'elle had been blessed with superior health so they'd never required the help of the medical profession. The only time M'elle had ever encountered a doctor was the day one had visited her home to pronounce her mother dead after a delectable fish supper. Her disdain had somehow permeated her sister many miles away, for Mabel had spoken about having extracted her own septic wisdom tooth in Joucous with leather and alcohol, rather than accept the skilled knowledge of a professional.

They took turns watching over Magdalena, guardians of her bedside, while she ground her teeth together madly in her sleep. But no matter how much they cooled down her brow, Magdalena burned up with an internal heat that nothing could abate.

M'elle watched her twin relinquish her seat every quarter of an hour to stand by the café's door, in anticipation of the doctor's arrival. She was transported back to when she'd stood there seven days earlier, tearing the door wide open to halt the banging from the other side as Mabel came up behind her. The musician had cradled Magdalena in his arms. M'elle had ushered him in gratefully, chiding herself for being unaware of her niece's whereabouts while she'd been fast asleep. Her sister had been similarly disoriented when she'd arrived, slurring her words. She'd assumed that Mabel had also been dreaming peacefully before they were disturbed.

At first she'd thought her niece had fallen and the musician had come to her rescue. But on closer inspection, Magdalena appeared to be sleeping. This comforted Mabel, who knew the fitful nights her child had been experiencing of late. They'd let Babylon place her carefully on her mattress – with barely an interruption to his breathing, despite carrying her sizeable mass – and they covered her with a sheet. In her slumber, Magdalena had swooned as the cover passed over her body. As Mabel offered the musician her thanks, they found his features laced with concern.

'She'll be all right,' her mother stated boldly. 'She's fast asleep.'

'No. She took something,' he replied, certainty deepening his voice.

Mabel was struggling to form her sentence when Babylon pulled a small item from his pocket. The packet still held some powder residue. M'elle had grabbed it, fingering it suspiciously before bringing it up to her nose.

'Her pulse was very faint when I found her,' the musician disclosed.

He stroked Magdalena's cheek as he spoke and pushed her hair back behind her ears. She moaned deeply, recognising his touch even in her comatose state. If they hadn't been so gripped with fear over her condition, they would have been embarrassed at the guttural sound that escaped her as her body quivered. A half-smile adorned her flaky lips, prompting a small train of drool to make the short descent to her chin.

'She's safe now.' M'elle heard her sister speaking with a wisdom she knew eluded her. 'She's home.'

Mabel mopped her daughter's spit with the edge of her dress before approaching Babylon shakily. She tore the pocket from her outfit and offered it to him. He took it and bowed his head knowingly. No words were uttered to complicate their implicit understanding. He'd saved her child.

M'elle refused to plague her mind with memories, to unravel the sequence of events that had brought them to the present day and the unquestionable role the musician had played in the events leading to her niece's illness. It was enough that he'd rescued their precious Magdalena. It wasn't just up to Mabel. She was also in his debt for ever.

Magdalena hiccuped like a baby unable to support breast milk and gurgled loudly before waking. It was the first time she'd opened her eyes in over a week, since Babylon had brought her home from the fields. A crusty yellow substance had formed over the edges of her lids, clumping her lashes together. Even though the curtain was drawn, the light from her awakened pupils startled her. She brought her hand over them quickly to shield them, mesmerised by the wobbly rainbow her arm carved through the air.

Through the haze, she saw the other inhabitants of the room waiting patiently for her sight to correct itself. After her vision cleared, she glanced around the room. Her gaze rested on her two primary carers. Their furrowed brows were knitted together, forming a collective blanket of fear. Familiarity flooded her chest and she tried to smile, to issue a voice from

280

her chapped lips. But there was someone else in the room and a voice she didn't recognise called her name softly.

She tried to turn in its direction but her hair was glued to the pillow from days of feverish sweat. She decided to wait until the voice approached her instead, which it did, coming to a stop just above her head. As the room around her spun, Magdalena searched for something sturdy to anchor herself to. Finding nothing to hand, she fell into the piercing blue eyes of the stranger.

Babylon grimaced as Driver tugged at his shoulder. He wished he'd followed his first thought, which had been to beseech Corál and her lissome fingers for a massage. He'd stopped himself because he didn't know if he'd have the strength to fight those fingers off were they to seek payment after their task. Now, however, the thought of her fingers was far preferable to Driver's harsh grip that pulled his muscles free.

'I didn't know Magdalena was that heavy,' Driver joked, digging his knuckles deeper into his friend's flesh.

Babylon closed his eyes and tried to pinpoint when he'd first started experiencing the pain he could no longer downplay. He relived the night he'd found Magdalena ragged and barely on the edge of living. As he carried her homeward, his mind had toyed with him fleetingly. He'd imagined that it was another he rescued, guilt piercing his core as soon as he'd thought it. Not that he wished Jericho harm, but had he been her saviour for some reason, she would have been indebted to him. That would have forced her to look upon him differently. With kindness?

It was as if she'd disappeared from the village entirely. At a time, he'd had a good sense of her, could picture her clearly in the square before he turned the corner and walked beyond the promenade of trees, and there she would be in front of him. Now all his walks were mysteriously Lwembe-free.

He considered the possibility that she'd gone back to Angel, and even though he could have confirmed it by walking to her house, he couldn't persuade his legs to make that journey.

He'd wondered from time to time whether she'd been real at all. Perhaps she'd been a summer spirit, a hallucination sent to question his sanity while more physical devils tormented his fingers and musical ability. There had been one small moment of hope, one afternoon when what seemed like the endless rainfall had ceased briefly, allowing a moment of clear sunlight to reign. As he packed Guitar into his case, he was convinced he saw her leaving the market. He shoved his friend into his case unceremoniously and took off after what appeared to be her shape but it was difficult to follow her among the bustle of shoppers and the moment they locked eyes, she'd melted into the throng of people. He found himself pirouetting at the edge of Manuel's Meat Market. He accepted the incident as a figment of his overactive imagination. She couldn't have been so ashamed of their kiss that she would avoid him. But the sweat that had pricked his skin suddenly was an indication of his embarrassment, causing him to question his thoughts and eyesight.

He'd suffered a similar attack of uncertainty when he'd come across a painting a week later while walking through the square. He'd idly scanned the items on display on a makeshift stall erected for the Manna fundraising sale. He did a double-take when he saw the small canvas amidst the other offerings. He recognised the boldness of her strokes immediately, the haunting colours of her painting even though the image itself had been tame. He'd looked around him, hoping that she would be there, somewhere close to her work, but he could feel she wasn't. Relief flooded him when the woman who held its corner relinquished it, opting for a clay vase instead.

If he was surprised at his sentimentality, he hadn't let it deter him from buying the portrait of the Kissing Trees.

Thankfully, the rainy season provided some respite. He wasn't in the mood for company, and with the rain he didn't feel duty bound to entertain. The unpredictability of the elements allowed him more time indoors, away from any shock or speculation in regard to his dwindling musical proficiency. He knew Guitar thought – and Driver concurred – that his pain was linked to an emotional issue rather than a physical injury. They preferred to hold Jericho Lwembe responsible for his muted demeanour. Guitar claimed that she'd grabbed hold of him and was turning him inside out with a series of calculated manipulations that were making him unrecognisable. When he'd argued forcefully that if he was in fact changing then it was into a more compassionate, sentient being, Guitar had remained unmoved. For him, that Babylon was changing was enough; or rather, too much.

Babylon knew that what worried his other friend most was the speed of this transformation. Driver believed in a natural order to things, a pace at which life flowed, a rate at which flowers grew and water ebbed. According to him, any disturbance of this rhythm could only lead to harm.

Babylon rubbed his shoulder absent-mindedly as Driver toyed with Guitar, attempting to coax some sounds vaguely resembling music from him. Long as his two friends had known each other, they still appeared to be speaking different languages. Guitar's sound hole coughed noisily as Driver strummed away oblivious, the instrument's frets a mystery.

Babylon brewed some tea. He would have preferred something stronger, but he would need a clear head if he were to make any sense of the last few days. Everything in his life was shifting, like skin shedding itself in preparation for something new. As much as he didn't want to admit it, he was afraid. He'd spent his life embracing the well-practised order of things without a care or obligation in the world, and only the music dripping from his fingertips; now the newness of his experiences and emotions troubled him. It wasn't changes he minded, after all: they provided surprises and hidden wonder. It was *changing*. The more he thought about it, he didn't like changing at all.

He poured the tea into two cups with his left hand, aware of his increased reliance on this side owing to his deteriorating right. Jericho rose in the steam from the cup. His smoky temptress. He smiled into the dark liquid and watched her features swirling in response. She was a vision of perfection until she pursed her lips and mouthed the words 'It's no one' over his head. That had been the needle in his paw ever since.

'Now you know how I feel,' Driver said, blowing on the tea Babylon handed him.

'Eh?'

'Jericho. Now you know what it's like to lose in love,' he chuckled.

Babylon remained pensive for a moment but watched his hand curling around his cup before slinging it at the wall just above his friend's head. Driver held his position, swigging from his own cup unperturbed. Miraculously, he wasn't graced by a single drop of the scalding liquid.

'I haven't lost,' Babylon replied, agitated. 'Especially to that, to that . . . *Dorique*.'

He paced the small space, consumed with a sudden anger. He searched for a suitable solution to the quandary he found himself in while Driver continued sipping his tea quietly as if he'd failed to notice the temper tantrum.

'Why don't you ask your guitar what he think?' Driver teased. 'Play something.'

'No. Not for her,' he replied tersely.

What Babylon didn't say was that he was reluctant to play in case his fingers failed him again. He no longer trusted himself to complete even his most familiar tunes but he wasn't ready to share this truth with his friend.

'You're not serious?' Driver asked him, salivating at the vehemence of Babylon's statement.

Babylon held his ground until he could no longer bear his friend's scrutiny.

'No,' he sighed heavily. 'Just tired.'

'Of course,' replied Driver, picking up the proffered olive branch. 'You worry about Magdalena.'

'Yes, you're right.'

'Think she dead if you didn't find her?'

Babylon didn't answer his question but pretended he was thinking about it sincerely. Shameful as it was, he didn't have room in his thoughts for Magdalena even though he'd been her saviour. Right now, Jericho and his fingers were more than enough. Besides, there was no way he could embrace his hero status, particularly when he was feeling like such a loser.

Driver had outstayed his welcome at the house but was trying to avoid delivering his wares in the deluge. Babylon had begun by answering all of his questions with mono-syllables. But he grew bored quickly and proceeded to ignore him outright. Not even Waranga updates could draw him out. Offended, Driver slipped off into the rain, his spindly legs shivering as he pedalled towards the centre.

Babylon watched him leave, feeling surprisingly little at the image of his friend being pummelled by the merciless tears of the Creator. He moved around his house, looking for something to occupy him. Guitar called to him sheepishly but he was in no mood for conversation. His head throbbed with the sound of the rain and he felt as if he was underwater. He relaxed into the sensation until it seemed he could no longer hold his breath and choking, he gasped for air. Reluctantly, he re-entered his living room.

'*Why were you ignoring me?*' Guitar whimpered as Babylon picked him up from the far wall where he'd been propped.

'I'm not.'

'*Remember when we rode the back roads of Tigris?*'

Silence.

'*Remember . . . Come on! Sing.*'

'Not now. I'm tired.'

'*You're tired! You're always tired, since she came along. But yet, you're not tired of her,*' he pouted. '*Easy! That hurts.*'

'Sorry,' Babylon apologised as he accidentally bumped his friend's headstock. 'How about this?'

'*Better,*' Guitar responded churlishly, his strings still singing from the sting of the musician's touch. '*If you're angry with her, don't take it out on me.*'

'You say what?'

'*For calling you a nobody,*' Guitar clarified.

'No.'

'*Liar.*' Guitar's voice reverberated around the walls and the rain outside echoed his statement.

'Shut up,' Babylon threatened. He tightened his grip on Guitar, who yelped in response, and for a little while Guitar dropped his line of questioning while they talked about different things. But he soon steered the conversation back to the girl who had run off with Babylon's mind.

'*Do you love her then?*'

Babylon grunted in response.

'*She must really be something if you can't talk to me any more, if you can't play—*'

'Who says I can't play?' he squealed.

'*Pues, of course you can play. Just not well,*' Guitar confessed sincerely. '*What? It's not as if I'm telling you something you don't know already, is it?*'

Guitar waited intently for a response but was met with a stony silence.

'*Something has happened to you, Babylon, to us,*' Guitar continued. '*We shouldn't stay here ... If you weren't so obsessed with Jericho maybe—*'

'Leave her out of this. Why do you keep mentioning her? This is nothing to do with her.'

'*It has everything to do with her. You've changed ever since—*'

'That's not true.'

'*What do you see in her anyway? I understood with that woman from Muntogo. Lulabelle! But Jericho? She's—*'

'Be careful what you say, my friend. She's what?'

'*Tempestuous ... You'll never please that one. Believe me when I say—*'

'Look at you! You sound jealous.'

'*Me?*' Guitar snorted incredulously. '*Jealous of what?*'

'Of who, don't you mean?' He cut his eyes at his instrument. 'Jealous or afraid. Maybe I've found a greater love than you.'

Guitar shrank in horror at Babylon's wounding words. He moaned deeply, emitting a vibration that moved right through the musician's core.

Babylon felt his shack closing in on him, making it harder for him to form clear thoughts. As he knelt down to put Guitar in his case, he retrieved the tarot card Allegory had placed in there when he'd played in front of Borrow's. Immediately he knew where to find some clarity.

'*Where are you going? Don't leave me ...*' Guitar cried frantically but Babylon tore the door open to the rain and despairing clouds.

As he walked under the deluge, the noise soothed him. With every step his drenched sandals sloshed in the water that caused the gutters to overflow, backwashing all the village's garbage. With superior skill he navigated the refuse swimming along the roads. The streets played host to only a few Mannobans brave enough to endure the unremitting weather. Aside from that they were deserted.

Babylon actually liked rain; it reminded him of his travels with Gogoa and *le Cirque d'Orgeuille*. They'd ridden through vast jagged canyons in the midst of monsoon season, entertaining the hill tribes and mountain people with their colourful tales. He'd followed his mentor in awe, marvelling at how Gogoa could make any and every instrument his own, courting attention from all angles. Whether it was men or women, Gogoa had that gift of turning them from whatever they were involved with to make them focus on him alone. As his protégé, Babylon had studied the giant's every move before painstakingly replicating them later in the solitude of the camp, desperate to command that level of admiration one day.

Accompanied by the memories of his past, his feet led him faithfully to his desired destination. He arrived at Venus Oracene's house completely soaked.

Venus's thatched hut was surprisingly adept at keeping the water out. Outside, the goats harnessed in her compound were bleating for redemption, a speedy sacrifice proving a more preferable alternative to the slow drowning they were currently enduring. But indoors, her house was eerily soundless, and he imagined that the rain itself was too afraid to fall on her house, knowing what she could do to it.

Babylon acclimatised himself to her surroundings, inhaling her dusky scent. She'd been waiting by the door when he arrived. It was as if she'd been expecting him regardless of the downpour. There was an energy in the still air, the particles between them charged so that the atmosphere pulsed with sheer excitement. It reminded him of the sensation he felt whenever he connected with some woman in

288

his concert audience who was yearning for him. He scrutinised the ugly obeah closely but as she seemed ambivalent about his presence at her home, he attributed his incorrect channelling to the heady rush from her incense – shivering columns of smoke by each doorway.

She led him to her small table and lit two black candles before motioning for him to sit. She allowed a wide smile to grace her lips then held her palm out to him, clearly expecting something. Instinctively, he reached inside his pocket and handed her the tarot card, face down.

'Blessed be,' Venus exhaled heavily. 'My deck always feels empty without the five of swords.'

He hoped his poker face was sufficient to mask his astonishment but his heart had jumped out of his chest. Venus slid the deck to one side and faced him squarely.

'You want me to tell you what it means,' she stated, without a hint of a question in her tone.

'If you would, Madam,' he drawled, wondering why he felt as if she'd tied a noose around his neck and was raising the cord.

'Very well. But you're not going to like it.' She eyed him carefully. 'But you're a big man; you can handle it.' She chortled deeply from her belly. 'Let's see what Oracene sees.' He watched her eyes roll to the back wall of her skull. 'Five as a rule speaks of a split with the elements. Now the five of swords . . .'

She shook her head and inhaled so deeply that the air made a whistling sound when she drew it into her chest. He was filled with an immense sense of foreboding but forced himself to listen to her reading right to the end.

'The five of swords means failure, defeat or degradation. Humiliation, and a sense of betrayal . . . Sometimes it can predict a tragic situation ending in mourning. You were expecting other news, yes? *Ewo*, this is *your* news, musician, because this is your card. The five of swords.'

289

She shuffled the deck before lifting the top card off the pile at the table's edge and twirling it. The card rotated between her fingers and he saw it was indeed the card given to him by Prophet. He felt his throat tighten and tugged at the imaginary noose squashing down his Adam's apple. His eyes burned with the smoke that had seemed so inviting at first. The obeah appeared to be enjoying his discomfort.

'The five of swords is conceited, self-assured. It likes to stand out in a crowd, to cause a scene!' She pointed at him knowingly.

'Your life has been changing recently, yes? Well, the worst is yet to come,' she revealed ominously. 'You're in for a struggle, no doubt about it, and there's more work and obstacles ahead than you are aware of at this time. Things will not go as they should and you will have a clash with another. It is inevitable. This card is about self-interest, Babylon. We are instructed to be self-sacrificing, yet we oppose it. But we must remember that our self *is* the world. And what we do to the world we do to ourselves.'

His mouth fell open but she waved it shut. She was on a roll and didn't want to be interrupted.

'The cause of your disaster will be weakness rather than excessive strength. However, the time of defeat is the best period to sow the seeds of future successes.'

Each word drained through him like the downpour he'd braved to seek her counsel. Again, he had the feeling that something greater than his comprehension was being handed to him, but a chalice he was disinclined to sip from.

'Be careful of who you trust in the near future. It's just a small thing, but you could be hurt by gossip, and the cost will be very dear. Either way, you must hold on to a larger view of who you are and all will be well.'

When she finally fell silent, the only sound he heard was the candles drawing their breath; even the rain outside was

290

temporarily speechless. Oracene turned her back to him and made her way over to her crowded shelves. She sniffed at certain bottles briefly before putting them back where she found them. She called over her shoulder as she ransacked her stockpile.

'She's a tricky one, isn't she?'

'Who are you referring to, Madam?' he said quietly.

'We both know who I'm talking about,' she chided him. 'Jericho Lwembe.' She enunciated each syllable of the name, her voice playful in its tease.

'I guess,' he sighed in admittance, his eyebrows knotting into a frown.

Finally, the obeah selected a particular bottle. Positioning herself behind him, she placed a heavy hand on his left shoulder.

'You shall have her,' she stated matter-of-factly. 'You want her, don't you?'

'Yes.'

On his response, she plunged her fingers into the thick of his hair and began kneading his scalp rhythmically. He was startled by her touch, but her strong fingers eased the pressure that had been building in his neck and shoulders. He let out an involuntary moan as her fingers wove their magic.

'Be careful what you wish for,' she whispered into his ear.

'Why?' he replied drowsily. 'Because I might get it?'

'Depends. Sometimes we have to lose something in order to gain what we want, *music man*.' He noticed her change of reference to him but didn't say anything. He was entranced by the movement of her forceful hands around the base of his neck. Her skilled massage was sending him slowly to sleep, so much so that when she began to unfasten his shirt, revealing his shoulders, he offered no resistance.

'Are you prepared to relinquish something in order to win her heart?'

'Of course. I mean . . . I don't understand.'

Her hands hovered over his exposed back as he battled for lucidity.

'Would you like me to show you?'

'Okay.'

Oracene reached for a curved bottle and poured out some ointment into her palms. As she made a big show of rubbing her hands together, he noticed the candle flames behind her dancing with glee. She imprisoned his left shoulder and rubbed the grease into his flesh. Babylon let out a huge sigh as the medicine began to flow through his arms, liquefying his muscles. His fingertips flexed, responding with more fluidity than they'd done in days, and he exhaled as he felt the weight he'd been carrying lifting from his bones. Oracene smiled greedily as she gripped his arm and applied heavier pressure so that her fingernails scratched his skin.

The fire that ripped through his veins was quicker than the space between two heartbeats. His flesh began to burn so ferociously that he screamed. He watched the candlewicks spit and hiss before extinguishing in the reflection of the obeah's melanoid pupils.

'*Aye! You dey craze!*' he shouted, yanking his arm free from the satanic vice of her grip. The pain subsided once he broke her connection with his skin but the imprints of her nails still marked him. He sent the bottle flying as he got up from his stool, but she caught it in her right hand.

'It's only now you know?' Oracene howled at his naked back as he fled into the rain.

'*Cora?*'

'Eh?'

'What do you think of Allegory?' Mabel was startled by her sister's question.

292

'What?'

'I mean, you and him spent time together now? Is he a good man?' Her sister's cheeks reddened.

Mabel placed her head over the large cooking pot to hide her expression in the steam that rose from its mouth.

'He's a good man,' she answered evenly. M'elle giggled and drew her knife down on the chopping board, separating a chicken's thigh deftly from the drumstick. 'Why are you asking?' she said over her shoulder with a bright voice.

'I'm just making conversation,' she heard M'elle's lying tone. 'He looks like a good man. There should be more of those in the village.'

'Mmm,' Mabel replied noncommittally, thinking of her past actions. It wasn't that she disagreed with her sister. But she believed the village was in greater need of better women.

'I wish the rain would stop,' Penny sighed.

'It suits my mood,' Jericho replied sombrely. As demoralising as it was, there were some advantages to the endless downpour. The rain had cooled the soaring temperatures that had accompanied this year's Sol season.

Putting down her paintbrush, Jericho wiggled her fingers to dislodge the cramp that had set in. She'd been trying to correct her background and had mistakenly added too much blue. She placed a hand on her stomach subconsciously, removing it when awareness set in. Penny squeezed her palm and peered at her anxiously.

Ever since she'd whispered feebly through her window, bloody and confused, Penny had been hesitant to leave her side, fearful of what might take her if she were alone. Jericho blinked rapidly under Penny's scrutiny and tried to dislodge the imbrued image from her mind.

They'd stumbled to the creek under the cover of that oyster moon, Penny carrying most of her weight as she shifted in and out of consciousness. Penny had cleaned the blood caked on her clothing gently, placing her in the shallower water until the flow of blood that issued from her raw womb ran clear. Penny had cried for her, had known that she was too tired to do so, too damaged to let the tears flow from herself. Her friend had understood intuitively that Jericho couldn't afford to lose any more of her essence, even in the form of tears, to mourn the life she'd poisoned out of her body.

They'd remained on the banks of the creek until the moon turned to the ground and kissed it tenderly, causing it to blush the first light of dawn. Then they'd sneaked to Jericho's home to bind between her legs, listening out for her mother.

The elements had conspired to help them. The rainfall that had begun the night before provided a valid excuse for Penny's prolonged presence in Jericho's house this week.

Her mother would most certainly have guessed that something was amiss had Penny not been there. She could only mask red, swollen eyes for so long. Luckily, her mother left the two of them alone to gossip and whisper quietly, the way young women do.

Jericho was still trying to piece together that night in Silas's fields, the events fuzzy to her. She recalled the disorientation the morning after: the room had spun so fast that she'd held on to her centre only to snatch her hand away once she remembered the emptiness of her belly. She contemplated her loss alongside the throbs that plagued her body since she'd swallowed Venus's medicine.

It was then that her eyes discovered the comb. She squinted at the table in her room, identifying each of her possessions and sensing the pain in her body ebbing away as a result of her fixed concentration on something else. She'd searched her room up and down after the ball and

294

that comb hadn't been there. It was strange that it should appear now, so ironic that its return was preceded by an immeasurable deficit. Yet the presence of that little ivory comb had lessened her anxiety. She thought she'd never see that gift again but there it was, blinking at her amongst the jumble of objects on the table. Whilst her other loss was a thousand times more poignant and its effects less ephemeral, it could never really be gone because her memory of it would live.

Jericho sobbed over that comb until her throat closed and her nose ran out of mucus. Until her nails drew blood from her palms. She'd fallen asleep with her friend's breath against her temple, hoping her dreams might ferry her to where her father had taken her unborn.

Jericho tried to hide her furtive glances out of the window but Penny caught them easily, having long ago catalogued all of her many expressions.

'You think he'll come back again?' Penny enquired.

'I know he will.'

Her voice held the conviction her heart lacked. She smiled at her friend, squeezing the hand that enclosed hers affectionately. She welcomed Penny's strength. It buffered her when she felt so weak and so empty. All power had been drained from her body along with the life she'd cradled and refused to acknowledge for months. Initially she'd felt invigorated when a supine energy had begun to climb back into her lithe frame. Biting back on her sorrow, she'd welcomed the colour darkening her sallow cheeks. She'd had the courage to face her destiny; finally her eyes had opened.

Now, weeks later, she wished the obeah had warned her about how different she would feel with this new awareness. She was constantly tired but terrified of sleeping, in case her dreams transported her back to the jumbled depths of Costa Lina and the unripe baby her mother had spurned. That *she* had ejected from her own body without so much as an apology or a prayer up to the heavens to govern its premature passing.

That was when she'd started to paint. Busying her fingers occupied her mind and gave her less time alone with her thoughts. Her canvases had been ominously dark at first, so much so that she wouldn't let Penny near them. But gradually, a little light shone through.

She'd dismissed the idea when Penny first mentioned painting in the village, but suddenly the prospect seemed more real. She'd developed her craft in the city, had learned how to experiment with colour and light. The paintings that normally sold in the village were more traditional but maybe she would be the one to challenge their opinions.

She thought about when she'd first met Babylon, their first conversation. He'd asked whether her work was for sale. He'd been flirting, of course, but for a moment his question had made her pastime a reality.

She couldn't determine when her feelings for him began mushrooming. They'd been growing in the dark but now they appeared to be running out of room and coming into clear view. She'd tried to ignore them because they brought with them large, parasitic guilt weeds about Daniel. About the baby. It wasn't that she wanted to forget the musician, but things would be simpler if she tried, and for the most part she was succeeding.

Although there had been one slight mishap at Manuel's. She'd obliged her mother one afternoon in case she became suspicious of her sudden agoraphobia. She braved the market crowd, imagining they all guessed her secret. Eyes downward, she accepted the jostling of more aggressive customers and sellers as worthy punishment for her crime on Wishing Day.

Her heart ballooned when she saw him in the centre of

the market. Emotions conflicted; part fear – or was it excitement? – at seeing him, when she'd wanted to go unnoticed. It was as if her determination to avoid him had drawn him out.

She wasn't ready to socialise with anyone she knew. She hadn't expected to accomplish her market run without human contact but she wasn't prepared to be challenged or, worse still, to be admired, especially after what she'd done in the orange grove. Her rudeness at their last encounter, when Daniel had been there, replayed, over-whelming her. But while she realised this, she knew there were apologies far more pressing than the one she perhaps owed him. Thankfully her feet kicked into action long before her brain. She'd allowed them to dispatch her speedily from the marketplace, far away from an awkward confrontation.

Jericho scrutinised the painting she was working on. She looked at it again with one eye closed and her paintbrush extended to guide her lines. She bit her lower lip as she imagined her mother's face on seeing it. This was the first real painting she would give her, not the childish efforts her mother had loved simply because she'd made them, the ones she knew her mother secretly dismissed as a hobby. Because of this, it was taking her longer than she'd expected and she knew Penny was getting bored with being kept in the dark until it was complete. Jericho mixed some yellow into the white paint and moved her brush gently over the canvas, satisfied at the warmth that now peeked through. The piece was important not only because it was a demonstration of her skill and her heart's desire, in terms of a profession; it was also a form of apology to her mother.

Her easel wobbled again and she looked down at its legs; one of them was undoubtedly shorter than the others. She left Penny and went back to her bedroom to find something to level it. She hunted around the room before spying some paper underneath her table. It wasn't the paper snake – that was still lying next to her crane on the table. Her eyes scanned it fleetingly, the delicate tissue paper with one torn edge. She tried to decipher the illegible scribbles but gave up and folded the paper again along its seams while heading back to the kitchen. She wedged it under the leg and tested her efforts by shaking the frame. Satisfied, she resumed her work, humming an unfamiliar song.

She sensed his car before she heard it; divining the stillness in the air before the unmistakable grumbling of its motor. She'd been too exhausted to communicate with him in those first days and sent Penny to be her mouthpiece, briefing her not to allow his entry to the house. As her mother left for work at the bakery early in the morning and there were no neighbours on either side of their compound, there was no one to witness the repeated visits.

He'd come with the rain, or maybe he'd brought it with him. The first time had been successful: Daniel hadn't breached her home. Penny had relayed the whole story scene by scene at the foot of her bed, exaggerating the encounter to will life back into Jericho's still form. Only the subtle movements of her eyes had indicated that she was still among the living. On day three, as Penny walked her friend around the house to release the pressure building up in her stomach and thighs, they'd heard his car approaching again. Friend and loyal protector, Penny had obediently headed for the door to carry out her bodyguard duties but Jericho stopped her, instructing her instead to help her into a chair. She'd run her tongue quickly over her lips and smoothed the hair at her temples in preparation. Penny opened the door to him and slipped through it quietly to leave them their privacy.

Only a steely look from Jericho kept him on her doorstep; he made no further progress into her home. Something stood between them, an incredible force that hindered his footsteps but that also kept him from dropping to her feet, the way he usually did when he needed to gain ground.

'*Cara*,' he began before drifting into silence. He removed his driver's cap and fidgeted with its brim. She'd known he was ransacking his mind for words to woo her with. A thin film of sweat broke out on her face as she waited for him to speak. She wasn't sure she had the strength yet for this confrontation.

'Are you sick?' he asked. His face leaned forward for a closer inspection of her countenance, but his feet remained planted in the same spot.

'*Ewo*, I've been better. What do you want?'

He'd stumbled over his words, intimidated by her steely look. He sensed the change in her, the front she was projecting to stop his endearments from penetrating, and didn't know how to combat it.

'I wanted to apologise for my behaviour the other day.' Her look of disbelief caused him to stammer. He'd obviously hoped that she would overlook his weeks of silence. 'I mean, when we last spoke . . . I told your friend . . .' His words trailed off as he realised that Penny had no doubt already conveyed his message and more besides.

'Jericho, I was wrong to imply that . . . I mean, I was wrong to question your honour.'

He waited for her to react, for her features to soften and for her to wave her arms in his direction so that he could cover them with kisses, but she stayed firm behind the wall she'd erected.

'You finish?'

She waited for him to shape words out of the emptiness in front of him. He implored her with his face but got no response.

'I don't want to lose you, *Coco*. If you're carrying my child, we'll work it out. I'll talk to my father again. Make Papa see sense. We'll deal with it together,' he said softly.

'Really? Thank you for your timely concern, but don't worry yourself. I've already dealt with it.' Her words tripped off her tongue.

'What are you saying?' His eyes narrowed.

'What do you think I'm saying?'

'You're not pregnant?' His tone was high but his hat still twirled in his nervous fingers.

'Not any more.'

She'd averted her eyes, choosing to look at her ashy feet. Once, she would have been mortified to face her *nonno* in an unkempt state. Now she didn't care. When she looked up, she found him staring somewhere over her head. The guilt her words had produced in him wouldn't allow him to look her in the eyes. The knowledge energised her and she felt warmth creep into her vacant bones.

'I don't know what to say,' Daniel said, embarrassed.

'Maybe you should come back when you do.'

She got up dramatically on her heel and retreated as quickly as her convalescing body would allow. In the safety of her room, she listened for the sound of the back door opening and closing.

But he'd returned. Every single day after that at almost the same hour, he'd returned. The first couple of days after their conversation he'd said little but proffered gifts to appease her: exotic linens with hand-stitched embroidery; little chocolates in the shape of little doves. Penny pored over the treasures after his departure, draping expensive fabrics over her clothes and parading around Jericho's home. But while Penny's foolishness amused her, Jericho's laughter always faded quickly. Her resolve was weakening; she and Penny knew it.

300

The day before, Daniel had changed his tactics. They'd both been disappointed when they hadn't detected the distinctive sounds of his engine rattling down the road outside her home. Jericho downplayed her let-down but she knew Penny felt it. They spent the day not talking about his absence and because they weren't expecting to hear his car in the night, they hadn't registered the sound when it approached.

Her mother had entered the kitchen with an expression Jericho hadn't seen on her face in years. In fact, she could have sworn her mother's cheeks were flushed, and not with the usual fatigue that pinched her features after a day's hard toil at the bakery. Her mother moved fluidly with the sacks of groceries she carried and Penny had run to help her.

'Eh, Auntie! Why didn't you tell me you wanted to buy things? You know I would have gone for you.'

'It's okay, Penny, you are a good daughter, you will marry well. Anyway, I didn't walk far. I got a lift.'

She brought the last bag in and stood awkwardly by the doorway. They'd wanted to peer around her but her mother's body blocked most of the opening. They saw her wave into the darkness and heard a horn sound in return before the engine purred into the distance.

'A fine young man,' her mother enthused before drinking a glass of water and running the empty cup down her neck to cool herself. 'Pity.' She pursed her lips. 'It's a real shame. We don't breed villagers like that any more.'

At the sound of the car horn they both jumped and lit up like candles for separate reasons. However much Jericho fought it, Daniel's persistence temporarily dulled her pain, while Penny was enjoying the drama of the situation.

Penny ran to hide in the bedroom while Jericho positioned herself at the table. Daniel knocked boldly at the door and

301

she shouted for him to enter. He smiled at her, now well accustomed to her frosty reception. She couldn't help noticing that he seemed restless today, charged with renewed vigour. He approached her cautiously, as he'd done in the days before. When he arrived within a few feet of her, he knelt down. She followed his movement, opening her mouth to speak but rapidly deciding against it. Jericho's heart didn't stop as he searched his pocket to retrieve another present that she would accept in silence like she had all the others. But it did when he extracted a velvet string-purse slowly and held it out to her. Her eyes narrowed as he opened it to reveal a ring shinier than a phosphorous moon.

'What happened?' Penny squealed against the roar of the motor as Daniel sped away. She'd run from her hiding place as soon as she heard the door slam.

'See for yourself,' Jericho replied, sliding the blue purse across the table to her.

It took three glasses of water to wake Penny up after she fainted.

Driver hated to drink by himself. He didn't like to be alone with his thoughts, especially as alcohol had a way of putting a slant on them. It was early so there weren't many people inside Borrow's bar. Still, he kept a watch on the door in case Babylon entered. That way he could make a swift getaway until his friend was ready to apologise.

He wasn't mad at Babylon per se, but it annoyed him the way the musician acted as if he was the only one that had suffered the blows of love. At least *he* got to experience it. The Creator knew – some men were still trying.

Hamid raised a glass in his direction before draining the drink and leaving. Driver looked around him; there were some new faces inside Borrow's. From the cut of the clothing, or more particularly, the fact that their clothes weren't cut, or sullied or re-stitched, he knew they were outsiders. He'd also seen a spectacular car parked outside Borrow's and had stopped to shine his teeth in the reflection.

If his friend were here, they might have heckled the strangers for a card game, knowing their pockets would be fat with coins, not matchsticks like their own people. But since he was alone, he kept his distance, content that nobody was bothering anyone else.

One of the musicians, not really much competition for his friend, played the guitar while his friend accompanied him on the flute. The music wasn't great but it helped the millet to slide down his throat and it was enough to make Corál poke her head round from the back before coming to watch them play. Driver felt his sweet potato twitch, suddenly grateful for the thick table that hid his lower half. They hadn't had much contact since the festival, but he remembered her smell, it teased his nostril hairs as it soared towards his brain and created pictures of their tangled bodies in his mind.

Corál's entry coincided with a large disturbance on the table of foreigners and he watched a fury of back-slapping break out among the men. He assumed they were celebrating. Some of the men stood to circle the musicians, clapping their hands offbeat – not that they knew it. One man – he looked slightly familiar but Driver couldn't place him – rose to join his friends in front of the musicians. He signalled to Borrow, who nodded his head. The man moved towards the right side of the bar and plucked an object off the wall. It had hung there as long as Driver could remember and he'd assumed it was an artefact of some kind. If it was an instrument, no one had ever attempted to play it.

The man placed it on the table and stood behind it. The

303

musicians watched him but weren't deterred by his proximity, even though his friends had begun to clap double time. He shrugged his sleeves back and began to play the thumb piano. *Well*. The guitarist stopped playing and threw him a look of approval before the jamming continued. The man smiled and closed his eyes as he continued to master that wooden board with its metal keys that were staggered like Nbira's teeth, the poor bell ringer who could never close his mouth properly.

Driver looked over at Corál, who was concentrating intensely as she watched the men. Disappointment lanced his chest. In a village with competitors like his friend, and visitors like the man playing, there was no way he stood a chance with someone as beautiful as the waitress. He should have paid more attention to Magdalena, before she'd noticed Babylon.

The music accelerated as if the players were engaged in a race, reaching a spectacular crescendo. They all lifted their instruments to the ceiling when they finished and clapped each other while drinking in the applause from the scanty group that watched. The man on the thumb piano accepted the embraces of his friends and returned the instrument to the wall. He shared a quick joke with Borrow, then reached over the narrow bar to kiss the man on the cheek.

'A drink for all of you!' he cried, waving his hand to everyone he could see. His friends brayed liked hyenas and raised their glasses, looking for service.

'What would you like?' Corál's question startled Driver.
'Sorry?'

'The man offer a free drink. What do you want?'

'Oh. Another beer. Please.' He smiled sheepishly at her and watched her bottom as she walked away from him. She stopped at a few tables to get people's orders and then went to the bar.

Driver plotted different conversation starters in his mind while surreptitiously watching her assembling the new drinks. She returned, balancing a tray, which she placed on his table to pour his beer.

'You liked the show?' he asked.

'It was good, eh? Who knew people could play so? But don't tell your friend,' she giggled.

'No I won't,' he replied, suddenly crestfallen. 'I know he take your fancy . . .'

She gave him a look he couldn't decipher.

'*Babylon?* Please,' she laughed. 'That was a long time ago, but my interest for him done pass. Now I have a fancy for someone else. Someone close.' She smiled.

'Oh.' He wanted her to leave so he could down the beer she'd poured. Then he could look around the bar for the object of her affection.

'Take this.' She slid a plate of yam covered with palm oil along with a meat pie off the tray and on to his table, grazing his fingers along the way. 'No charge,' she winked, stealing a quick look for her boss who was in the back. With her free hand, she pointed at the man who'd played the piano. 'I put it on Dorique account!'

Dr Poniche held Magdalena's hand loosely as he timed her pulse, unaware that its racing had more to do with his proximity than the illness she'd endured. She'd been decidedly unsettled since waking from her coma. Although her matriarchs hadn't sought his counsel before, they all knew who Mr Mapicchu was – Mannobe's senior physician with so many years' medical experience under his belt: a man who'd forgotten more over time than he currently knew. When the man now at her bedside had presented himself as the doctor, Magdalena had been understandably confused; first that he'd gained entry to Le Papillon despite the presence of her mother and aunt in the room, and secondly, that the man staring at her wasn't the proprietor of the halitosis and sprouting nostril hair that best described Mapicchu, but an extremely handsome gentleman who looked no more than ten years her elder. Poniche had promptly explained his presence in Mannobe; he'd been sent from Lugobiville as a temporary replacement for the old doctor. He explained at great length that it in no way reflected on his elder's skill, whose misdiagnoses were usually dismissed as quirky faux pas. But, apparently, a strange woman had delivered a cake to Mr Mapicchu on Biko's Eve as payment for a service, and her kindness had left the good doctor latrine-bound ever since.

Poniche made his visits to the café every morning to check that her fever had completely broken. In the beginning, Magdalena had been battling some delirium that manifested itself in her trying to remove various items of his clothing. Her mother and aunt had been there to assist him in extracting her tentacles from his outer garments. On his third call, however, M'elle was occupied with the task of feeding the masses that had taken shelter during the rain and demanded her mother's help in appeasing their hungry house guests. Magdalena was in bed taking shallow sips of air into her chest as he approached, her expression becoming more animated when she saw him. He called out her name brightly, then repeated it in the form of a question until she acknowledged him verbally. But when he tried to place the small wooden spatula inside her mouth to analyse her tongue, she'd gagged dramatically, releasing more and more phlegm. He withdrew a small handkerchief to remove the ghastly sight and this kind movement set her off, so she'd resumed her previous assault on his clothing. Luckily, he was able to distract her long enough to inject a syringe into her hip and she released her hold on him slowly. Before slumping into her dreams she spoke so softly her voice was barely audible.

His brain must have intercepted it where his aural canal had failed.

'I'm sorry. This is not me.'

She fell asleep quickly, oblivious to his tender touch as he wiped her face free of its emissions.

Her remarkable recovery was attributed to the prayers of the throng currently occupying the café. Candles lined the path to her room, and voices could be heard singing into the early hours of the morning, praying for an end to the tireless rain as much as the well-being of Miss Codón. Try as she could, Magdalena remembered very little of the events that had rendered her bed-bound, but with the advent of Dr Poniche, she could think of no place she would rather be.

Her friend Tebo had paid her a visit, uttering the musician's name softly as she introduced it into their dialogue, but Magdalena remained unaffected. No wound had resurfaced requiring emergency surgery at his mention. It was as though she'd been transported from the previous melancholy that had eaten her alive. She slept deeply, longing for night to bring forth the day so that she could gaze into the watery depths of the doctor's eyes as he observed her vital signs. When her speech returned fully, she begged little stories of him, some flesh to add to the skeleton of his physical features. She longed to turn him into a man, for him to become real to her, not just her professional consultant. Soon, the woman in her noticed that his café visits were consuming greater amounts of his time. Now, he warmed his hands carefully before checking her pulse. Also, when he'd checked it a few days earlier, their eyes met for what seemed like an eternity. Then he'd apologised and had to begin his count again.

'When are you going back to Lugobiville?' she asked with her eyes steadfast on the window to deflect her avid interest in his response.

'I don't know,' the doctor replied in his mixed accent. 'I was annoyed when I was first sent over here. Rumours are that Mapicchu is ready to retire and looking for a replacement, even though the position pays less than the Lugobiville post. But this place is growing on me, I feel like I've been here before. You know what I mean?'

Poniche looked to her for comprehension and she nodded knowingly. 'Yesterday, for instance, I was on my way to deliver a child outside Costa Lina when my tyre burst in a pothole. I got out of the van, I could barely see – the way it was coming down last night – but my feet knew exactly where they were going. It was as if they'd experienced the journey before.'

They gasped at the same time, watching the thick grey clouds congregating in the sky. His finger touched hers where they rested on her bed. Even after they both realised, he didn't move his away.

'I suppose your family would miss you if you didn't return?' she enquired hopefully.

'I have no more family.' Although he smiled she caught the sadness behind it.

The doctor cleared his throat and offered her the story of his childhood. He'd been adopted when he was younger. He was raised in Taro before settling in Lugobiville and all the family he'd known had passed over. His adopted father had been a doctor, but his choice of profession had been solidified when his younger brother had died as a result of their childhood antics. Poniche had pushed his brother down as they were chasing each other around the compound. When he fell, he'd impaled himself on a nail that left a putrid hole in his toe. Fearing their father's chastisement more than the injury, they'd kept the accident hidden. They'd been unconscious of the fragility of his brother's blood; different to the blood that Poniche carried in his veins. A few mornings later when his mother had asked him to wake up his brother, he discovered that he couldn't.

His memory didn't evoke any sadness when he shared it, and it was the most natural thing in the world that his fingers should brush away the pulsing in her right temple after he'd told her the story.

'Since you were adopted,' she teased lightly, 'perhaps you were born in Mannobe before you moved? It's possible.'

'Yes,' he agreed readily. 'It's possible. For my heart appears to beat to your time.'

On witnessing Magdalena's recovery, Mabel wondered whether she should have diverted some of her commissioned prayers to Waranga because they had clearly worked. She wasn't concerned that her daughter had transferred her affections to another man, even one from the medical profession, in her eyes more questionable than Babylon's profession of musician. Mabel was simply relieved that her daughter appeared to be reverting to her normal countenance. In fact, peace radiated a beauty in Magdalena none of them had witnessed before.

Babylon had nestled himself at a corner table in Borrow's bar and was steadily drowning his sorrows. Although his black mood could be blamed on the obeah's prediction, he couldn't hold her wholly responsible for his flagging spirits.

The place was dead apart from the So-So brothers, two touring musicians who answered every yes–no question religiously with the words 'so so'. Borrow kept the drinks flowing, seamlessly interpreting Babylon's nods and finger gestures that indicated changes to his alcohol consumption. There was nobody around to start a card game with – the So-So brothers being renowned cheats – so he toyed with the deck by himself. But each card he turned over reminded him of the five of swords and of Venus. Scattering the cards on the floor, he dropped his head on the table and began to doze. Borrow wouldn't disturb him about the strewn cards; well, not unless he refused to pick them up after his nap.

'These poor people don't understand politics. They are all enemies of progress. Take this Waranga business for example.'

'It's a difficult issue. It's their land . . .'

'It's not an issue! It's business. Tell me, how many Mannobans have ever been up there? You think they can even spell Waranga? Yet they must protest because that is their only power.'

'I know, but—'

'But nothing. Cutting trees will create jobs. No more meatless swallow day after day! They'll be able to build better houses – not those nonsense ones where you blow your nose and the roof disappears. But all villagers want to do is complain. It makes me sick.'

Snatches of conversation bored tiny holes into his dreams like word-rain flooding his rest as Babylon allowed his ears to stir before his eyes. The words seemed more elevated than animated, but their pitch inside his Sting-clogged brain was causing him great discomfort. He imagined he'd inhaled a fly during his sleep and it was still somewhere inside his skull, searching for an exit. He prised his eyes open cautiously, making out the shapes assembled around the card table. At least things were picking up inside Borrow's. Maybe some money in his pockets would brighten his decidedly gloomy future.

He lifted his head and swayed when the blood redistributed itself into the appropriate places. He prised his tongue off the roof of his mouth with a popping sound. It alerted the other table to his awakened state and a gaggle of eyes shifted in his direction. Most of them sized him up before reverting to their covered hands. All except one. A look of recognition flew between them on scarlet wings and Babylon averted his eyes from Daniel's beady ones and proceeded to gather the cards he'd flung to the floor earlier. Suddenly he had no desire at all to be at Borrow's.

Daniel left the table, heading in the direction of the latrine. As he knelt on the ground to gather up the discarded deck, Babylon watched him, yelping as the pain in his arm fought for his attention. He reached for the last card and had just wrapped his long fingers around its tip when the remainder of it disappeared under an impeccably polished shoe. His eyes moved from the moccasin over the dark linen trousers and then the jacket until he was staring up at the feline features of the Dorique.

Daniel smiled down from his height advantage, a sneer which rendered his features all the more feminine.

'Excuse me,' Babylon growled.

'Oh, I'm sorry,' Daniel chirped. 'I'm not accustomed to looking beneath me.'

Daniel smeared his shoe across the card before releasing it and Babylon retrieved it slowly, righting himself. He towered over the city man as he stood to his full height.

'No harm done, *non*?'

Daniel flared crimped nostrils at him and Borrow, sensing trouble between the new card players and his regular, coughed loudly behind the bar, making his presence felt. One of Daniel's companions pulled on his jacket and ushered him back to the game, and Babylon left his table to sit by the bar. Borrow handed him a bottle of brew, capping it expertly with the inside of his elbow, and Babylon drained the bottle, trying to let the bubbles quell his foul humour. He wondered how Jericho could be enamoured of such a buffoon.

311

His head ached. His hair felt like coiled springs leaking rusty metal into his bloodstream. Every part of his body was tense, ready to strike. Everyone was right. Guitar, Driver, even Venus Oracene. Maybe Jericho was troublesome. Maybe at this time in his life, peace was what he needed.

He settled his tab and was preparing to leave when he picked up a loose thread of their conversation. Daniel was pulling on the end of it and surreptitiously drawing him over to their table – he knew – but he couldn't help himself.

'You see, that's the thing about village girls. They're so eager to please they'll believe anything.' He looked over the table at Babylon as he spoke, his eyes flashing from generations of superiority over peasants like the one before him. Babylon got down from Borrow's high stool to a standing position.

'What about Lara?' one of the table occupants asked.

'In Darkloof with her family. If the two of them are separated I see no reason for either of them to open their mouths and complain. It's simply a matter of editing the truth. And if my little jungle-cat still wants to fight, I have plenty to keep her satisfied.'

Daniel tugged on his belt suggestively and the table rumbled with undignified braying that mellowed to a quiet hubbub as Babylon approached, with the exception of Daniel who was banging his hand on the table to complement his laughter. He raised his head to Babylon in query.

'I don't think you should speak about women like that.' He heard the anger in his own voice as he cautioned Jericho's *nonno*.

'Was I speaking to you?' Daniel looked from Babylon to his friends around the table. 'I was just minding my own business and talking to my friends. *Abeg-oh*, this no be your concern. Besides, do you see any women here? I

312

don't.' Daniel shrugged, looking around his table for complicity. Borrow had moved from the shelter of the bar towards the percolating trouble.

'You know what I'm talking about,' Babylon's voice boomed, annihilating any subordination from the group. But Daniel was impervious to hints.

'Ah okay, you mean Miss Lwembe?' he asked innocently.

'Yes, Miss Lwembe.'

'Okay! You're quite right, I'm sorry.'

Daniel held his hands up in an act of mock contrition and seemingly dropped the conversation. Suitably appeased, Babylon turned away from their table. He was moving towards the door when he heard Jericho's *nonno* snigger.

'He definitely wasn't talking about a *lady* then, let me tell you—'

Although Borrow reached the table with remarkable speed for a man of his size, it was too late. Babylon's fist had already connected with the Dorique chin, dislodging the other's tooth with the ferocity of the blow. Everybody that heard the noise his punch made on impact assumed it was Daniel's face crumpling as he fell backwards clutching his jaw, trying to catch the blood that spouted from it like a tap. But they were wrong.

For while Daniel's cheek had indeed imploded, another more sinister casualty had also occurred. That crisp sound, distinctive as the snapping of wood, was really that of bone splitting, ligaments tearing, and arteries repositioning themselves inside the musician's hand; the damage to his arm irrevocable.

Sixteen

Allegory viewed his reflection in the creek. He'd stopped bathing there recently, after noticing a metallic tinge in the water that tasted like blood; it held a sadness that unnerved him. He bent down to inspect himself properly, pleased with what he saw. He was decked out in his finest regalia, a clumsy one-piece tunic that resembled a pair of cropped dungarees, completely fashioned from African pine. It was one of the by-products of his recurring insomnia: the intricate weaving relaxed him whenever he couldn't sleep.

He tugged carefully at an overhang near his crotch before tidying the bundle of dreads masquerading as hair on his head. Satisfied with his appearance, he set off in the direction of the Eternal Compound. He whistled a tune as he mentally prepared his farewell speech for Mama Abandela. Part of him was grateful that she'd departed before the village acceded to the future's will. He wasn't sure she would have sat comfortably in the new Mannobe. Too many changes upset the old.

Funerals were a colourful time in the village, regardless of who had passed over to the other side. Some attended only to ogle the body as the priest placed red poinsettias on the deceased's eyes, pressing some seeds into their palm to spark the reincarnation process after burial. But mostly, people came to pay their respects.

Mannobans were reluctant to refer to their place of worship as a church. They preferred to consider it as a spirit house, in keeping with their ancestors' language and their belief that those who passed over left their essence there. It was indeed a house full of spirits. The wooden structure was dark on the inside, which kept the interior a much needed cool for their lengthy assemblies. Large banyan branches had been woven together to form the complicated latticework of the high ceiling. The walls were also made of a mixture of wood, although portions had been cemented over time to halt nature's assault on the old edifice. There were carefully placed holes in the walls that housed the candles and incense lit during the sermons, and a few chairs in the front, facing the altar, for elderly members of the congregation who might never rise again were they asked to sit on the floor. A sprinkling of bamboo mats lined the remaining ground for people to sit on. The wooden doors at each side were left open during assemblies to allow for cross-ventilation on days when occupancy was near capacity.

Funerals never took place in the covered part of the spirit house but were reserved for the annexe outside, the open space next to the burial plots. People assembled under the wide bamboo canopy erected after a senior elder was buried in the Eternal Compound during a tireless rain. They'd resolved after that to make some essential improvements to their place of worship.

Villagers chatted and nodded vigorously in Mama's remembrance, tutting at the life no longer. After the rain that assaulted them for weeks on end, half-naked children were giddy with delight at their newly found freedom and held their hands skyward as if to cradle a lemony sun. Mannobe crackled with energy, a veritable manifestation of life, despite the fact that they were congregated to lay one of their own to rest for eternity.

Mama Abandela, the cantankerous old gem from Halome, had outlasted the bitter rainfall, according to her eldest son; the only one with skin thick enough to be impervious to the many lashings of her tongue. But the very first day the sun had finally pierced through the clouds, banishing them from the sky, she'd sneezed theatrically. He moved to fetch a shawl for her shoulders but she raised her hand to stop him. Then, scrunching up her face as if to avoid sneezing again, she'd held her breath and never released it. The sight was so enthralling he'd stared at her for half an hour, poised in her chair with that grotesque expression, before running for the doctor.

Nevertheless, Mama had had a good innings. It was widely believed that acrimony was the preservative that kept her going as long as she had, well after her husband's passing in his early sixties.

Allegory feasted on funerals the way most did on weddings. Butterflies effervesced in his belly, and he was always craning his neck for a better look at the deceased. Most Mannobans dressed in white as befitted the occasion, but they had long since accepted the madman's eccentricities, and since his pine costume was of a pale yellow hue, it was not altogether inappropriate.

Mama was encased in white cloth, ready for the public viewing. Father Lovewell – also known as Holy Moses – smoothed the grimace from her caustic features so as not to frighten the young children eager for a glimpse at death. Observers separated for Allegory to pass through them and he positioned himself by the less ornate outdoor altar, his unofficial station at these ceremonies. Only Mama separated him from the priest. Allegory sat cross-legged, patiently waiting for his turn to address the crowd, and went over his alternative closing several times, his teeth clicking together like prayer beads.

'It brings me joy to see so many of you out here today,' Father Lovewell began. 'We come here to bless the spirit of our departed angel, Irene Abandela. Mama was a memorable woman . . .'

As the priest spoke – his gentle voice oscillating through the people gathered – several heads in the crowd bowed in grief. Her eldest son was called forward to cover her face with the remainder of the cloth. His sorrow-filled tears dislodged the flowers from her eyes, delaying the ceremony considerably as he fought to reposition the poinsettias and still his hands long enough to wrap her properly.

Once she was completely bound like a pharaoh, the priest invited the crowd forward. As he was the closest to her, Allegory was the first to press his lips against the dry cloth that covered her. With his spindly leg poking out of his wooden jumpsuit, he looked like a life-size insect feasting on a humungous cocoon. After the conflicted procession of mourners – those stricken with sorrow and those celebrating another of life's transitions – had paid their respects, Allegory silenced the hum resonating from them with a sweep of his wiry arm.

'The Creator will wipe away tears from off all faces. For whosoever believeth should not perish.'

Heads nodded in tacit agreement with the self-appointed prophet. He surveyed his people with a penetrating look, knotting their chests with faith. He conjured Abandela up with words, clothing her in her infrequently worn garments of charity and compassion, eroding the memory of her brittle bark and unaffectionate manner. He placed his hands over her body while he spoke, as if he was a mere conduit for what she herself wished to impart before returning to the earth and the universe.

317

'Mark the perfect man, and behold the upright: for the end of that man is peace,' he continued, his voice growing deeper and his words more pronounced with the scriptures he extolled. 'My flesh and my heart faileth: but the Creator is the strength of my heart, and my portion for ever. Neither death, nor life, nor angels, nor things present, nor things to come, nor any other creature shall be able to separate us.'

His voice broke off after he'd serenaded the crowd with a shower of spit. He saw Mama's family swooning after his sermon, the tears on her son's face dried so that his cheeks appeared taut, with only two grey tracks marking where they had been. Male members of the crowd were called upon to lift her from the wooden stretcher where she lay, and with Allegory taking the helm and the priest her feet, they shuffled towards the hole waiting in the earth. A moment's silence was granted after Peon, the gravedigger, and his apprentice covered her with the red clay of Mannobe soil along with the sweat from their glistening limbs following their hard labour.

From the sighs and hollow cheeks of the attendees, Allegory was satisfied that Mama had received a good service. Even those who merely tolerated him at the best of times cherished his performances at the Eternal Compound. Whilst Father Lovewell's wisdom was invaluable and his position necessary in the village, Allegory knew he had a way of transporting them to loftier spiritual planes, so that they floated high above the sadness they were supposed to feel.

The air was pregnant with the smell of harvest. Farmers, called prematurely from their dreams, combed the fields during unheavenly hours of the morning, stoically unearthing their crops with cobwebs of sleep still clinging to the corners of their eyes. Allegory soaked up the view of the field-workers as if it was the oxygen he needed for survival. He plucked a tomato from a cluster growing nearby, relishing the plumpness of the fruit and its salty aftertaste. It reminded him of the skin on Mabel's neck; elsewhere she tasted of cocoa beans and pears. But he didn't want to think about Mabel because inside her he saw M'elle, and inside M'elle he saw a palpable grief that he didn't know how to assuage, that he was afraid to be swept away by.

He let his feet dictate his journey and walked through the moist tenderness of the morning, smiling as his internal compass steered him in the direction of the Ten Rivers. A shiver crept up his neck and his ears pricked. He marched quicker now, his eyes seeking out what his gut felt. As he approached the agate water, he saw a bundle in the mass of reeds immersed in the quickening current. Nearing it, he realised it was a body. Allegory reached down to pull it out of the water properly. Sweeping the hair from its face, he waited until he saw the gentle movement of the man's nostrils as they drew air into his sleeping chest. The fist around his heart unclenched, and he relaxed finally. For the second time, he'd rescued his charge.

Jericho sat motionless on the bank of the creek. The damp soil cooled her bottom but she couldn't be bothered to move. She dangled her feet in the water and felt tiny ripples working their way through her toes. The paper in her hand remained blank, the pen untouched. She allowed her tears to join the creek at her feet, a union of water, remembering. The emptiness that clawed at her insides and threatened to bore a hole in her stomach was bigger than the loss of her child. In that moment, she realised that she missed him. It had crept up on her so slyly that she hadn't been aware of it, and now that she was she mourned his absence. She'd begun to rely on his attendance and adoration the way one takes each breath or sunset for granted, assuming the presence of another inevitable.

She had to return, to deliver her answer on her terms. To reclaim Angel for herself – independent from the memories of men. But it had been stained with the memory of Babylon's company on her last journey into the city. She'd seen his sinewy shoulders on every street corner. His face was in every child she saw walking the streets unaccompanied.

She'd turned her head, double-taking at every dread-locked hairline, subconsciously scouring the city for him. She hadn't allowed herself to admit that she liked him until now, in her quiet communion with nature. A family of clouds temporarily hijacked the ruby sun, bathing her in darkness. In the sudden coolness she remembered why she'd come here. She retrieved the pen from her side and held it over the paper, willing her hand to voice her thoughts. Her wrist glided along slowly in determined strokes, and she moved her hand aside to see what she'd written. The two words repeated, staring back at her: I'm sorry, I'm sorry, I'm sorry. Gripping the paper's edge with her fingertips, she allowed the wind to carry it away and watched it wistfully as it skated on the water before sinking into its shallow depths. She left the creek for home, wondering how long it would take to feel its forgiveness.

As Claudia pored over the squabble in Mannobe again, Jericho found her affections secretly divided about the fracas between her two duelling suitors, and decided it best to keep quiet. She knew from experience that her friend would interrogate her mercilessly until she broke down. Claudia embellished the fight between the two men, so that in her version Daniel's gums had stuck together, vacant of all his teeth, which Babylon now wore around his neck as a memento.

She realised how long it had been since she'd truly laughed, inwardly, not just arranging her external appearance so as not to alert anyone to the true feelings cowering

320

underneath. For so long she'd been pretending to be someone else; sliding into the painting everyone had etched of
her likeness. When the paints had dried, she'd been stuck
there, powerless to change the image from the inside, until
Venus had blown her eyelids off with that herbal remedy.

It could even have begun before then.

She tried to think back to a time when she'd experienced
a true emotion, and a catalogue of events, all incorporating
the musician in some form or another, fell open in the back
of her mind, its pages turning rapidly with the chill accompanying the recognition.

She was grateful that Claudia had broached the subject;
she couldn't have invoked his name without her features
giving her away.

'Why are you asking me? I haven't seen him much since
he gave me a lift back to the village,' she replied haughtily.

Claudia eyed her suspiciously before heaving a sigh.

'Really? Such a pity. He was very nice, you know?'

'Please. The musician?' she moaned, excited yet anxious
all the same.

'So what? What's wrong with that?'

'Nothing. It's not—'

'Babylon's a real man,' Claudia enthused. 'He's not
afraid to embrace life. He has no airs, graces, he's a man in
the most natural sense of the word, just existing.'

'Bush meat . . .' Jericho joked weakly, regretting the
words as soon as she said them. She knew they didn't
mirror her thoughts, she'd been referring more to his atti-
tude than his status, but it was as if her tongue could only
speak ill of him, if only in denial.

'You're so spoilt, Coco. *Eh*, you're from the same place!
What has Daniel, non-peasant that he is, ever done to
you?' Claudia waited for her response, but she bent her
head into her chest, using that as a welcome excuse to say
nothing. '*Eh-heh*. Exactly,' Claudia continued, vindicated.

'Did Daniel pedal all the way here from Mannobe for you to find your *nonno*? Or fight a man for you? Remember – he even sold your painting! Ignorant so-and-so . . . At least the musician knows how to love. *Pues*, he can certainly kiss, *eh*?'

Jericho propped her chin against her collarbone to disguise the blush working its way up to her eyebrows. The sweat on her scalp was already crinkling the hot-press they'd laboured over for an hour. She refused to confirm Babylon's orificial prowess. She didn't want her friend to know she was an official member of his harem, and she certainly didn't want to share the warmth the memory gave her at this time. She would revel in its heat, a quiet bubbling in her swadhisthana chakra, alone.

She left Claudia and made her way to Yalla's for a welcome break. Claudia was precious to her, yes, but there was only so long she could listen to her friend's bright voice or live in her borrowed clothes. Her stay there had only really been prolonging the inevitable. Sooner or later she would have to take hold of the reins and steer her life instead of always being dictated to by it.

If there was one thing Jericho was good at, it was making decisions. Making decisions showed strength of mind. Carrying out decisions, however, required a strength of character that failed even her from time to time. She'd wanted to see a world bigger than her village and one-storey houses so she'd gone to the city. She'd wanted to rid her womb of the cells multiplying inside and so she'd been to see Venus. She'd wanted to procrastinate about whether to accept Daniel's proposal, so she had.

She was happy to come to a decision about becoming more proactive, so long as she didn't have to actually *do* anything. To do something would mean being willing to accept the blame if that something didn't work out to her

322

liking, and blame was what other people were for. Yes, in her heart she'd wanted the child nestled under her heartbeat out of her belly, but really it was Oracene who had seen to that, not her.

Without the drama of Daniel, Angel had been different. It wasn't the first time she'd noticed the absence of greenery but it was the first time it affected her. She'd also been struck by the people's reserve compared to Babylon's outpouring of energy. Buildings that threatened to block out the sky. They were so impressive before. Now, they were industry obstructing nature.

Gone was the thrilling perspective, or maybe it had never been there, and she was seeing the city as it really was for the first time. With that realisation, she acknowledged that she'd been doing her home town a disservice – viewing Mannobe with visitor's eyes ever since her return. Physically she'd gone home, but mentally she hadn't accepted that reality. She'd been waiting for Daniel to take her away. Life in Angel had always been intended as a temporary move, a way of stretching her legs before accepting the position society had mapped out for a young woman. She hadn't anticipated meeting a man who would shake up her universe. But even if he had, that didn't mean that she had to blindly accept his world. Surely she could shape her own, even within the constraints of the village?

She was taken aback when Daniel showed up outside Yalla's. The feeling was quickly followed by disappointment and fear; fear because she knew he'd come for an answer and wouldn't leave until he received it. She watched him, pacing outside the store with the sun setting behind him, the hem of his white trousers just skimming his woven sandals. For a moment, he looked exactly as he had the first time he'd ever come to visit her, clutching an armful of flowers.

She touched her hair absently as she greeted him, more

for courage than to see whether the style was still in place. Daniel wiped his palms on his trousers: she took it as a sign that he was nervous, which reassured her. He smiled awkwardly, aware of his lost tooth. He hadn't yet acclimatised to the gap created by the musician. Her eyes concentrated on the hole, delighted. The absence of one little tooth had totally transformed his features. His teeth were once a row of diamonds, but now the setting was awry. He was no longer beautiful. She made a face and he closed his mouth instinctively.

'Hi, I'm Daniel,' he joked, shrugging his sloping shoulders.

'Hello,' she replied.

'I've been looking for you.'

'*Ewo*, I'm here.'

He seemed encouraged by her response, as if her words marked the return of someone he recognised as opposed to the lacklustre woman that had ignored his best efforts in Mannobe. She crossed her arms casually, strengthened by the manner in which he looked at her. It made her feel feminine; it was a sensation that had escaped her since her womb fell silent.

'Have you given any thought to what I said?' he asked boldly.

'You didn't actually say anything, as I remember it.'

Her courage grew with each breath. She was amused by his discomfort. As she toyed with him she wondered what her final answer would be, were he to ask her again. Properly. He always seemed so composed, but now he reminded her of Babylon's infantile attempts to get her attention when she came back home for the festival.

'You know. My proposal.'

'*Okay*, your proposal,' she echoed. 'When would that be, exactly?'

'When?'

'Yes, Daniel. What date? When are you planning for us to get married?'

'*Pues*, what I'm thinking is this . . . Why don't we . . . I mean, there's no hurry, now that you're not—' He stopped himself abruptly, knowing the only natural destination for such a sentence, and although she flinched she didn't attack. They stood quietly for a few moments. He took a couple of steps towards her, touching her shoulder tentatively like a cat deciding whether its paws were on friendly terrain. 'I mean there's no rush, *non*?'

'*Vero*,' she replied slowly. 'Sometimes, Daniel, in life you get what you want before you realise that you don't want it again.'

'What gibberish are you talking?' He looked at her, confused.

Jericho felt her confidence slipping and thought quickly of another angle from which to approach him. His probing energy encroached on her space, making her uncomfortable, and she wondered why she hadn't noticed this before. Perhaps it hadn't been like this, she told herself. Maybe he too had been changed by life.

On Yalla's archaic steps they seemed worlds apart. Sporting his new, altered teeth *he* looked like the pauper. Even in her favourite wrapper she carried herself like a city girl. Suddenly Daniel looked foreign in her landscape; he didn't blend in with the steps, the small shop window with the magenta dress hanging from two nails inside, the rickety staircase with the peeling paint leading to her small room. Not so long ago she'd longed for the security and the life he could provide. Now she wanted him gone. She remembered how lonely she'd been one morning when she'd woken up in his bed and he wasn't beside her. As she'd pottered through the vast house, the rooms that had seemed so elaborate the night before looked empty and unloved because they were unlived in. They were only there for show. She'd longed for her home town then, Mannobe, where you could tell where everyone was simply by closing your eyes and listening. You could call a name out loud and it would echo back almost as soon as you'd opened your mouth – the village was so small.

She smiled to herself and he mirrored her action. Watching his expression change, she realised that she didn't want him. For a brief moment, he'd allowed her to be someone else, and she hadn't stopped to question why the real her wasn't enough in the city. But it was only through that pretence that she'd been awakened to who she really was, who she wanted to be.

All she could remember now was the familiarity of home, and the unbending loyalty of loved ones, of family. Her thoughts went to her mother, the day before, before she'd run to catch the bus to the city. The noise she made had evidently disturbed her mother's sleep and she'd entered Jericho's room with an irritated expression. Jericho had finished the painting she'd been working on the night before and knew it was the time to give it to her. She'd watched her mother rub the sleep from her eyes, her arms coming up to grip the canvas that was held out to her. Breath held as she waited for her mother's reaction.

She'd modelled her childhood mother on herself, changing the mouth slightly so that her mother's more generous bottom lip was present along with her eyes that were set further apart than Jericho's own. The scar, partially hidden by her hairline, evident. In the painting, the wedding dress was restored to its former glory as she was dressed in it, sitting in profile underneath an iroko tree.

Her heart unclenched as she watched her mother admire the painting. She saw the film of tears glazing her mother's eyeballs.

'When . . . Why . . .' Her mother had been unable to complete her sentences as she stared at the portrait.

'I know I can't fix everything, but it's the least I could do, Mama.' Surprisingly, emotion had clogged her throat, making it hard for her to deliver her apology. 'Anyway . . . you know how bad I am at sewing.'

'Do you believe in destiny?' she asked Daniel, roused suddenly from her memory.

'What kind of nonsense question is that?' His features curled in annoyance.

'It's simple. Fate, kismet, destiny – do you believe?'

He bit his bottom lip, thinking up a response. Then, pointing at his chest, engorged with his own boasting, he replied pompously, 'Do I look like a person who needs to believe in fairy tales?'

'No.' His response saddened her temporarily, but she felt lighter once she'd absorbed it. 'But the problem is, I do.'

She stood on her toes to kiss his cheek. Then she stepped past him towards the stairs.

'*Ah-ah.* What is this? What's happening?'

'This is not what I want for myself any more, Daniel. I thought I did but . . . You are free,' she waved her hand. 'Go and marry your cousin.'

'*Eh!* Is it because of the baby?' he stammered.

'Maybe . . .' She shrugged her shoulders. 'I don't know. No.'

'It's that fool with the guitar? That's the one you want?' He laughed madly. 'You think I didn't hear about that? How he was serenading you at the ball?'

She held his gaze but offered him no answer. He kissed his teeth, his expression moving between indignation and fear. 'So, you won't marry me? You don't want to? *Hmm* . . . you think you're tough? Stay there, village girl.' He waved her off like she was his servant but his lips trembled nervously. 'You think I will ask you again? I won't, you hear me?' He spat on the ground before striding off, his back tense with anger.

'Thank God for small mercies,' she said, heading upstairs for the remainder of her things.

'Morning, *hijo*.'

Babylon looked up at the familiar smiling face as Gogoa blew fat smoke rings over his head to celebrate his awakening. The long-forgotten scent comforted him and he returned the giant's smile. Age hadn't changed his dear friend greatly, only his hairline had receded so that a half-moon shape was displayed on his scalp and his once black hair was sprinkled with a white dusting. As they studied each other, it was as if the old man relayed all the happenings during their years apart in the light of his eyes.

'Your friend brought you,' Gogoa revealed, as if anticipating his question. He rubbed his shoulder gently the way he'd done when Babylon was younger and Babylon noticed that the dull ache in his arm had dissipated, almost as if it had finally accepted its fate.

'What day is it?' he croaked weakly.

'Does it matter? Just be satisfied it's as beautiful as it is.'

They both looked skyward into the vast whiteness peppered with streaks of cobalt blue. Then Babylon dropped his gaze to take in the horizon. As the heat from the dry, baked earth crept through the tattered blanket he'd been sleeping on, Babylon observed his surroundings slowly. He was astounded when he realised where he was.

'We're, we're . . .' he stuttered.

'That's right, *hijo*. You're home.'

They rose to their feet, brushing the dust from their trousers. Babylon stretched like a man who'd been asleep for years and his old friend eyed him affectionately. They were now roughly the same height; it was only Gogoa's

328

ballooning width that allowed him to outrank his former protégé.

They left the fields and Babylon re-familiarised himself with the slate-grey building they walked towards. Compared to the beauty of the Mannoban landscape he'd grown to love, it was an eyesore, but his heart still flipped in remembrance of his upbringing there. His eyes caught the sign, a slender piece of wood knocked on to a post. It had long since decayed and was hanging off to one side like a broken flag. The once white paintwork was brown with age and some of the lettering gnawed off by the elements; all that remained was '*Glori__ for the child_*'.

He fingered the sign gently, memorising the grain of wood that was smooth against fingertips that were hardened from his playing. He could recall the sign perfectly in his memory, the day they'd knocked it into the unyielding ground, Titus and Chika wielding a hammer so large it had looked terrifying from his boyish standpoint. After the arduous task had been completed, they stood back and appreciated their handiwork. '*Gloriama's Home for the Children*' was displayed in pristine white lettering for all passers-by to see. Finally they belonged somewhere.

Gogoa was silent behind him, allowing him some privacy with his memories. When he moved towards the step, Babylon couldn't bring himself to enter the house, to commune with the ghosts of his past and account for his extended absence. He already knew the answer to his question, but he felt compelled to voice the words out loud.

'Gloriama . . .' He lapsed into silence.

'Yes,' the gypsy responded. 'Gloria is gone. A long time ago.'

Babylon wept the bitter tears of a man, stored up from hurts he hadn't allowed himself to acknowledge, rivers of salt water from wounds he'd run from without dealing with the loss. As his lips caught them, he tried to remember when he'd last cried.

'I can't go in.'

'*Si*. You can.'

'Really, I can't. Why are we here?' he demanded tersely.

'Sometimes, even when something seems lost, it's still here,' Gogoa said, leading him up to the derelict building.

Babylon shook his locks, exasperated. He allowed Gogoa's chest to prop him up briefly while he fought for composure. He missed Guitar then and wished for his company. He would know what to say at a time like this.

There was no longer a door marking the entrance; only a lattice of cobwebs decorated the narrow doorway that looked like the mouth of a dead man. They entered cautiously, trying not to disturb any debris or any spirits residing in the crumbling building. Babylon felt himself being pulled through the bare rooms that were at once resurrected by his memory. It was as if Gloriama was alive and her energy vibrated throughout the whole home down to the foundations below. He peeked inside the small, barren rooms where he and other children had rationed portions of night, huddled for comfort and warmth. The decaying walls had buffered their nightmares, rebuked by Gloriama's will.

He stopped in the schoolroom at the back. It had seemed so large when he was a child. Now he imagined if he lay on the ground with Guitar in front of him, they could touch the wall at the far end. Remembering the older children who had tried desperately to instil some authority and education into the younger ones, he laughed to himself. He bent to retrieve a discarded stencil and ran his finger over its surface before blowing the dirt off it. His brother Ramón came back to him then, in the cloud of dust that surrounded both him and Gogoa, who hovered behind him. Babylon remembered the two of them in the

330

corner of the room, dividing a candied apple they'd stolen from the kitchen. Gloriama's attention had been diverted by the mass of sticky fingers that tugged her apron, like the tentacles of a gigantic jellyfish, and Ramón's quick hands had spirited away the dessert.

His silent laughter interrupted his vision and dispelled the ghosts of his memory, propelling him back into the naked walls of the deceased building.

They exited the house from the other side. Babylon stood on the small porch and looked out to the trees. He thought back to the time they'd navigated the low branches to uncover the gathering of gypsies. The landscape – his own childhood Waranga – had been much richer then, but had thinned out now, much like his friend's scalp. Gogoa removed sunflower seeds from his pocket and offered him some. Then they squeezed on to the small swing-chair erected at the back of the house. It seemed to be the only thing untarnished by the onslaught of time.

The sound of their teeth clicking as they extracted the seed from its hull echoed through the afternoon. A short while later, Gogoa reached into his pocket again and removed a tiny harmonica. He placed it to his lips then intercepted a look from Babylon, and handed it over without saying a word. Babylon took it and turned it around in his hands, observing the elaborate markings on its brass surface. He recalled the first time the man at his side had placed an instrument in his boyish hands. The disaster of sound that had ensued. Gogoa motioned for him to play but he refused with a simple nod and passed the harmonica back to him. The gypsy calmly accepted it; wetting his lips in an easy motion, he delivered a fruity tune. Babylon listened to the music sliding from the chambers of the tiny instrument that was almost completely hidden inside Gogoa's palms. The beginning of the tune was strange, but the old musician steered it towards one that Babylon recognised instantly. It was the song he had always played to him when he was younger and pining for Gloria's comfort. Babylon's heart warmed in recognition, anticipating the twists and turns in the melody like the familiar streets of a journey home.

'What's happened to me? What's wrong with my hands, why can't I play?' he beseeched Gogoa after his song ended.

Gogoa exhaled heavily before responding. 'You've forgotten where the music comes from.' The old man wiped the harmonica against his trouser leg before sliding it back in his hip pocket. 'It's not your body. That's just a vessel, an instrument for it to speak through. Some corrode quicker than others.' His words were earnest but he seemed detached from the musician's torment, as if it were merely self-pity he mustered.

'You mean I can't play the guitar any more?'

'I'm saying that once you've truly found the music, you can't lose it.' Gogoa pulled out a half-smoked cigar and lit it. He inhaled deeply, savouring the dusky flavour he drew into his throat, and released a small cloud through his nostrils. 'Life is a bitter leaf, my friend. But at the end of the day, we grow again.'

Babylon was confused in the perfumed fog. He heard what his friend was saying but he didn't really understand it. He simply wanted to know why, whenever he attempted to play, the hands that once anticipated every chord change before he himself knew them were suddenly foreigners to him. Why Guitar had become a traitor, changing the music so that he couldn't keep up.

Babylon looked down at his Judas hands. When he played, his knuckles were out of his control. His brain refused to translate the correlating messages to his fingers. Then Guitar would sulk, and they'd spent more and more

332

nights apart in silence, neither of them willing to address the situation.

'Music is all I have, Gogoa. If I can't play, then . . .' His voice faltered. His friend placed his burly hand on his neck and rubbed it, reminding Babylon quickly of the winch back in the village.

'It is not all you have,' his mentor corrected sternly. 'It's all you know. All you've allowed yourself to know. You have been running all your life. Even when you joined us, you were always rushing to learn, to do everything! You couldn't just *be*. Maybe nature is telling you to stop.'

'But without it, how will I be enough?'

'Enough for what?'

'For her,' he revealed softly.

'*Eh-eh*, so there's a woman . . .' Gogoa shook his head at him. 'Is that all you think you have to offer?'

'Why would she want me?'

'Gloriama did. I did.'

'But she loves somebody else—'

'Technicality.' The gypsy winked with paternal pride. '*La musica* is love. That's all it is. And that is what you must remember.'

'I don't understand.'

'You needed to lose something, to find out what you have. To find out what you want.'

'You mean the search isn't over?' he asked cautiously. 'When I was small, you said we were searchers. What was I meant to be looking for?'

'The same thing we're all looking for, Babylon. The elements of peace.' Gogoa pushed him away playfully before hugging him around the shoulders. 'Now, go back to Mannobe. Find your beloved, and win her hand. Then tell Guitar the whole story . . . It'll be the tale you pass down to your children.'

As Gogoa rose from the swing, Babylon followed him,

falling into step with his father figure easily. They circled the house and strolled back to the fields where their bedding was and gathered their belongings.

'Gogoa,' Babylon called out to his mentor.

'Yes?'

'What are the elements of peace?'

'When you find out, Babylon, you let me know.' Gogoa grinned, releasing from his cigar more smoke that rose to meet the crystalline clouds.

Seventeen

Mannobans learn from birth that nature, in its infinite wisdom, blessed us with senses to help colour our experiences in the universe. Any villager worth their cornflour would declare that of all the senses, sight and not hearing is the most powerful; for what one sees, one believes. So when Driver passed Jericho Lwembe's house on his wagon and saw her with a man who could only be Daniel, from his finery, he naturally assumed a tryst was unravelling before his eyes.

Driver didn't think it strange that she had handed her *nonno* what appeared to be a ring, he only witnessed the energy that surrounded the moment. Sensing the heightened voices that accompanied their meeting, he mistakenly attributed it to their passion. His skin prickled with heat as their encounter unfolded before him, and his armpits became clammy. When Daniel leaned down and kissed Jericho, he'd seen enough. He pedalled away as fast as he could, consumed with how to tell Babylon what he'd witnessed.

Driver could speed off on his wagon quicker than any other delivery man for three villages. He never looked behind him but kept his eyes fixed on the way in front. Because of this, he didn't see the slap that Jericho gave her ex-love after he pressed his lips to hers without permission. Driver also didn't see her slamming the door in Daniel's face or him hurling abuse to the closed portal because of the fact that she could choose a life of poverty – or, worse still, a peasant over him, a Dorique. All he'd seen was more than enough to make a poorly filed report to his friend, and to reconfirm his belief in nature's rhythm.

'How is the patient?' Poniche asked with a voice so bright it could rival the sun.

'Better, Doctor,' Magdalena sighed in his direction. She'd risen hours earlier to take time to prepare for his arrival. She was perfectly positioned against her background of feather pillows, her hair draping behind her like a fancy cape. Her bedroom was light and airy, the Mannoban sunshine the only intruder on their conversation. He dropped his small bag by the door and perched on the end of her bed.

'How did you sleep?'

'Like a lizard,' she replied quickly then cursed herself. Inwardly she'd no idea where that had come from and instinctively reached up to trace her lips as if that would recall the words.

'How do lizards sleep?' he asked jokingly. 'Well, I should imagine. We don't see many of them during the day, so I suppose they must dream like us?'

'Exactly. Yes,' she responded breathily, grabbing his lifeline with all her might.

'Your colour is much better, Magdalena,' Dr Poniche said loudly. 'Soon you'll no longer require my visits.'

She lowered her eyes to mask her disappointment. Had she detected an inflection of sadness in his voice?

'Anyway, until then,' he added nervously, 'I shall like to

336

test out this theory of yours. About whether lizards sleep,' he offered, catching her confused expression.

'Outside? You mean I can go? I thought you said I had more days of bed rest?'

'Yes, that is true,' Poniche replied gravely. He scratched the non-existent beard on his chin before waving his finger in the air as if he'd stumbled on a solution. 'Then we must move your bed.' He scooped her up in her cocoon of blankets and swept through Le Papillon, to the amazement of the dining clientele and Magdalena, who was the most surprised of all at being the order of the day.

'What are you thinking about?'

'Your vehicle, Doctor. I mean, Ibrahim,' Magdalena stuttered, flushed.

It was the first time she'd ridden in a van. He'd driven slowly, navigating the bends on the roads so as not to frighten her lying in the back. He watched her in the mirror, and it was different from how Babylon used to look at her. She realised it was how she'd caught Babylon looking at the Lwembe girl, after her beauty had captivated him.

The wind swept Magdalena's hair off her round face, and her eyes were aflame as the van wheels undulated along the nooks and crannies of the dusty road's uneven surface. He'd wanted to talk but felt it would be impolite to deprive her of this simple pleasure. He said it was like distracting a child with the scientific machinations behind flying a kite when all she wanted was to gaze at the coloured dart riding the breeze, so he laughed at her pleasure instead and told her he would wait to let loose his tongue.

She stopped herself from stealing another glance at him as they sat by the Belago. She knew it was happening, but she couldn't quite believe they were actually engaged in their quizzical courtship. She wasn't sure when his interest in her had changed from a medical perspective to an emotional one, but she was enjoying it. It was so different to her dalliance with Babylon, this dialogue felt so much more encompassing to her that it was wrong to even question it or query his intentions, as she'd done constantly with the musician.

Venus Oracene's voice played in her mind in quieter moments. The woman's counsel had reassured her, but her words weren't a guarantee. Still, there was something inside her that had changed for the better, and she knew that the man beside her had been instrumental in that.

When they came to a stop, she sucked in her stomach as Poniche came round and carried her from his doctor's van. He placed her delicately under the extended arm of a tree as if she were fashioned from the most precious of porcelain, and wrapped her thoroughly in a prison of blankets. She sat quietly as he unpacked the large basket he retrieved from his vehicle. He uncovered dishes of sweet potato salad with coriander seeds, peppered beef, plantain, and cheese that smelt of smoke, sliced so thinly that she was afraid that merely looking at it would cause it to crumble.

She squealed with delight at the feast he unpacked, before her stomach reminded her brain of its fragile state. 'But I can't eat all this. My appetite is still a stranger since my, my illness . . .'

'This? *Eh*, this is not for you.' He swept his azure gaze over the magnificent array of food. Then he removed a flask from the basket and poured its contents into a bowl. The familiar aroma of her aunt's chowder washed over her, triggering a large growl from her belly. She coughed, embarrassed.

'So who's going to eat all that?' She pointed at the food.

'Me,' he replied indignantly, his telltale dimples appearing.

'But you'll be sick!'

'*Eh*, that won't happen. But if it does, I know a very good doctor.' He winked at her before demolishing an entire chicken breast.

Four hours later, the doctor was still unable to test Magdalena's theory. The riverbank was completely devoid of the pesky reptiles. Not one to dwell on the negative, Ibrahim Poniche surmised loudly that *that* in itself was a form of proof; the lizards must surely be sleeping if they hadn't appeared. He looked so undignified with his trouser legs rolled up revealing thin ankles, almost completely masked by hairs heading towards his calves. He'd graced the water to retrieve a flower that danced across the translucent surface. A blessing from the gods, he'd remarked, when he placed the limp pink flower against the thickness of her hair, and she was thankful she could disguise her blushes under the pretence of her heightened temperature.

'Can I ask you something?' His voice cut through the conversation of the birds on the branches above them.

'Of course,' she replied eagerly, looking at him.

'Why did you do it?'

He didn't raise his eyes to hers, embarrassed at the boldness of his question, and she remained silent for a while after his words had dissolved into the day. She thought of the sequence of events that had led to her moment of insanity at Silas's grove. She was looking for an explanation that wouldn't push him away when he seemed so close to her reach. The obeah's features were clear in her mind as she recalled the woman's words perfectly. Had she really known the hidden message behind the obeah's words when she'd taken her medicine or had she simply wished for an end to the images pounding against the back of her brain? She'd carried too many secrets, and some of them didn't belong to her, she reminded herself, thinking of her mother and the philosophic tent-dweller. Although her eyes had been heavy with all the things she'd seen, the weight of them hadn't allowed her to rest. Then, the death Venus had hinted at had seemed so alluring.

'I think I wanted to die,' Magdalena revealed, finally, her voice barely above a whisper. 'If I could die, I must have been alive.'

'What made you think you were not? Or who?' he implored, moving closer.

Her lips quivered involuntarily. All her life she'd felt invisible, as if no one could see her. Now she felt transparent, as if he was able to peer into the depths of her soul with such ease. She wondered if her outer self had ceased to exist. Overhead, the birds stilled their dispute as the air between the doctor and her became charged. The time for speaking, for her denial, had passed. Now she couldn't utter a word.

Poniche sighed heavily as if he was about to deliver the gravest of prognoses to a hopeless patient.

'If you allow me, Magdalena, I would like to make you feel alive again. I mean, you *are* alive . . . I would like to spend my days reminding you of that fact.' He reached for her hand apprehensively. 'The heart is an organ, a muscle capable of tremendous growth. It has room for many people, for many loves. It would be selfish to keep it guarded for just one.'

'What are you saying?' she stammered.

'I'm a simple man,' Poniche continued. 'A doctor, a listener, a friend. I want very few things from this life: my sight, so that I may always enjoy the beautiful creations the earth has to offer, a faithful woman by my side whose cooking can incite me to sin; a brood of children. Since I arrived here in Mannobe,' he paused emphatically, 'you are the only thing that I have seen.'

Magdalena's features flushed deeper at his confession.

340

She remembered the description she'd given the obeah regarding her heart's desire. Suddenly her whole body felt very light. She was grateful for the swathe of blankets that anchored her to her position.

'Don't worry. I don't expect an answer straight away. I mean, I'm assuming because of your family, but I don't even know if *you* can cook, *sha*.'

His humour broke the tension between them and she emitted a laugh that shook a feather off one of the birds. He watched it float down in slow motion as if it was being dangled from an invisible wire, a puppet from the heavens. It landed on her auburn curls and he was momentarily lost for words. She gasped as the doctor diagnosed that his heart had in fact stopped beating in that moment. He declared boldly that maybe it was she who would remind him that *he* was alive.

'Are you serious? Do you really want to—'

'But of course! As soon as possible,' he cut her off, impatiently.

'*Pues*, but so soon . . . Is it because of my . . . age?' She blushed, embarrassed.

He placed his hands against her temples and closed his eyes. 'What are you doing?' she asked when he seemed reluctant to exit his trance.

'I'm not sure; I trained in the body not in the brain, but I was trying to check for signs of your intelligence! *Pues*, how can you ask me such a thing?' he asked over her giggle. 'When you see a gem on the roadside, do you snatch it up before someone else, or do you leave in the hopes that you'll find another on your path? I, for one, don't intend to take that chance.'

He leaned in to remove the feather from her hair, and placed it into her waiting hands.

'It's good luck,' she whispered, twirling the pearl-grey quill around.

341

Poniche took it from her and held it between two fingers in front of her lips.

'Make a wish. Then blow,' he commanded.

Magdalena closed her eyes tightly. She was spirited back to the tent of the obeah woman, when a similar request was put to her and suddenly the totality of the Oracene's reading struck her. The force of it caused her to sigh dramatically. Of course, Poniche read her motion as proof that her wish had been dispatched and decided to act upon it.

'Finished?' he enquired abruptly to her nodding head.

Pouting her lips, she blew the feather from his grasp. She didn't have time to track its flight path; she felt his mouth at the end of her pursed lips.

The sky was darkening by the time they finally parted, the retreating sun highlighting their profiles. A lizard lazily approached the basket and sniffed suspiciously at a stray olive before tracing the craggy riverbank, but the pair were oblivious.

'What did you wish for?' he asked her as he drove back, almost as an afterthought.

'*No importa*. I think it already came true,' she replied, shy again.

'And if we had a girl, what would you call her?' Magdalena laughed over the noise of the engine as the van hugged the road back to the café while he shouted out boys' names for their imaginary children. Under her breath she made a silent plea bargain to the Creator not to give her a boy so he would be spared the horror of Ibrahim Junior.

'What about Cleo?' Poniche's voice was pensive.

'After your mother?' She pulled herself up from her horizontal position to hear him better. There was still so much to learn about the good doctor.

'No,' he replied softly. 'But isn't it a beautiful name?'

*

342

Babylon arrived back in Mannobe with a heavy heart. It had been difficult to say goodbye to Gogoa, harder than he'd imagined. He'd been bombarded with images of Gloriama; in particular, the morning he'd bid her adieu never to look upon her face again. If the fates had taken her away, he wondered when they would unite him with the old gypsy again. Although Gogoa had seemed physically unmarred by time, he had aged spiritually. He'd always believed Gogoa would be around for ever, but with everything he'd experienced recently, he knew now that nothing was for certain, and that knowledge weighed heavy on his head.

He was deep in thought when he saw Driver hanging by the village fringes, even more fidgety than usual. They hugged and Babylon smiled weakly when Driver patted him down as if he was checking for injuries. He allowed Driver to steer him towards Borrow's supposedly to soften his larynx with some brew. Borrow cast him a stern glance when he entered. Evidently, the squabble he'd been partly responsible for in his establishment hadn't yet been forgotten, and he returned a look that he hoped was suitably apologetic. When Borrow brought a steady supply of the thick bottles to their table he knew he'd been forgiven.

On one of the owner's trips to their table he placed something next to Babylon's brew that looked like a nut. He reached out to inspect it and discovered it was a tooth.

'Corál was to give it you. She found it on the windowsill after your punch-up,' Borrow laughed. '*Souvenir.*'

The heated topic lay between the two friends in the form of an incisor. Babylon pocketed it swiftly. He knew Guitar would enjoy it later on. He'd wanted to go and look for Jericho, he'd been thinking about her nonstop since seeing Gogoa, but Driver held his wrist.

As his friend conveyed what he'd witnessed, all the sounds in the background faded away: the crisp sound of

343

cards being tossed down in defeat; the clink of glasses against teeth; the bubbles of conversation rising to the surface; the fiddler in the corner serenading himself. He watched Driver's mouth shaping brutal words through a liquor-fuelled haze. He suspected his friend had chosen them carefully – they seemed somewhat rehearsed – keeping them small to minimise their effect.

Babylon's ears filled with blood. He saw the gates around Jericho Lwembe closing. She would wed Daniel Dorique. It was over. At last, it was finally over.

The moon hung full in the sky like a perfect shilling coin, illuminating his convoluted steps home. He was glad he'd refused his friend's offer to accompany him. Driver had been in a worse state, having consumed far more than him, first with guilt and then consequently in sympathy.

Babylon waited until he saw only one back door in front of him, not the three meshing together in his pulsing brain, before venturing inside. The door creaked noisily behind him but he couldn't find the handle to close it. The house smelt stuffy after his brief absence, the blinds still drawn from his last days at home. He ransacked the shelves behind his food sacks. He normally stashed some millet bottles away from Driver's spying eyes, but his hands came up empty.

He swore in frustration. He wanted to increase the periods of black in his head, to reach a place where there were no thoughts at all. Holes in time, where he didn't have to endure the technicolours of reality. Another period of blankness occurred and he found himself fully clothed on his mattress. Guitar was whispering, but mixed with the alcohol flooding his thoughts, it sounded like a hyena-pitched whine prising him from the barren lands he so desperately wanted to inhabit.

'*Are you sleeping?*'

'Uh-huh.' His reply was gruff.

'*Are you awake? Where have you been? Babylon!*'

He covered his head with a pillow to drown out Guitar's voice, but it seemed to mushroom through the fibres, clearer, louder, more persistent.

'*You left me here over a week ago without a word! The least you can do is talk to me.*'

Waves of nausea paddled up from his liver, through the choppy waters of his stomach and pounded on his Adam's apple. Babylon sat bolt upright in bed. Pulling his lips together like the mouth of a string purse, he waited for the sickness to subside. Each sentence from Guitar seemed to trigger a pain in his temples. He just wanted everything to stop.

'*Anyone would think you don't want me any more. Now you have her,*' Guitar wailed.

'I *don't* have her,' Babylon revealed. 'She's to be married!'

'*Oh,*' Guitar replied, stunned. 'Pues, *you'll see it was all for the best. Yes, she was lovely, but if she was the one for you then she'd be marrying you, no?*' He looked at his friend, who was trying to focus his eyesight. '*So, that's why you came back then? And now I suppose you'll be wanting me again,*' Guitar threw at him churlishly.

'Shut up your mouth. My head . . .' Babylon pleaded, terrorised by the pounding in his skull.

'*Ah-ah, but we haven't talked for a while!*'

'Please, not now, I beg you. I have a headache.'

'*I know how to remove it,*' Guitar cooed gently. '*I can make it go away . . .*'

His friend began to sing ever so softly, a simple melody of dulcet Ds and angelic As to smooth away the ripples of piercing pain. Babylon allowed his tears to fall freely on Guitar, causing sweet notes to slide into each other and his partner's strings to slip dangerously. Scenes of delicious music intercut with the blackness in his brain. Music. Black. MusicBlack. Music. Guitar's inflection was strained in those waking moments, haunting, unlike he'd ever sounded before. He tried to keep his head clear but his eyes wanted to close. His eyelids became magnetised. His heart yearned for the black.

Suddenly Guitar's voice magnified until there was no thing bigger than it. Babylon had lived for such moments in music, when a mutual recognition – utterly seamless – between creator and that which is created exists. Those evanescent exchanges permeated his solitude, not the quiet introspection that each human enjoys from time to time, but that space no other thing can ever reach. When these times occurred, he felt uplifted; connected to something much greater than this physical world. But with so much Sting in his system, his most holy transcendence couldn't be sustained. Babylon tried to hold on in that place but when he felt himself being transported into a valley of despair, he began to disengage from his friend's aural seduction.

He misheard Guitar through his tears, couldn't punctuate his instrument's sentences properly with the liquor still coursing through his veins, boiling his blood.

'*Don't stop . . .*' Guitar purred longingly. '*Don't stop. Don't. Stop! DON'T! STO*—'

Babylon played deep into the night, fuelled by the demons in his chest. Every song he'd ever composed came through him, his fingers fighting for freedom from the music. The water springing from his eyes stained his vision and his hair covered his beloved instrument with bruises.

Every time he opened his eyes, he saw her painting. It had been resting against the far wall in his main room. Each brush stroke on the canvas was her voice repeating her rejection, quickly followed by Guitar's incessant whine. It was better in the darkness; there he could drown

346

out their sound. Eyes closed; there was only the music and himself.

Babylon retreated willingly into the ether, satisfied when the periods of emptiness in his brain lengthened. Sleep finally came, prising him from his beloved instrument. He fell on his bed, unaware that his hands were bleeding.

When the first sounds of morning penetrated his eardrums, he pulled himself from a vacuous dream. Daniel's tooth blinked at him from the pillow as if it had guarded his sleep all night. He remembered he'd brought it home to show Guitar. Rising from the bed, he ignored the hangover throb in his temples, eager for his friend's complicity and comfort. But Guitar wasn't in his case.

Babylon threw a sweeping glance around the room and screamed when he saw his friend trembling in the corner. His partner's veins were slashed and humming faintly as the life left his body. Letting out a gasp, Babylon sank to his knees and pressed his hand over the gaping soundless hole of Guitar's mauled centre. But his friend was too far gone. His eyes darted around the room in horror at Guitar's carcass. Had someone come in and wrecked his most precious thing while he slept? His gaze moved to the door that was still ajar from the night before. He was sure he'd closed it when he came home. He caught sight of Jericho's painting, intact against the wall, apparently the only witness to the night's tragedy.

His fist clenched angrily at the thought of the imagined intruder. When he looked down at his hand, he saw the dried blood on his raw knuckles. A violent cold rushed his chest as he gazed down at his worn clothing, mapping specks of crimson. Repelled, Babylon turned his attention back to Guitar. He surveyed his friend's torn bridge and the broken pegs lying beside a shredded fingerboard,

347

trying desperately to patch the pieces of blankness together in his mind.

He was completely unprepared when Guitar slid to the floor by his feet and emitted a final strangled gasp before his strings stilled, to play no more.

Eighteen

A bitter chill swept up the morning, blowing under poorly constructed doors and through the hairline cracks of cemented walls. The winter season Hivierno had evidently come a-calling, leaving its trademark footprints in the greenery, frosty kisses making the grass curl into itself for warmth while leaves shrank back inside their trunks for greater protection. Mannobe turned insular as it had done during the rain. Villagers preferred to remain indoors, only venturing outside when necessity absolutely demanded it.

For the first time in Le Papillon's history, the doors and shutters were drawn. Mabel ignored the fists that pounded angrily against the wooden frames in disbelief, unflinching even when they jiggled the handle roughly in the hope that the door would suddenly yield. She knew her customers were confused – and incensed – that the wafts of food leaking through the restaurant's joints weren't for them. She chuckled to herself and threw a bowlful of onions into some hot oil, thinking how much the crackling sizzle sounded like applause.

M'elle would join her, when she rose, to help with the celebratory feast she was preparing, but Mabel was relishing the morning alone with her thoughts. She'd always wanted to cook a wedding-announcement dinner for her daughter. Now that the day had finally come, she wasn't exactly sure how she felt. Magdalena had told both her and her sister after she'd returned from her picnic with the doctor. He waited anxiously outside the back door of the café even though he'd previously hinted to Mabel about his intention.

Nonetheless, Mabel had hidden her approval behind a gruff exterior. Poniche might have restored their faith in doctors and he was clearly a decent man, but it wasn't good for her daughter's future partner to like her too much. Fear was a very good motivator for a man and none of them knew what the future held.

In contemplating life's uncertainty, her mind drifted to the forest. After her unsuccessful trip to Joucous, she hadn't let the disappointment deter her completely. She'd set about trying to arrange an inter-village meeting that would inform all the neighbouring villages and settlements of the pressing issue concerning Waranga. The council members would be forced to address their concerns if many people got involved, and at least she was doing her part. She'd thrown herself into the activity, invigorated by her revived youth and keen for an escape from her crimes of the flesh. The meetings with other villages took her away from the café, but M'elle had covered well in her absence. The trips also had an added advantage: they widened the distance between her and Allegory.

She rubbed the bruise on her shoulder, a gift from Hamid, anxious for the Joucous update. He'd embraced her tightly in the café two days earlier on discovering she'd kept aside some guineafowl surprise especially for him. Alone in the kitchen she pondered his obliviousness about his daughter. Hamid had never exhibited discomfort in Magdalena's presence or any paternal recognition and if it hadn't been to her advantage Mabel might have felt disappointed. But his behaviour had taught her something: how to overlook a mistake. Sometimes people only saw what they wanted to, sweeping the rest aside like waste. That was what stopped him from recognising his daughter, and she decided this was how to handle her indiscretion with Allegory.

Mabel heard her sister's distinctive shuffling footsteps and poured out a cup of tea. M'elle took the cup from her and sat down on a stool close to the fire. She pushed her headscarf away from her eyes and sipped loudly on the brew.

'You have to season the goat meat—'

'Already done,' Mabel interrupted her. 'I made the chicken this morning, but I left the pork and mango for you as well as the fried rice.'

'I was thinking of making coconut brittle.' M'elle rose to pour herself another cup of tea. 'Weddings and coconut go so well together . . .'

'You can make what you like as soon as you wake Magdalena and tell her to go to Al Rais for the shrimp. You can't do the rice without it, and I want to finish quickly so we can relax. If we're going to close for the day then I don't want to spend the whole time on my feet.'

'Listen to you, old woman,' M'elle grumbled, slurping her tea.

'You want to talk about age with *me*?' Mabel eyed her sister, who laughed.

Mabel made room for her sister beside her. She felt M'elle looking over her shoulder into the pot of cowfoot she stirred, sniffing expertly at the vapour coming off the top. Without tasting it, M'elle added two more pinches of salt and took the spoon out of her hand. Mabel kissed her teeth playfully in feigned annoyance. Moving away from the pot, she began to slice some okra.

Their cooking was heavily peppered with grunts and

sighs. To strangers, these would have been unintelligible, but Mabel could decipher every one of her sister's exclamations and her sister could do the same, having spent years in this fluid tango in their kitchen. The conversation was light between their preparations, M'elle equally reluctant to dwell on anything too pressing on a feast day.

'You prepare for your meeting?' Mabel heard her twin ask before frying some peppers.

'What can I do? We will hold it and hopefully something good will come. But . . . we'll have tried, *non*? We have to believe in the power of our people,' Mabel replied sagely. 'What – you don't think we can change the council's minds?'

'Hmm . . . Those greedy men?' M'elle pursed her lips as she squinted over the smoke. 'You'll have more luck feeding a rabid dog vegetables.'

Mabel relaxed in the relative silence of the kitchen. Pot lids sang with the heat of their dishes. Utensils clanged, deep in conversation, but she and her sister were quiet. Their pace was leisurely, the normal pressure of cooking for large numbers of hungry villagers absent. The peace was a welcome break from their usually frenetic days; more so since Waranga, that had added to her workload.

'You like the doctor?' Mabel asked, her eyes fixed on the knife she worked with.

'Of course, what's not to like?'

'You think he's too fast?'

'Nonsense!' M'elle boomed. 'The man has good sense . . . When you have good sense, why you have to wait? You want to come back from the Eternal Compound to see your child marry?'

Mabel allowed her sister's words to sink in. She wondered if her twin was aware that she'd struck a painful nerve. M'elle was ageing at the same rate as her, more so,

352

if her restricted agility was taken into account, but she seemed at peace with it. Magdalena's good news had undoubtedly infected her.

It seemed odd that one of them was now going to get married. They were a strange household that seemed to function entirely on female energy. Now that would change, along with everything else.

There was so much movement in the air, winds of change stirring up her emotions as they passed territorially through the village. Mabel wasn't sure if she could keep up with it. Mannobe's pace of life had quickened and she found herself suddenly short of breath.

With her sister by her side, they palmed ingredients to each other for the meal that they would share with her child and her future husband before they received any well-wishers who had already heard the news. Mabel allowed her sister's joy to accentuate her own happiness. Today, they would celebrate her child's blessing. There would be plenty more days to worry about everything else.

Allegory shuddered as guilt wormed a convoluted path to his brain. Then he reprimanded himself for dwelling on his mishaps with Mabel and alcohol, especially when there was something more troublesome pressing against his lobes. As the musician dominated his thoughts, he felt an immediate warmth for him along with a sense of foreboding. It had perplexed him initially, the young man's obstinacy, but he'd grown to admire it. The musician had stayed, waiting to repay a kindness, and all his attempts to release Babylon from the debt he was convinced he owed had failed. Now that he'd saved his life again, he tried to meditate on the younger man's future. After ten minutes he gave up, relieved that no picture of doom arose.

Removing the neckerchief from his face, he allowed the

intoxicating fumes from Le Papillon full-nostril access, wondering what the dishes were.

'*Chiy!* You always put too much seasoning . . .' M'elle pulled a face after she sampled Mabel's stew.

'Hmm . . . and you put the wrong meat,' she replied cryptically.

'Eh?'

'Remove your tongue.' Mabel's lips spread out into a grin. 'It will taste much better then.'

She heard her sister's raucous laugh. Then M'elle began to hum one of their favourite tunes. It was the song they waited for as children. Even when their mother shooed them out of the kitchen as she cooked, her telltale song had always informed them of her menu. Mama Codón would whistle – her fleshy lips puckered as she pushed the air out over her tongue. Then she would hum, quietly at first, until her voice reached a startling crescendo as she whipped her meringues into peaks with savage strokes of her cooking fork.

M'elle broke off from her humming and pointed the end of her spoon at Mabel.

'You know, Magdalena marrying . . . it's a sign of things to come. It makes me think, *pues*, I don't know, but maybe it's not too late for all of us . . .'

Mabel threw her sister a sideways glance. 'You planning on getting married?'

M'elle giggled childishly. 'I wasn't saying that, exactly . . .'

'I was about to say,' Mabel could feel the insult she was formulating tickling the back of her throat, 'like we would ever find enough fabric to go around those hips of yours.'

M'elle snorted insolently and Mabel couldn't contain her laughter any longer. She chortled until she was bent double. M'elle took the knife from her hands before she dropped it or accidentally pierced herself. Mabel saw the upturned edges of her sister's mouth and knew M'elle wasn't upset by her words. The only reason she hadn't laughed as madly as her was because she'd already resumed her humming as she cooked.

Mabel wiped her tears away and waited for her sister to reach the chorus before accompanying her seamlessly. Then, closing her eyes, she let her notes dip so that M'elle's pitch could soar above hers, knowing that before their song came to an end, they would have met somewhere in the middle.

Nineteen

Sometimes when something is lost, another is remembered.

It was time to go.

Babylon wandered through his house, crestfallen. It was lonely without the familiar lull of his friend and each wall was clogged with memory. He'd held on to the lifeless Guitar for as long as he could, until it was forcefully removed from his hands. Even though there was activity all around him, he couldn't drag himself out of a dream-world where his oldest companion was still intact and singing out joyfully.

Driver had enlisted Allegory when he was unable to rouse Babylon from his trance. The old man had bent to gather the broken guitar together. Even Driver had stared, horrified by the mutilation of the carcass. What was once a comrade and co-conspirator was now just a broken, inanimate object, shards of wood and steel. The faceless garbage that lay in mountainous heaps in the refuse dump. Unclaimed, unmourned, unremembered.

Babylon lay slumped, immobile as a professional life drawing. The two of them picked him up and moulded his stiff body into a chair. Driver pottered about in the kitchen, brewing a strong batch of canela tea in the hope that the familiar smell of the brew might revive him. But Babylon was oblivious. His piceous eyes flickered as though they were reliving the past, recalling the lilt in Guitar's voice as they'd whispered conspiratorially, sharing their own private jokes.

Out of nervousness, Driver made idle conversation with Allegory, questioning repeatedly how the old man had known to wear his pine outfit. Allegory wasn't altogether despondent, but even he was a more subdued version of his normally vivacious self. It was clear Babylon's mood had permeated his body, weakening his tempestuous spirit. They brought the cup to his nostrils and urged him to drink. Babylon performed the mechanical action completely unaware. He kept his eyes fixed on the jumble of wood that lay in the corner. The ashes of his friend.

'Shall I remove it?' Babylon heard Driver ask Allegory in a voice barely above a whisper, not that there was any need. He was lost between two worlds of present and past.

'*Tranquilo*. It's not yet time.' The spiritualist steadied his friend with a hand on his shoulder. Then gorging themselves on unnatural amounts of tea, they watched him closely, like evangelists awaiting a new god.

When the moon hung high – like a ball kicked with so much force it had impaled itself on the dark sky – Allegory rose from his haunches. He'd been squatting in that position for hours, watched keenly by Driver, who needed something to occupy his thoughts while Babylon was temporarily catatonic.

'Go and fetch a bag,' Allegory ordered him in a strange voice and Driver yawned widely like an impudent servant before assuming his task. The old man pointed at the remains of the guitar with his skeletal arm and Driver began to place the gutted pieces into an empty grain sack.

Babylon's eyes registered a small interest in their activity but his lips didn't interrogate them. Once all the strewn pieces of Guitar had been collected, the old man went over to Babylon and lifted him up by his armpits, like a child.

As the three of them walked slowly in the night, the stars were reflected by the edges of the old man's costume, lighting their way on the road.

It seemed that all the belongings Babylon had amassed, the sum total of his life, could fit into Guitar's now-vacated case. There was no longer anything of value in his home without his friend; the meagre possessions he elected to keep were solely to preserve some lasting connection to what had been. His eyes fell momentarily on the painting resting against the wall. He'd considered destroying it a hundred times, eviscerating it with the same anger that had vanquished his dearest companion. But his arms had refused to comply. It was as though they couldn't consciously repeat the massacre they'd carried out on Guitar, and the knowledge had left him slightly relieved. Still, there was no way he could take the painting with him.

He took one last look at his surroundings, the limp purple curtain that waved him off like a heartbroken relative, the wooden floor beneath his feet that creaked, echoing the cry 'alone, alone' to his retreating back. He closed the door behind him, wincing as it clicked with finality. After a few steps, he swore and strode back to the house. Pushing the door open, he worked quickly in case guilt stopped him. Babylon reached for Jericho's painting and pulled the canvas off the frame. He folded it roughly and added it to his other belongings hurriedly before turning to leave a second time.

He slung Guitar's case over his shoulder, wistfully remembering the old leather one – with the adder's teeth-marks – he'd lost in a card game long ago. There were few people on the roads that morning: the little boy pulling his barrow of ice around in preparation for the morning rush; the school brigade balancing their books on their heads as their falsetto voices jousted with the early sounds of day. Villagers recognising him called out and he nodded in return. Women tried to lance him with their loaded stares but his eyes were impenetrable.

He found himself at the Eternal Compound. He paused outside the wrought-iron gates marking the Mannobe cemetery and threaded his fingers through the rusty grille. In the daylight, his eyes found the spot they sought instantly, where the ground dipped like a concave stomach. He pushed the gates open apprehensively and drifted to the remembered spot. Then, bowing his head with the respect befitting his surroundings, he said his goodbyes.

In the darkness, it had been impossible to know where they were going. Only Prophet had seemed guided by the night-lights of nature. Babylon had shuffled behind his two friends like a zombie. Followed, because it seemed the only thing to do: there were no other choices left. There was nothing left.

The ground beneath their feet felt different when they arrived. The earth was warm, charged, replenished by the decomposing bodies that fed it with the essential nutrients it survived on. Prophet had bypassed the altar in the dark and gone directly to the grounds and Driver looked about him shiftily, not wanting to come across a spectre but anxious to anticipate it, if the worst were to happen. Babylon watched the old man expertly selecting a piece of earth where the ground seemed to curve from the pressure of the moon that hung above it. He dug a deep hole with his fingernails and then reached out for the bag. Driver handed it to him in silence.

Prophet removed the broken pieces of the instrument

359

slowly and buried them in the earth. He covered it over with soil when he'd finished, packing it down solidly with his bare feet. The three of them surrounded the small plot, straining to see each other in the blue-blackness. Prophet had reached for Babylon in the darkness and handed him something wiry. He knew immediately what it was: Guitar's bracelet, the lock of Gloriama's hair worn around his headstock for protection. Prophet's clamouring voice cut through the night sky. Even though Babylon couldn't see the old man, he knew his eyes were rotating wildly in their sockets as he spoke.

'Awake and sing, ye that dwell in dust: for thy dew is as the dew of herbs, and the earth shall cast out the dead.' The old man pointed at him and his words began to soar, stirring the souls present with them in the cemetery. 'But though our outward man perish, yet the inward man is renewed day by day.'

Prophet called Babylon forward and together they laid Guitar to rest. Under the vigil of the moon, without the interruption of the village indigents, without the flowers to cover his eyes. Guitar went to his new world fully aware.

They left the Compound in a line, Babylon the last to turn around. He wanted to memorise each stone in the earth, each grain of dirt so he could always find his friend. When at last dawn broke, they heard the strains of a melody; the beginnings of a familiar waltz, and knew that Guitar had arrived.

Babylon removed a poinsettia from his pocket and placed it on the sunken ground. Its petals flapped gingerly as if they'd been seduced by an impromptu breeze. A pathetic hello from the afterlife. Still, a greeting all the same.

He turned and continued on his journey out of the village.

When he reached the outskirts, he took one last look for

360

memory's sake. His glance swept greedily over the curve of trees, the slope of sky, the grooves in the dirt. The place that had stilled his feet from their former nomadic existence. He shifted the case on his shoulder and braced himself for the road ahead.

As he turned around, he was knocked over by a bunch of scattering boys, their laughter strangled in their throats. The boys carried a large hunk of ice between them, undoubtedly the loot from their heist. They rushed past him without an apology in their haste, their fear of him overpowered by the adrenalin rush from their robbery. But the smallest one, striving to keep up with the ostrich legs of his peers, hesitated. As Babylon's eyes met his, the boy stopped running immediately.

'Sorry, *sah*,' he apologised sheepishly and bent to pick up Babylon's meagre possessions from the squashed case.

'Don't worry. But be careful. Look where you're going next time,' he replied to the top of the boy's nodding head. 'I mean, where are you running to anyway?'

As soon as the words left his mouth, Gogoa's voice penetrated his skull. Babylon's hands dropped the guitar case he'd just retrieved. The little boy, startled by the transformation of his features, sped off, shouting his terror of the music man as he escaped.

Suddenly, Babylon was back at Gloriama's home for the children. In the wagon with his mentor. By the creek with his ghosts.

He smiled widely, seemingly for the first time. As the epiphany washed over him steadily, he allowed what was left of the sun to baptise his body in its glow. The question was, where was *he* running to?

It was approachng nightfall as he made his way back home and he found his feet taking him past Jericho's place. He faltered nervously, reluctant to look directly at the house, yet incapable of taking another step without a glimpse. He entered the compound, sensing its emptiness as he proceeded. She was probably out spreading the news of her impending marriage, being fitted for a dress made from pure ivory – or, given that she was marrying a Dorique, a golden fleece.

For the last time, he tipped his non-existent cap at her abode. A final farewell to his queen.

Twenty

Edith Lwembe busied herself with jars in her kitchen. She'd been collecting them steadily throughout the year for this very occasion. Lining up a barrage of vegetables beside her, she began the time-consuming process of pickling them to preserve them for the season to come, and to alleviate her boredom at being cooped up inside.

As nervous pinpricks assaulted her body, she attributed the sensation to the upcoming Widows' March. Her feet always wanted to join the annual line of mourners as they covered the village's length with ashen crosses on their foreheads, but something held her back each time. Although she wasn't a widow in the real sense, she was certain her wailing could rival those who had genuinely lost loved ones through death. How could you convince those who thought otherwise that abandonment was worse than death? Dying, for the most part, couldn't be avoided. When the Creator asked you back, you went.

Edith pictured the group of mourners as they came to a stop at the Crescent with tear-streaked faces. Every year the gathering seemed to her to grow in numbers, as if they were losing more than were born to repopulate the village.

Hijacked by their individual grief, their blending voices became magnificent oral libations as they belted out sorrowful songs until nightfall, in the hope that their common sadness would resurrect the dead.

She was glad her daughter had come home from her most recent trip to Angel, but she saw very little of the child she once recognised. Although Jericho was under house arrest due to the cold, they hadn't really spoken properly, preferring to keep to the niceties that made the days roll by without a hitch. It seemed as if their conversations lay on the surface like insects floating on water, not weighty enough to allow them to reach any depths. Just like her father. That girl was just like her father.

She wondered whether her daughter would ever settle back into the village properly. The city had changed her, opened her eyes too much. It wasn't exactly restlessness; more as if Jericho was a formerly sighted person that now had to acclimatise to blindness. She seemed awkward in her new situation. Not that a village existence was akin to a life of darkness, Edith reminded herself sharply.

Her fingers attacked the vegetables quickly, revealing the table beneath as she worked. The vegetables rested, embalmed like foetuses suspended in amniotic juices awaiting consumption. She heard Jericho rising, the distinctive cough she made to clear the remnants of fantasies from her throat followed by the subtle click of her jaws whenever she yawned. Jericho padded sleepily into the kitchen and kissed her gently from behind, and she temporarily paused her pickling to receive her daughter's embrace.

'Mama, I had the most amazing dream,' she began but paused, distracted by something. 'Wait – can you hear that?'

Edith sighed and resumed her task while her child pitched her ear to the wind. Every morning – without fail – since the full moon, Jericho had been plagued by music trapped in the confines of her aural canal that no one could corroborate. Edith had taken to concocting ways to keep her inside, away from the whispering tongues of the less tolerant, frightened they might dismiss her daughter as demented. Even the smallest of labels could become the biggest of burdens in a little village.

She remembered only too well when the Mtoba girl had been pronounced crazy; Edith had seen children pelting her with stones while she strolled hand in hand with her invisible admirer, defenceless. Even adults had exchanged knowing glances, relieved that they weren't responsible for the irregular being.

Edith looked over at Jericho. Aside from the brief musical interludes, her child appeared to be lucid. But still, she couldn't dislodge the doubt that made her throat close over at random times. She sent a prayer to her guardian angels for sending Hivierno early this year; at least being housebound kept the busybodies to themselves.

'Don't you hear it, Mama?' Jericho asked again giddily.

'No, *bona*. I can't hear anything.'

Jericho shrugged off her grimace and squinted as she concentrated on the imagined music. 'Maybe it's only meant for me,' she twinkled, swiping a bean off the table before floating out of the room.

M'elle drew the shutters vigorously and allowed early morning light to fill Le Papillon. She inhaled the crisp air and grinned. This truly was her favourite time of year. She affected a light skip – as light as her heavy gait would allow – to the cupboard where the linens were kept. Surely it was time to stir things up a little. She removed the yellow napkins, confident they would lift the spirits of their diners.

Magdalena's happiness was truly infectious. Ever since Dr Poniche's proposal, their small house had seemed to levitate, as if the woe previously weighing it down had disappeared. Finally after all these years, one of them had been chosen. It really didn't matter which one, M'elle decided. A Codón was to be married.

She inhaled deeply, acknowledging an emotion she hadn't recognised before. Her chest was filled with hope, she realised. *Her hope chest*. She exhaled loudly, her breath a cluster of stars.

Mabel was surprised to find Edith Lwembe pacing on her doorstep, looking behind her almost as if she'd been followed. Hamid had been her first unexpected visitor of the day. He'd informed her of his decision to join his daughter in Odin. Better to get out with good memories than watch what he'd built disappear. He was too old for that. She'd listened to his admission quietly, ordering her tear ducts to cease their activity. There'd been little point in objecting; Hamid wasn't a man that was easily dissuaded once his mind was set on something. But his news hit her hard. The blow marked the beginning of Mannobe's transformation, and not in a good way.

Curiosity won out over Mabel's apprehension and she held the door open for Edith, who made a great show of wiping her feet before becoming distracted by the smells circling their kitchen – she was roasting meat. They listened to the skin cracking with the intensity of the flame, the rich juices glazing the goat's tender flesh before sizzling in the fire below. Mabel watched Edith lick her lips nervously and placed a bowl of cocoa in front of her, topped with cream and a cocoa bean. Edith warmed her hands on it while Mabel poked at the meat on the fire. It was cooking perfectly well without her assistance but she sensed her visitor was struggling to relay the object of her visit, so she pretended to look busy while she waited. They heard the meat popping above the flames and succumbed to the heady aroma of the ingredients seasoning the air. After wiping away her cream moustache, Edith squared her shoulders and began.

'I need you and your sister's help.' Mabel nodded knowingly, intrigue quickening her heartbeat. 'I'm taking my daughter to the Koye.'

It didn't happen all at once. It always started slowly, a note colliding into a thought before another came to join it, surreptitiously at first, so as not to draw too much attention to the nine-piece orchestra forming in her head. The music was so sublime that its presence didn't alarm her; she knew intuitively that it hadn't originated from a bad place.

Jericho leaned back into the rich chorus as the dulcet voice tickled her eardrums. The guitar took centre stage; its strings repeating her ennui in double-time until it faded into the background as the other instruments had done and allowed the voice to take the lead again. When she was small, she would lie down on the ground in the compound with her eyes closed, waiting for the sun to roll gently over her. She used to revel in the sensation of each limb warming up as the sun blessed it. The singing in her head reminded her of her former pastime, a split second of bliss and abandonment.

She contemplated her mother's kitchen expression, that mixture of worry and sadness that had become her dominant countenance these days. Faced with the reality of a permanent village existence, it had been safer inside Jericho's head. She'd taken refuge there, away from her mother's constant questioning about her future. Without Daniel, her plans were more precarious. She couldn't bear to tell her mother she had no real interest in pursuing medicine and that her passion could truly be her profession, so started helping out in the bakery. They attributed her tearful eyes to the smoky oven.

Babylon had been a part of her village decision. She'd realised that more since their paths had uncrossed. She felt the loss of something that had never started deeply, taking that anger and sadness out at work by pummelling her frustrations into the dough despite her mother's advice. Last week, her guilt had even stopped the malt bread from rising. She'd thought about the baby so much during that shift, they'd had to throw the entire batch away.

Jericho held her breath in anticipation of the last note, that final graze of string that brought her safely back to the present. As much as she welcomed these musical interludes, an unfortunate side effect was that they led to repeated thoughts of a certain musician that were almost as bittersweet as the symphonies themselves. She frowned at the ceiling as her mind ran through her routine of admonishments in the hope of quelling all thoughts of him. If only she'd inspected the tiny, pink flowers whose petals they pulled off to suck the honey-like substance on the stamens as children, things might have happened differently. She should have stopped for a drink of water or to remove the stone that had worked its way under her arch, but she'd wanted to speak to Babylon before she over-analysed things or her nerves hijacked her. As she'd walked towards his home, she imagined the different scenarios that might have ensued on her arrival, but never had the possibility of another woman being there arisen.

She revisited her apprehension on that day. She'd felt such exhilaration after returning Daniel's ring and the feeling would have been magnified by sharing it. She was surprised when Babylon popped into her mind before her girlfriends as the first recipient of her news. They'd been linked since their trip to Angel; Babylon had been patient while she'd searched for Daniel, offering no objection as he'd followed her through the city. After his kiss in the grove, that would have been hard for him to bear. For a man she'd dismissed as somewhat pretentious, he turned out to be rather softly spoken.

She contemplated his behaviour; so different from her ex-*nonno*. Daniel's gestures had been lavish, but it was usually the smaller things she remembered in those moments before dreams, like his first gift of wild flowers. Unfortunately, that Daniel hadn't lasted very long. Babylon, on the other hand, was an amalgamation of so many little things that the totality of him was grand. He was like a connecting device; she'd seen that during his interactions with the locals, watching him closely with the children. He enticed people's joy to the surface. Despite her residual frostiness towards him, he'd conducted his curious alchemy on her too.

It was right that she sought him out; her news about Daniel belonged to him equally. Even so, her pace had slackened when she eventually reached his house, and she'd trained her ears for sounds of his whereabouts. She'd been excited when she heard footsteps approaching but that had turned to alarm on discovering their owner. If she'd only hesitated, even for a few minutes on the road, their paths might never have crossed.

The woman had smiled at her warmly but there'd been a question in the subtle tilt of her eyebrow. Jericho had eyed her quickly: she was vaguely familiar. She was the kind of woman a man would find attractive but women would be suspicious of. Her flowery scent had been so overpowering, Jericho remembered. That must have been why her eyes began to sting.

'You looking for Babylon? He's not at home.' The woman placed a hand on the door territorially. 'I was waiting but . . .'

'It's all right,' Jericho managed to stammer before backing away.

'You can stay. I can tell him something for you?'

'It's okay . . . It doesn't matter.'

She'd marched for hours after that, waiting for her embarrassment to leave her before she went home. Maybe not coming across him was for the best. After all, she hadn't been sure what words would come from her in her compulsion to explain herself. It was funny really. The universe had given her a taste of her own medicine.

Of course, there would have been others. She was foolish to have thought that his words were anything more than his standard prelude to a conquest. He'd probably even written the same song he played at the ball for a dozen other women, substituting their names when he grew tired of one, so that the latest interest believed she was his muse.

She was lucky that he hadn't been there to see her. Even if his current lover and he had laughed about her momentary lapse in judgement afterwards, at least she'd been spared the humiliation of his pity.

Jericho chased away the lingering blue devils in her heart, assuring herself unconvincingly that the songster in her head was the only musician she needed.

Babylon rose to a blood orange sky. The air still held the crispness of the previous rainy season. He inhaled deeply, the rich mineral fragrance of earth tickling his nostrils. A perfect morning for composing. He chased the thought down bitterly and pulled his dreadlocks off his face, tying them in a ponytail. He pulled on his oldest pair of trousers, a worn shirt and a jacket before filling a container with some bush tea, and took to the road.

He wasn't exactly sure where he was going. He walked past Borrow's, lamenting that he couldn't go in. Even though it wasn't officially open at this early hour, the establishment never really closed, there would still be a few diehard drinkers swaying on stools. He licked his lips, imagining a bottle of millet. He hadn't thirsted for a drink since the night Guitar . . .

Babylon shooed away the memory before sadness overtook him. That he was unable to recall the act was what terrified him the most. How his hands that had once shaped the wind into song could have brought about such destruction, particularly to another that had been so close to him. He squeezed the tooth in his pocket, and a rush of adrenalin flooded him at the thought of the other man's wounded pride and loss of face at Borrow's. Then he remembered. He too had lost something at the hands of Daniel Dorique. As his mind formulated the thought and contemplated his own loss, he was surprised when Jericho's face didn't come to him.

They would all have learned of Guitar's fate by now, Driver – bless his heart – would have been unable to keep the story to himself. But Babylon had no time to spare on explanations. Seeing Gogoa again had made things clearer to him. Now was a time for action. He'd made his living from his hands his entire life. They would be useful again.

A cluster of men hung about on the patch of dirt between Kano's farmland and Puwenga Way where the road forked. They seemed accustomed to an early start, dozing with eyes open, some lying flat on the ground. To a passer-by these men might have looked like friends prolonging their late night revelry, reluctant to cut short the party and return home to their families. But a local knew: these men were seasoned labourers.

Whenever men were out of work in Mannobe, there was always one industry where they were able to boost their self-esteem – after the tongue-thrashing they received at home – and earn some money to line their pockets: labouring. There was never a shortage of work, things always needed building or dismantling. Employers were in need of a constant supply of able-bodied, quiet-lipped men.

Babylon had often seen these men. He admired their physique and their work ethic; these men were life's backbone. He'd considered their work time and again, during those difficult patches when he'd put his hand into his pocket only to draw out the lining instead of a few coins, but something always held him back from going on the crew. He knew what had given him pause. Labourers' bodies bore the scars of their precarious travail. He hadn't wanted to endanger his hands, the curators of his musical gift. Not that it mattered now.

The others glanced at him when he joined them and sat down. If they recognised him as a musician they didn't say anything. In fact, none of them spoke to each other; there was only a curt nodding of the head in acknowledgement as another person joined the group. He waited patiently, trying to mirror the posture of these habitual workers. He'd expected conversation, an exchange of information at least. He was mildly disappointed. He'd spent the night before dreaming in spurts while perfecting his tale of introduction. *Where the B in the village's name came from.* Now that these men found no need to talk with each other, the silence made him remember the earliness of the hour, causing his heavy eyelids to droop.

The rumble of an engine stirred him. When the battered vehicle finally appeared, its noise sounded more like the aftermath of a cold; a persistent wheezing interspersed with random coughs. The indigo truck stopped abruptly in front of the gathering of men. He looked inside and saw two men in the front. Both were as dark as tar and their skin glowed like polished tiles. One held a chewing stick in the side of his mouth and the other one had a weather-beaten cap made out of straw, whose brim seemed to be unravelling with the slightest friction from the air surrounding him. The one with the hat jumped out of the truck, although it took him a while to complete the manoeuvre as the door

372

was stiff with rust. The back of the vehicle was empty and there was some loose plastic sheeting that was fastened on to the driver's cabin at the front. He wondered if they were to cover themselves with it if it rained. He also noticed that there was nothing for them to hold on to. The sides of the back were shallow, and only sheer willpower would keep them upright as the vehicle navigated the bends in the roads. The truck had a poster on the side that had been painted on, probably when it was new, but it was partially hidden by clumps of dirt. He made out a few letters – 'ALVA' – and guessed that whatever the whole message spelled out, it included the word 'salvation'.

The man with the hat scanned the line quickly. He pointed at some men, motioning for them to climb into the truck. Babylon saw the man nod in his direction. The ones that had been refused looked down at the ground, saddened temporarily at the loss of money, but secretly relieved at the reprieve from back-breaking work, and began their journey home.

As the truck pulled away, Babylon felt the fire brewing in his lungs. He wanted to yell 'stop' and 'wait', hoping the driver would halt the vehicle. Then, he could climb down and substitute a reject in his place. But he didn't. Biting down on the words, he guarded them closely in his mouth, like the chewing stick of his new boss.

When Edmund – the man with the hat – had shown him how to work the two-man saw, Babylon had been glad that he didn't have to wield the axe all morning by himself. As masterful as it seemed, carving a curve through air to shatter the spine of a sapling, he imagined the toll the labour would take on his shoulders. His joints might have been flexible enough for him to play a *bachata* but that didn't mean they could withstand such physical exertion.

In the daytime, the forest seemed dense, relentless. A huge knot of green and brown that stretched as far as his eyes could see. He felt constricted and claustrophobic, but looking up at the sky at regular intervals helped ease his tension. The men from the truck hadn't really given them instructions, except to create a clearing. The regular labourers knew exactly what to do, approaching their weapons of habitual destruction swiftly, leaving the unsavoury implements for the more naïve newcomers. Observing the physiques of the men that worked, spread out around him, he knew why he'd been chosen. For his sinewy, yet strong, frame. He was part of a team.

The two-man saw was hard work, but it reminded him of a dance. It required absolute symmetry with his partner, who liked to relax as Babylon brought the handle towards his chest before pulling back the tool with all his strength. As they worked, wood clippings competed with jungle flies for occupation of his eyes. Sweat oozed from his pores, drenching his shirt. He now understood why the men wore oversized, holey vests to work despite the cool temperature. He'd balked at some of the smells emanating from these men, the raw stench that assaulted him every time one of them moved his arm, exposing his armpit, but he understood it now. After a while, he surrendered to the rhythm of the saw and his muscles accommodated themselves to their extended exercise. Thoughts left his mind as he worked; all he registered were states of being. Hunger, exhaustion, thirst.

Chewing-stick Willo sounded the truck's horn, two sharp raps to signal home-time. It was then Babylon realised the day had escaped him. The sky was tangerine with navy edges; the colour of nightfall. He was exhausted, but it felt good, the pain in his arms deserved. The men mounted the back of the truck, struggling this time with the feat. The return journey was peppered with

374

mild conversation. It was as if they could risk it now: their energy levels no longer needed to be conserved for cutting. Their strength had been drained under the sun, and the tiny portion that remained was only good enough for speech. The introduction he'd rehearsed the night before had completely vanished from his mind. He was one of these men now, he'd no reason to entertain them.

After climbing down from the truck he walked by Borrow's in the moonlight. He heard the hubbub of joyful drinkers bleeding through the windows along with the strains of a guitar. Babylon stopped and listened intently to the sounds of his past. When the guitar player fell silent he started walking again, laughing quietly to himself. For the first time in forever, he was actually looking forward to an empty bed.

His ears still rang with the sound of the buzz saw. He marvelled at how it cut through trees as easily as a piranha could chew through a person's leg in the Belago, given half the chance. At the end of the day Willo had pressed on the horn, but Babylon held back as the other workers climbed on board. He'd waved them off as the truck coughed down the road, leaving a trail of toxic fumes in his face. He peeled his shirt off the rock he'd rested it on after it became too soaked to wear. He slid his arms into it even though it was still damp, then he sat on the rock and drained the rest of his bush tea. In the darkness, he tried to inspect the work they'd been doing.

It was nice being back in the forest again. As they waited each morning for the blue truck, they had no way of knowing what their destination would be. They were simply provided with tools and incomprehensible grunts, then they copied the worker with the most experience. Follow the leader. He'd arrived at the fork in the road surprisingly early the day after his first; he'd been afraid to sleep. By the time he'd arrived home, the pain in his muscles was so acute and the tiredness so encompassing, he was scared he wouldn't be able to rise again for work. He'd been surviving on inertia and bush tea, chewing surreptitiously on ungacha leaves to keep him alert.

The next few weeks had taken him to farms, fields and building sites. He'd had his turn on various bits of machinery, but the work was always the same: demolishing, never building. He was happy that the back-breaking toil of labouring didn't afford him much alone time with his thoughts. He focused on the job, observing the skyline to see which direction the trees were coming down as they went about felling part of the forest, or making sure his part of the chain was effective as they passed bricks down to each other to take away in the truck. The work made him feel useful in a way that didn't require any applause or congratulation at the end of the day.

He made a conscious effort to push all thoughts of the Lwembe girl aside, although she inevitably floated across his eyelids at the randomest of times. These moments always sidelined him – he used them as breaks to mop his brow or tweak his ponytail – until he remembered her rejection. Once he resurrected that, all his losses came flooding back to him in an almighty wave and he threw himself even deeper into his job.

It was hard to make a living in the village. Not that they all wanted to live like Doriques; to be comfortable was plenty, but comfort still required shillings. There were very few openings for a middle-aged musician, roles that would give him a sense of worth. That had some meaning. He thought of his best friend, riding through the village on his home-made device to peddle his wares. He knew Driver would immediately have offered to cut him in on the trade but he barely made enough for his millet stash at the end of the week. Labouring was an honest profession and it paid.

A pineapple-headed shadow appeared from behind an enormous tree. In the past, Allegory's sudden presence might have scared him, but this time fatigue eroded his fear. The old man's eyes burned like fired coals in the dark as he moved towards him, stopping near the rock.

'Babylon.'

'Prophet.'

He wished he had some tea to offer him but he'd finished the remainder moments earlier. Allegory's eyes were closed as he rested on the edge of the rock next to him; Babylon wondered if he might be praying. When his friend spoke, his voice was heavy.

'You're a labourer now.'

'Yes.'

'How you finding it?'

Babylon thought for a moment. 'It's good work,' he replied, satisfied.

'You're sure about that?' He felt the old man staring at him in the darkness. 'What are you doing here exactly?'

'Working,' he answered defensively.

'No,' Allegory said. '*Destroying*.'

'How so?' he replied. 'Besides, it's not just here, we work everywhere, all over the place! On people's farms . . . What's the difference between what we are doing and what other workers have done in the forest for years?'

'You're killing the land.'

'And other people aren't killing the land?'

'Not like this. Those people live from the land, not off it. They take just enough to survive. They are not clear—'

'I don't understand.' He felt too tired to argue. 'Those are who I'm working for. Edmund is a common labourer. It's an honest living.'

'How do you know?'

'Come again?'

'How can you be sure that's who you're working for?

377

You don't think these caners are smart? You just look at small boss man and don't see the bigger picture? You don't think he may be working for someone else. *Hmm*, I expected more of you.' The old man sounded disappointed. 'When you come into the land which the Creator has given you, you shall not follow the abominable practices of others.'

Babylon was relieved the darkness sheltered the old man from his glare. He knew his friend was full of wisdom but after a day's hard work he resented his criticisms. Couldn't he see that he'd lost so much already? He'd suffered more than most with the loss of his music. The woman that had captured his attention had slipped through his fingers: now he was trying to find a new way to survive. Who was Allegory to look down on him? What had he done to safeguard the forest? Whether they complained or not, the council always had a way of pushing through their agenda. Was he so wrong to try and make a living?

'What did Gogoa teach you?' the old man asked him then, and before he could reply, continued. 'Does the work you're doing now make you happy like when you were a musician? Do you go to your bed rested, pleased with the results of your day's work? I thought you were a traveller. You explored many territories with your mentor, sleeping under the stars. Tell me, does your new job fill you with peace?'

Babylon heard that word again, the elusive destination they all spoke about but couldn't divulge the directions to. He might not have found peace, but at least he was still.

Allegory took his silence as comprehension. 'You must look inside yourself, Babylon. The universe has given you an opportunity to find out what you are made of. I believe it is this,' he said, patting the rock they rested against with his aged hand. 'And this,' he continued in the darkness, and Babylon vaguely made out the man's arm sweeping the trees around them.

'What are you saying? You asking me to quit my job, Prophet?'

'It's not for me to tell you, Babylon. Right now, you are seeing money, not living things. For all you know, this could be where your guitar was born.'

Allegory's words chilled him. He saw gnarled strokes against shadows, the outline of trees. A forest full of Guitars. Every blow he'd dealt under the sun, collecting his coins at the end of the day that jingled in his pockets on the journey home – reminding him of his friend's strings humming in the case that used to adorn his back – every stroke was another death at his hands. He hadn't given it any thought before.

He'd been as mildly concerned as any other villager about the state of affairs with Waranga but that was all it was, an issue, something intangible that would only be made real once an official law was passed. And this had a habit of taking years to happen. It had all seemed so far away from climbing on the back of a truck and doing some sawing. He understood now that he was part of the problem. In his attempts to become disaffected, he was affecting something much more valuable.

He felt Allegory move away from him. He fought for some words to heal their silence, but he couldn't think of anything suitable to say.

'I'm sorry,' he replied after a time.

'It's to be understood. You're still searching for the answers. That is all.'

Twenty-One

According to Mannobe custom, the Koye could only be consulted by five women; five denoting completeness. The number of fingers comprising a hand. Whilst one could be lost to tragedy and the hand remain largely functional, it would no longer resemble the five-pointed star, so it was considered impaired and consequently inferior to the one nature had created.

The Koye was the elder of all elders; the oldest woman in Mannobe. A hundred and four years old at last count, there was really no one living to refute her claim. No one ever used her real name and so over time they forgot it, but they always knew where she could be found. She'd been relocated to the tall, white house in Apapa because it was the only one that maintained its original colouring. The building seemed miraculously impervious to dust, wind and rain. Plus, it meant that everyone had no problem pinpointing the elderly woman's now permanent residence.

Once a gathering of five women was established, they could proceed to her house and put their request to her. As the Codóns were well respected in Mannobe, most women invariably asked them second to form part of their hand. Mama Abandela had regularly been the first port of call.

Edith had recruited a strong team of five with the twins, Penny's mother – her lifelong friend Corlette Azevo – and Mercelline, who ran the bakery where she worked. She refused the women's offer to contribute to the gifts required to present to the woman whose counsel they sought. If her daughter was mad then the gifts of the others would feel like pity. She knew the hoard of shillings she'd kept hidden since her husband's departure would always come to her aid. Even after Jericho had gone to Angel, she'd begun to save money again out of instinct, despite her daughter's assurances that she would never again need the earnings from her mother's hard labour.

She squared her shoulders, thinking of the task ahead. She might not have the most lavish offerings to bestow on the Koye, Edith reasoned assuredly, but the woman was old. It would be enough.

Along with her, the group was ready to make the trek to Apapa. They were prepared. All that remained was to convince her child.

'What? So she can throw bones on the floor and blow smoke over me?' Jericho complained noisily.

'*Ah-ah*, she's not a witch doctor,' Edith explained to her daughter's rolling eyes. 'She's a sage.'

'She can be bay leaf for all I care, I'm not going. Did she *ask* to see me?'

'That's not how it works.'

Edith threw up her arms in exasperation; why she was blessed with such a troublesome daughter she didn't know. She remembered when Corlette had taken Penny to the Koye two years previously. She'd been adamant that Penny had gone willingly, unlike her daughter, who was pouting like a catfish. 'I thought you might like to see her.'

'For what?'

'Things. You know . . . The singing?' She saw her daughter's quizzical look. 'The music you're hearing.'

'Oh. You think I'm mad?' Jericho's jaw dropped in understanding. 'You do? *Eh-eh*, what will the village say about your crazy daught—'

'Stop talking nonsense,' Edith scolded quickly. 'But you have to admit it's not normal.'

'Yes, but Mama, *you* must admit that singing is not a sign of madness. Can't I just go to the obeah instead? I'm sure she has a potion to cure me.'

'Are you afraid of an old woman? Why won't you go?'

'Why do I have to talk in front of people? You elders and your beliefs . . . It's no one's business,' Jericho argued crossly.

They stood in Jericho's room, locking horns, each refusing to relinquish control. Edith sighed heavily and laid her body – tired from their verbal battle – on her daughter's mattress while Jericho observed her, bemused. Edith tried every argument, but could think of no way to persuade her child to cooperate with her.

Jericho smiled, prematurely celebrating her victory as she spied her mother's waning expression. But Edith was a seasoned manipulator.

'*Hmm*, I suppose I paid for you to learn how to disobey your elders in Angel?' Edith countered, twisting the corners of her mouth downward. If all else failed, she could rely on her maternal command.

'Fine, *abeg*,' Jericho conceded, grudgingly. 'If we must go, let's go now. Penny's coming here to see me this afternoon.'

They arrived with matching scarves and congregated outside the house waiting to be ushered in. The Koye was now blind but it was rumoured that she sometimes responded to the colour red, and so over time all visitors had adopted the appropriate attire.

This was not the case at all, however. If Mama Abandela had still been alive she would have told them that, after the Koye lost her sight, she began asking her daughter what she was wearing so she could recreate the picture of her child in her mind. Whenever her daughter declared it a red day, the Koye became animated; remembering when her husband-to-be had sped past her on his bicycle drenching her red dress with rancid gutter juice. Consequently, her daughter had taken to wearing red on most occasions, and visitors to the house had eventually picked up on its symbolism.

The carer led them into a reception room before blending inconspicuously into a corner. The interior was deceptively dark in contrast to the sunny exterior; any bright light, including the caress of the sun, somehow affected the Koye's unseeing eyes and unsettled her otherwise temperate nerves.

Edith and her group entered; the Codóns in the lead and Edith at the rear, pulling her daughter with an iron will and subtle clicks of her tongue. They fanned out to occupy the space.

'The ladies in red.' The Koye spoke in a gravelly voice weathered by age.

This statement was correct but the gathering squirmed uncomfortably at her accuracy because she had her back to them. The carer exited her corner to turn the Koye's large raffia armchair round to face them properly and Jericho stifled a giggle. Edith pinched her daughter's behind, causing her to promptly behave herself. The elderly woman chewed steadily through a pile of senna leaves in her lap before brushing off the remnants that her carer jumped to catch as if they were blessings.

'Who has brought the girl to me?' The old woman's voice was weak but stern.

This time they were all stunned into a tense silence. There was no way the Koye could have known a girl was the reason behind their visit.

'Me. Edith Lwembe, Madam,' Edith chirped, moving further into the room. She curtsied in front of her elder, even though the action was lost on the elderly woman.

'What is the problem?'

Edith coughed lightly, suddenly embarrassed in front of the group she'd assembled. 'She hears music.'

The gathering looked at each other but said nothing. Their wide eyes were loquacious enough.

'*Eh*, that we should all have that good fortune,' the Koye replied. She waved her hand, beckoning them forward. 'Let me see her.'

Edith prodded her petulant child and Jericho approached slowly, stopping a few feet in front of the old woman. Edith sensed her daughter's trepidation and willed all her strength into the body of her child, supporting her despite the small gap that separated them. Jericho's chin jutted out defiantly and seeing that simple action, Edith's heart flipped tenderly. For as long as her daughter's obstinacy was still present, Edith reasoned, there was much less room for the crazy to inhabit.

The Koye's hair was completely white against her black smock. It had been braided into one long plait that was coiled around her head. It looked to Jericho as though someone had planted a row of wheat on her scalp. The old woman had had a darker complexion once, undoubtedly, but her extended exile in the shade had starved her skin of essential nutrients. The old woman's pupils, glazed over with cataracts, riveted her. The gloop in their cracks glistened like crustaceans under water.

Jericho took the Koye's outstretched hand. Her palms felt like leather inside her own; the backs like trunks of a

384

tree. She could feel each groove in her skin as if it was engraved with wisdom. Instinctively she knelt before the old woman, who placed both hands on her face and kneaded its outline gently.

'*Eh*, how fine you are,' the old woman chuckled.

'Jericho.'

'A mighty name for a woman.' The Koye gripped Jericho's chin and lifted her face to look at her as if she was still capable of sight. 'Do you think you are strong?'

'I don't know. I guess so.'

Again the Koye laughed the laugh of a parent humouring their child. Slipping her hand inside her blouse, she pulled out a sweet and handed it to Jericho who glanced at her mother anxiously before taking it. Jericho unwrapped the warm rice paper and popped it under her tongue.

'Now, tell me your dream,' the Koye asked.

The old woman's request took her by surprise. What did she know of her dreams? Jericho hadn't mentioned them aloud.

Standing so close to her, Jericho found her energy comforting rather than intimidating like she'd expected. If she were alone with the blind woman she would have spoken readily, but the twelve spectator eyeballs boring a hole in her skull made her shy.

'Here? But there are so many people,' she stuttered, looking behind her at the gathering. She wished the Koye would command them all to leave, to wait for her outside, giving them some privacy.

'In here?' the Koye mimicked her protest. 'We are all women, *venga*.'

Jericho swallowed her candy and threw another helpless look behind her at her mother. She gulped audibly before revealing her dream.

'*Ewo*, I'm in a cloud,' she stammered, closing her eyes. 'At first it is dark, the atmosphere is choking me and it's difficult to breathe. I'm shouting for someone to save me but because I'm in the middle of this . . . black cloud, no one can see me. I begin to cry and my tears leak through the cloud, forming rain. When I look down at my feet, underneath me is nothing but the earth's surface. It's like I'm sitting on a star very far away, watching the rain drop as if someone is pouring water out of a bucket.

'When it has stopped raining, the sky is ice blue and my cloud is white and fluffy like yam. I put my arms up and begin swinging through the sky, my cloud now my seat. And then suddenly, I hear singing, only it's not really *singing*, it's more like music. But in my heart it feels like singing. Like a *voice*. I ask myself who it could be in the dream, and then I look down at the cloud. Now, it looks like a long train of steam. I blink again and it becomes a staircase leading down to the ground. Words are written on each step but the handwriting is *jagga-jagga*; I can't read it. At first I walk slowly, watching my footprints disappear through the cloud. Then the music grows loud and I begin to run faster until I am on the bottom step. And then, and then . . .'

'*WHAT?*' she heard the women squeal in unison behind her.

She hadn't realised her eyes were closed as she spoke. Shocked out of her account by the older women's interruption, she lost her footing in the dream. The Koye slid a beefy arm across Jericho's body until she located her shoulder. Then she squeezed it gently, coaxing her back to the last step.

'I'm . . . I'm on the bottom step. I step on to the ground to see where the music is coming from and I'm standing by the Kissing Trees. I can feel another's presence; I'm not afraid. It's not a stranger, I don't know how I know that but I just do. Someone is there with his back to me. I go over to him. When I tap for him to turn around—'

386

'*Who's the person?*' Mabel hissed uncontrollably, before her sister hushed her mouth with her hand.

'*Yes, who is it?*' she heard her mother's voice.

'I don't know,' she whispered and turned to face them. 'He disappears.'

There was a collective intake of air from everyone except her – the storyteller – and the Koye.

'But you do *know* who he is, don't you?' the Koye whispered, drawing her attention back.

'I think so. Yes,' she admitted, breathily.

The old woman sighed, a gesture that made her shrink deeper inside her chair. She motioned for Edith to come forward.

'There is nothing wrong with your daughter at all. At least nothing I can fix. She is simply in love.'

Edith Lwembe swooned at the elderly woman's words, and was kept upright by the beaming women behind her. Jericho came and stood beside her and clasped her hand tightly. The gathering shuffled forward, knees bowing in respect in front of the Koye, and Edith offered the old woman her gifts.

As they turned to leave, Jericho heard the Koye calling her back.

'What does this music sound like?' the woman asked, her voice suddenly childlike.

Jericho pondered her response momentarily then smiled. She knelt down and placed the leathery hand against her bosom, to the heart underneath, and watched the woman's face light up as her fingers latched on to its beat.

'*Ah!*' The Koye let out a heavy sigh. 'We should all be so lucky.'

Babylon rested against the tree trunk pensively. He tried to imagine the life emanating from within it. *A forest full of Guitars*. Ever since Allegory spoke to him he'd seen his friend inside of every tree he passed. He battled the guilt from his unthinkable act all over again each time.

Stubbornly, he'd joined the gang of men the day after the old man's scolding. He didn't like being told what to do or who to serve – even by Prophet. The day had seemed endless, primarily because of the torturous work he endured: some trees fell willingly and easily, while others seemed as heavy as the pillars of concrete that they were then forced to move. But their conversation played on his mind throughout his shift. He was relieved when night fell around them and he heard the truck's horn sounding the end of their work day.

The men had left him there, alone once again in the forest. His gaze narrowed on the greasy tarpaulin that covered some of the saplings they hadn't moved that day. In the moonlight, they looked like covered carcasses. He remembered the brown sack in the Eternal Compound and shivered. The remains of his friend.

He closed his eyes and breathed deeply, the way he used to when he'd been waiting for a song to come to him, Guitar in his arms. It seemed he was there for an eternity, waiting for something magical to happen. The rock he was sitting on was hard, drawing his attention to his aching thigh muscles. His bottom grew cold. His concentration was wavering, when he heard something. He strained his ears to the darkness, his body stilling as memories flooded his cells. The ghost of a melody, so faint. But the hairs prickling at the back of his neck told him his fear was real. He jumped from the rock and fled the forest with a guitar's unmistakable music in his ears, every jagged rock or tree limb that grazed him in the dark a touch from the dead.

He was grateful that Driver had been waiting in his compound when he'd returned from the forest. His terror had seemed stupid to him now that he was safely home. They shared a bottle of millet together. When that was finished Driver removed a bottle of Sting from Borrow's latest batch and waved it at him. Babylon was reluctant at first, but once the potent fumes wilted his nostril hairs, he'd gulped the firewater willingly, pushing the bottle away after a few large sips. Driver was watching him carefully so he'd made sure to keep the conversation easy, lighter than how he felt. But eventually, his interaction with Allegory poured out of him.

'You give me truth serum?' Babylon joked afterwards, looking at the bottle curiously.

'Let me test it . . . *Pues*; where you keep the rest of your millet?' Driver grinned.

They talked long into the night, passing the bottle between them. Only a thimbleful breached his lips each time, but it was enough. The cock crowed at exactly the same time as the bottle slid from Driver's hand, dangling low from the hammock. It was then Babylon remembered that he'd wanted to remove his friend from the hammock. But he'd forgotten in tiredness, and remained on the ground where he'd first sat, half dozing.

As more and more pinpricks of light seeped through his eyelids, his thoughts took him further away from his dreams into the land of the living. He would have to get up now to make the truck.

He wasn't sure if he'd come to the decision, or whether the Sting decided for him. As the old man's words replayed themselves in his mind, he reordered them in his head, playing them simultaneously with the words of his other mentor, Gogoa. He'd have to take the time to listen, to stop moving away from things, and truly listen. Search for what his heart yearned for.

He allowed his thoughts to rest on Jericho, not to turn back from the hurt as he imagined her with another. He waited for the pain in his heart, for it to trigger the wound in his chest, but nothing came. Words as familiar to him as his own name tapped on his temples. '*Va passar.*' All he needed was time. Babylon smiled. It would all pass.

'You not working?' Driver asked as they watched the sun coming up. Babylon shook his head and watched his friend's eyes closing as he spoke. 'You want work for me instead?'

Deep dimples appeared either side of Driver's face.

Babylon bridged the distance between them quietly, but his friend opened his eyes when his shadow standing over him clouded the sunlight. He didn't hesitate but tipped Driver out on to the ground as if he was emptying a wheelbarrow. They both laughed as he climbed into the papoose of material and rocked it into a leisurely swing.

'What you going do?' Driver asked him after a while.

'I don't know,' he replied honestly. 'I have to think about it.'

'*Hmm*? Labourer to layabout. Farmhand to philosopher, in a day? Is no easy ting, *o*,' Driver chuckled.

The Sting bottle Babylon tossed caught his friend dead on the shoulder.

Mabel uncorked the bottle of *anis* with vigour as the ladies whooped with delight. The pungent perfume of the drink tickled her nostrils as she poured the potent liquid into tiny tumblers.

'I stole this from a bartender in Irrobor.' She winked mischievously at Edith. The drink would certainly kick their revelries up a notch and keep the chill at bay for the rest of Hivierno.

The group had returned to the warmth of Le Papillon after their tepid encounter with the wise woman of Mannobe. Tepid because no one knew how else to categorise the event. Being in love was no small thing, especially in their village.

Still, the fact that the Lwembe girl wasn't possessed of a great affliction was mildly anticlimactic.

Their homeward journey had been quiet, each of them reluctant to start a conversation while Jericho swayed gently to the waltz playing in her head. Occasionally, one of them emitted a sigh from deep within her longing that was magnified in the chill and although no one had suggested it, they automatically made their way towards the Codón café.

M'elle settled herself inside the kitchen and filled a blackened pot with goat's milk and cocoa. She added a pinch of cayenne pepper and stirred. The drink would stave off the cold that was filtering through their bones. Shivering hands welcomed the steaming bowls of cocoa readily when it was offered; the only sounds heard, the melody of the six women blowing and sipping the chocolate broth. Mabel had been the first to speak in her unofficial position of host. She cleared her throat dramatically for her intimate audience as she recalled the day she'd first been kissed.

'*Vero?*' Mercelline the baker guffawed, suckling greedily on the story.

'Of course,' Mabel scoffed. 'He was very good-looking in those days, no?' She looked to her sister for confirmation. 'Who knew that nature would be so cruel?'

The 'he' in question was Ricket Ladipo, whose now bald head could rival the gleam off the sundial in the square. Back then, he had a full head of hair, thick black curls that framed his sculpted features so finely it was impossible not to look at him. But he was an old man now, barely capable of staying upright even when he gripped tightly on to his broom.

'I was coming back from Manuel's when he accosted me by the crossroads,' Mabel explained. 'M'elle was supposed to go that day but she'd eaten too many cashews the night before and her stomach was churning.' They turned to look

391

at M'elle nodding in agreement, this tale as familiar to her as her own.

'He took the bags I was carrying from me and we walked back through Silas's place. It was late summer at the time, the smell was intoxicating. Finally, we couldn't stand it! Ricket dropped the bags and climbed up a tree to pluck fruit. I was so excited I couldn't breathe.' She rubbed her collarbone as she remembered the past. 'He brought down two oranges and only peeled one as we sat under the huge tree in the shade. My hands trembled like so as I tried to take the fruit from him. On the last piece he said, "Wait. *Tranquila*," and placed it between my lips! I was going to swallow it but he put his fingers to my mouth, motioning for me to wait. *Ewo*, he put the other end between his lips. When our mouths met, *deus*, I swear it began to rain!'

Mercelline clapped her hands together in delight, relishing the tale even more since the man she spoke of had turned from a young Lothario into the wrinkled old gardener that maintained the Dorique compound.

'It was like two planets colliding,' Mabel embellished as Mama Azevo and Edith laughed at the thought of the unlikely union.

'*Ewo*, it's not that funny,' she added when finally tears began to roll from her eyes, the women's amusement contagious.

'*Eh – eh*, all that from a kiss?' Edith eagerly enquired.

'Of course. One kiss can change the world,' Mabel argued evenly. 'Cici, what's wrong with you?'

'Nothing,' Mama Azevo hiccuped from her doubled-over position. 'It's just – my sister can tell you the exact same story with Ricket. Only it was by Togo's guava trees!'

Allegory's thoughts rested on the musician; or rather, the ex-musician, he corrected himself quickly. Their last conversation had caused a film of guilt to wash over him. It was a feeling he'd become more acquainted with since his union with Mabel. His harsh words may have been directed at Babylon but they were really his way of chastising himself for his Joucous behaviour. Still, he'd wanted his charge to take responsibility for his actions, to realise that they had consequences.

He would atone through others, he decided firmly. That had been what his acerbity towards Babylon was about. His role in the village demanded devoutness, and that could only be brought about with a stern hand. He and Mabel had decided to keep their transgressions a secret; no benefit could come of them being brought to light. She was a woman who stored secrets well – he'd learned that from Joucous – preserving them at the back of her pantry in an undisclosed chamber. She'd kept a discreet distance too since their return, busying herself with the forest's salvation, ensuring they were never in each other's presence too long.

They would be safe, he reassured himself, and if he was lucky, he'd be resting in the forgiving hands of his Creator before she could ever call in the favour that silence had bought.

He was impressed with the meeting she'd planned between the neighbouring villages. It must have taken a formidable force to round up all those people; she was obviously paying more than lip service to the forest issue. The depth of her passion encouraged him. There were still many villagers with fire in their blood. Admittedly, some of the forest they would lose, that was a certainty. But he knew he was fighting for more than that, for the preservation of his village's identity and its traditions, and that meant standing up when outsiders threatened all that in the name of profit.

It was inevitable that change would come, even to their

sleepy backwaters. As people searched for solutions for fuel, food and building, and even sought a way to make money, Allegory had seen more and more of his precious forest vanish. The knowledge caused him physical pain. He tried to weigh the benefits from so-called progress against the losses and calculated the patent deficit. To the elder council, each leaf in Waranga represented a shilling. Eventually, it would all be gone.

He thought back to decades earlier, when he'd first set eyes on Mabel Codón. She'd flounced back home with all the arrogance of a foreigner, ordering him to clear his load so that she could build her café. He smiled to himself at her petulance, and his smile widened as he remembered his refusal. She'd been stunned at his boldness but he'd won in the end and she'd reworked her building.

He would need to summon that strength again, only on a larger scale. He would be a rock. He would ensure that as many villagers as possible became an impenetrable force that the council would be compelled to listen to, to build around. He knew that give was inevitable. Big money was involved so neither the mercenary councillors nor industrialists would go away without a fight. Part sale of Waranga was the most probable outcome: he envisaged it clearly when he closed his eyes. But he could still protect the forest by determining how much of it would be sold for profit and destruction. He would teach the villagers that, poor as they were, they had always been surrounded by things of value, and that they too had power.

Allegory let the flowing water caress his ankles, washing away the image of Miss Codón that assuaged him and then the one of her twin that followed. He moved into the water slowly, deliberately, calling all his scriptures to the tip of his tongue. Then he lay back on the water with his arms outstretched, allowing the creek to receive his weight. His tears ran into the water, finding their home in his ritual of cleansing. He opened his mouth a fraction to let in fresh water, tasting salt and endless apologies.

Jericho escaped from the cackling erupting among her elders – who had moved to Le Papillon's eating area – into the quiet sanctuary of their kitchen. She stole a glance through the beaded curtain that rattled noisily as she eavesdropped on the conversation. The older generation. They were no different from Penny and herself, the way they tittered, exchanging stories and useless information. But in other ways these women were part of the old village; the dinosaurs that didn't ask anything from life. Most of them had no larger ambition – to travel or to learn, for example – Mabel Codón being an exception. To marry was enough. To raise children, to be blessed with children was plenty. Not that there was anything wrong with those desires, she thought, but surely they could see the world was changing.

Even their beloved village was transforming. Developments of a greater industrialised civilisation were chomping at their home town from the edges and steadily working their way ever closer to their epicentre. Soon the forests would disappear along with people; then, their red roads would be replaced with the smoother, greyer, wider plains of the city's surface, that didn't care how close it came to someone's house; that devastated smaller compounds and the poorer villagers who were powerless to defend themselves against its onslaught. But there these older women sat, swapping stories of love, like the first people the Creator made.

Jericho always considered herself a woman with ideas. When her mother said it, it had seemed like a challenge. But when Daniel had echoed those words, it had felt like an insult and she'd wondered why her heart shrank. If the city wasn't the place for her, could she happily blend into

395

the village's tapestry with her head full of ideas? If she was lucky, the change coming would create space for women like her, to be *more*, not to be bound to traditional roles. She'd been mistaken in thinking that Daniel, with his helter-skelter lifestyle, could carry her away from this life, or that he could provide for her a stability that her childhood hadn't offered her with her father's absence. She'd also been wrong to make her desire paramount, as if that was all being a woman involved.

She reflected on the ball – women dressed up and beautified to tantalise the men of the village, herself included. Now, the Codóns were busy toasting the success of their daughter who had finally secured herself a husband. Yes, the music in her head whispered different things to her, but what was so wrong with standing alone? Even the Koye had declared her a woman with a mighty name. Maybe she didn't have to be heading towards someone to be heading towards something.

The sounds from the café drew Magdalena from a restful sleep. She'd been in the midst of a vivid dream where her stomach had been full with the doctor's child. She'd been cradling her newborn in her arms with Ibrahim looking affectionately at the two of them just before she woke. The child she held in the blanket had been the spitting image of her auntie. She'd turned to face Ibrahim but his face had transformed into Allegory's, whose features betrayed no age. He'd blown his pepperminty breath over her daughter who gurgled with pleasure, long eyelashes fluttering gently in acceptance. '*Por courage, for luck,*' he'd whispered, before vanishing in the cacophony of voices flooding her dream.

She rose grudgingly, stretching her sleep-softened limbs before wrapping a blanket around her shoulders. Voices grew louder as she left the house quarters and made her way towards the restaurant. Her mind separated them as she came closer, identifying those of her family first before the baker woman's and others heard less frequently. She wanted to grab a snack in the kitchen without the formality of having to greet people, anxious to return to her dreams with Poniche's baby. She stopped in her tracks at the entrance, astonished at who sat in the kitchen. Jericho's back was to her as she looked to the window outside, apparently oblivious or superfluous to the goings-on in the café.

Magdalena observed Jericho from the gap. She waited for the jealous viper to coil itself around her heart and squeeze the life from her chest the way it used to, but she couldn't feel its presence. The snake inside her had died. Maybe it had been underfed because of her lack of insecurities, stemming from her newfound joy with the doctor. It must have passed away quietly, evaporating with the sweat that ebbed from her body during her weeks of illness.

She watched Jericho without making a sound; taking in her regal profile, her unfettered nature. Apart from her size, the girl wasn't so dissimilar to her. Then she sensed another resemblance between them. Jericho was in the depths of a passion greater than her mind could contemplate. Magdalena had never noticed it before, or maybe she'd overlooked it because she'd still been firmly in Babylon's grip. Jericho must have felt her gaze on her because she looked around, startled.

'You scared me. I thought everyone was in there,' Jericho said softly.

'I was sleeping,' Magdalena replied, moving forward. Up close, she sized her up and noticed Jericho doing the same thing. 'I'm Magdalena.'

'I know you,' Jericho laughed. 'We've met, danced even. Jericho Lwembe. Congratulations on your marriage,' she added gently. 'Your mother gave us your news. You must be very happy.'

'*Tanka*. Yes,' Magdalena beamed, unable to stop her mouth from widening.

'We went to see the Koye,' Jericho confessed. 'I mean, they took me . . .'

'Okay? Was it? *Pues*, you don't have to say anything . . .'

'No, it's fine. Just – I keep hearing noises. *Music*,' she whispered. 'My mother was concerned; no one wants a mad daughter! Who will take her?' she laughed hollowly.

'Yes,' Magdalena agreed with a half-smile.

'Maybe I should go back before Mama starts complaining.' Jericho glanced at the beaded curtain. She rolled her eyes, attempting to bridge the silence that had formed between them, and Magdalena flashed her eyebrows at her in return. As Jericho turned to leave, Magdalena stopped her.

'Hold on, let me talk small . . .' She held her hand up cautiously. 'Well, it's nothing really, just a thing somebody told me once. That music comes in many ways. You have to be quiet to hear it.'

'*Da vero*?' Jericho responded sharply and Magdalena wondered if she'd offended her in some way.

'No,' Magdalena explained quickly. 'I can only see it in you now because I hear my own. I have my own musician.' She giggled, watching the comprehension dawning on the girl's strained features.

'There is a piper for everyone, I guess.'

'*Eh-heh*,' Magdalena agreed. 'You know, I've stayed in the village all my life. He has never played like that for anyone before. Only you. *Ewo*, you know who I'm talking about.'

She placed her hand on Jericho's shoulder tentatively and the girl leaned into her touch.

'But what can I do?' Jericho appealed desperately. 'I don't know . . . There has been so much—'

398

Magdalena shushed her words. '*Tranquila*. Just be quiet. Be very quiet and listen. It will come to you. You will know.'

Their conversation was broken by the clatter of the beaded curtain. Mabel burst into the kitchen and began hunting through cupboards in search of her private stash of liquor.

'Ah, *bona*,' she called out, wobbling over to Magdalena. She embraced her tightly, curling her face into the soft wool of her blanket. Magdalena kissed her teeth even though she wasn't genuinely annoyed at her mother's display.

'Stop it. *Abeg*, Mama.'

'*Ah-ah!* What will I do when you're away from me? See how the doctor has stolen your heart . . .' Her mother feigned a pained expression and squeezed Magdalena to her bosom. 'Come, come and greet everyone. What are you girls doing in the kitchen? Come where we can see you.'

Mabel pushed her daughter towards the café, her quest for booze forgotten. Jericho hung back, reluctant to join the animated women in the other room. She could hear her mother extolling the praises of a young man who had helped her with her shopping, while the other women commented loudly.

She tiptoed to the back door and went outside. She stood still and waited patiently. Quiet and just listening as instructed by Magdalena Codón. Slowly a note made its way over the mound of land, a shallow hill on the horizon hooded by the bluff of trees. Another came to join it where the sky and earth touched fingers, until gradually the hypnotic lullaby became more pronounced.

By the time the charcoal clouds overhead separated, allowing the late afternoon sun to declare his presence, the orchestra inside her head was complete. Rousing music echoed through her fibre, rich sounds that could lure the sirens from their watery depths to contemplate a life on land. The fiery timbre of a telltale voice *soñando, soñando, soñando*.

Twenty-Two

Man confident enough not to swagger
Cock left limb
Loose right
With bravado worthy of the most reputable
Pamplonian bullfights
Sucked gut in tight
Like a balloon exhaling its lifeblood
And began his journey . . .

Springtemps was stirring. Babylon knew this when the velvet returned to the air, pushing out the rough cold of Hivierno. He was happy to see the season passing. More and more he caught sight of the flowers that had hidden throughout the winter poking their heads tentatively out of the grass that had increased its height, as if it too was stretching itself after a period of hibernation.

He looked around the village affectionately, enjoying his new sense of lightness. In a few days, preparations for the Uprising would start. Mannobans took their celebration to welcome in the spring very seriously. The youngsters had already begun rehearsing their hymns for the three-hour service at the spirit house. After that, spring's returning blooms were deposited on all the resting places in the Eternal Compound.

Somehow, the weight that had plagued him since Guitar's passing was lifting, and even though he knew it wasn't solely attributable to the new season, Babylon was grateful.

He yawned loudly as he rose. He bent to retrieve the placard that he'd laid under the trees, next to him. This would be a good place for him to set up. He could reach the older Mannobans who rose early, unable to sleep through the heat of the morning sun. They liked to while away their days with a friendly game of rudón.

Whenever his brain was too quiet, he could hear the vague echoes of that ghostly music, but it no longer made him afraid. It was still in him. He thought the music had gone along with Guitar.

He contemplated his fight with Daniel Dorique. The punch had cost him his gift, yes, but maybe for a higher purpose. He'd been robbed of his hands so that he could find another instrument with which to reach the people – *his people*. He called himself a traveller, yet he'd made a home here in Mannobe's welcoming bosom, just as he'd done in Gloriama's once upon a time. This was his land as much as anyone else's. Prophet was as much the reason as the excuse. Nevertheless, a grown man had to set roots some time. Better to plant roots and transport them to flourish elsewhere than to remain eternally rootless, no? Where the B in the village's name came from . . .

He would be the village's talking drum, he decided again, his eyes lighting up with his confirmation. It wasn't so much about the forest: what mattered was furnishing the villagers with truth. The same voice that seduced women from their clothing could also be a beacon of news and education. He knew how much pleasure his visits to the homes brought those lost children, society's discards. His new work was simply an extension of that. Looking back on it, a life of frivolity had brought him little. He envied the fulfilment people like his protector had, people who gave of themselves for something greater than their own benefit.

News had gathered momentum around Mannobe about the forest that divided the community in their opinion but united them in their emphatic discussion of the outcome. The council had weighed up the concerns of its locals but had still proposed the clearing of over six thousand hectares of Waranga to facilitate the expansion of sugar-growing – almost a quarter.

Prophet, Mabel and others had fought valiantly but the real battle was just beginning. Now was the time to ensure that what remained was protected, for them and their children's children to enjoy.

He reflected on the subtle irony that it had taken an outsider – even though that outsider was a Dorique – to show him where he belonged. He'd fought to protect the honour of his people, of a woman, at a higher cost. He was now ready to face the question that he dared not speak out loud, that was always on the tip of his tongue: had she been worth it?

He laughed to himself, knowing that if Guitar was here he wouldn't have waited so long to put the question to him.

Market day was normally a lucky day. If he could get older villagers to take an interest, they could educate their children; after all, they were the ones to be affected by the progress of the village. *The young shall grow*. It was an old proverb Gloriama had liked to use with all of them in the home, reciting it whenever a little one had been aggrieved by an older sibling. 'Never mind,' she would say, wiping away hot tears. 'The young shall grow.' Everyone's time will come.

From now on, he'd think of that phrase with an additional meaning. The young trees would be allowed to grow like their ancestors whose roots were anchored deep in Mannobe land. He would find a way to help them. Maybe that way he could undo what he'd done to Guitar. To repay Prophet. Maybe he would finally find the peace they'd all spoken of.

He twirled the placard in his fist determinedly. Its wooden shaft reminded him of the spears the bushmen used for hunting. It seemed appropriate, given that this was his new weapon, his new ally. He laughed heartily into the leaves, enjoying his own sound, full and rich. It was the sound of release, of freedom. He smiled to himself, in the shade, then started to hum.

Jericho smoothed down her rose dress for the second time and waited for her attack of nerves to subside. Sliding her ivory comb into her hair, she double-checked its grip so that she wouldn't lose it carelessly again. She reached for her sandals then decided against them. They were far too time-consuming to tie and the song that called her was too strong for her to ignore any longer.

She left her home and headed towards the centre barefoot. The sprinkling of dew on the road reminded her of a snail's phosphorous trail as her feet left their damp prints in the sand, evidence of her determined passage. No one was on the road; not Joyce with her fruit cart, not Dungu on his way home from satisfying the neighbourhood strays.

Lured by the music, she allowed the notes to lead her. She crossed the sundial in the square slowly. She remembered the game she'd played religiously when she first came back from Angel, to determine her future with Daniel. How long ago all that seemed now.

As the symphony crescendoed by the two magnificent Kissing Trees, she stopped, mesmerised by the music as well as their large umbrella of leaves. It was exactly like her dream, only this time she was awake and the earth beneath her feet was terracotta instead of green. In her sleep she was always excited: here she was afraid.

Then she saw his outline against the tree. It was as if it had hollowed out a space in its trunk for him. She took a fortifying breath and allowed the memory of her past dreams about this future to guide her. Moving up behind him, she extended her hand tentatively to touch his shoulder, waiting for him to turn around. Waiting.

'*Señorita*,' Babylon spoke, surprise arching his eyebrows.

'You called me,' she whispered breathily. 'Your music . . .'

'You must be mistaken,' he replied with what sounded like sadness in his inflection. 'I don't play any more.'

'Oh.'

She took a step back, embarrassment not yet penetrating but cooling her clammy skin all the same. She wondered whether she was still dreaming now, at home in the safety of her bed, and dug her nails into her palm.

'Congratulations on your wedding,' he offered in his baritone, his eyes resting on the tip of her nose. She wondered if he was struggling not to look at her or whether his ambivalence made it easy.

'What? But I'm not marrying.'

'Oh. I see.'

It was then that he looked into her eyes. Jericho held his gaze properly, latching on to the crack in his reply, that minuscule word 'oh', as if it was a portal to happiness. She placed her whole being inside it; hoping.

'Our village is small, *sha*. You don't think the whole of Mannobe's gums would be flapping if a Dorique was marrying?' she continued boldly.

'I heard . . .' He dropped his outstretched hand, letting the wind carry the remainder of his sentence away.

'You heard wrong,' she finished for him. 'Maybe you should see the Koye.'

Babylon stared at her intently, enjoying her looking back at him. She was still the loveliest thing he'd ever seen. From the quarter-moon dimples in her cheeks to her eyes like liquid promises. She was the only love he'd ever known, and yet the only woman he'd never known. Their story was just beginning, much like everything else in his life. The young shall grow. He spotted the comb tucked behind her ear and smiled inwardly. He studied her lips, their perfect bow shape on which he suspected he could play the most delightful of symphonies.

He seemed changed to her: still, centred, at peace. His ever-present smile, his angular face that looked like it had been cut out of a rock, fashioned from the earth. She felt his energy vibrating through her, *his cells*, syncopating with her own internal rhythm. *The blues in his eyes.* Finally, she understood Venus's meaning.

They had no words left. No breath for apologies or to correct miscommunications; no energy to rehash the past or old pain, feeling for scars and bruises. She focused only on the present moment. The blood pumping through their bodies; the space they occupied in nature; the universe that conspired to unite them in reality and the uncharted territories of dreams and illusion. Their shadows merging beneath the leaves, that neither life, nor death, nor things to come could separate, as long as they both could hear. The rest could wait. The future would be theirs to shape like a sonnet, to fold like paper-made cranes.

Jericho shortened the distance between them, surprised at how much she wanted to taste the burn after his kiss.

She felt her womb open at the thought of his hard body against her softness, and as the first musical note sounded in her mind, she wished it was him beating inside her.

Reaching up, she buried her fingers in his hair. She pulled his head down towards her but when they were less than a breath apart he stopped her.

'Wait. Let me play a song for you.'

'I thought you didn't play any more,' she teased quietly.

'Maybe not the guitar,' he replied: 'but I play.'

Babylon lifted her arm as he'd done once before and arched it towards the sky. Whittling a bow from a slender branch of the banyan tree, he shaped the air around them into a perfect prism of song.

'*That's it*,' she cried out as the sound flooded her eardrums, her body swaying theatrically under its spell.

'That's what?' He stared at her magnificent possession, bemused.

'*La musica . . .*'

Acknowledgements

To God be the glory!

Thank you to my family and friends for their faith, farce and funding. To early readers: Ofordi Nabokei, Khary Jones, Donna Muwonge, Kerri-Ann Grant, Marina Warsama, Iyabode Olajumoke and Chika Okereke, bless you for your enthusiasm and diplomacy. Thanks to all the people who offered their support and to the writers who aided and encouraged me along the way. I am indebted to Andy Hine and Jessica Leeke for their unwavering belief and advice.

To my agent Juliet Pickering, your conviction and optimism have been a delight every step of this journey. Thank you for taking a chance on my work, without which none of this might have happened as spectacularly as it has!

I'm very grateful to all the people at Virago, staunch supporters from the offset. To my editor Elise Dillsworth, your insight helped me walk more firmly on that terracotta soil . . . *Tanka*.

To everything that fed and watered my imagination . . . and to the people of Mannobe who embraced me as one of their own – thank you for your patience, your humour, and for offering your histories so unreservedly.

Finally, thank *you*, the reader, for whatever compelled you to peer through the covers of this book into this foreign landscape, and for your willingness to travel alongside me.